"Displaying a flair for comedy and witty dialog, Miller is clearly an author to watch…with clever, snappy repartee, creating an exciting and fast-paced read." ~ *LIBRARY JOURNAL*

"Carolyn Miller keeps on turning out these beautifully written, tender hearted books!... There was humor and brilliant bantering conversations, heart stopping romance, as well as exciting descriptions (and sometimes dangerous passages of play) of hockey games. Well worth the late night/early morning read!" ~ *KAYE'S REVIEWS & NEWS*

"A sweet love story that continues the Original Six Hockey series by Carolyn Miller. The setting of Montreal with the Gardens and all the French woven throughout was delightful!" ~ *GOODREADS review*

"I am emerging out of my book hangover after reading *Checked Impressions* by Carolyn Miller....The romance, humor and themes of identity are so enjoyable and make for a great read!" ~ *BECKY'S BOOKSHELVES*

"Adrenaline, chemistry, romance, and lots of wooing!... You do not have to be a fan of sports or even knowledgeable in hockey and short track to appreciate *Love on Ice.*" ~ *GOODREADS review*

"Carolyn Miller scores another win with *Love on Ice*, the second book in her Original Six Hockey series. I absolutely loved the faith thread in this story. It's message that success does not lie on what we do, but who we are is powerful." ~ *GOODREADS review*

"*The Breakup Project* is a fun, charming, and faith-filled contemporary romance with adorable characters set in the competitive North American ice hockey world. Highly recommended." ~ *NARELLE ATKINS, Author of Solo Tu & Her Tycoon Hero*

MUSKOKA BLUE

CAROLYN MILLER

Dawn's Untrodden Green

Regency Brides: Legacy of Grace
The Elusive Miss Ellison
The Captivating Lady Charlotte
The Dishonorable Miss DeLancey

Regency Brides: Promise of Hope
Winning Miss Winthrop
Miss Serena's Secret
The Making of Mrs Hale

Regency Brides: Daughters of Aynsley
A Hero for Miss Hatherleigh
Underestimating Miss Cecilia
Misleading Miss Verity

'Heaven and Nature Sing' from the Joy to the World Christmas
novella collection

CHAPTER 1

*I*t was the perfect time to be brave. The sun shone, bouncing brightness off the smooth blue glass of Lake Muskoka. *Musk-oh-ka.* She rolled the word around in her mouth as she drank in the postcard-like scene. Tall, deep-green pines leaned over the shore, watching expectantly, guardians of this beautiful sapphire two hours north of Toronto.

Sarah glanced around. Nobody was here to talk her out of it. Nobody was here to say, "Sarah, are you sure?" and start the second-guessing that was all too familiar now. Nobody was here to see the scars that marked her side and look at her with pity or, worse, ask those questions for which she didn't have answers.

She stepped off the small patch of sand into the water.

"Ah!" She screeched as the icy water bit her skin, pressing her lips together to stop another groan. Of course Canadian summers would differ to those back home—but surely the water should be warmer than this!

Be brave.

Memories flashed: moving to a new country. Singing in front of thousands. Learning to walk again. She lifted her chin.

Took another step. Sun-warmed air made the cold shock all the more, but she plowed on regardless. Things were never as they seemed. Superficial calm could hide pain so deep—

No. *Don't think about it.*

She took another step. Gritted her teeth. Then plunged in headfirst.

The water slapped her face, her chest, her skin tingling with a million pinpricks. She gasped, heaved air past the rocks in her lungs, and sliced her arms through the water. *Stroke. Stroke. Stroke.* Movement eased the chill, bringing a modicum of warmth. Once the icy fire in her lungs abated, she could see the red-and-white buoy in the lake and, over on the lake's far shore, small fir and spruce sheltering under the arms of larger trees. Kicking with her good leg, she pivoted to study Aunt Angela and Uncle John's small, homey cottage. It huddled under a pair of poplars cathedral-high.

She glanced across at the three-story mansion next door, all gleaming windows and big fancy deck. It even boasted its own hot tub, little jetty, and cute red boathouse. She made a face at it and turned toward the buoy, forcing her left leg to kick like her physical therapist back home had taught her and slowly carving her way closer.

Her hip felt better today. Maybe those sadistic exercises over the past eighteen months were working. Her hip hadn't seized up for...almost four days. Not since that ultra-embarrassing episode on the plane when she'd started cramping halfway through the sixteen-hour flight from Sydney to Vancouver, before needing sedation to stop her gasps and whimpers from scaring the other passengers. Her skin crawled at the memory. Cowering in the aisle. People staring, probably thinking she was deranged. Bile rose—

No. She sucked in a breath. *Don't think about it.*

She scooped her way closer to the buoy bobbing happily in the lake. Fifteen meters. Ten. Five. And touch. She began treading water as a smile threatened to escape. Yes. She'd done it. Victory.

She flipped over onto her back and gazed at the blue bowl of sky, cloudless, open to the heavens. "See, God? See what I can do without You?"

No answer, but that wasn't surprising. God had stopped answering her prayers eighteen months ago. He certainly wasn't going to start talking now.

Sarah closed her eyes. The splash of water played against her ear as she floated, drifting like a broken stick on the sea. It would be so easy to stop trying, to cease this struggle to stay afloat, to just let go and sink to the bottom of a foreign lake...

She frowned. Except if she did, her parents and sister would be devastated. And her aunt and uncle would never forgive themselves for going into town today. And anyway, she'd already spent way too long at the bottom.

Be brave.

She opened her eyes—and stared straight up into a pair of deep brown ones.

Bump. Her head hit something hard. Then water filled her nose and she was underwater, long strands of red hair swirling in front of her. Her heart hammered: *Can't breathe! Can't breathe!* Hands grabbed her upper arms. She clawed at them. The pressure released. Her head broke the surface and she spat out water. Gulped in precious air. Saw the brown eyes again. Kicked away.

Her hip cramped, the spasms shuddering up her left side. "Ow!"

"Hey!" The man stretched a scratched hand toward her. "Want a hand?"

She shook her head and tried to swim away. Dumb move. Her hip was on fire, her left leg a dead weight. Drowning wasn't on the agenda today. *Oh God, please help me!*

"It's at least a hundred meters to shore. Can you make it that far?"

Cramps continued ratcheting up her side. Sarah bit back a moan to study the shoreline. She gulped. Glanced back.

The man leaned over the boat's side, dark eyes concerned. "Do you need help?"

No. She was sick of people needing to help her all the time, sick of being pathetic, sick of being sick. But something in his face suggested kindness. And hopefully he'd be like all those plane passengers and she'd never see him again either. "Yes."

Sarah inched her way to the side of the boat. The man reached down, grasped her right hand, and hauled her up like she was a feather. Her knees scraped against the metal rim, then she landed with a grunt in the bottom of a sleek, modern runabout. She eased into the seat he gestured to, pressing deep into her side as she glanced about. Fishing rods were propped into narrow slots, their lines stretching taut into the water. The smell of bait penetrated her nostrils, threatening to send her insides out. She fought the nausea and studied her rescuer.

Brown hair, unshaven jaw, tanned skin, dressed in a scruffy beige T-shirt and khaki shorts, he looked very…brown, like an advertisement for Mr. Wilderness. Judging from the muscled arms he'd used to haul in her not-so-dainty self, he probably wrangled bears in his spare time while off camping somewhere hundreds of miles from civilization—and a decent coffee shop. She drew up her knees and wrapped one arm around them, grasping the side for balance as the boat gently rocked.

"I'm Dan." He smiled.

Her heart fizzed. Good-looking guys always made her feel tongue-tied, like she was still the pale ugly duckling she'd been years ago in high school. "Uh…" She swallowed against the squeakiness. "I'm sorry."

His mouth curled up one side. "Well, hello, Sorry."

She blinked. "I meant I'm sorry for scratching you." She

motioned to his gouged hands. "I didn't know what was happening."

He shrugged, his gaze dropping to study her knees. "You're bleeding."

"I'll be right."

"As long as the sharks don't get a whiff of it, we'll be okay."

"Sharks?" Her eyes widened. "There aren't any sharks around here." Were there?

"Hey, I need an excuse for the lack of bites today. Not everyone will believe a mermaid chased them all away." He turned to reel in a line.

Her cheeks heated. There was a limit to how much apologizing one person should do per lifetime. "I was just trying to get to the buoy."

"Did you say boy? What boy?" He frowned and moved closer to the front of the boat, stripping off his shirt as he scanned the water. "Why didn't you say so?"

She blinked. The man's torso screamed muscle definition.

"Hey!"

Her eyes snapped back up to his face—his frowning face.

"Where'd you see him?"

"Who?"

He muttered something under his breath and shook his head. "The boy!"

"What boy? I meant that buoy!" She pointed to the red-and-white floating structure.

"Huh?" He blinked. "You mean the boo-ey?"

She nodded.

He stared for a moment, then cracked up, his laughter echoing around her.

She stiffened, his mirth layering new ice around her heart. Laughing off tease was like worship leading—she couldn't do either anymore. She studied the lake's far shore until a huge shiver betrayed her self-control.

"Hey."

She looked back, and he gently lobbed a blue towel at her. "Get dry, then you can show me where you belong."

Sarah wrapped the towel around her shoulders, huddling into its soft warmth as his words pierced her soul. Where she belonged? How about back home in Sydney, or maybe in PNG. Better yet, next to Stephen—that was where she really belonged. Grasping the ring on her left finger, she blinked away the hot sting in her eyes.

Be brave.

Dan started the engine, then glanced at her, amusement still sketched on his face. "Now, where shall I take you?"

Throat clogged, she pointed to the jetty belonging to the big house next door.

He raised an eyebrow. "Really?"

She tilted her chin at his odd look, then nodded before glancing away.

The boat's motor throbbed as it quietly cruised the short distance to the dock. He pulled up, killed the engine, tossed a rope around a pole. The boat rocked as he hoisted himself out onto the dock, then he turned back to her, a hand outstretched. "M'lady."

Was he still making fun of her? She stood, carefully folded the towel, and left it on the spare padded seat in the back, moving gingerly as the boat dipped and swayed.

"Here, take my hand."

She grasped his hand and clambered onto the dock, wincing as her hip protested the sharp movement.

He glanced down at her leg, eyes widening as he saw her scars.

Humiliation flowed, lava-hot. Why hadn't she worn board shorts today? She backed away, turning to hide her degradation. "Thank you."

"You're welcome." His smile made her heart quiver.

Stop. She had no right to find another man attractive. She forced herself to walk slowly away and not scamper like she wanted. *Don't look back, don't look back—*

"See you around."

She glanced back to where he stood, hands on hips, mouth still tilted on one side. "I doubt it." She tossed her hair and veered off onto a stone-strewn path that led to the cottage. And tripped.

Scrambling to her feet, she swiped hair from her hot cheeks, ignoring his yelled, "You okay?"

She picked up pace, heedless of the small bushes slapping her legs.

Forget trying to be brave.

Now was the perfect time to run away.

"Look who I found!"

Dan swallowed a smile as the woman in the hammock jerked, blinking, her eyes widening as she peered from her aunt to him. Yep. He'd felt much the same when Angela had called earlier—his melted muscles protesting, brain rebooting too slowly after his nap to make sense of her invitation at first.

"Dan, this is my niece, Sarah Maguire." Ange's fine features melded into a slight frown. "Sarah, you remember me telling you about Daniel Walton, don't you?"

"Um, no." Sarah's gaze flicked from her aunt to him. "Hi."

"Hey." He dipped his chin. "So, you're not 'Sorry' after all."

Her lips twitched, then her gaze skimmed away, back to her book.

He turned to her aunt. "We met yesterday and had a slight miscommunication over boys and buoys."

Ange's eyebrows rose, and she stared at Sarah, blue eyes wide.

Sarah shrugged. "I didn't think it worth mentioning."

She didn't, huh? His lips notched up another degree. "Ange invited me to dinner."

Ange nodded, the June sun bouncing off her wavy auburn hair. "Dan is staying next door. No doubt you'll come across each other occasionally."

"Next door?" Sarah squeaked.

He nodded. *That's right, Princess. Trying to bluff your way onto my dock, saying that's where you belong.* He knew a moment's satisfaction to see her so disconcerted, followed by a ping of relief that she wasn't some crazed stalker fan, as some of his teammates had occasionally dealt with. Muskoka was for relaxing, not wondering about who might be out to find him.

He rolled his eyes at himself. Please. Like he was any real celebrity.

Movement behind him signaled John's arrival. "Dan. Good to see you, my friend."

"Hey, John." He gripped the pastor's hand. He'd first met John and Ange McPherson when he'd started attending their Toronto church, then they'd moved here five years ago. His living here over summer meant John was still his pastor more than anyone else. It was often hard to get to church once the season's schedule released. "How are you doing?"

"Can't complain. You?"

Dan shrugged. "Can anyone complain when they wake up to that view each day?"

"God's country."

"For sure." He glanced back to where Sarah was gingerly sitting up in the hammock. "So, is it true?"

"Pardon?"

"'I'd rather be reading…'" He quoted the phrase emblazoned on her T-shirt.

She nodded, clutching her book to her chest as the hammock began a wild swing. Then, before he could blink, she'd rocketed from the hammock only to stumble at his feet like a beggar.

"You okay?" He offered a hand to help her upright.

"I'm fine," she muttered, ignoring it.

"Falling for me, eh?" he teased.

She stiffened, startled green eyes shooting to meet his before she ducked to collect her book. "Excuse me." She slid open the glass door and slipped inside.

He turned to John and Ange, eyebrows raised.

"You must forgive her. Sarah has...well, let's just say things haven't been easy for her." Ange eked out a smile. "She may be a little prickly at times, but she used to be one of the warmest, loveliest girls you could ever hope to meet."

"Uh huh." Uh oh. He appreciated his pastor's wife, but not Ange's hopeful look, nor where this conversation seemed to be going. Better change the subject. He nodded to John. "We'll have to go fishing soon." The fish seemed to like John, almost leaping onto his line whenever he was out.

John's expression lightened. "That'd be good."

Fishing consumed most of the conversation for the next half hour as the sun began its slow descent through the pines. An aroma of garlic and onions tickled his senses, digging anticipation for when they finally sat down at the dining table.

Dan gestured to the vase of pink and red roses Ange slid to the table's end. "They're pretty." And looked expensive.

"Sarah gave them to me for my birthday yesterday. And a voucher for the Muskoka Shores spa, too."

He nodded. "Did you enjoy your day?"

"How could I not? We had a lovely meal at Muskoka Shores, thank you." She patted his hand. "You and Sarah are both so sweet and thoughtful."

"Glad you enjoyed."

Sarah plunked a steaming dish of lasagna onto a hot pad in

the middle of the teak table, then slipped into the vacant seat, opposite Dan. She didn't look at him.

"That smells fantastic," Dan said. "Is this another secret family recipe, Ange?"

"Ask Sarah. She made this."

He eyed the cook. Nope. Still not playing.

"Let's give thanks." John reached across the table to hold his wife's hand.

Dan reached across to grasp Sarah's hand, her soft fingers barely holding his as her uncle prayed a blessing on their food. As soon as John finished, she dropped his hand like a hot tong. The action lowered his defenses a fraction more. Yeah. Definitely not like some of those other women.

The next minute was a frenzy of plate passing as they loaded up with garden salad, garlic bread, and the baked pasta dish.

He forked it in. Nearly moaned. "This is really delicious. Sure beats whatever I would've had to throw together."

Sarah seemed surprised, then pleased. Well, she didn't smile exactly, but her features eased a little.

"So, do good cooks run in your family?"

A glimmer of amusement touched Sarah's face before she replied solemnly, "I don't think Ange runs, and I prefer swimming."

"I meant—oh, right."

Huh. A flash of humor.

The meal progressed amid polite nothings about the weather, the tourists, and what had changed in past weeks. Sarah seemed to be relaxing, peeking at him every so often like she wasn't sure what to make of him. That made two of them. He wasn't used to women so aloof they could be mistaken for an ice princess.

He took a sip of water and eyed her. "So, Sarah, your accent tells me you're not from around here."

"No."

He swallowed a smile along with his mouthful. "Where did you grow up?"

The green eyes met his warily. What had her so withdrawn?

"You don't have to answer if it's too personal."

"It's not that," she finally said, glancing at Ange. "It's not easy to condense into a sound bite."

"Try me."

She studied him a moment longer, then gave the tiniest nod. "Papua New Guinea."

"Seriously?"

"Yes."

"Wow." He leaned back in his chair. "I don't think I've ever met anyone who's been there."

"I was a missionary kid." She sipped her water, eyeing him over her glass. "My dad is from the US, Mum is from Australia. We left PNG when I was twelve and moved to Sydney, where Dad pastors a church."

"So that accounts for the accent."

She shrugged. "Growing up between various cultures always marked me as somewhat strange."

"Oh, Sarah, you don't still believe that, do you?" Ange protested.

Another shrug.

He studied her. He didn't think her strange. Intriguing, maybe, despite the prickles and frost.

John motioned to Dan's nearly empty plate. "Help yourself, Dan. There's plenty more."

"Thanks." Dan served himself another portion of lasagna, then glanced at Sarah again. "You're pretty lucky having family in different parts of the world."

"I think it's important to encourage family members to live in places one would like to visit, if at all possible."

He nodded. "Amen."

The rest of the meal continued with conversation with Ange

and John, Sarah answering the occasional question in monosyllables. What was her deal? Was she shy? Proud? No, the self-deprecating humor suggested otherwise. He stole another look. She was pretty, with that milky skin and glowing hair, but seemed pretty cold, too. Glacial, even.

He was still puzzling it over when Sarah excused herself to go wash dishes.

"I'll help you," he offered, pushing back his chair.

"Thanks, but I don't need help."

You sure about that? He bit back his response, instead passing his empty plate across as she requested. Light flashed from a ring on her left hand. She was engaged.

Later, after Sarah had pleaded a headache and said goodnight, Dan joined Ange and John for coffee on the deck. He slouched into his seat, the pungent scent of Ange's homemade anti-bug lotion tickling his nose. Distant lights twinkled from across the lake as the breeze sighed through the pines. He rolled his shoulders, trying to release the tension.

"So, Dan." John placed his mug on the table. "How long will you stay in Muskoka?"

"I've got two months before duty calls me back. How about you? Do you get much of a break this year?"

John's graying head nodded slowly. "A few weeks."

"You deserve it."

John gave a tired smile. "For once, I think maybe we do."

The night sounds grew louder—the hum and whir of crickets and cicadas, the lake's gentle wash, the slap as a mosquito found a patch of unprotected skin. John and Ange sat at the table, the porch light revealing the strain of the past few years in the fine lines around Ange's eyes.

John reached over to hold her hand. "At least Sarah's here."

"I didn't realize how hard she was still—" Ange bit her lip and glanced over at Dan.

"God can work things out for good," John murmured.

"I know." Her eyes sheened as she nodded. "We keep believing."

Dan chewed his lip. The past two years had been tough for John and Ange as they'd struggled through church issues, the funerals of friends, and some family drama for which Ange had gone away for several weeks. He'd spent many hours praying for them, had upped his weekly offering and sent them anonymous gifts and donations for their own needs. John and Ange were good people and a blessing to so many. They really needed a break.

Dan stretched out his legs. "So, what's her deal?"

His pastors glanced at each other. So, there really *was* a deal. He'd found it oddly amusing, the bedraggled kitten with the big green eyes and claws that he'd plucked from the lake who then turned her nose in the air and her personality down to frozen. But the earlier glimpses of humor and generosity had signaled Sarah's personality might be more like her aunt's than the initial ice princess act had suggested. So, what had happened?

John steepled his fingers. "Sarah was…hurt a while back."

Oh. Remorse bit as he remembered her scars. And judging from the tension he sensed, any explanation was likely complicated. Still, she was engaged, so life couldn't be all bad. The knowledge she was engaged eased a knot of concern. He must've misread Ange's look earlier.

"Have you heard of Heartsong Collective?" Ange asked.

"The music ministry with all those albums, right?"

"Sarah was involved with them for a few years. She was one of their best…" Ange's voice faded as she glanced at him, then offered a wobbly smile. "Excuse me for a moment."

She left, leaving Dan to exchange glances with John, who murmured, "She's okay."

"You sure?"

Apprehension lifted at John's nod. Dan took another sip of coffee, then plunked his mug on the table. Change of subject time. "So, John, are you free to go catch some walleye later this week?"

"Just tell me when."

They discussed details, and Dan gave a small smile of satisfaction. Yeah, even with an ice princess around, this summer would be good. Water, sun, fish…what could be better?

CHAPTER 2

"Sarah, are you interested in coming to Pilates with me?"

Sarah looked up from her copy of *Pride and Prejudice,* her ultimate favorite novel, the perfect escape from reality. Who didn't fancy herself as Elizabeth or want to spend time with someone like Mr. Darcy? "Um, sorry?"

"*Sorry* you don't want to come, or *sorry* you didn't hear because you're engrossed in the world of Austen?"

She smiled guiltily. How well her aunt knew her. "The latter?"

Ange laughed. "I'm going to Pilates over at the resort. Are you interested in joining me?"

She loved spending time with Ange. And the therapist had wanted her to do some form of regular stretching. "Will there be coffee and cake later?"

"You know the point of exercise is to get healthier, Blue."

"I know that nobody in Australia calls redheads Blue or Bluey anymore, Ange. I also know if I'm to leave the hallowed halls of Pemberley, I'll be needing coffee and cake."

"You're incorrigible." But her aunt's eyes held warm affection.

Sarah smiled. These past few days had been so good. No counseling, no deep and meaningful conversations, no doctor's appointments or visits from the do-gooders in her father's congregation. Nothing but the quiet ease of family.

She swung her legs over the side of the hammock, the momentum propelling her upright but without the fall factor of last week's embarrassment. Why did the spirit of clumsy always attack in front of new people? So much for good first impressions. Not that she wanted to make a good impress—

"Sar?"

"Oh! So, um, how fancy is this resort?" She gestured to her leggings and T-shirt, a long-ago gift from her older sister, Rebekah. "Do I need to change?"

"I think you'll be fine. Just grab some shoes. I can sign you in as my guest."

A half hour later they were in the gym studio of Muskoka Shores—one of the largest resorts on the lake, so Ange had informed her when Sarah had exclaimed on its size.

Sarah glanced around from her position near the back next to a wall. Most of the attendees were older women with squishy bits that suggested they'd be none too flexible. But classes back home had proved her wrong before. She unrolled her mat and covered it with a towel, then slipped off her sneakers and socks. Ange introduced her to some of her friends, the interaction easy —nothing like the awkwardness of dinner with Daniel. She cringed again at how she'd behaved. That standoffish girl wasn't her. Not really.

Once upon a time she'd known how to be friendly, known how to recognize social cues and not blurt out awkward stuff that dismayed. Her father used to say how Sarah could talk to anyone, that she was as comfortable chatting with people who were homeless as she was standing out the front of her class-room inspiring rambunctious teens. Now, playing nice was just exhausting. She'd much prefer to hide in her bubble of denial and pretend Mr. Darcy or his equivalent could come riding on his white stallion and rescue her from this life.

"Good morning, class," the perky instructor said. "I see we have a few new faces today. Welcome!"

There came a buzz of greetings from those so inclined.

"Now, before we begin, let's shuffle those mats forward just a bit. Great! Now, I have to ask, is everyone feeling well?"

"Yes!"

"Is anyone expecting a baby?"

Pain flashed. No.

"Are we ready to get limber?"

"Yes!"

The Pilates cheerleader led the class through a series of stretches, most of which Sarah was used to, even if some had different names. She leaned to her right, careful not to go too far as she stretched her left arm above her head. Maybe this was helping. She had spent a lot of time lying around in the hammock lately, and if Pilates helped prevent another hip spasm, well, good.

Back to the other side, then it was down to the floor, knees under her shoulders. Floor work tended to be trickier. The therapist had warned her to be careful, so she took her time, gauging her back muscles as she did a cat stretch, then released. Another cat stretch and release, then it was down with arms outstretched in a resting child's pose. So far, pretty good.

"Well done! Now, let's go on our sides. That's it. Don't forget to go at your own pace and take a break if necessary. You know your body better than anyone, and we don't want to push it. We want gain, not pain, okay?"

A cheerleader *and* a poet, Sarah thought, following the

instructor's movements as she raised her left leg. Still, gaining movement, not creating pain, was exactly what her therapist had advised. She gritted her teeth as she held her leg in the correct position. Her core shook, and she clenched her fingers, exhaling with a rush as the instructor bade them.

Ange looked across and mouthed *okay?*

Sarah nodded, taking a moment to sip her water bottle before tackling the next move, one that required the right leg to extend behind.

"Good. Now, hold. Hold. Hold!"

Who was Perky Pilates Instructor yelling at? Sarah glanced up. Judging from the death stare being levelled in her direction, she knew who. Wait. Hadn't she just said to go at your own pace?

Sarah ducked her head, cowering back into position.

Be brave.

She blinked. That's right. Courage. She lifted her chin, eyeing the instructor, who immediately barked, "Head down!"

Way to make a newbie feel welcome. Sarah pushed to all fours, rolled her eyes at Ange, and reached for a drink. She'd come to exercise, not be yelled at.

Sitting on her knees, she glanced around the room, avoiding the glare of the now not-so-perky Pilates instructor, and froze. Behind her was a man. A dark-haired, tanned man, whose T-shirt did nothing to disguise the rippling muscles she'd seen recently. Since when did Mr. Wilderness-types do Pilates? Weren't they supposed to prefer fishing and hunting and the like? And guys his age—he had to be late twenties, like her—and with muscles like his usually did weights, not classes that emphasized balance—or the lack thereof. Her chest tightened. Oh no. What if he recognized her? She swiveled back to the front and sipped more water. Then started choking.

"Miss?" Miss Perky Pilates drew near. "Are you quite all right?"

"Yep," she muttered. "I'll be right in just a moment."

She wouldn't look behind her, *wouldn't* look. Wouldn't!

"Sarah?"

She glanced up. "Oh! Daniel. Hello." She held her breath, working desperately to clear her throat. By now, half the room was looking at her. She snuck another peek. Or maybe they were looking at him. Age was no barrier to admiration of the human form, it seemed.

"Would you like to leave?" the instructor asked—or was it pleaded?

"I'm fine." Sarah pushed up to a sitting position. "I just need a—oh!"

Pain speared her side, felling her, and she was back on that plane, back in the water, as her hip protested the sudden movement. She gasped, dragging in deep breaths in an attempt to ward off the spasms. She glanced at Ange, who nodded and rose, apologizing to the instructor, who still hovered like a scrawny bird of prey.

"Can I help?"

"Thanks, Dan. If you could just collect her things, that'd be good."

Sarah closed her eyes. Dialed her expression up to pleasant as she vainly tried to stretch out the cramp. Oh, this was ag-o-ny.

"Here." The soft voice in her ear provided a mite of comfort. As did the arm around her shoulders as he helped her to her feet. She caught a whiff of Eternity, the clean scent one her dad used to wear, a subtle nod to his profession.

Sarah hobbled outside to where Ange opened the car, then collapsed into the passenger seat in a haze of heated-skin awkwardness. She peeked up to where Macho Man studied her with a frown. "Um, thanks for helping."

"You sure you're okay?"

Hardly. But, "The pain is improving, so I'll be fine." Maybe.

She rushed to change the subject, shifting to look at Ange. "Guess we won't be getting that cake and coffee now."

"You really need to eat?"

Maybe not. But she *really* needed to escape Mr. Wilderness's intense perusal. "Since when did need factor into eating?"

Dan's look of concern melded into amusement. "I can't disagree." His smile was just the same as she remembered from last week—wide, white, and disarmingly friendly. "You're definitely okay?"

"Yes. Thanks again."

He dipped his chin, and she drew her legs inside the vehicle. A minute more and she could escape, could head back to Pemberley and its associated gentlemen, could pretend this unfortunate episode had never occurred.

"Dan, would you like to join us for a coffee?"

Dear God, no. Sarah closed her eyes. God bless Ange's gift for hospitality, but she *really* didn't want to have to make small talk with the man who'd now rescued her twice.

"Uh, maybe another time."

She snapped open her eyes. Had she appeared too rude again? "You can come. If you want. I mean, I didn't intend to interrupt your workout or anything." Heavens, that wasn't exactly gracious. "I mean, you obviously like to keep really fit..." She faltered to a stop as his lips curled up in one corner. Yep. Foot-in-mouth disease. Had she really just said that aloud? She might as well just call him Thor and be done with it.

He swiveled a look she couldn't decipher at Ange, then shrugged. "I think the class is close to finishing now anyway. So maybe I will, seeing as you're so insistent."

"I'm not—" Sarah bit back the rest of her reply and bent her lips upward in something that probably looked more grimace than smile. But at least she wouldn't have to deal with Ange's patient looks of compressed lips and sympathetic understanding. She turned to her aunt, changing the subject. "So, where is the best place for coffee around here?"

"Ask Dan. He's more of a connoisseur than I am."

She reluctantly turned to the he-god, whose brawny arms were crossed, revealing every sculpted muscle. Was he a professional body builder or something? In addition to his chief role as rescuer, that was. Maybe he was a fireman. Had his own calendar, where he posed with kittens he'd personally saved from trees.

He shrugged. "The Coffee Blend is the best place in town, but the cafe here isn't too bad, if you feel like venturing back inside."

And potentially see all those who'd just watched her inglorious exit?

Be brave.

"Fine." That didn't sound terribly polite. She pasted on a smile—one that didn't exactly move her cheeks, but it was the best she had right now. "That sounds good."

Again, he had that disconcerting tweak to his lips, like he found her amusing or something. "Let's go, then."

And shrugging off their concern, she reluctantly followed them inside.

He still didn't know what had made him agree to coffee with Ange and the princess. He sipped his coffee—tall black, no sugar —making small talk with Ange while Sarah gazed out the lakeview window and nibbled at her chocolate brownie. He'd barely seen Sarah these past few days. She seemed to have perfected the art of disappearing whenever he came on the scene. Still, he was supposed to love his neighbor, right? And yesterday's sermon on loving the unlovable had struck deep, the knowledge that he was supposed to actually put it into practice pushing him past his initial reluctance to be friendly. Or maybe—his lips quirked—he simply wanted to hear whatever outrageous thing would fall from her mouth next.

"So, is the instructor always like that?" Sarah asked, her gaze shifting between them.

"I think she's new," Ange said, brow pleating. "And perhaps a *little* too focused."

"I think I'll stick with swimming rather than come back here." Sarah grimaced.

"You're not going to let a pushy instructor stop you coming, are you?" he dared.

Sarah's gaze narrowed.

"Or are you simply living up to your T-shirt again?"

She glanced at her shirt—today's line read *My good opinion once lost is lost forever*—and shrugged. "I can't help it if Mr. Darcy is right."

"Mr. Darcy, eh?" Who the heck was he? He glanced at Ange. She was looking at him curiously again.

Ange's phone chirped, and she excused herself to take the call.

"So, how does this measure up?" he asked Sarah as her gaze flitted back to him.

"Do you mean the coffee, the company, or the view?"

"Any, all of the above."

"Okay"—she ticked off her fingers—"good, and lovely."

He rated as good? That was better than okay, at least.

"Actually, scrap that. It's not good. More like gorgeous."

He choked on his coffee. She thought he was gorgeous?

Her eyes rounded, cheeks pinking. "I meant this Muskoka area is gorgeous. Not that you're not attractive, because obviously—I mean—" She faltered to a stop. "Kill me now," she muttered, pushing back her chair. "Excuse me."

His lips twitched as she snatched her purse from the table and stalked away. Someone who appreciated Muskoka like he did couldn't be too bad. He watched as she swerved through diners to the cashier. Wait. She was paying?

She turned to point out their table, saw he was still looking at her. He lifted a hand. She spun back to the cashier, said something else, shook her head.

He grew aware of the buzz of nearby conversation and turned to see a young boy—who looked the spitting image of Dan's brother Sam fifteen years ago—holding a hockey card and a nervous smile. He smiled, signed and briefly chatted, all the while conscious of regret kneading within. The boy looked to be the same age as what his own—

"Thanks, Mr. Walton!" The kid beamed, then hurried to a waiting man and woman who offered Dan a wave, which he returned as Sarah slipped back into her seat and sighed.

"You know I didn't expect you to pay for my coffee."

"Who says I did?"

He blinked.

"Don't worry." Her mouth twisted. "I paid for yours as well, especially since you're only here because of my little breakdown before."

Yeah, that. He'd known cramps before, but her episode had seemed next level. He wanted to ask but figured she'd think it rude. Even if she seemed to have recovered now.

"Hey, can I ask you a question?" she continued.

"You just did."

She raised a brow at his pathetic humor. Guess that didn't even rate an okay. "What makes a guy like you do Pilates?"

"A guy like me?" He placed his cup on the table. "You'll have to tell me what you mean by that."

"I just mean—"

"I'm sorry," Ange said, returning, brow pleated. "That was John. It seems the husband of one of the congregation has been taken to hospital, and Patty needs to be driven there immediately." Ange looked at him apologetically. "I'm sorry to ask, but Dan, would you mind taking Sarah home?"

Sarah shot him a look before turning to her aunt. "I don't mind going with you—"

"I'm afraid I really don't know how long this will take. Henry's been sick for a while, and I suspect I'll be caught up for hours."

"I don't mind," he said. The engagement ring made it safe.

"Thank you," Ange said, visibly relieved.

"I'll take care of dinner." Sarah rose to give her aunt a hug.

"Thanks, Sarah. And thank you, Dan. See you later."

He watched Ange leave, then turned back to see Sarah studying him warily. The ease had gone, replaced by almost palpable tension.

He gestured to her half-eaten brownie. "You nearly ready to go?"

She pushed aside the plate and rose. "I'm ready now."

They moved to the resort entrance, and he nodded to Serena Williamson, the resort's assistant events manager he'd met a few times before. A toddling boy raced inside as a mother maneuvered her baby's stroller through the revolving glass doors, only to trip and let out a loud scream.

Sarah crouched and picked the boy up, soothing him. "Hey, it's okay."

The woman hurried forward and reprimanded her son before sighing and thanking Sarah.

"No worries," Sarah said before giving the little boy a wave as the trio moved away.

Another glance at Sarah showed her smile had faded and she was gnawing her lip, strain on her face. He knew a strange twist of sympathy.

"Ready?"

She nodded, following him to his Jeep.

He steered onto the road that would take them to Gravenhurst. The dark green of the black spruce flashed by, and he admired the fancy fretwork of leaves arching across the road, filtering the high summer sun. Muskoka at this time of year was beautiful. He smiled to himself. Actually, Muskoka at any time of year was beautiful. "Anything you need to do, seeing we're passing through town?"

"I wouldn't mind going to the post office, if that's okay."

"Sure."

The minutes passed in silence, leading him to wonder again about his passenger. He wasn't any expert on women, but most he knew talked way more than this.

He pulled into the commercial area and parked. "Canada Post is just there." He pointed. "They're pretty efficient. Meet you back here in twenty?"

"Okay. Thanks." She exited, her gait a little uneven as she walked up the street.

He frowned and went inside a small grocery store to collect the next few days' necessities. As he lined up to pay, he noticed the young blonde cashier give him a second glance.

"Excuse me. Don't you play defense for the Maple Leafs? You're Daniel Walton, right?"

Dan forced a smile as she started the customary small talk. Years of the limelight had taught him to respect the fans. But still, it'd be nice to enjoy a vacation anonymously for once.

Her smile widened as he paid then hefted up the bags. "Bye, Daniel. See you next time!"

"See ya." He headed outside. Better avoid that store next time. He'd seen that look a few too many times before. He shuddered, recalling Jai Mullins's recent wedding, where he'd over-heard a woman whisper something to a friend about the NHL. They'd smiled at him, speculative gleams in their eyes. He'd exchanged glances with his NHL Bible study friends, Brent Karlsson, Beau Nash, Mike Vaughan, and Tyler Woletsky. Guys had been burned before. He knew that only too well.

Sarah waited by the Jeep, her long red hair windblown. She clutched a small paper bag.

He loaded his groceries into the back of the vehicle. "Anything else you want to do?"

She shook her head.

"You got your postcards?"

"How did you know?"

Dan unlocked her door. "You're a tourist, you went to the post office, and those shapes in the bag kinda look like postcards to me."

She climbed in. "I didn't know you were a detective."

He laughed to himself. And Little Miss Frosty was back. Good luck to the fiancé. Sarah was an ice princess, for sure.

He exited the parking lot, escaping the town's tourist traffic as he turned onto the county road that led closer to the lake. At least his passenger's silence meant he could think. And pray.

Lord, I know You've blessed me in lots of ways—with a good family, great church friends, an awesome job, and a super nice house. I'm thankful, really I am.

But he was still lonely. The house still seemed empty. There was too much space.

He changed gear again to climb the steeply graded hill, glancing over to where Sarah fiddled with her ring. His grip tightened on the steering wheel as he fought a spike of envy. Most of the other guys in the NHL online Bible study group had found wives or girlfriends in recent years. John said God would bring along the right woman at the right time, but where was she? Someone to talk, laugh, and live life's adventures with —surely that wasn't too much to ask. But another year kept clocking by with no prospect of his life ever changing. Yeah, he'd had a few first dates, but he'd never felt any real connection or been intrigued enough to want more. And he always wondered if the glossy, made-up faces were just that—made-up, shiny veneers to hide someone totally different underneath. Like Lana.

Shame shivered up his spine. Could he ever fully trust a woman again? And how good did he need to be for God to trust him with a wife and family?

He took the bend a little wide. His passenger gave a muffled cry. As he grappled with the steering wheel, he glimpsed Sarah bracing herself between the door and the dash. He gritted his teeth, wrestled the Jeep back on the road, and pulled up safely on the shoulder. *Thank You, God.*

He exhaled, willing his heartbeat to slow as he turned. Sarah was even paler than usual, staring straight ahead, still clenching the door in a white-knuckled death grip.

"Hey, Sarah." He waited until she finally looked at him, her eyes' usual emptiness replaced by stark fear. "Hey, you're safe, we're okay now. I'm sorry if I scared you."

If? He bit his lip. She still seemed terrified. Compassion shot through him, and he leaned across to touch her arm.

Her flinch felt like a slap. He drew back, waiting until Sarah finally nodded, then he shifted the Jeep into gear for the final stretch home.

Dan shook his head. How could he think about having a wife and family if he couldn't even keep his mind on just getting home safely? His stomach tensed. Maybe he'd never be good enough. He'd done some stupid things in the past. But God was full of mercy, wasn't He? That's what John kept saying, anyway.

He carefully rounded the final bend. *How long, God?* The plea was never too far from his heart these days, usually followed by *I'm trying to trust You.* But, man, waiting was hard.

He pulled up outside John and Ange's cottage and watched Sarah slowly exit. She turned, her eyes meeting his for the briefest of moments. "Thanks for the ride."

"You're welcome. And hey, I really am sorry for scaring you before."

She inclined her head a few degrees, as if she were the queen, then turned and disappeared inside.

He frowned as he drove off in a cloud of dust, wondering about his new neighbor. A mix of what seemed like grit and fear, humor and reserve, fire and ice. John and Ange seemed to treat her with kid gloves, but he knew from personal experience they could speak pretty straight. Why all the tiptoeing around the princess?

CHAPTER 3

"Give it some thought, Sarah. People need to hear about the benefits of mission work overseas."

"But I'm not good at talking to people anymore."

"You can do this. You're stronger than you think."

Her uncle's words hung heavy in the air, teasing her to believe. She shook her head, exchanged a wry smile with Ange, and redirected John's attention. "Have fun today."

"Have fun yourself." They moved to the small blue sedan.

Ange blew her a kiss as John started the engine. "We'll be back tonight."

As the car disappeared around the bend in the road, Sarah smiled. Being alone had proved a rare pleasure growing up. Maybe it was all the meetings her parents had held at home, or all the people who'd come and stayed. Just one of the hazards of being a minister's daughter. The smile slipped as she recalled some others, like the expectation from certain congregation members that she look and behave a certain way, as if she was supposed to be extra holy simply because she was a preacher's kid. That bubble had certainly burst over the past year. After the accident, people didn't know what to expect of her anymore.

She moved through the front door, down the short hall, and eyed the bathroom. She'd offered to clean, but Ange had declined assistance. Oh well. Cleaning Fairy was about to appear anyway. That burst of energy lasted just long enough to also tackle the kitchen, leaving it gleaming as brightly as the chrome on the French coffee press. She took her coffee to the dining table, pulled her laptop near, and puzzled over her uncle's comments. No way was she ready to stand in front of strangers and declare the wonders of the Pacific Mission Organization. But maybe there was another way.

A few clicks later and she had the makings of a slideshow, the words and images seared in her brain. Tropical jungle. Mountain vistas fading into blue. People engaged in education, health, building houses. Her parents' ministry base high in the New Guinea mountains had hosted many short-term missions teams over the years, offering a place to stay for a variety of people to make a positive difference in the world. Offering their daughters the chance to later meet men who had ultimately altered their lives in ways unimaginable.

Heart dipping, she gazed at the image on the screen. Stephen.

Her lips quivered. She shut the laptop. Pushed away from the table, away from the memories. *Distraction, distraction.*

She moved to the little living room out the back. It held an open fireplace, some comfortable couches, the dining table, and big windows overlooking the back deck. She slid open the glass door, gazing out across the great view of the lake. But she needed something more than a pretty view. She needed to *do*. And that could be achieved with the help of the prize sitting against the wall, something she'd been itching to try since she'd first arrived.

Sarah lifted off the dust covers and settled in front of the old Yamaha. Hopefully it was in tune. She held her breath, struck middle C, and completed a quick run up the keys. Resonance filled the room. After some scales, she began her limited repertoire of classic melancholy pop songs. Ease settled into her soul. There was something divinely relaxing about playing the piano, creating music as the mood took her. And here, with nobody around, the mood could take her to the usual place, and nobody would ask any questions.

A half hour later, she was in the midst of the familiar dark swirl of emotion, the minor chords deepening the heaviness of her heart, her voice blending with the piano's surprisingly good tone. She began singing "Kissing You," a haunting tune from the 90s film *Romeo and Juliet*. It had become one of her favorite songs—guaranteed to release some of her pent-up emotion.

Tears escaped. She swiped them away, pushing through the break in her voice as the music swelled around her like a cocoon. She was safe. Nobody could hear, nobody could see the broken heart being played aloud or the tears splotting on the ivories. She sang the final line, finishing on an unresolved note, the sound fading into silence. Placing her head in her hands, she exhaled a ragged breath, heart raw with the grief that wouldn't leave. *God, this still hurts so much.*

Something creaked. She lifted her head, then jumped. Dan stood at the screen door, his features soft.

No. She couldn't deal with pity. Best defense was attack. She rubbed damp cheeks, willed her voice to normal. "What do you want? Are you some kind of stalker?"

"What? No, I, uh, came to speak with John. I didn't mean to intrude. But when I heard the music..." His eyes held hers. "That was...beautiful."

No. That had been way too revealing. Honest. Real. "No one was meant to hear that."

"Why? You're really talented." He leaned against the doorframe, studying her, his dark eyes intense, like he was trying to puzzle her out.

Her skin prickled. She slid off the piano stool to stand at the window. "I...I like playing if nobody's around. I don't have to worry if I hit a wrong note."

"You shouldn't worry. You're so good you could perform in public."

If only he knew. Obviously Ange hadn't said anything. Relief was followed by the slightest sense of disappointment. She folded her arms. "Did you say you wanted John?"

"Just to see if he wanted to go fishing."

"He's not here. They went to Port Carling."

"Oh. Well, I'll leave you to your music."

She shook her head. "I'm kind of done now." There was a flow to music, a space that was hard to find once the rhythm had been broken. She couldn't go back there right now.

"I didn't mean to interrupt." Dan continued standing there, a lopsided smile on his face, hands jammed in his back pockets. But that grin was a little disconcerting. And he'd proved surprisingly kind and thoughtful several times now. Not that he'd ever be her type, of course. Although, as she'd sat in the car after church the other day, she couldn't help but notice the number of girls who thought he was exactly their type, ogling and giggling their way up to speak to him. Please.

"Well, uh..." He shoved a hand through his hair. "Do you want to go fishing?"

She choked. "Me? I don't fish." The few times she'd accompanied her father as a child had been a waste of a good sit down as far as she was concerned. What was the point if you didn't catch anything?

"Want to keep me company while I fish, then?"

"Is this a pity invitation?" Not more pity.

"No." The tough-guy mask slipped a little. "I, uh, I'd just like some company."

"Oh." Loneliness she understood. And if she stayed inside, she'd only feel more of this stifling, sickening melancholy. "Well, I suppose I could."

"Is that a pity acceptance?" He bit his lip, as if trying not to smile.

The corners of her mouth twitched. "Maybe."

SARAH TUGGED down her wide-brimmed hat against the sun's bright glare on the water. Why had she agreed to this? This sitting around waiting for things to happen… She yawned. If only she'd brought *Emma*. Maybe she could make up some excuse and go back.

"This is good, isn't it?"

Good? Well, maybe compared to being covered in honey and left in a pit with hungry bears. "When do the fish start biting?" She snuck a peek at the man sitting beside her.

His lips curved. "Patience. They'll bite when they're ready."

Sarah adjusted her oversized sunglasses and bit back a sigh. She so didn't do patience.

"You're not really having fun, are you?" he said after a moment. "I knew you said yes because you felt sorry for me. What d'you want to do instead?"

"Read. Sleep." She concentrated on her ring, studying the diamond facets as they sparkled in the summer sun, twisting it again so only the thin gold band showed. Sometimes she liked to pretend she was married, that Stephen was only away on a long vacation and this was all a bad dream. She couldn't take it off. The ring was her last tangible reminder of him.

"Sociable, huh?"

"Not anymore." After an initial flurry of hospital visitors, she'd begun isolating herself, making excuses not to see people. Who could ever understand her pain?

"You're enjoying it here, though, aren't you?"

"It's beautiful. So serene." The loud whine of a motorboat powered across the lake in front of them, sending rippling waves to the shore. "Yep, real serene."

He laughed. "That's the downside of all this beauty. Everyone wants a piece of it." He propped his fishing rod up with a rock. "I guess that's the end of the bites for a while."

"You're such an optimist. I still think you didn't attach the bait properly."

"Pessimist."

"Nope." She followed a droning dragonfly's lazy acrobatic display. "Realist."

He snickered. "You're kinda fun when you want to be."

Sarah stared at a tiny rocky island proudly waving a Canadian flag. Fun? For all the peace and tranquility of her surrounds, tension still coiled inside her like a snake—tension that could never leave her. Over the years, she'd been accused many times of having a temperament to match her fiery-colored hair, but now anger really did bubble away, like in a pressure cooker, ready to spew out. Sometimes she felt so angry her skin could barely hold it in.

She was angry with Stephen for leaving her. Angry with God for allowing this to happen. She even felt perversely angry with all the well-meaning people who tried to help but ended up saying those same stupid, meaningless things, like *He's in a better place* or *God must have wanted him home.* She wanted to scream at them *He should be here with me! We should be married by now, planning to have babies!*

Babies? Her breath suspended, her eyes filling afresh. She bit her lip hard, trying to breathe past clogged tears.

"Want to talk about it?"

"Not really."

He picked a blade of grass, neatly sliced it with his thumbnail. He didn't push; just waited, as if he knew she'd eventually crack.

"Why? Why would you want to hear my story?" Why would anyone want to hear her heart bleed, let alone a near stranger?

He shrugged. "I like to hear you talk. Your accent is cute."

"Cute?"

"Besides, bottling stuff up isn't healthy. Sometimes you just gotta let it out."

Maybe, but not today. Emotion felt too close to the surface, with no guarantee her façade wouldn't splinter into a million tiny pieces. *God, I need some help here.*

The line bobbed. Then dipped again.

"Hey, I think we caught something." He moved to grasp the line, then with a careful flick and quick reel, brought up a large silvery bass. "Look at the size of him!"

"You like to catch fish."

"I gotta admit, I usually end up feeding the fish rather than actually catching them." He grinned. "You're good luck. We'll have to do this again."

She groaned. But maybe, if he asked, she might even agree.

"This is really good, Sarah."

John's praise tugged at the corners of her heart. She clicked to the next slide. "It's not much, but it's better than nothing."

"It's really good, Sarah." He eyed her kindly, as if willing her to accept the words.

She ducked her head. Why was it so hard to accept affirmation these days? Rarely did it settle. Had the forced cheer of the do-gooders led her to doubt people's words?

She had to get out of here. She closed the laptop, pushed back her chair. "I might go for a swim, before it gets too hot."

"Good idea. I would, too, if Ange and I weren't going to Bala today. Enjoy."

"You too." She nodded to the tray of cookies Ange had set out to cool on the counter.

He laughed and patted his rounded stomach. "I always do."

Her answering smile lingered as she wandered down to the small beach situated between the cottage and the mansion next door. She dropped her towel on a handy boulder and waded through the shallows out to the deep. The water was still a little chilly, but at least nobody else was around. *Thanks, God.*

She swam out to the little buoy. Her smile broadened—her leg *was* improving. She touched the buoy, then dived, the water so clear she could see the rocks and tiny green weeds on the bottom. She swam underwater for a while, then resurfaced with a grin and a wet hair toss that would do a mermaid proud.

"Morning!"

Sarah turned. Dan stood on the beach, prime witness to her Ariel impersonation. Oh. No. "Uh, hi."

"Nice in?"

"Yeah." She continued treading water. "John and Ange might still be at the house if you want them."

He lifted his towel. "I'm swimming too."

Great. She still felt weirdly nervous around him, but maybe he wasn't so bad. "You can come in. I won't bite."

"Promise?" He smirked, then stripped off his T-shirt and waded in.

Oh. She didn't know where to look. The man obviously worked *out*, and his skin was such a nice even brown. Definitely what her sister would've labeled "an excellent physical speci-men." She glanced away, forcing herself to concentrate on the correct breaststroke kick.

"Sleep well?" Dan was like a seal, slipping through the water beside her. A playful, brown-eyed, rather-too-cute-to-look-at seal.

"Yes. You?"

"Yeah. Gonna be a hot one today. Maybe a storm later." He pulled ahead of her slightly. "So, you like to swim."

She nodded, then realized he couldn't see her. "Yes."

"Play any sports?"

"Does Pilates count?"

"Nope."

"Well, in that case, no. My face goes bright red whenever I exercise and stays that way for hours. People always think there's something wrong with me."

He laughed. "Well, you're an excellent musician. Can't be good at everything, I s'pose."

"Do you always talk when you swim?"

"Sick of my voice, huh?"

Actually, no. His voice possessed a timbre that soothed the jagged spaces of her heart. "I don't mind."

"Good."

The water gleamed, the warmth in the air nothing like the summer heat she remembered from the tropics of her childhood but enough to make her glad for the chance to cool off. She concentrated on her stroke, on her kick, on her breathing, trying to ignore the man swimming nearby. Fortunately, Muskoka wasn't short of attractive outlooks. She closed her eyes, heard the pines sing in the light breeze, and felt the tiniest easing of tension.

"Hey."

Sarah gasped and opened her eyes.

"You okay?" Dan was treading water, watching her carefully.

"Yeah."

"Having fun?"

"Yes."

She was? Sarah began a fast crawl back to the beach.

"A race is it? You're on." He powered through the water, easily overtaking her to reach the shore first.

Men were the same the world over. "Hey, that's not fair! You're so much bigger and stronger than me. Anyway, what happened to ladies before gentlemen?"

He chuckled. "I guess I'm not always a gentleman. And I definitely don't like to back down from a challenge."

Dan toweled himself off as she waded through the shallow water. He handed her the towel she'd dropped before, looking away as she quickly dried herself. As she sat nearby, he glanced at the scars on her leg.

Yep, they sure helped her feel beautiful. She wrapped the towel more tightly around her. Thank God for one-piece swimsuits that mostly hid the web of angry red ridges around her left hip and across her stomach. Such ugly, raw reminders. If, by some miracle, she ever did get married, her husband was in for a nice surprise.

"I have a few of my own." He pointed to the side of his jaw, his knees and hands.

"Yeah, no. Thanks for playing, but I think I win."

He did the half-smile thing again. "Mmm, maybe you do."

Sarah hugged her knees, her hair hanging in damp auburn clumps. She drew in a deep breath, appreciating the sun's warmth on her back and how it highlighted the cloud shadows drifting across Muskoka's vibrant blue. There was something just so peaceful about this place. Or was it something about the company? Dan was so easygoing. "So, how long have you been coming here?"

"For years." He stretched out his legs. "My family camped up this way when I was a kid. Now I come for the fishing. It's a great place to escape from the hockey world."

"The hockey world?"

His eyebrows shot up, and he studied her a moment longer. Then shrugged. "I play pro hockey, which involves a lot of travel, training, and practice in cold rinks. I love my job, but coming here, where there's great scenery, and doing what I want when I want is awesome."

As he described his personal piece of paradise, her heart grasped at his words. "That's exactly what I've wanted. To be away, free from people's expectations, to take time out. I love it here. I can just be. I don't have to look a certain way, or smile, or pretend everything is okay." She shot him a wry glance. "I've pretended for so long now, I barely know what's real."

Why was she saying this? She barely knew the man. But somehow he seemed safe, like he was someone she could talk to. Someone whom, if he offered to listen, she might dare to finally share with. She *ached* to talk about Stephen to someone who didn't know him, whose feelings she wouldn't have to protect, with whom she could just be real for once.

She peeked across. He was gazing at the clouds scudding across the sky, like a man without a care in the world. The pale scar on his jaw dipped in, dipped out. He turned, and she quickly averted her gaze, pretending interest in the glistening lake.

"It's hard to leave the past behind."

The gentle words pricked her heart. "I don't really know how to," she whispered. "Stephen..." She drew in a pain-tinged breath. Exhaled.

"Your fiancé?"

She nodded, wondering again how much Ange and John had told him. Maybe nothing, judging from that question. "He was."

"Was?"

Was. Three little letters that encapsulated a world of grief. "We...we were going to a party on New Year's Eve a year and a half ago when our...our car slammed into a tree." Pain roared up her throat at the memories. She shook them away, swallowed. "He died."

"I'm so sorry," he murmured.

She shrugged as if his words didn't stroke the underside of her pain. "Now everyone wants me to be this happy, bubbly girl again, like they want me to forget and move on. Like he wasn't important to them."

"Is that why you still wear his ring?"

Sarah nodded, twirling the diamond around her finger, surprised at his sensitivity.

"People care about you."

"Sometimes they care too much." Her breath caught, her

chest growing taut. "I...I feel like a huge part of my heart is missing. I don't know who I am or what I'm supposed to do with my life. I feel so lost, like I can't cope anymore."

As if to prove her words true, emotion swelled, tsunami-like, pausing for a fraction of a second, then pummeling through her, a relentless wave straight from her heart to line the backs of her eyes, nose, and throat. Oh no. She breathed out slowly, desperately trying to hold it in as she hunched away, but it was too late, her silent tears leaking to drip onto her towel. One. Two. A dozen. More. She wiped at her face, willing him not to notice, even as her sniffling whimpers refused restraint. How excruciating. She needed a tissue. She *really* needed to leave. She shifted to scramble away, felt a touch on her shoulder, and froze.

"I'll be back in a few minutes."

She heard the crunch of pebbles as Dan walked away, probably to phone Ange to say her niece was a basket case. She didn't blame him for leaving. A shudder shook her as her chest swelled with new emotion. Suddenly she didn't care what she looked like. How long had it been since she'd cried it out? Had she ever? The doctors and nurses and counsellors had all wanted her to focus on getting well and not give in to grief. But they weren't here. Neither were her parents. She didn't have to pretend anymore.

"Oh, God. Why?"

Breath hitched, the tears trickling down her cheeks quickly turned into chest-heaving sobs wrenched from the deepest part of her soul. Sorrow writhed, like a living presence trapped within, as she cried for Stephen, cried for herself, cried for her lost future. *Why, God? Why?* It wasn't fair. Would never be fair.

It just was.

The weeping continued, then gradually lessened, escaping in a series of rib-bruising wheezes, then she exhaled shakily. Drew in another ragged breath. Wiped her eyes with the heels of her hands. Noticed a tissue box had mysteriously appeared. Great.

So there had been at least one spectator to her grief. Oh well. It wasn't like she was trying to impress anyone here. She snagged a tissue and blew her nose—loudly—to emphasize the fact. Pushed out another shoulder-slumping sigh.

Footsteps behind her stilled her movements, tension bracing her as Dan resumed his spot, near but not too near. Had he heard her banshee wails before? She cringed. How could he not? Oh, what did it matter?

The sounds of the lake gradually stole into awareness again: the hush of breeze, the sigh of pines, the song of waves. Far above, an eagle wheeled and whirled. Into her soul stole a measure of...

Peace.

It had been so long since she'd felt this way she barely recognized the feeling. The tight coldness encasing her heart had eased, like an iceberg splintering into the sea. She felt lighter, as if the grief had been weighing her down, holding her prisoner, seeping out in anger and bitterness. Funny. She didn't feel angry like that anymore. Embarrassment, however...

She peeked across to where Dan sat, eyes closed, leaning back on outstretched arms. How *awful* to weep like that with such a stranger. But holding back the tears had been impossible, the sorrow squeezing from the furthest corners of her heart. She'd needed to cry to get rid of every drop.

Those months in hospital, she'd been told to focus on getting better and not give way to grief. Tears at night had only led to concerned questions from her parents. She'd pasted on courage with Stephen's family for their sake, and the charade had continued, the tears pushing down into some cold, dark well inside, damming up her heart, increasing the pressure in her soul.

But she felt better now.

Sarah grabbed another tissue, grimacing. If only she had a face that could cry pretty, but no. She always managed to do what Oprah would call the ugly cry. Her nose felt swollen, the skin on her face had to be bright red, and she could barely see, her eyes had puffed so much from all the tears. She shook her head. Stupid vanity. What did it matter?

She gazed across Muskoka's vivid blue as the sun warmed her. *God, that was really embarrassing, but thanks for the freedom to cry here. Thanks for Ange and John.*

The gentle wash of the water was punctuated by a faraway squabble of ducks. She glanced at the man sitting peacefully nearby. "Hey, Dan?"

He opened his eyes. "Mmm?"

"Thanks for being here."

"Anytime." His gaze was soft. "I'll be praying for you."

"Thanks." Tears? Still? She blinked them away. "I obviously need it."

"Hey, we all do."

A faint insect buzz began nearby. Dan stretched, yawned, then lay down on the grass, closing his eyes again, muscles popping as he rested his head on clasped hands.

She studied him, the picture of controlled strength. "You know, for such a macho man, you're really kind of nice."

His brow wrinkled. "Macho man?"

She bit her lip. Was he offended? "I didn't mean—"

"And what do you mean by 'kind of nice'?" He opened his eyes and flicked her a crooked grin. "I'll have you know, I *am* nice."

Maybe he was. Sarah dropped her gaze, as the diamond twinkled impudently up at her. She slowly turned the ring around until she could only see the gold band. And frowned.

CHAPTER 4

*Y*esterday's storm had scrubbed the world clean. Dan leaned against the wooden railing of the deck as he finished his juice. It was a new day, a fresh start, and Muskoka shone in all God's glory. The lake sparkled, the trees were brightly washed, the sky was clear, the world held hope. Days like today—fresh, invigorating—made him glad to be alive.

Last night he'd caught up with some of the Bible study guys. Mike, Tim, and Brent had been distracted with their little kids, the sight of which had tugged envy again, and he'd been glad for the distraction of Beau, Tyler, Luc, and Ryan as they shared about their summer plans. Beau had apologized for not being able to help out at Dan's camp this year, which had helped Dan refocus from such stupid emotions.

His thoughts slid to next door. Hopefully the storm had also washed away more of Sarah's sorrow. He chewed his lip. He'd never been good with emotions. As the middle of three brothers, he'd never really needed to be. But that same little prompting to invite Sarah to fish had insisted he stay, even as everything within had protested.

And now he was kinda glad. Learning her story—her

tragedy, really—had prompted some googling last night that had revealed more of who she'd been. He'd barely recognized her as Heartsong Collective's lead singer on the YouTube videos, and he'd found himself watching clip after clip, his heart tugging to know more. That vibrant, sassy, rock-star-like chick moving around the stage like she owned it was Sarah? Who would've thought? He even recognized some of the songs she'd written as ones he'd sung in church. He struggled to reconcile that confident woman with the broken one from yesterday, but knew he shouldn't have been so quick to judge. *Sorry, God.* At least the ice princess had thawed enough to show him those cracks. He hoped she was doing better now.

He took another deep breath of the pine-scented air, placed the glass in the kitchen sink, then headed over to check on his neighbors.

John and Ange were drinking coffee on the deck and greeted him with a smile. "You survived last night all right?"

"Sure was a wild one. Fun to watch, though."

"You've got a great spot for storm watching."

He chatted with them for a while, then entered the back door to find Sarah in the kitchen, holding a cup of tea. Her face seemed a little swollen and pink, but also lighter, less shadowed.

"Hey."

Her gaze dropped to study the wooden floorboards. "Hi."

"How's it going?"

"Better." Her lips half curved. "Sorry you had to witness my emotional train wreck."

"Seems like that was a crash that needed to happen."

"Maybe." Sarah pointed to the carafe. "Do you want a coffee? It should still be warm."

"Why not?"

Dan leaned against the dining table as she flitted about, checking if he wanted milk and sugar. She seemed different today—happier, although clearly self-conscious, avoiding his eyes. As she passed the mug to him, he noticed she'd moved the ring from her left hand to her right. Huh. Yesterday really *had* helped if moving the ring was any indication.

"Want something to eat? Ange made these earlier." Sarah motioned to a plate of macadamia and white chocolate cookies.

"They're my favorite." He devoured one, the rich, buttery cookie melting in his mouth, then picked up the plate and joined the others out on the deck. "So, what are you all up to today?"

"We've got branches to clean up." John sipped his coffee. "Then Ange and I are heading to Toronto to see Doris Easterbrook in ICU. We'll be back in a few days."

"Tell Doris we're praying for her." *Mental note: send flowers.* "I can help with the branches and stuff. I've got some down as well." He glanced over at Sarah, who'd finished her tea. "You going too?"

Her gaze met his. "I'm staying."

"Well, if you need anything, you know where I'll be."

"Thanks."

SARAH WATCHED, hands on ears, as Dan used a chainsaw to rip through the last of the bigger branches felled by the storm. They'd waved goodbye to John and Ange hours ago, then spent the time working as Dan turned into Action Man, finishing cleaning up John and Ange's yard, then his, before chopping up weathered logs for kindling.

Well, he'd worked. She'd attempted to look busy stacking wood, but it was hard not to stare. Growing up in a tropical forest, she'd seen her father chop wood. And she vaguely recalled Stephen using an axe on the mission trip when they'd first met. But she didn't remember either wielding an axe quite like Dan did. There was something so fiercely masculine about it. Of course, women could chop wood, but they'd never look like Mr. Wilderness. Dan looked so strong. Her lips twisted. No way would she ever be let near an axe—that was an amputation waiting to happen.

She was still smiling about it later when they'd finished and were drinking tall glasses of iced water on the back deck of the cottage. Dan shifted his gaze from the lake to study her again. She'd noticed his glances a few times today.

"You seem happier."

She paused. Happiness was something she'd not expected to feel again. And while she wasn't exactly *happy*, she'd concede something like… "More accepting, maybe."

"Acceptance is a start." Dan glanced at her. "Maybe you need to give yourself permission to live, to feel new feelings. And not feel guilty about it." He drained his glass of water and settled the glass with a thud. "Hey, I'm getting hungry. Want to have dinner?"

"Dinner?"

"Yeah, food."

"I don't know." She hadn't eaten alone with a man for a long time.

"It's just a meal. I'm hungry; I need to eat." His tan seemed to take on a reddish hue as she studied him. "Don't worry. It's not a date."

"I wasn't worried about that."

"Just friends having dinner."

He thought they were friends? She tried the word on for size. It felt… "Okay."

"What do you want to eat?"

"I…I don't cook much."

"Apart from amazing lasagna?" He raised an eyebrow. "Well, I don't feel like cooking. Let's order in. But you don't have good phone coverage down here, do you?"

She shook her head. Phone signals—and the internet—were temperamental at best.

"We'll need to phone from my cottage, then. Let's go."

They moved through the grove of trees separating the two properties, past the dusty black Jeep in the driveway, to the three-story cedar house. From the lake it appeared massive: the term *cottage* definitely a misnomer. Uncle John had a real cottage: two bedrooms, small living areas, country-styled furniture, and homily comfortable. This place seemed at least five times the size. For such a rough-and-ready-looking guy, he seemed to be staying in a pretty fancy-schmancy place. He must know some rich people to stay here.

He led the way up the stone steps to the front door. "Come in."

Sarah walked through the massive entrance and stood on the flagstones, staring at the lovely home. Late afternoon sunlight on the red timber paneling and exposed brick created a rustic, cozy feeling, while the high ceilings and huge picture windows gave a sense of space. The back windows of the large living room overlooked the extensive back deck, and she could see through the trees to the hot tub, boatshed, and tranquil lake beyond.

"Nice." Massive understatement. She gazed around at the comfortable furnishings, leather lounges, huge flat-screen television, gigantic stone fireplace. He took her on a brief tour. Six bedrooms, four bathrooms, several living spaces—for a holiday cottage, it was way larger than an average home. The people he'd borrowed it from must be loaded.

"Happy with pizza?" She nodded, and after debating the pizza options, Dan ordered. "They usually take a little while. Want a coffee while we wait? I can make you a cappuccino if you like."

What, like one of those cappuccino-in-a-packet things? No, thank you. Then she noticed the chrome machine sitting in the corner of the kitchen. Her taste buds switched to high gear. "There's a real espresso machine!"

"It's nice to not have to travel into town when I need my coffee fix."

"I'd kill for a real coffee. I mean, the plunger's okay, but it's not quite the same."

"You're not an addict, are you?"

"I prefer the term *aficionado*." She offered a half smile.

He studied her a beat longer, mouth tucked up in one corner. "So, what'll it be?"

"Can you make a latte?"

"Sure."

She sat on the barstool as he switched on the machine and plugged in the electric grinder, whose high-pitched whine soon filled the room. Well, hello, Mister Barista.

"Want any flavoring?"

"No. I like to actually taste the coffee."

"Hey, me too."

As he described where he bought his organic beans, Sarah bit back a grin, chastened about her initial preconceptions. And when she tasted the coffee, she knew just how wrong she'd been. It was like liquid gold hitting her bloodstream. She closed her eyes and smiled. Okay, she'd been way wrong. Seriously nice, smooth, dark, delicious…

Whoa. Her eyes snapped open to meet his gaze. The coffee was delicious—nothing else.

Her cheeks heated as he continued studying her. "What?"

"You have some froth…here." He leaned over the marble counter, eyes intense, and touched her lip.

A tingle shot straight through her. She jerked away.

His surprised gaze held a question she wasn't up to answering, so she swung off the stool, carrying her mug over to a large bookcase. She sipped coffee, tracing the spines, while he excused himself to make a phone call. John Grisham, Tom

Clancy, Robert Ludlam, Lee Child. Someone liked to read. Mostly action thrillers, but she noted a few authors she liked also.

He hung up the phone and glanced her direction.

"I love this book." She held up a hardcover copy of L.M. Montgomery's *The Blue Castle.* "Do you think it'd be okay if I borrow it?"

"Sure."

"Did you know it's set here in Muskoka?"

He shook his head. "Take it. I know you enjoy your books."

"Thanks." She looked up at him—baseball cap on backward, barefoot, lounging against the wall, biceps straining against the faded blue maple-leaf-emblazoned T-shirt as he crossed his arms. Classic jock. "So, do you read?"

Amusement crossed his face. "Believe it or not, we have schools here that teach us to read. I'm reading C.S. Lewis at the moment." He shrugged. "A book is a great way to unwind after a game."

Hmm. So maybe her pride had engaged in some prejudice. Dan kept surprising her, proving to be kind, insightful, patient, funny...sweet, even.

Next to the big screen TV she found the DVDs: some comedies, classic movies, TV adventure including the *Man vs Wild* series, and wonder of wonders, the complete James Bond collection.

"Someone wants to be a tough guy, huh?"

His eyes crinkled. "Some of us don't need to try."

She snickered. "Modest, too." She examined the box set.

"Don't tell me you're a fan?"

"Pierce Brosnan was the best. I like Daniel Craig, but can't get past the blond hair."

He looked at her thoughtfully. "You like 'em suave but ruthless, eh? I'm more of a Connery fan myself."

"He sounds a little too Scottish for me."

"Picky, picky."

"Maybe you don't mind accents."

A smile hovered on his lips. "Maybe."

She willed her cheeks not to blush and turned back to the film titles. "Could I borrow one sometime?"

"Sure. Or we could watch it here."

The doorbell rang, Dan disappeared, and Sarah slowly exhaled. The way he looked at her sometimes was so disconcerting. Fortunately, the pizza's arrival seemed to signal a return to the casual banter of before, the lightheartedness a welcome change to the heavy conversations of past days.

Afterward, they settled on the leather lounges in front of the window, the gathering twilight bringing forth a glow of lights across the lake. Sarah sank into the soft cowhide, content. Somehow this place made her feel quite at home, the relaxed atmosphere making her at ease to ask the question that'd had her curious for a while now. "So, you've heard enough about me. What's your excuse? Why isn't there a Mrs. Walton?"

THE FRANK QUESTION took Dan by surprise. A whirl of memories flooded through his brain, mixed with the deeply buried guilt. He settled for the safe yet honest answer. "I just haven't found the right girl."

"You must meet plenty of women," she scoffed. "Come on, who wouldn't want to date you? You're a single Christian guy! I've been in church long enough to know that's a big deal in itself." Her head tilted. "You're nice, you have a job—and you're not exactly horrible to look at."

He shrugged. "I just haven't been that interested in anyone."

"A little fussy, are we?"

"I've dated, but it's always hard to know who is genuine." Her raised eyebrows demanded further explanation. "It's hard to tell if girls like me or the lifestyle." So hard. And some women were mighty good actresses.

Sarah kicked off her shoes, tucked her legs up on the lounge. "The lifestyle?"

"You do know what being an NHL player involves?"

"What's the NHL?"

This was different. "The National Hockey League. I play for the Toronto Maple Leafs."

"Oh." She blinked. "Oh! So that's why all those girls were checking you out after church the other day."

He lifted a shoulder. Fans came with the territory.

Her brow wrinkled as she studied the décor. "Does that mean this place is yours? I thought you'd borrowed it from someone. I didn't realize..." She bit her lip.

"Yeah, it's mine."

"So you're rich?"

"Some might say so." He shrugged. "Hey, you never told me what you do for a living." He knew she'd been part of an international worship group, but she'd left that a few years ago. Would she consider them friends enough to admit that?

She took another sip of water. "I, uh, used to teach high school."

Huh. So maybe they weren't quite at friend status then. "Let me guess—music?"

She nodded. "Mostly piano and voice. But I play guitar, clarinet and saxophone too."

"Really?"

"Yep."

"Do you enjoy teaching?"

"Mostly."

"Will you do it again?"

She pressed the bridge of her nose. "Maybe one day. I've invested too many years of study and practice to give it up completely, but right now I don't really have the confidence to handle a classroom of teenagers."

"I don't know how high school teachers do it. I remember when we were at school, how much grief we gave our teachers. Some teenagers these days have no clue about respect."

She exhaled. "I have to admit it's nice to hear someone sympathize and not complain about all the time off teachers get."

"You should hear the people who complain about professional sportspeople and their vacations."

"Yeah, it must be so hard, being so rich, having to suffer in holiday homes like this." She waved a hand.

He remembered she'd been brought up as a missionary's kid. Okay. Fair point.

She offered a small smile he guessed was meant to be conciliatory. "I guess all jobs have their challenges. Not everyone would cope with big men trying to squash them just to get a little piece of plastic."

"I see I'll need to educate you about my sport."

Sarah shoved her feet into her sandals and stood. "Maybe, but not tonight. My head feels like a bread knife is sawing through my brain. I'd better get home."

"Want an aspirin or something?"

"No, thanks. I just need to go."

"I'll walk you."

Moonlight glinted on leaves, dappling the path with shadows as they walked to the pastor's cottage. She unlocked the door and turned on the lights while Dan waited at the base of the front porch steps. "Thanks, that was fun."

"Glad you enjoyed yourself. Maybe see you tomorrow?"

"Maybe." Her gaze found his.

Then she smiled.

He blinked, took a step back. "Sleep well."

He waited until she closed the door, then exhaled, almost

walking into a tree on his way home. That smile. When her face had lit up he'd caught a glimpse of the radiant girl he'd seen on the YouTube clips, and—wow. With that hair and those eyes and that smile…

Sarah was beautiful.

He stilled. Looked at the twinkling heavens. *Hey, God?*

An owl's long, mournful hoot broke the silence. Something rustled in the top of a nearby tree. A gust of wind rippled coolness up his spine—and common sense to foolish dreams.

He shouldn't be attracted to her. She was the daughter of a church minister, and obviously innocent—she'd always be too good for him. Nope, it could never work, for so many reasons. He'd need to treat her as a friend.

He dragged in a breath of night-cooled air, then slowly exhaled. He could do that. How many times had John spoken about exercising self-control? It mightn't be easy, but he couldn't fail God again. Dan gritted his teeth. *Wouldn't* fail God again.

That night, after he'd finished his book and turned off the light, thoughts about his neighbor refused to stay neatly locked away. For all her issues, Sarah had a fun sense of humor. And she wasn't shy of asking the difficult questions either, like that one tonight.

God, how long must I wait for the right woman to appear? He rolled over, shifting the pillow. *Lord, help me trust You.* He punched the pillow into shape. *And help me not to think about her.* He closed his eyes. *Or that smile.*

CHAPTER 5

"*M*orning."

Sarah looked up from her alfresco breakfast to check out the clear blue sky, which made Lake Muskoka gleam like a newly cleaned mirror. "Look at that! So it is."

Daniel's lips lifted. "How's the headache?"

"Better, thanks. Sleep always helps."

"I'm glad." His expression lit as he offered a twin-dimpled grin.

Her heart fluttered. So he was good-looking. That was no reason to act like a hormonal teenager. "Um, John called earlier. They're staying in the city for a few more days."

He nodded, his gaze dropping to the table. "Your Bible, huh?"

"That it is."

The chair screeched as he pulled it out and sat. "What are you reading?"

"One Thessalonians." Where the old koala-shaped Sunday school bookmark had been. Maybe it was time to give the Bible reading another go.

"Where are you up to?"

Dusting the crumbs off the pages, she slid the Bible toward

him, pointing at chapter five while she swallowed another piece of blueberry jam-covered toast. Mmm. This stuff tasted *so* good.

He glanced up at her again, eyes lit with amusement. "You like that, eh?"

A sip of tea cleared out the crumbs. "What?"

"You moaned."

It was way too early in the day to begin this blushing business. "No, I didn't." Had she? The jam was *really* good. And it wouldn't be the first time she'd become overly excited about food.

"You did."

"Are you gonna poke fun all day, or will you let me finish my brekkie?"

"Finish away, then." He waved a hand at her while he started reading.

She concentrated on slowly eating like an adult and not a ravenous wildebeest. Best not to think about why she cared.

"I like this part about being joyful always," he said. "Giving thanks in everything."

Memories rose of the hospital ward, when she'd been told to be thankful she'd been unconscious while the emergency crews extracted her from the wreck, thankful she hadn't seen Stephen's horrific injuries, him broken and bloodied against the windscreen. Thankful? How could she thank God? Her fiancé was dead, her injuries so extensive she hadn't known about his funeral until weeks later.

She dragged herself from the mental abyss. "Life is a little more complicated than simply believing everything I used to as a child."

Dan's smile faded. It was like the sun had disappeared behind clouds. "Complicated, but not impossible."

Why did conversations with this man always leave her floundering, the minister's kid treading water while the rich hockey star powered ahead? For that matter, why were they having such an intense conversation before she'd finished her breakfast? "Didn't you sleep very well last night?"

He frowned. Opened his mouth. Closed it again.

His hesitancy sparked frustration. Didn't he think she could handle what he had to say? "Go on. You might as well say what you think. You haven't held back before."

His gaze lowered to the scuffed boards of the deck, then met hers directly. "Look, I get it. Your fiancé died. And that's really sad. But you didn't. You should be thankful you're alive."

She gasped. He so didn't understand. It wasn't that simple at all. "What would you know?"

He glanced away, his scar dipping as his jaw clenched. "I've had my share of pain."

She shook her head. "You've got no idea what I've been through. You could never understand—"

"So the only person to ever experience any problem in life is you?" His gaze swung back to her, sharp, poking past her defenses. "Sarah, when are you going to ask God to help you let it go? That's why you came here, isn't it?"

Breath sucked in. Words couldn't even form in her brain. She blinked back hot tears.

"There's plenty to be thankful for, if you bother looking." He scraped back the chair and stood. "When you're tired of feeling sorry for yourself, let me know."

Her jaw dropped. That wouldn't be anytime soon. She clenched her fists as he disappeared through the trees, her heart writhing at his words.

How dare he?

She pushed from her seat, gathering the plate and cup with force, and moved inside. Irritation with her neighbor triggered a whirlwind of energy that soon saw the cottage sparkling from top to bottom. But that still wasn't enough to release the pent-up emotion or the frustration that still lingered. Where had mild mannered Dan gone? How could he act like her friend, then say such things? His words still slithered inside.

A slight breeze shivered the silver-green leaves of a white poplar beyond the kitchen window. Did she feel sorry for herself? Well, if she was brutally honest, maybe she sometimes entertained the *teensiest* amount of self-pity. But wasn't she entitled to? After all, her fiancé had died, and with him, any chance of ever having a family. Her eyes blurred, emotion cramping her throat. Couldn't she regret that?

"God?"

There came no rushing wind of reply from heaven. Not even a tiny whisper. But her thoughts did flick back to the Bible verse she'd read earlier.

"'Give thanks in all circumstances'?" What a crock. "How am I supposed to do that, God?"

Another verse flickered to mind, one that used to be one of her favorites: *I can do all things through him who strengthens me.* How long since she'd thought about it?

She moved outside and sank into the chair from earlier, the heat in her chest fading as the view soothed like balm on a burn. Yet her mind kept ticking, ticking, ticking. For too long she'd fought the way this chapter of her life had been written. Doctors, counselors, her parents—everyone—had urged her to accept things, and while at times she thought she'd reached acceptance, moments like this morning proved otherwise. And where had that left her? Isolated. Miserable. Lonely. Forever locked in the past.

And maybe she couldn't thank God for Stephen's death—as if God wanted her to, anyway—but with God's strength, she could trust Him for her future. Couldn't she?

Definitely, whispered a voice, as a refrain from a song penned long ago slid through her mind. *We can trust Him, we can trust Him with it all.*

Her insides tensed. How had she ever believed so blithely?

But even here, now, the grit of experience didn't change that truth. So maybe God did want her to see beyond the immediate and learn to thank Him for still being with her. For protecting her. For still loving her. She could still thank God in the midst of—even *despite*—her circumstances.

She exhaled, liquid once more slipping from behind closed lids. "I'm sorry, God." She heaved in a breath, conscious of her self-centeredness, conscious of her self-pity. "Thank You for all the good things You've done, like letting me live, letting me come here. Thank You for Ange and John." She swallowed. "And for Dan."

BE BRAVE.

Sarah braced, grasped the plate carefully, and rang the doorbell.

No answer.

"Hello?" She twisted the door handle. The door swung open, but all remained silent. She stepped through the entryway into the big lounge. With its huge windows and feature fireplace complete with mounted deer head, this room looked like something in a magazine: welcoming, tranquil, relaxed. Her lips twitched. Well, relaxed except for the poor deer. Her smile faded. If only she could absorb some of the soothing atmosphere. She needed more peace.

"Hello?" Sarah padded through the thick cream carpet to place the plate on the dining table. She glanced around—still no sign of him. Went outside to the deck. Nothing.

"Hello! Dan? It's Sarah."

He wouldn't hide from her, would he? No, he was much tougher than she—he'd face his demons, not run away. She moved back to the front door. She wouldn't venture upstairs—that'd be too much like trespassing. Looking around on this level? Only visiting. She rolled her eyes at her stupid logic, turning to exit, when a faint sound arrested her step. Downstairs. She knew from her earlier tour that the basement contained the laundry, garage, and gym. Maybe he was down there working on something.

She tiptoed down the stairs, thankful they didn't creak to give her away. The noise came louder now—a clanking sound, like a machine. She peered round the corner and saw him on the far side of the room, straining against heavy weights, determination on his face as he held the barbell then released it. Sweat had stained his T-shirt dark blue, but the smell was oddly inoffensive. It just smelled like hard work. She watched, fascinated, as he completed a set, unable to ignore the muscles in his arms and legs that said this workout was nothing new. Nothing wannabe about this tough guy indeed. He paused to bend down to take a swig of water.

"Uh, Dan?"

He ignored her.

Hurt swathed her chest. He moved in front of a mirror, balancing on something like half a large ball, pushing off to one side in a series of lunges. She blinked. He looked superhero fit.

She stepped forward. "Dan?"

He met her gaze in the mirror and stumbled, turned, wincing as he rubbed his knee. "Sarah." He pulled out earbuds.

"I'm so sorry, Dan! Are you okay?"

He looked so focused still, like she was an unpleasant intrusion in his day. "I'm fine."

Her throat closed. His voice held an edge she'd never heard before.

"What do you want?"

"I, uh, just wanted to say you were right, and I'm really sorry for before."

A beat. "Okay."

"Well, um, sorry for interrupting." He obviously didn't want her around, but she gave a small smile anyway. "Maybe catch you later?"

His lips pushed up on one side, as if reluctant. "Maybe."

She turned and hurried up the stairs, half expecting to hear him call after her, wholly disappointed when the sound of his exercising resumed instead.

DAN EXHALED, his muscles protesting the sudden onslaught of intensity after weeks of inattention. After his earlier clash with Sarah, he'd tried to fish in his favorite section of dark lake, but the quiet setting had done little to ease his frustration. The patience people knew him for both on and off the ice had just about run out.

He rubbed his eyes. She'd been right about one thing. He hadn't slept well, unwanted dreams interspersing with rotten memories and regrets. But it didn't change the fact that bemoaning the past seemed to be Sarah's default position, so when she'd started—again—he'd snapped. The only one who could really sort her out was God. *She's all Yours, God. I'm over it. W-a-a-y over.* Nope. Even though at times he'd found her strangely attractive, he couldn't afford to get caught in her emotional mess. He had enough of his own stuff to deal with.

Two biteless hours later, he'd packed up and headed back, wondering how to fill the rest of the day. The sunlight flashing off the basement windows reminded him he'd let his training slide, too busy enjoying his vacation. Off season meant building endurance and strength for a good fitness baseline come training camp in September. Intense workouts always demanded full attention and might prove a better way to clear his head.

Ten minutes of warming up on the exercise bike had led to isometric exercises: squats, shoulder rises, leg extensions, and his favorite, the plank. His trainer's go-to exercise always accompanied his motto: pain is just weakness leaving the body.

Dan's lips curved, recalling a few of the choice comments his teammates had made about that particular mantra. He didn't mind it so much. The innate patience that usually served him so well was excellent for these trials. Just hold position, stay focused, and push yourself to keep going, even when you felt the burn, even when it hurt.

His traitorous mind flicked to next door, and he scowled. Was God trying to say something to him? It wouldn't be the first time God had shown the analogies between exercise and spirituality. But if He was, well, Dan would rather use the weights to push aside the heaviness caused by his next-door neighbor.

He wandered upstairs to the kitchen, wolfing down two bananas before noticing a plate of cookies on the dining table. Macadamia and white chocolate. She'd paid attention to his comments the other day. The attached note read *Please forgive me* with a smiley face next to the name. He lifted off the plastic wrap. They smelled really good. Well, maybe he could try just one.

He forced himself to stop at three. Whoever said the way to a man's heart was through his stomach probably had major health issues, but they sure knew what they were talking about. It worked. He felt far more forgiving now. Dan smiled ruefully. He was such a sucker.

He glanced at the note again. Stilled. His words from the morning marched across his brain, trampling him with guilt. Sarah had revealed the vulnerable, dark spaces of her heart, and he'd all but stomped on them this morning. Forgiveness? Sarah didn't really need his forgiveness—but he probably needed hers.

HE FOUND Sarah slowly swinging on the hammock, staring up at the pines, a closed laptop on a chair beside her. Her bright hair tumbled around her shoulders, the green tank top contrasting with her creamy skin.

"Hey."

"Oh!" She eased upright. "Hi."

"Uh, about before—"

"I'm so sorry," she rushed to say.

"Me too."

Her eyes glistened, and his throat tightened as he nodded and looked away. He wasn't used to girls crying on him. Growing up with brothers, and now working and living surrounded by guys, tears weren't too commonplace.

A tiny sparrow hopped along the deck's wooden rail, pecking at invisible crumbs. "Those cookies were pretty good."

"I'm glad."

Silence stretched. The sparrow flew away in a rush of brown feathers, like it sensed the awkwardness here.

"Daniel?"

He glanced at her.

"I'm trying to accept things." Her voice dropped to a whisper. "But it still feels like it's my fault."

He lowered himself into a white Muskoka chair. "So, you intended to crash the car?"

The green eyes widened. "Of course not."

"Did Stephen?"

"How can you say such a thing?"

"Was it an accident?"

"Well, yes, it was raining, but if I hadn't insisted we go to the party, and if we hadn't been arguing, he'd still be here." Her bottom lip trembled. "I can't get away from that."

Compassion filled him afresh. He dragged the chair closer, leaned forward, and touched her arm. "Sarah, it was an accident. And even if it wasn't, is anything too hard for God to forgive?"

She bit her lip, those big green eyes searching him. "No," she whispered.

"I—" He swallowed, memories taunting his convictions. "I know it's hard, but God promises to help us. We can trust Him."

She nodded. "I was reminded of that earlier."

His heart softened a fraction more. He settled back in his seat, listening to the hush of the spruce in the breeze. The hammock's faded ropes protested as she shifted.

"Dan?"

"Yeah?"

"I really am sorry about before. I know I get a little carried away sometimes."

He lifted an eyebrow.

"Okay, maybe a lot carried away." She sighed. "I know I can get pretty emotional."

"Really?"

Her lips lifted at his tone. "And believe it or not, I don't actually like being this way."

He shot her a look filled with skepticism.

"I don't!"

His lips twitched.

"Well, okay, maybe I do a *tiny* bit."

His grin grew.

"It's just, I can't stand those stupid sayings anymore. You know, like 'let go and let God.' It's easy to say, but forgiving yourself is really hard to do."

"Yeah, it is."

DAN'S SMILE DROPPED AWAY, and she wondered again at his story. He'd hinted at chinks in his armor before but hadn't been particularly forthcoming—funny from a man who didn't mind poking his nose into her business. It was weird, but she did sort of appreciate his bluntness. People had been tiptoeing around her feelings for so long it was kind of refreshing for someone to tell the unvarnished truth.

"But Sarah, you need to stop blaming yourself. Guilt is a never-ending cycle. God doesn't hold you responsible for Stephen's death, and neither should you."

His words swirled, then settled feather-soft into her soul. God didn't blame her for Stephen's death? It didn't seem right that someone should die and nobody be held responsible. Guilt at being the one left alive had become a constant soundtrack in her mind, constantly whispering her faults and shame. But maybe God wanted her to play a different tune, something guilt-free.

She swallowed against fresh emotion. "Have you ever had to forgive yourself?"

He nodded. "I became a Christian at twenty-two. By then I'd done several things I really regretted." The light in his eyes dimmed. "When I began playing in Pittsburgh, I got caught up acting like this guy I'm not and treated some people—some women—pretty selfishly." He looked down, his cheeks red over his tan. "That's probably why I'm cautious about relationships now. I don't want to mess things up again."

Sarah's insides twisted in sympathy. In trying to follow Jesus since a child, she'd not made too many choices whose consequences she regretted.

He glanced up again. "I realized God had forgiven me for everything, that I couldn't keep focusing on my failures. It was a constant battle at first, but focusing on good things helped, as did choosing to be thankful."

Thankfulness was a choice. She'd forgotten that this past year, just like she'd forgotten how good it felt to play the piano and worship God—kinda dumb from someone who'd led thousands in worship. It was funny how Dan, despite being a much younger Christian than her, really seemed to know his stuff when it came to things like thankfulness and forgiveness.

She exhaled. "It's good to know it's all forgiven."

"Very good."

Forgiveness was one thing, but there was still so much more to consider. She bit her lip.

"What?"

She met his dark gaze, the patience there tugging out the truth. "I still feel lost," she admitted. "Like I don't know who I am or what I'm meant to do with my life anymore."

He was silent for a beat. Two.

"When did you feel most like yourself?" he asked.

She thought about it. Had it been when she'd been teaching? Or had it been earlier, when she'd been leading worship around the world? Her gut clenched. As if she could ever be that girl again. She'd burned those bridges years ago. Or had them burned for her.

"Ange mentioned you were part of Heartsong Collective."

She had? "When?"

"On that first night."

"You never mentioned anything."

"Neither did you," he pointed out.

"Yeah, because that part of my life is over and done with."

"Is it? Really?" he asked softly.

Regret gnawed within. It had never felt like she'd ended that part of her life well. Touring the world with her friends one minute, then feeling like it was yanked away. Maybe this forgiveness thing needed to stretch to cover the reasons behind that decision, too.

"I might've looked you up on YouTube," he said. "You were —wow."

"Once upon a time, maybe."

"Hey, for what it's worth, that woman I saw singing onstage was so free, so strong, so vibrant," Dan said. "You can be like that again."

"I don't think so," she scoffed.

"God hasn't changed. He remains faithful. You might not sing quite like that on stage again, but you can own that confidence again."

Could she? It seemed fairytale impossible.

"God hasn't finished with you, Sarah," he said softly. "He has good plans for you and greater things still in your future."

His words drifted past the doubts to seed in her heart. Maybe she could trust that God had good things still in store. Memories of who she'd been—filled with faith, filled with boldness—tantalized, like a hazy mirage she suddenly yearned to be true.

"I was listening to a podcast the other day," Dan continued. "The preacher said we need to lean into God and lean on God. If we remember who He says we are, we can stand tall in that again."

She nodded, his words spinning through her soul, carving away at the weight of fears she'd worn for so long. God *was* for her, not against her. What more did she need to remember in her quest to be brave? Her chin rose, and she met Dan's eyes. His warm, faithful, faith-filled eyes. "Thank you."

"For what?"

"Your encouragement."

His lips turned up in a crooked grin. "It's gonna be interesting."

"What is?"

"Seeing more of just who Sarah Maguire can be."

"Are you sure you're ready for this?" she said, only half teasing.

"Bring it on, Sarah."

She smiled across at him, holding his gaze a fraction longer than necessary. Gee, Dan was nice to look at. His eyes, those dimples, even that scruffy five o'clock shadow...

"What?"

"Nothing." She dropped her gaze, conscious of some weird

vibe. What was going on? Here she was, trying to figure out the smashed-up foundations of her life, and skimming across the top of her emotions was this…awareness. Almost like…flirting. This was so not good.

She turned her attention to gracefully exiting the hammock, but the sudden shift in weight swung her too close to the edge.

Dan chuckled and pushed to his feet. "Need a hand?"

"Nope, I'm fine." Clumsy factor was definitely operating right now, as was her signature blush, judging from the heat in her cheeks.

"You sure?"

Wonderful. Just as well she wasn't trying to impress him. She extracted one leg and placed it firmly on the floor. "Stop laughing!" With a sudden lurch, she hurtled from the hammock, crashing into him, sending him to the deck. "Dan! I'm so sorry. Are you hurt?"

"I'm tough, remember? You'll have to try harder to hurt me." He rubbed his elbow.

"You told me to bring it on."

Amusement filled his face, and she relaxed. Grinned. And as she extended a hand to help him up, relief coupled with joy gurgled up and escaped in healing laughter.

CHAPTER 6

Vacation days that had seemed too long and too quiet now seemed too short. Dan glanced over as Sarah fanned herself with a battered straw cowboy hat, her book face-down as they attempted to catch a breeze on his back deck.

She swiped her brow. "I didn't think Canada could ever get this warm."

"What can I say? We're full of surprises."

"That's for sure."

She smiled that smile that made his heart glow, and he grinned back. It was nice to be back to this ease, the drama of two days ago a distant memory. She reached down, grabbed a tube of sunscreen, and smeared it on her face and arms. After a minute, she turned. "Am I rubbed in?"

He pointed to the side of his nose. "Apart from here."

She rubbed in the tiny smudge of white. "Better?"

"There's some on your forehead."

"Really?" Her brow creased as she dabbed at the non-existent mark.

"Okay, Princess, now on your cheek."

Her eyes narrowed. "I don't think I believe you."

"Hey, believe what you like." He held up his hands. "Just wanna be helpful here."

She picked up her glass. "So do I."

The water caught him front and center. "Ah!"

"Just being helpful." She laughed with that husky burble he'd heard so rarely. "I thought you looked hot."

He stared at her. Then snickered.

The green eyes widened and—there it was, that cute blush. "I meant warm, Dan. Honestly." She jammed her hat on and dived back into her book, embarrassment highlighting her cheeks as she slapped over a page, muttering to herself.

Dan wrung out his saturated T-shirt as best he could, then settled into his seat. He glanced at Sarah again, at her straw hat tipping forward as she squinted at the page. Between the past few days' robust discussions, the laughter, and the relaxed nature of swimming, fishing, and movies, she was becoming a good friend. After all her initial icy spikiness, he now appreciated her sassy spunk and spontaneity. He liked her. He'd not had a female friend like this since—well, not ever.

She sighed, closing the book. "It's so hot I can't even read. I really need some ice cream. I don't suppose Mr. Fit and Healthy has any lying around the house?" She eyed him hopefully.

"Nope, nor in the freezer either. But…" He studied her as an idea sprang to life. "I could get you some—for a price."

"Name it. I'll do anything. I need something chocolaty and cold."

"Wait here." He hurried downstairs and hauled two bikes from the basement. He checked them over, found the helmets, grabbed his wallet and phone, and motioned her outside.

Her jaw sagged. "You're kidding."

Dan grinned, then handed her the smaller helmet. "Nope. It's the only way."

"What about your car?"

"What about 'I'll do anything'?"

"I see you gotta earn your fat food around here," she muttered, placing the helmet on.

"Sure do." He swung up. "C'mon, follow me."

FOLLOW him she'd gladly do, as long as it led to a chocolate sundae. Sarah smiled. For someone who hadn't ridden a bike in years, she was doing okay. Despite some initial wobbles, she hadn't fallen off and was keeping up. Sort of. And rushing through the sticky heat did have a cooling effect. It was even kind of enjoyable.

She coasted down another long hill, feeling as free as a ten-year-old kid. Her hair whipped behind her as the sun tried to penetrate the extra-thick layer of sunscreen she'd applied before. She chuckled. Dan's sense of humor was almost as warped as hers. She thought back to the latest hammock cata-pult mishap. Thank goodness Dan had seen the funny side, because she hadn't laughed like that in years. It'd felt cleans-ing, like the old tidemark of bitterness was being washed away.

He turned. "You having fun?"

She gave an exaggerated sigh and resumed pedaling. "'Fun' is a little generous, Dan."

"Just keep thinking how good the ice cream will taste when we get there."

"Can't wait." Ice-cream incentive sure worked in this direc-tion, although some of these long hills would definitely be a challenge on the way back. At least she'd be freshly fattened up.

He flashed his dimples. "See you at the finish line."

"I didn't realize this was a race!"

He laughed, stretching his lead as they rounded the corner before the highway. Bitumen made the ride smoother, but the traffic was a little scary. She took a shaky breath, glancing up to see Dan way ahead of her, like he was competing in the Tour de France. He wasn't worried. Why should she be?

She pedaled on, wiping sweat onto her shorts, and chanced a look at her thighs. It probably wouldn't hurt to get a little more exercise now and again. Must be the effect of hanging out with someone who looked like he could be on the cover of a sports magazine. He probably had been, she mused, or maybe fronted an advertising campaign. Mr. Rugged Sports Star Celebrity...

But in addition to his looks, Dan was good company, easy to be with, with no pretense. These past few days they'd talked for hours about all kinds of things: their churches, sponsor kids, theology, teaching, music, mission trips, Toronto, Sydney. He'd shared about hockey. She'd talked about her two years writing and singing for Heartsong. They'd discussed favorite movies, food, songs, Bible verses—the last driving her to wrestle with what she thought she knew, to dig deeper, just as their argument about thankfulness had done. The past eighteen months of social distance had obviously created a backlog of conversation—she hadn't talked this much in years. Something about this place made it so easy to be open. Or maybe it was just being with Dan. Ange and John were right—he was a genuinely good guy.

She glanced up to realize they'd pulled into town. She'd happily tootled along behind him, but the sudden near whiz of the cars set her heart racing.

"Sarah, over here!" Dan waved from the other side of the road, having somehow made it across the busy highway without her noticing.

Oh no. Her confidence drained away. Cars kept flying by as Dan waited, wearing that same patient look she'd seen him sport a dozen times before. Traffic drove on the opposite side of the road here. Which way was she supposed to look again? Was it right, then left, then right, or the other way around?

Be brave.

She sucked in a breath, steadied her wobbly bike. She could do this. Time to just screw up her courage and go—

"Sarah! Look out!"

BANG!

"Sarah!"

Terror clawed up Dan's throat as he raced past the line of honking cars to where she lay crumpled on the side of the road. She'd pulled straight into the path of a car turning left, then in a crazy, miraculous maneuver, had somehow swerved, missing the car but skidding into a roadside barrier where she lay prone now. Why on earth had he thought this was such a great idea? *God, let her be okay!*

He reached her side, dropped to his knees, and touched her face. "Sarah?"

Her eyelids fluttered open.

Warmth rushed through his chest.

"I'm so sorry! I didn't see her! Is she alive?" The elderly female driver climbed from her sedan, gasping, shaking, looking like she was verging on hysteria.

"Yes." Dan exhaled. Thank God Sarah hadn't been hit. Thank God for people helping calm the driver and move traffic away. And thank God for bike helmets. Otherwise, Sarah might be—

She groaned.

Dan smoothed some hair from her eyes. "Hey, Princess. You're gonna be okay." He glanced at her legs. Winced. It looked like she'd trailed her skin halfway across the road. Blood was smeared down her legs, oozing from a hash of grazes. Her elbows hadn't fared much better. His stomach turned. Blood always made him queasy. "But, Sar, I think you need a hospital."

Her slightly unfocused green eyes suddenly cleared, and she

shook her head, groaning again as she tried sitting up. "No, no hospital."

"You might have a concussion. You need to get checked over and have those scrapes dealt with."

"No." She shoved his arm away, pitching forward with a gasp. "I'm fine. I might need some Band-Aids maybe, but no doctor—and definitely *no* hospital."

Her fierce look pushed further argument down. He'd just call a doctor later. Hockey had shown him potential concussion couldn't be dismissed lightly.

"Help me up?"

Dan wrapped an arm around her waist, noting her grunt of pain as she finally made it to her feet. "Feeling light-headed?"

"No. I just feel like a fool. I forgot which way the cars go here." She grimaced again as she finally noticed the blood trail. "I did a good job, huh?"

"Spectacular."

"Good thing redheads have such a high pain threshold."

She wasn't crying but making jokes? He so didn't get this woman. He ushered her to the relative safety of the parking lot. "Come on, let's get you cleaned up."

"Then do I get my ice cream?"

"Princess, you can have all the ice cream you want."

AFTER HELPING her hobble to the nearby ice-cream parlor and ordering something appropriately called a "rough and tumble"—a smashed up version of a sundae heaped with chocolate sauce, nuts, and sprinkles—Dan discreetly phoned the paramedics, who visited, checked her for concussion, and patched her up. Sarah wasn't impressed.

"I look like a five-year-old"—she motioned to the big white bandages on her knees and elbow—"who can't ride a bike properly."

He hid the smile. Yeah, it did look like that. "It could've been worse." How the old lady had missed her was amazing. Maybe an angel had stood between the car and bike or something.

He watched as Sarah finally finished her sundae, scraping out the last traces of chocolate fudge sauce with her finger. "How are you feeling now?"

"Ice cream helps." She sighed. "But it feels like all Gravenhurst has come out to see the clown."

Yeah, there'd been some of that. He'd politely shooed away some tourists who'd asked him for an autograph. They'd been none too subtle in checking out the girl with him. "Good thing you don't care about what other people think."

"It is, isn't it?" Sarah gave a twisted smile, then eased up. "Can we go now?"

"Sure. I'll call a cab."

"I can ride back."

"What? No, Princess, you can't do that. You're not exactly roadworthy—"

"I know *I'm* not exactly worthy of riding on Canadian roads, but the bike still is." She nodded as if to convince herself. "I can do this."

"I don't think you should."

But she wasn't listening, was already moving to where he'd propped their bikes earlier. She strapped on her helmet and gingerly got back on.

"Sarah!"

She ignored him and pedaled away. He sighed, retrieved his bike, and caught up with her at the next cross street.

"This is really dumb, Sar."

She lifted her chin, moving on as soon as the break in traffic allowed.

Dan gritted his teeth. He could shake her for this stupid stubbornness. He glanced across. The determined tilt to her jaw suggested more than simple pride was at stake here. He had a long time to ponder the cause as they walked most of the way back, up those big hills they'd so lightheartedly flown down a couple of hours earlier.

By the time they finally arrived at John and Ange's cottage, Sarah's face glowed as bright as her hair. She hadn't been joking about that exercise thing. "You look like you need a really big, cold drink. You're pretty red."

"Thanks. I *love* it when people notice and feel they have to say something." She dropped the bike, then collapsed into a Muskoka chair. "I'm completely wiped."

He retrieved several bottles of water from inside, handed her one, then another as she drained the first in world record time, complete with water dribbling down her chin. His lips twitched. Classy. Halfway through the second, she put her head in her hands and groaned.

"Sar?"

"I think I need to lie down." She stood unsteadily.

He grabbed her elbow and helped her inside, settling her on the couch with a blanket and a book. He examined the cover. "*Sense and Sensibility?*"

"Don't start. I don't want to hear about my lack of common sense."

He forced a small smile. "Do you want anything?"

"I can always go for a cup of tea."

He nodded, glad for the simple task, returning soon with her tea and some cookies. After placing them on the coffee table, he straightened. "Will you be okay?"

She nodded, yawning. "Thanks so much, Dan."

He chewed his lip. He didn't like to leave her, but the medics had cleared her of concussion, and he didn't want to make her uncomfortable by insisting on staying. "I'll be round to check on you first thing tomorrow."

"Okay, thank you." She smiled drowsily. "You're so lovely."

Her sweet words caught him square in the chest. Lovely?

Not a word he'd choose to describe himself. But it made him feel taller, stronger, *cleaner* somehow.

After casting her a final look, Dan slowly slid open the glass door and headed home.

DUSK WAS FALLING. Dan placed the hand weights back on the rack and picked up his water bottle, Sarah's accident still flashing through his mind. When she'd lain on the roadside, bloodied and still, he'd thought he'd gotten her killed. Once she'd opened her eyes he'd been so relieved he could've—

No.

He sucked in a breath. Walked outside, down the stony path to the end of the dock.

No. She was only a friend. Still hung up on a dead man.

He sat on the still-warm boards, drained his water bottle, and stared across the violet lake. Memories flickered of the last time he'd been so scared, eight years ago. He shivered. Imagine getting a minister's daughter killed. Imagine telling his pastors their niece was dead.

The thoughts kept pecking at him. Maybe it was practice-what-you-preach time. *Think about what's good, true, lovely...*

He frowned. Nope, that didn't help him not focus on Sarah either.

CHAPTER 7

The soft thump kept intruding, chasing sleep away. Her heavy eyelids refused to open. Her brain felt like thick soup. What *was* that noise? And where had the sweet spot on her pillow gone, where she'd been blissfully asleep before that noise woke her? Why couldn't she sleep more?

The noise continued, accompanied by faint shouts. Just sitting up was an effort, and now she had to go deal with whoever was outside.

She shuffled to the door, squinted out the window. Sighed. Mr. Knight-in-Shining-Armor.

"How's it going?"

Bright morning light hammered her brain. She mumbled something.

"Don't answer that question. I think I get the picture." Dan snorted back laughter as she peered through eyelids that only wanted to close. "You're 'crabby in the morning'? I never would've guessed."

Sarah glanced at her red pajama top, decorated with little crabs and a sentence that gave people fair warning, before crossing her arms. "I like to make a statement."

His laughing eyes softened. "How are you feeling? You took a while to answer the door."

"I was *very* happily asleep."

"Sorry, Princess, but I was worried about you."

Now she was more awake she could see the concern edging his eyes. Annoyance ebbed away. "I'm fine. Well, a bit stiff and sore, but if I don't do much today I'll be right."

After the pain she'd experienced during the accident and in the months of rehab that'd followed, yesterday was nothing—nothing but embarrassing. Although, seeing Dan stunned by her grit *was* satisfying.

"Are you sure? I felt so bad—"

"Why? It wasn't your fault. I'm way too good at falling over. It's a gift, I think."

"I'd feel better if you were nearby." Worry clouded his brow. "Today's supposed to get cooler, maybe rain. We could watch some movies?"

She rubbed her matted hair. It was kind of sweet to have someone show this much concern, especially with Ange and John still away. "And drink your coffee?"

He nodded.

"Well, when you put it like that…"

An hour later, Sarah was ensconced in the leather lounge at Dan's place, watching one of the old James Bond films, sipping another creamy cup of coffee. But as they laughed at some of the corny sequences, her thoughts kept drifting. This friendship with Dan was so different to that with Stephen. Stephen had always seemed super-holy, his attention flattering, her awe leading to a deep, intense relationship, with little of the relaxed ease she felt with Dan. With Dan she didn't try to be something she wasn't. He seemed to like her—as a friend, of course—just the way she was, mess and all. Like he got her and they were on the same wavelength or something.

She studied him on the lounge opposite. Jeans, another faded T-shirt, bare feet, dark hair curling slightly at the ends, scruffy jaw. Dan looked like he needed a good haircut and a closer shave. Rough and ready, definitely, but also kind, and steady, and—

He shifted and caught her gaze, offering a small smile. "You enjoying it?"

Something low in her stomach tightened. She swallowed, nodded, and hid hot cheeks behind her hair as she watched the film again. He might be attractive, but that didn't mean she'd let her stupid hormones get carried away.

As Dan had predicted, the day turned rainy. The giant picture windows made this a great place to watch the rain sheet down, the gray lake gradually merging with the heavy sky. Dan didn't say much, but from the way she caught him watching her, she suspected he still felt guilty. Distraction through films with even more ridiculous stunts than hers seemed an effective remedy.

After an early dinner, the phone rang, and Dan disappeared for a few minutes while she cleared up. He soon returned. "That was my friend Boyd, checking to make sure everything's cool for tomorrow's camp."

"Camp?" Some first impressions may have been wrong, but others… "Bingo."

He raised an eyebrow. "Anyways, I wondered, do you want to call your folks?"

"Oh! Thanks. That's really thoughtful." And after yesterday's scare, probably wise.

He pointed to the phone, and soon she was chatting with her parents. After a good catch up, she glanced across to where Dan wiped down the table. "I better go."

"It's wonderful to hear your voice, Sar. We love you."

Sarah's heart filled with warmth. "Love you, too. I'll call again soon."

She gently placed the phone back. "Dan, would you mind if I ring my sister?"

"No problem."

"Thanks." She dialed the long string of numbers. "Hi, Bek."

"Sar! How are you?"

Her nieces squealed in the background. They'd head to school soon. "Sorry about the hour. I know you're busy. I'm borrowing a friend's phone."

"No worries." A deeper voice murmured something and her sister laughed. "Joe says g'day to Blue."

As her sister chattered on, Sarah filled with deep contentedness from talking with someone who really understood her, who knew her inside out.

"And this friend of yours, what's her name?"

Sarah glanced over to where Dan stood at the sink, and dropped her voice. "Daniel."

"Danielle?"

"No, Daniel." If only this echoey phone would let her keep her voice down.

"You got yourself a new man!"

Sarah closed her eyes. "Don't be ridiculous. He's just the next-door neighbor."

DAN COULDN'T HELP but overhear that last comment and wonder why her words...hurt. Not that he liked her or anything. He rolled his eyes—how grade-school did that sound? But still, he thought they'd reached friends status, at least. He focused on carefully scraping away the last of the fish remains as Sarah hung up the phone and limped over.

"Thanks for that."

"Bet your family were glad to hear from you."

"Yes. I miss them too." Her accent had gotten crisper in the last hour. Cute.

"Anytime you want to call, help yourself."

"Thank you. They might not like it if I call anytime, though. These time differences are crazy, morning there while it's night here." She grinned, tilting her head. "May I ring Ange now? I don't feel too bad asking, knowing you're so *rich*." The tease was back in her eyes, along with something else he didn't recognize.

"Knock yourself out."

After talking briefly, she hung up. "They're coming back tomorrow."

"Good. Someone needs to keep an eye on you."

"I'm not a child. I don't need—"

"Anyone who gets injured like that needs looking after. And I'll be at camp."

She paused. Her smile grew. "Of course you will be. I should go so you can get some sleep before you go *camping*."

"I'll drive you. It's stopped raining but it's pretty slippery out there. I don't want you hurting yourself, especially now I know it's your specialty."

"I don't plan for it to happen—it just does. But I'm happy to walk. I'm tougher than I look."

Yeah. Those puffy bandages sure added credence to her claim for toughness.

They walked—slowly—through deep twilight to the cottage. When they finally reached her door, he was surprised at his reluctance to go. "Take care of yourself, okay?"

"You too. Enjoy the great outdoors." Her smile lit up her whole face.

Oh man. "G'night."

He stretched out the tightness in his shoulders and walked down to the dock. Thank God he headed north tomorrow to set up the campsite. Spending time with Boyd, Patrik, and the boys would be good—his neighbor was way too distracting. Ignoring the damp, he lay on the boards, staring at the couple of stars not obscured by the clouds, and spent some time talking with God.

Two hours on the piano pouring out her heart in worship was uplifting, but now her muscles complained. Sarah did her prescribed exercises, completed laundry, started dinner. The fish Dan had cooked last night had tasted so delicious she'd begged for the recipe, determined to try it out tonight.

John and Ange pulled in just after she'd placed the trout stuffed with Asian vegetables in the oven. After hugs hello—and appeasing Ange's concern at Sarah's injuries—Sarah made tea and they sat at the dining table, John and Ange filling her in on their time away. They'd visited Doris in hospital, her improved condition releasing them to spend a few days near pretty Stratford for their wedding anniversary.

"Definitely worth visiting the festival if you like Shakespeare," Ange said.

John massaged his neck. "But that trip in peak hour isn't fun coming home."

Ange sipped her tea. "You're looking happier, Blue."

"I do feel better. I think that cry was cathartic." That seemed so long ago now. "And it's so peaceful here, I think it's rubbing off."

"I'm sure women need to have a good cry every so often to cleanse the soul and get rid of the cobwebs." Ange patted Sarah's hand. "If you haven't cried for a while, that's a lot of cobwebs."

"There's a few less now. Make that a lot less," Sarah added with a chuckle.

John smiled. "It's good to see you laugh. We should all laugh more. It's good medicine."

"Seen much of Dan?"

"We've had dinner a few times." At their upraised eyebrows

Sarah's cheeks warmed. "No, nothing like that. Just pizza, some fish he caught." She shrugged, focused on slicing carrots for the salad. "He's nice."

"Maybe he should join us for dinner tonight."

"Aren't you both tired? Anyway, he said he'd be busy with some camp this weekend."

"Oh, that's right, the one for disadvantaged kids. Every year he sponsors some kids from the city to come and have a real camping experience."

"What, like tents and things?"

Ange shuddered. "Yes. I think 'roughing it' is generous. Think *Survivor*."

"That sounds horrible! And he chooses to do that?" Sarah's nose wrinkled. "Camping is for the birds."

THE NEXT DAY proved nice and quiet, a good chance to relax, read, and more fully recover. Mid-afternoon, John got a phone call and called Sarah's name. "It's for you." He grinned, handing her his cell phone. "It's Dan."

She frowned as excitement trickled through her veins. "Hello?"

"Hey, Sarah. Uh, I've a really big favor to ask. I told you about this camp I'm involved in, and…well, we have a problem."

Her stomach tensed. "Mmm?"

"There's been some kind of mix-up." He sighed. "We've a girl here called Georgia. Her name was down as George, so we didn't realize she was a girl until she got here. She's the only girl, a cousin of one of the kids…"

"And?" She closed her eyes. *Please don't get to the point. Please don't get to the point.*

"And we'd hate to send her home. But she can't stay unless there's a female counselor here, and I was hoping—"

"No."

"It's only two nights. And it means she can stay. Otherwise we'll have to drive her home, and she'll be so disappointed."

"I hate camping. I do not do camping, Daniel."

The silence at the end of the phone spoke volumes.

She sighed. "Can't you ask someone else?"

"Not who's had experience working with teenagers and is only thirty minutes away." A beat. "I suppose I could ask Ange."

As much as every fiber in her wanted to scream *Yes, ask Ange!*, she'd witnessed her aunt's exhaustion. Camping with a bunch of teenagers wouldn't help. "No, don't do that. She's really tired." Sarah bit her lip. The seconds ticked away.

"I promise, we'll make it easy on you. It's a really beautiful spot."

"That's nice, but I *really* do not like camping. Besides, I'm not great with teenagers these days." Why she'd ever thought teaching was a God-thing she'd never know. Especially after her last experience with teenagers. To prove a point, she'd gone back to work early—which had proved instead to be the catalyst for her exile to Canada. The students, knowing something of her story, sensing her vulnerability, had acted up so badly that she'd cried. They'd been disciplined, but the entire experience had proved so thoroughly humiliating she hadn't dared teach again. Her parents had warned her she wasn't ready, and they'd been right. But she'd been so tired of people's protectiveness all the time…

"They're good kids. You'll have fun."

"I doubt it."

"Please?"

His husky plea melted the last bastion of resistance. Just as well he wasn't here, pleading with his beautiful eyes—she'd have been a goner long ago. She sighed. "Fine. I'll come. As long as you have zero expectations of my camping proficiency."

"Zero."

"And I get a tent, don't I?"

"Yes."

"And I'm only there to keep Georgia company—I don't have to lead any activities or anything?"

"That's all."

She groaned. "Tell me what to bring."

CHAPTER 8

*D*an glanced over the fire pit to where Sarah stood, confusion on her face as she watched Patrik's demonstration once again. She hadn't been joking. She wasn't camp literate at all. Ever since John had dropped her off an hour ago, Sarah had seemed more helpless than a kitten on an iceberg as the boys flew around the site putting up tents, getting the fire going, preparing the evening meal.

He swallowed laughter and continued stirring the stew. Even blowing up air mattresses seemed beyond her ability. Patrik, a Swedish exchange student, had explained the procedure several times.

"And the spout thing goes in where?"

"In the hole."

"But it's not working! It's not going up."

"Maybe there's a hole."

"What hole are you talking about?"

"This hole!"

"Man." Dan looked up to catch Boyd shaking his head, and they shared another private chuckle. "She's nothing like your friend Beau, is she?"

That was for certain. Being a Christian and having a cool accent was about all Sarah shared in common with his goalie friend Beau Nash, who had helped out last year.

He'd warned them about the princess's self-confessed ineptitude—she hadn't sold herself short. But at least she seemed to get on with Georgia and the boys okay. When he'd introduced her, Dan hadn't been able to help but notice the effect Sarah had had on some of the boys. He didn't blame them for drooling.

Three hours later, the boys—and Georgia—were all in their tents, but not asleep judging from the giggles coming from multiple tents. Dan glanced over to where Sarah sat on the other side of the fire, her book propped on her knees as she tried to read by torchlight. The wind shifted, sending smoke her direction. She shuffled up the big log, then resumed reading.

Quiet descended, broken only by the soft strum of Patrik's guitar and the sizzle as Boyd added leaves to the fire. The brighter glow illuminated the gold in Sarah's hair, hanging loose around her shoulders. A few minutes later she coughed and moved again.

"What's with you and that campfire?" Boyd said. "Smoke follows you wherever you go."

She sighed. "What can I say? I'm a smoke magnet."

Dan caught her gaze. Smiled. "Smoke follows beauty, Princess."

She stared at him, wide-eyed, before ducking her head in her book again. He glanced away to catch Boyd's mouthed *Princess?* and raised brows. Dan shrugged and settled back against the log, gazing into the fire as blue flames slowly licked the charred wood. He chewed the inside of his bottom lip, while in his heart, questions flirted with dreams.

～

Sarah yawned and shook her head at the slumbering Georgia, whose loud snores had punctuated every minute of every hour last night, rendering sleep impossible. She crawled from her sleeping bag, unzipped the tent fly, then tripped over the dew-damped sneakers she'd inadvertently left outside last night. Wet shoes. Good times.

Blinking at the too-bright morning light and a bird's overly enthusiastic morning song, she stumbled over to the fire Dan was coaxing to life. "Those birds are so loud."

He glanced up. "Good morning."

"It's morning, anyway." She rubbed her eyes. "So, what can I do?"

Dan stopped fiddling with twigs and smirked.

"What? Surely there's something I can do."

"Can you make pancakes?"

"Yes." She crouched by the fire as Dan wandered away, then finished mixing the batter and slowly poured it in the griddle for the first batch. Finally, she was being useful. Who wanted to look helpless, even if it were true? But even something as basic as sitting around the campfire had proved challenging, last night's smoke making breathing—let alone reading her book —difficult.

And then Dan had made that comment about "smoke follows beauty."

She flipped the pancake carefully. He had to have been joking. Maybe she had a couple of nice features, but most of the time she looked—and felt—like a sloppy mess. It was probably just some old campfire saying, anyway. Stupid to read anything into it.

She gingerly scooped out the first pancake, placed it on a plate, and poured batter for the next. She swiped her hair from her eyes, waiting until small bubbles indicated it was time to flip. Yawned again. Why *had* Dan's comment kept her awake? Did she want him to find her attractive?

"Hey, Princess, you know there's batter in your hair?"

Great. Attractiveness would have to wait another day—or century. Mess was nothing new. But Dan leaning close to carefully remove the caked-on batter was. As was his fingers in her hair. And the way his eyes crinkled with—amusement? happiness?—when he saw her. And the color of his eyes in the morning light, more like nutmeg than the dark chocolate she'd always assumed. And his impossibly thick, dark lashes...

She swallowed. This wasn't good. Wasn't good at all.

DAN RINSED his fishing gear in the lake and glanced up along the shoreline to where a big pine lay weathered and white on the sand. Georgia leaned against it, chatting with Sarah. His heart eased. For a self-proclaimed non-camper, Sarah had settled in pretty well. He'd kept an eye on her this morning to make sure things went smoothly like he'd promised. At least, that's what he kept telling himself—and Boyd, who'd looked at him questioningly more than once.

"Hey, Dan, where should I put the fish?" Travis, Georgia's cousin, looked ready to explode with excitement.

"You did a great job, buddy, catching so many this morning." Dan nodded to Boyd. "Let's see what the boss says."

Boyd led Travis to their makeshift kitchen area, leaving Dan free to study the girls again. How "George"—as apparently she'd always been known—had come to be here was still a mystery, but thank God they hadn't needed to drive her back to the city. Georgia's demeanor suggested she'd experienced plenty of rejection. He didn't want to be responsible for more. She only knew Travis—who wasn't the most socially adept thirteen-year-old either—but Sarah seemed to have some magical connection to Georgia, drawing her out of herself. Quite ironic, really, considering the frozen princess of several weeks ago.

"Hello? Earth to Walton!" Boyd waved a hand in front of Dan's nose. "You know you're supposed to be keeping an eye on *all* our campers, don't you?"

"I'm glad things are going okay."

Boyd frowned. "I'm still not convinced—"

"Hey, she's a teacher, she's worked in church ministries before, and the pastor—who just happens to be her uncle—vouches for her. What more do you want?" Dan's jaw tightened. Despite being one of his best friends, Boyd tended to be pretty hard on people—quick to judge, slow to excuse. Even though he'd pointed Dan to Jesus all those years ago, Boyd lacked a little grace. Maybe because he'd never gone through any personal trauma, and he expected people to think and act like him.

"Maybe you're right." Boyd sighed. "At least we didn't have to drive Georgia home. That wouldn't have looked right."

Dan bit back a retort. Why did appearances have to count more than the chance for Georgia to experience God's amazing creation and hopefully find His love, too?

Nope. It was much better to have Sarah here. He glanced up again. Even though her presence proved personally distracting, as always.

"What happened to your leg?"

Sarah stopped rubbing sunscreen on her arms. Her knees had caused much comment the first night, even though she'd swapped the puffy white bandages for more discreet skin-colored Band-Aids. She'd worn board shorts today to try and hide the red scars on her legs, but obviously they weren't quite long enough. She tugged at her shorts, then leaned back against the smooth wood of the tree trunk before finally answering Georgia.

"I was in a car accident a year and a half ago. The car ran off the road into a gum tree, and my leg was pinned in the wreckage. I was trapped for hours, then in hospital for months in a coma, then recovery. It took ages to learn to walk again."

A beat. Another. She winced. Too much of an overshare?

"I don't like hospitals," Georgia muttered.

"Why's that?"

Georgia picked at her T-shirt's frayed edge. "My mom died of cancer two years ago."

Sarah's breath caught. As terrible as it had been to lose Stephen, she couldn't imagine being a young girl growing up motherless. Although Boyd had warned her last night about the no-touch policy, she couldn't let this moment slide. She wrapped an arm around Georgia's shoulders and lightly hugged her. "I'm so sorry, sweetheart. It's tough, isn't it?"

Georgia shrugged.

Oh. Sarah dropped her arm, her heart still throbbing with compassion. *God, touch Georgia's heart.* She took a deep breath. "My fiancé died in the car accident." Somehow, saying that aloud didn't hurt so much today. "I...I was depressed for ages."

Sarah sat in silent surprise. Was it really past tense? Was she really starting to get better?

Georgia turned, eyes wet with unshed tears. "What helped you?"

～

"Did you see that?" Boyd hissed. "Sarah stuck her arm around Georgia. After I told her not to!"

Dan rolled his eyes. Boyd was such a stickler for the rules. "She's just being kind."

Boyd dropped his gear to the ground. "I better talk to her."

"No." Dan caught his arm. "I'll go." He moved before Boyd could argue, praying his chat with Sarah wouldn't be edged with lingering irritation with Boyd.

The girls were in deep discussion and didn't hear his bare-footed approach on the sand. He stopped behind the fallen tree, the twisted branches affording him some cover. He didn't want to eavesdrop, but neither did he want to interrupt anything really important.

Sarah's soft voice continued."…and I realized, instead of focusing on my scars and feeling sorry for myself, I needed to focus on the fact that I'm alive and can walk." She gave a wry-sounding chuckle. "A good friend recently reminded me I have to choose to be thankful."

He was a good friend? His chest glowed. That was much better than "just a neighbor."

"It's really hard, because for ages I've only seen the negative. I'm trying to change." Her husky burble came again. "I think my friend thinks I'm just pretty trying."

Dan smiled. No, he didn't think that at all. Intriguing, definitely. Funny, for sure. Pretty? No, if last night's Freudian slip was a clue, she was in a class much higher….

Georgia mumbled something, and Sarah hugged her again. "Sweetheart, don't say that about yourself. C'mon, there's plenty you can be thankful for." Sarah switched into schoolmarm mode as she ticked off her fingers, listing various good qualities until she ended with "…and you've got the longest eyelashes I've ever seen! You're so lucky. I have to dye mine, otherwise it looks like I've got none."

"The boys don't notice. They just think I'm fat."

Sarah sighed. "Yeah, some guys are pretty shallow, looking only at the outside, wanting what's cheap and easy."

Dan flinched.

"But we're not that sort of girl, are we? You and I, we're not like those eating at a fast food restaurant, we're more like…" She paused, and Dan strained to hear her next words. "We're more like princesses at a gourmet feast prepared by the king of kings in a mountain-top castle, waiting for the man who is brave enough to meet the obstacles life has thrown in the way—to face the dragons, scale the walls, and finally reach the top. And then, when the king proclaims this man as worthy, he's allowed to dine with us." Sarah laughed, then nudged Georgia again. "So don't settle for cheap and easy junk food, Georgia. God loves you and thinks you're so much more valuable than that."

Her words inched him closer.

Sarah slumped against the tree. "God wants the best for you, Georgia. That may mean there's a special guy for you, or"—her voice hitched—"it may mean there's isn't. But we keep on trusting God that He knows what He's doing. And in the meantime, we find things to be thankful for so we can start liking ourselves some more. If we don't like ourselves, it's hard for anyone else to." She paused, adjusting her long red ponytail under her straw cowboy hat. "So, what do you reckon? Are you up for the challenge?"

Georgia mumbled something, shifting slightly.

Uh oh. He didn't want to be seen. He stepped back and jogged down the beach, heart tingling. *God, please touch Georgia. Help her know how much You love her. And thanks for Sarah. Bless her too.*

"Hey, Dan!" Several boys held sports equipment. "Can you help set up the volleyball net?"

"Sure."

Ten minutes later, he tied off the final rope and looked up. Sarah and Georgia stood nearby, the latter copying Sarah's posture, a hand on her hip, squinting against the sun.

"You gonna play?" He grinned. "You even know how?"

Sarah smirked. "Believe it or not, I do know how to play."

He stood, dusting off his hands. "Want to be on my team?"

"I'll think about it." And she and Georgia sauntered off.

~

THWACK!

Sarah rubbed her forearms. Why on earth had she agreed to play this stupid game? That's right—the tease in Dan's eyes, coupled with Georgia's murmured desire to play, had led her here. She readied to serve. *God, please let it go in, if only for Georgia's sake.* She couldn't let her team captain down, especially when she was Georgia's prized first pick. First pick! She'd never been that before, thanks to her lifelong reputation for clumsiness. She lined up the ball, closed her eyes, and hit. "Ow!"

"It's in!" her team shouted delightedly.

"Practice makes perfect." An hour must've passed since they'd finished a hot dog lunch and started playing. In that time she'd had *plenty* of practice. It made a nice change to actually score a point rather than be the chief cause of the other team's points.

"Sar, it helps to open your eyes."

Dan's comment from the other side of the net required a glare as she took the ball again. Her sunglasses had kept falling off as she'd floundered around, and the bright afternoon sun only enhanced Dan's tanned torso. Major distraction. Opening her eyes didn't help.

Thwack. The ball went in again! Sarah high-fived her team and celebrated another rare point. She sent Dan a smug look and went back for the ball. Maybe she'd finally found her sporting niche: volleyball server extraordinaire. She smiled at herself. The fact the ball had a mind of its own and landed wherever it wanted—thus confusing the opposition—had nothing to do with it. She lined up again, hit, and prayed. Another ace!

"Sarah! You're a rock star!"

She couldn't stop the grin. So *this* was how it felt to play team sports.

"Come on! She's on a roll." Boyd and Dan finally strategized their team into position.

She laughed, picked up the ball as Patrik cheered, "Go Sarah!"

Again it went over, but this time the opposition returned the ball. Georgia jumped up, pivoting the ball down at Dan's feet. He dived to return the shot, sending it straight to Sarah.

"I've got it!" Travis rushed into the space before her, knocking her to the ground, yet somehow angling the ball back to Georgia, who neatly plopped it over the net for another point.

"You okay?" Patrik jogged over from the net.

"I'm fine." If only her clumsiness didn't bring so much attention. Enough already.

"Sorry, Sarah." Travis's ears reddened.

"No worries."

Patrik extended a hand to help her up. But as she reached to grasp his hand, something wasn't right. Her mouth dried. "Where's my ring?"

SHE WAS SO FUNNY, flailing around the court, playing with her eyes shut, wincing whenever she actually touched the ball. Despite possessing little hand-eye coordination, Sarah kept giving things a go. But something wasn't right. She still sat on the sand. Surely she wasn't hurt?

Dan jogged to the other side of the net where Sarah and the rest of her team carefully studied the ground. "What's up?"

"Don't move!" Travis warned.

"Sarah's lost her ring." Patrik's voice came from below.

"Not—?"

Sarah looked up with agonized eyes. "I have to find it."

"We will." He hunkered down nearby, even as the sand shifting beneath him told him this was a fruitless exercise.

WHY? Why had she worn the ring here? Why hadn't she left it at home? Sarah glanced around with unbelieving eyes. How could it just vanish? *Oh God, help me find it!* She re-checked her clothes in case the ring had bounced off and gotten snagged somewhere. Still nothing.

Maybe one of the boys had taken it.

No. She shook off the unease, glancing over to where Boyd and Patrik had taken the boys canoeing. Everyone had happily abandoned the game to play archeologist for a while, until they'd gotten restless and needed distraction. But what if someone had found it and not said anything? Nobody would have stolen it. Would they?

At least with Boyd gone, she wouldn't overhear his mutterings about the imprudence of wearing jewelry to a camp. And at least nobody still asked her to describe the ring. Shame crawled up her spine. She'd *tried* to be calm, to tamp down the panic. But after being asked for the tenth time what it looked like, she hadn't been able to bite back the yell. "It's a gold ring with a diamond! And I need it!"

She'd immediately apologized to poor little Justin, who'd asked the fateful question. He'd nodded, but she still felt so bad. She glanced over at Travis and Georgia, still scouring the ground as did Dan, who kept shooting glances at her, like he thought she might burst out crying or something. Well, if they didn't find it soon, maybe that *would* happen. But right now she was too angry with herself and this whole stupid situation to cry.

"Sar, I don't think it's here."

She shook her head at Dan's comment, her eyes focused on the ground. Surely she'd see it—the diamond wasn't that small. "It has to be."

He moved over sand sifted a dozen times already and

touched her shoulder. His eyes softened. "I'm so sorry, Sar. We've looked this past hour. It's just not here."

"No." She needed that last reminder of Stephen. It couldn't be gone.

He angled his head. "You definitely had it at lunch?"

She nodded, even as her mind questioned her recollections. It wasn't like she'd focused on looking at her ring. It was simply always there, like the freckles on her hands were now a part of her. She didn't notice them all the time, either.

"You sure you had it on after your swim? Maybe it came off—"

"Don't say it!" Withheld tears made her voice squeaky. "It can't be at the bottom of the lake!" She stepped closer to make sure Georgia and Travis couldn't overhear. "Do you think one of the boys found it and took it?"

Dan's brows rose, making her feel even worse for suggesting such a thing. He shook his head no.

"Then where is it?" Her voice pitched up. "You don't even really care. I bet you'd be happy if I lost Stephen's ring, so I could just build a bridge and move on, wouldn't you?"

He drew a deep breath. "I do care. That's why I'm still here, trying to help."

It wasn't helping.

"Sar, what do you want me to do?"

She gulped. "Just find my ring." With tears blinding her eyes, she hurried away.

CHAPTER 9

Sarah sighed as a pot lid clattered. She'd lain here in the tent, trying to sleep, then trying to read, but the diminishing light had now made that impossible. The boys had returned from their canoeing and, judging by the clanking sounds and muffled voices, were trying to get something underway for dinner and not disturb her. Not that she deserved anyone's kindness.

The pot lid clanked again. She needed to face the music. She rubbed at the dull pain in her head, grabbed her book, then slowly unzipped the tent, trying not to topple over as she shoved her sneakers on.

"Hey, Sarah, how you doing?"

Even though Patrik's comment vaguely reminded her of Joey from an old *Friends* episode, her smile refused to come out and play. She shrugged, looking around to encounter the sympathetic gazes of Georgia and several other campers.

"I saved you some cake."

Sarah struggled to return Georgia's smile. "Thanks."

Boyd was frying some fish in a pan at the fire. It smelled good. He'd not really said anything much to her today, which was a surprise. He'd sure had a lot to say last night, from giving her detailed instructions in camp etiquette to wondering aloud if the Australian police checks done for those working with children were as thorough as those of the Royal Canadian Mounted Police. He didn't seem to like her much, so she was happy to ignore him now as she sat on a log, trying to focus on her book. She just hoped he remembered Dan saying she didn't have to be too involved in camp life. She sure wasn't up to "helping" right now.

Speaking of Dan, where was he? She peered into the gathering gloom but couldn't see him anywhere. Not that it'd be easy to face him again. She wanted to cry some more about how she'd treated him. It so wasn't his fault, but all hers, as usual. If only she hadn't worn the ring…

"Travis and Dan are still looking." Georgia's worried face generated more guilt. "Travis feels really bad. He keeps thinking if he hadn't bumped you then you'd still have it."

Sarah bit her lip. Maybe that was true, maybe not. Amid her tears, she'd realized just how powerful Stephen's ring remained. It was like a talisman, a symbol of hope, a validation of her womanhood. Maybe no one could ever love the scared, scarred Sarah, but she'd once been loved, she'd been found acceptable and desirable once upon a time. She couldn't lose that.

Her thoughts slid back to earlier in the day. Oh yeah, the ring had power all right. Power to heal, and power to hurt. Her chest grew tight as she recalled Dan's look of shock at her outburst earlier. She was busy destroying friendships all because of the ring. *God, help him forgive me.*

She sighed. Once her crying jag had finally abated she'd realized something else. Her words to Georgia this morning were just as important for her. Despite all her flaws, God loved and accepted her, and she really shouldn't rely on a guy or a ring to tell her that. She stared blankly at the page. Equally challenging was the knowledge that she'd need to come to terms with the fact that Stephen's ring was lost forever.

~

DAN SHOVED a hand through his hair, scanning the ground for the umpteenth time, then looked up at the young teen beside him. Travis had looked so miserable, Dan hadn't wanted to quit searching. "Trav, it'll be okay."

"But Georgia said it was her engagement ring, from the guy who died."

Dan nodded, heart going out to the wide-eyed youngster who looked so guilty. "It wasn't your fault, buddy."

"It feels like it is."

"Yeah, I know what you mean."

He knew he couldn't really blame himself, but still, Sarah's white-faced accusations earlier had haunted him all afternoon. Some camp this was turning out to be. After Boyd and the others had finally come back from canoeing, he'd shaken his head no, and Boyd's small shrug felt like another blow. When they'd eventually had the chance to talk, Boyd's whispered, "Why on earth did she wear it here?" had mobilized Dan's energy for another round of searching. They'd exhausted the possibilities around the volleyball court, including Travis's careful list of the trajectories of possible landing sites. Where could it be? Sarah was right—the bottom of the lake wasn't worth thinking about.

"Hey, Trav, we need to pray."

The teenager nodded.

"Lord God, you know where the ring is. We need to find it. Please help us. Amen."

Dan closed his eyes, trying to be still as a memory floated past. He looked over at Travis, who'd echoed his amen. "Let's go look again while there's still some light."

Shadows were deepening as they slowly wandered back up the beach. A strange hope thumped in his heart. *Please, Lord.* They rounded the gnarled old pine where Sarah and Georgia had sat talking earlier in the day. *Please...*

And there, right at the base of the tree, half hidden in the sand, the diamond ring winked up at them next to the abandoned bottle of sunscreen lotion.

He exhaled. "Thank you, God."

"Dan, you found it!" Travis was so excited and Dan so relieved, they burst into laughter.

Dan picked up the ring and examined it, unable to believe this tiny gold hoop and piece of carbon had caused so much trouble. He bit back a sigh. "You want to give it to her?"

"Sure!"

Travis bounded away, yelling about their find, the ring carefully clasped in his hand. Dan slowly walked along the sand, getting back to the campsite in time to witness Sarah giving Travis a giant hug, much to the boy's delight judging from his grin. Dan stood in the shadows as Georgia and the boys whooped and cheered and Boyd's face tightened in consternation as Sarah did her huggy thing again, exclaiming her thanks.

"But where was it?"

"Near the fallen tree up on the beach."

Sarah looked up from her prize to the tree. "It must've slipped off while I was sunscreening..." Her voice trailed off, and she looked back at Travis. "Why did you look there?"

"Well, Dan suggested it." A corner of Dan's mouth pinched up at Travis's admission. "He said you were sitting there earlier today."

"Oh." She looked up and somehow, through the dusky gloom, her eyes caught his. "Dan?" She stepped past Georgia and the boys and stood in front of him. "Can I talk to you for a moment?" She glanced back at the curious faces. "In private?"

"Sure."

They moved through the trees until they'd cleared sufficient space, then she turned around. He caught the faint glimmer of tears before she looked down.

"I'm really sorry." She blinked, then took a deep breath and looked up, her eyes sparkling with sorrow. "I'm really sorry for accusing you of not caring and for getting so upset. I shouldn't have done that." She looked down again. "Please forgive me."

The sight of her, penitent in the evening wash of darkness, would've moved anyone. How could he hold this against her when he'd been forgiven for so much more? "Already done."

She looked up then, and the relief on her face was so akin to what he'd experienced earlier it made him smile.

"Friends?" She smiled tentatively.

"Of course." As if there was any other option.

But as she stepped forward and gave him a hug every bit as close and strong as the one she'd given Travis, whispering a thank you close to his chest, his heart started racing and he forgot to breathe. Maybe there was another option….

HUMBLE PIE WAS SO DELICIOUS. **Not.**

Sarah sat on the log, gazing at the expectant faces turned to her. Why did she always overreact, leading to necessary moments like this? "Uh, I just wanted to apologize to everyone for earlier. I shouldn't have become so hysterical. I'm really sorry." She caught Justin's gaze and attempted to smile. It was so not cool to be here as a leader and be the one acting more like a child. She exhaled. "Oh, and thanks heaps, everyone, for spending so much time looking for my ring. I don't know what I'd have done if Travis and Dan hadn't found it." She sent Travis another warm smile. It was nice to see the other boys treating the day's hero with a little more respect. His cheeks reddened even as his chest puffed out.

"You're the man, Trav."

Sarah caught Dan's amused expression and quickly dropped her gaze. It was still so hard to look at him after all that had transpired earlier. His forgiveness still couldn't cover her shame.

"Now, who's up for a sing along?"

The chorus of groans greeting Boyd's suggestion mirrored Sarah's own feelings. She'd be very happy not to sing. It'd be nice to go to bed early and just have this day end.

"Come on, didn't you enjoy Patrik's guitar playing last night?"

Boyd was keen for some reason to extend the night's activities, even though they'd already toasted marshmallows and played spotlight with torches. After nursing fresh bruises from that stumblingly awful activity, she was *really* ready to find her sleeping bag. Maybe Boyd just wanted the boys to sleep in more tomorrow morning. Ha. Fat chance.

"No s'mores till we sing!"

Sarah swallowed a smile. Boyd really was a camp Nazi.

"Did I mention that Sarah's a musician?"

What? She looked up and caught Dan's smirk. Well, maybe she did deserve it, after the way she'd treated him today.

"Really?" Boyd shot her an interested look. "Do you play guitar?"

Sarah coughed. "Not very well." She'd had to learn the rudiments of several instruments in order to teach her classes effectively. If she was rusty with piano, then her guitar playing would be positively primeval.

But Patrik passed her the guitar—there was nothing she could do. Wonderful.

Sarah shook her head as Boyd and the boys suggested songs. "I don't really know any camp fire classics."

She absently strummed a couple of chords, reacquainting herself with the feel of a guitar, desperately trying to recall the chords of any song appropriate for this moment. How long since she'd done this?

"You play anything you like. It's gotta be better than what Patrik does. We don't understand too many of his Swedish songs." Dan's playful smile and thump on the exchange student's arm took the pressure off.

She strummed a couple of bars of "Amazing Grace" before she stopped. "Um, I think some of you will recognize this. The words are very important to me." Even more so tonight. "I really hope you'll sing along. I need your help." She looked at Dan and he smiled, giving her courage to continue.

"WHAT'S the deal with you and her?"

Boyd's question broke Dan's reverie. The boys were finally in bed, and the quiet of the campsite was perfect for dreaming. He'd been thinking back to when Sarah had finished the song and the entire group had sat in silence until Justin said, freckled face shining in admiration, "Gee, Sarah. You're an awesome singer."

Sarah had blushed, just as Dan had known she would. He shook his head. She really was getting under his skin if he could predict her movements.

Boyd nudged him again. "Dan?"

"Nothing. We're just friends." Was that like "just" neighbors? He had to be careful now; Boyd knew him too well. He subtly shifted to his game face, hoping the years of playing defense would help hide his inner turmoil.

"Friends, huh?" Boyd's searching glance and sardonic expression almost triggered the truth. "You could've fooled me, the way you've been staring at her all night."

"She's different." What a weak word for the wealth of emotion he felt. "I find her interesting."

"Just tread carefully, Dan. It's obvious she's not yet over the fiancé."

"Stephen," Dan ground out.

Boyd sent him another considered look. "She seems a little flaky."

"I don't think so." Dan shrugged. "She's passionate, but I think that shows something good about her."

"What?"

Dan stared across the flames at the woman with fiery hair. "She cares."

Boyd snorted.

"And yeah, maybe she can be a little temperamental, but at least I always know where I stand with her." Why did that sound so defensive?

"Yeah, well, I don't want to see you getting involved in a rebound that can only lead to heartbreak." Boyd frowned. "You don't want to go back there."

He certainly didn't. Dan slumped back against the log as painful memories floated up from the past. *Lord, I don't want to live with any more regrets.*

Boyd leaned closer. "Just make sure you're leading with your brain, not anything else."

Dan bit his lip, trying not to let the frustration show. He didn't like hearing what his heart already suspected. Especially when he'd thought maybe God was finally answering his prayers. He flicked a final glance at Sarah, sitting across the other side of the campfire as she watched the flames crackle and spark into heaven, then stood and walked away to the lake, trying not to notice how the stars and soft wash of the water made the evening resonate with romance. What was the point? Was he destined to be alone forever?

～

SARAH FROWNED as the two men conferred briefly before Dan set off. He didn't seem too happy. From Boyd's quick glance, it probably had something to do with her, but what? Apart from the ring incident, she'd been nothing but pleasant—as much as a sleep-deprived, non-camping person with bruises and a giant headache could be. And considering her previous behavior toward Dan, this definitely counted as pleasant. So what was the problem?

The evening chilled. She made her excuses and disappeared inside her tent, trying to snuggle down in the tattered sleeping bag John had found for her. She closed her eyes, but the questions persisted. Several times during the day she'd noticed Dan's attention on her—even the kids had commented. She'd laughed it off, saying something to the effect that she was just the camp clown and he had to keep watch to make sure she didn't hurt anyone else. That was all, wasn't it?

She shifted over, the air mattress protesting her every move. How did people ever sleep when camping? Maybe sleep came from utter exhaustion. Nights were so noisy, with creaky mattresses, snapping tent flaps, and sleeping bags constantly zipping open and shut. Then there were all those noises she just didn't want to know about. Canada had bears out there somewhere. Her heartbeat quickened. *God, don't let them smell tonight's chocolate. Please keep us safe.*

Georgia's snores indicated she was out. Sarah sighed. If only she could be, too. She heard a rustle and tried to cover her ears with the pillow. Ugh. How could she be so tired and still unable to sleep? A groan escaped. Surely part of today's overreaction was due to tiredness. A hollow ache in her heart still throbbed each time she thought about how she'd hurt Dan. She just wanted to see him smile, really smile at her, like he used to. She loved his smile. It made her feel all floaty inside.

She frowned in the darkness. What had Stephen's smile looked like anyway? He'd never been much of a smiler—that had always been her domain. She touched the ring, now safely back on her right hand, and her heart filled with warmth. How amazing Dan and Travis had spent so long looking for it. The fact that they'd do that for her made her feel…special.

Another rustle. Her skin prickled. She opened her eyes and found the small torch stowed near her pillow, but despite flashing the light around, she couldn't see anything other than the ordinary, now-familiar shadows.

She switched it off and closed her eyes again, tugging her T-shirt down and her shorts up to cover that cool patch on her back as she tried to snuggle down in the ratty old sleeping bag. It smelled musty, and the scent made Sarah long for the surprisingly pleasant wood smoke of the campfire. Maybe some things about camping weren't so bad after all. Like roasted marshmallows, or how big the stars were out here, or staring across glowing embers to encounter expressive eyes the color of molten chocolate…

There was that noise again. She opened her eyes and snapped on the small torch again. A pair of dark eyes gazed at her. Panic roared up her throat and she screamed.

CHAPTER 10

The noise was enough to wake the dead. As he scrambled from his sleeping bag, Dan's foggy brain somehow registered that the scream had come from the girls' tent. Thank God he'd gotten back so late from his walk last night he'd simply tumbled into bed in his track pants and T-shirt. He unzipped his tent, his heart hammering hard at the thrashing movement in Sarah and Georgia's tent.

"Sarah? You okay?"

"Help! Get it off me!"

Oh, God! Dan ripped open the girls' tent flaps, screamed the zipper down. In the darkness, he could just make out Sarah frantically trying to escape her sleeping bag. She was moaning.

"Sar?"

Georgia was still asleep, which was strange, and he couldn't see anyone else. What the—?

Finally free of her bedding, Sarah lurched toward him, bumping his head with a loud crack. "Ow!"

Dan winced, stumbling out of the way as Sarah staggered upright and outside. "What happened?"

Gasping, rubbing at the bump on her head, Sarah's frantic eyes found his. "It was on top of me! It was horrible!"

Her eyes were wild, hair mussed, and she was shaking. He stepped closer, stroking her upper arms to calm her. There were still no sounds of stirring in the other tents. Boyd's plan for exhaustion seemed to have worked a treat. Georgia snored on, oblivious. "Sar?"

"Huh?"

"Who was it? What did he do?" Dan's chest squeezed. How could any of the boys do something like this? *God, when I find who did this, so help me—*

"What's up?" Boyd and Patrik had finally poked their heads out of their tents.

"Shh!" He shook his head at them as Sarah looked distractedly around. He gently clasped her trembling arms. "Sarah, look at me." His heart continued racing. He took a deep breath to calm down. "Did you get a look at him? Who did this?"

Sarah finally focused those big green eyes on him. "What?"

He leaned closer. "Sarah, what happened?"

"It…it was—"

"It was what, Sar?"

She gulped. "It was a mouse."

"A mouse?" Dan stilled. How many years had he used up in the last five minutes, worried over a mouse? He dropped his hands and stepped back. "All this because of a mouse?"

She blinked. "A mouse was sitting on the top of my sleeping bag, staring at me." She shuddered. "I *hate* mice."

Dan stifled a snicker and turned back to Boyd and Patrik, who still watched them anxiously. "Mouse."

They smirked wearily before disappearing back into their tents, but he soon heard their smothered laughter. It triggered something, and his chuckles bubbled up and escaped, unable to be restrained any longer. He walked away from the tents so as not to wake anyone else, his sides hurting as he struggled to keep in the laughter.

Sarah stood scowling, arms crossed, as he slowly walked back. "It's not funny."

"It is." Another spurt of laughter gurgled up. Man, he must be tired.

"Stop it."

"Can't." He couldn't stop the sloppy grin. She was too funny.

Sarah moved toward her tent. "I should wake Georgia."

He gently caught her arm. "Why? In case the big bad mouse gets her?" She nodded and another chuckle escaped him. "I think Georgia is tough enough to deal with a mouse. And if she hasn't woken up with all your screaming, then I don't think she'll wake easily now."

Sarah turned back to him. "Well, I can't sleep there." She rubbed her hands up her bare arms, shivering. "I'm going to stay up."

Dan groaned. "Seriously? I don't think the mouse would even be in there anymore. I'm sure it ran off as soon as you started screaming. Most creatures would've."

Her eyes narrowed. "I'm not asking you to stay up. I'll be fine. But I am *not* sleeping in there." She shuddered. "I think it was in my sleeping bag. Urgh." She did a crazy squirming move that made him laugh again.

"Do you want to swap sleeping bags? Mine's new, with no mice colonies living there."

She seemed to consider it for a moment, then ducked her head. "Thanks, but I'll just put some warm clothes on and stoke the fire or something. I'll be right."

He sighed. "Get your sleeping bag."

"But the mouse?"

"I'll check it for you."

She shook her head. "No. I'll just change."

He must have a gift. Sometimes the words were just there. "As long as it's not in your clothes."

Sarah's jaw sagged. "You think it's in my clothes? Oh no!" She started shaking again.

Oh. Hadn't counted on hysterics. He grabbed her arms. "I'm joking. Of course it won't be in your clothes." He bit his lip. *God, please don't let it be in her clothes.*

She lifted her eyes, seeming to test his for veracity. "Please don't joke. It's not funny."

"Sorry, Princess."

Dan snickered again as she speedily retrieved a thick sweater, track pants, and socks, shaking them vigorously. Anything that survived that beating deserved to live. He added a couple of small branches to the fire, enjoying the sight of the sparks arcing into the blackness.

Dressed in her warmer clothes, Sarah joined him on the log. "Are you staying up?"

That sounded like code for *please stay*. Dan bit back the groan. He didn't relish being up half the night, then trying to deal with the boys tomorrow. "Let me grab something warmer."

SARAH SHIVERED, despite being rugged up in her sweater, long pants, and with the fire toasting her toes. Rodents—of all persuasions—should've been left off the ark. Even squirrels just looked like rats with big hair. As a child, she'd had friends who had always encouraged her to stroke their guinea pigs, but she could never bring herself to do that. It'd be like touching a snake —totally against nature, totally wrong. Yet Dan was still laughing about her mouse phobia, his shoulders twitching in silent amusement.

She hit his arm. "Stop it."

Of course, that set him off again, and she couldn't help but smile at his attempts to calm down. Maybe it was a *little* funny, but definitely not worth this much laughter.

Dan exhaled and leaned against the log she was sitting on, tilting his head to check out the stars. "So, Princess, do you even know how to stoke a fire?"

Why did people doubt her all the time? "You just chuck more wood on it, don't you?"

His teeth flashed white in the darkness. "Sort of."

A crack from the trees beyond the vehicles made her jump. "Um, Dan?"

"Yes?"

"Are there bears around?"

"Not here at this time of year."

"Are you sure?"

"Pretty sure."

That didn't sound entirely reassuring, but she'd have to trust him anyway. They sat in companionable silence for a few more minutes. Every so often he'd start that silent shaking thing again. Who knew guys got the giggles? That was supposed to be reserved for ten-year-old girls. She smacked his arm again. "Stop."

"Sorry."

At least he was enjoying himself. So was she. Sort of. The fire was mesmerizing, making her sleepy. But no, sleep was not an option. Who knew where that mouse was hiding? She shuddered again. "I wish I was tough."

Dan shifted slightly. "What?"

"I wish I was tough. Or at least tougher. Not such a wimp." Why was she saying this? Tiredness and campfire must combine for some lethal truth-serum effect. She huddled into her sweater. If only she were back in her bedroom at the cottage. How many hours until dawn?

Dan turned to look at her, his gaze searching. "Sarah, there's different kinds of toughness. You're one of the toughest girls I know."

He mustn't know many girls. "Why do you say that?"

"You've had to deal with stuff most people can't begin to imagine."

She made a face. "I haven't exactly been *dealing* with it."

He turned back to the fire and stirred up the embers again. "When you fell off the bike, it was pretty tough of you to get back on when you were so hurt. Gutsy."

"I had to do that, otherwise I knew I'd never do it again."

She blinked. Oh.

"See? You have been dealing with stuff, learning from the past."

But there was still so much to learn, still so much not dealt with, still stuff that was just way too personal to ever explain…

"But, Princess, I don't think I ever said 'build a bridge' or 'get over it.' At least, I hope I didn't."

She swallowed. "You didn't. I'm sorry." Always sorry. Such a sorry, sorry creature.

"Even coming here, knowing it wasn't going to be easy, took courage." His teeth glinted in the firelight as he grinned. "I gotta admit, when you said you weren't into camping, I didn't realize what lengths you'd go to to prove it." Another quiet burst of laughter erupted from him, and she couldn't help but join in this time, the infectious giggles coming in fits and starts over the next ten minutes. He wiped his eyes. "Sorry, Princess."

"I don't think you're very sorry at all." She slid off the log to sit on the ground next to him. "You've been laughing at me since I came here. I'm glad I'm such a source of amusement for you."

He chuckled. "But you have had fun, haven't you?"

Sarah looked up and held his intense gaze for a heart-stilling second before dragging her eyes away to focus on the fire. "It's been okay."

OKAY. He could live with that. The silence that descended afterward was comfortably thick and filled with peace, both of them happy to study the fire, stirring it up occasionally or adding more wood. Sarah's fears about mice and bears all seemed to have faded away as she sat next to him, legs stretched out toward the flames, shadows flickering across her face, firelight dancing in the depths of her hair.

Dan bit back a sigh. He wanted to hold her hand, touch her hair, do anything to maintain this connection. It was funny how this woman had the ability to make him feel like a hopeless fool one minute and her own personal hero the next.

He chewed his bottom lip as Boyd's words floated in the back of his mind. No, he didn't want to get heartbroken. He didn't want Sarah hurt either. He didn't want to be driven by emotion. He did want...what? *Lord, lead me, guide this...friendship? Relationship? Show me what to do.*

The last few stars disappeared in the gradual lightening of the sky as a faint glowing rim appeared across the spruce-fringed water. Sarah stirred, stretching from her awkward position near him. He was surprised she was awake—amazed he was still awake—but even though he liked to sleep in, part of him was always glad to see the magic of dawn.

They sat in silence as the sun made its quiet appearance, bathing the campsite in slow warmth. Sarah ran a hand through her hair, the sun catching the red-gold strands, making them almost glow. With her pale skin and radiant hair, she reminded him of a picture he'd once seen on a school field trip by an Italian artist who liked to paint angels.

Whoa. He blinked. He must be super tired.

"It's so beautiful."

Sarah's smile as she turned to him made his heart skip. Yeah, definitely beautiful.

"I saw a few sunrises over Lake Muskoka when I first arrived." She turned back to study the sky. "The different time zones made it hard to sleep properly at first. But there's something so lovely about seeing this, here, just us and nature, the way God intended."

Just us. What did she mean by that? *Just us* as in people in general? Or *just us* as in only the two of them? Tiredness was muddling his brain. "Camping has some pluses."

"Yeah, I suppose it does." She shifted over, drew up her knees, and put her head on his shoulder. "Thanks for inviting me and for staying up with me. You're a good friend."

As wisps of her hair started playing with his chin, he toyed with possible responses: *You're welcome; You're a good friend too.* Maybe even putting his arm around her shoulders—just to keep her warm. Didn't good friends do that? Not that he'd ever do that with Boyd…

But a stirring from one of the boys' tents put paid to any reply as Sarah threw him a wry look, then scrambled up and away.

TREES FLASHED PAST, green blurs, the Jeep eating up the miles as they drove back to the real world. Sarah yawned. The camp had been…fun. She closed her eyes. And last night had been…interesting. That quiet time by the fire last night—or was it this morning?—had been amazing, the peace all-enveloping, like a quilt that warmed her soul. She smiled. Not long after early bird Justin had made his appearance, the rest of the camp had woken and all tranquility had gone. Breakfast followed by morning devotions, then more activities before lunch and the pack up. They'd all been busy little beavers.

Sarah opened her eyes to steal another glance at Dan as he drove home. Late afternoon sun glinted on his strong, muscular forearms, turning the hairs golden. She blinked and turned away. No, no, no. Why did she notice things like that? Dan was her friend. That was all. She wasn't even really over Stephen anyway. Was she? *Oh God...what am I thinking?*

She peeked back at him, long enough for him to flash that great smile at her before she looked away. This was terrible. It felt like their friendship had shifted. That closeness last night had stirred up...something. But they were driving back into reality now, and this couldn't work. She had to go back home in a few months, so yeah, they could be friends, but anything more was just asking for heartache. It was best to nip this in the bud before anything could develop.

She shifted closer to the window. No. She'd be much better off thinking about people like Georgia and Travis. She'd promised to keep in contact with Georgia, whose tears at their farewell were proof Sarah's going had been worthwhile. Georgia was such a sweetheart. Sarah was so glad they'd had the time to bond, despite Boyd's concerns about her hugginess.

Sarah gave a mental shrug. Boyd didn't have a corner on relationships, even though he obviously thought himself some kind of guru. She frowned. He'd even had the nerve to give her some veiled warning about Dan. While Dan and Patrik had conducted a final game of volleyball, she'd been trying to help clean up some of the cooking utensils. She'd been getting more of the greasy soot on her than she'd anticipated when Boyd had approached. "When do you go back to Australia?"

She didn't know yet. What business of his was it anyway? "Why?"

"Just wondering." He'd shrugged. "You and Dan seem close. He's been my friend since high school. He's had a ton of girls after him over the years, and I don't want to see him hurt."

She'd needed to count to ten before calming sufficiently to answer. "I like Dan a lot, but I'm not *after* him. He's only a good friend. Is that all right with you?"

Boyd had muttered some sort of apology, but she still got the feeling he didn't really approve of her. So when Dan had mentioned as they started driving home that Boyd and Patrik were staying the next few days with him, she'd decided she wouldn't hang around. Nope, it was best to avoid all of them, for lots of reasons.

But avoidance wasn't so easy a few hours later, as Dan and his guests sat at Ange and John's dinner table. God bless her aunt's insatiable gift of hospitality. She'd insisted on having the guys come for a "proper meal," knowing they'd be tired from the previous few days.

As they conducted an informal debrief of the camp and what type of follow-up might be necessary, Sarah found it difficult to concentrate. It was hard to ignore the person sitting across from her and yet somehow draining to look away anytime she found Dan's eyes on her. It was like her eyes were operating differently to her brain, so constantly were they drawn to him. What was wrong with her?

WHAT WAS WRONG WITH HER? Dan couldn't help but notice the lack of eye contact with Sarah. Every time he looked up she shifted her gaze away, as if the ice princess was back and those fireside glances had never happened. Dinner had been nice, but the lack of attention from Sarah almost had him believing Boyd's words from earlier today, that she wasn't interested in him and would remain fixated on Stephen forever. That thought filled him with a jabbing kind of pain, and he tried to ignore it, tried to stay focused on the conversation.

Ange leaned forward. "So, Boyd, how are things progressing with Joanna?"

Dan swallowed the snicker as Boyd looked up from his steak like a scared rabbit. Maybe Boyd would realize how it felt to have his love life scrutinized, only this time under the pastoral microscope.

Love life? Oh man…

Boyd took a sip of water. "These things take time."

"Any more time and you'll be old and gray and in a wheelchair, my friend." Dan clapped him on the back.

"Better to take things slow than get it wrong and have to live with the consequences."

Consequences? That shut Dan up. He shot a quick look at Sarah, but she seemed oblivious to the loaded comment. He speared a slice of cucumber as a new pang shot through him. Sarah was so innocent that she and Stephen had probably never done anything more than hold hands. And she was a minister's daughter…

His guts twisted. Nope, much as he liked her, had even thought maybe one day she might like him, she'd always be much too good for him.

Dinner felt a little tasteless after that, and he was glad when Patrik's yawns provided sufficient excuse to head back. When his guests finally switched off their lights, he stole out to the dock, lying down to stare up at the sky. The heavens declared the hugeness of God: glorious, all-powerful, and majestic. The vast expanse of black velvet dotted with stars also reminded him of another verse, something about how God had taken his sins away from him as far as the east is from the west.

He sighed. If only his soul could remember that too.

CHAPTER 11

Sarah lay on the hammock, trying to read *Persuasion*. Silly Anne Elliot. Fancy giving up on the man you loved just because somebody else persuaded you to. How dumb was that? She slapped over another page as her uncle's voice wafted from the open kitchen window.

"We haven't seen much of Dan lately."

Sarah's ears pricked up. Then she slumped back down. Why'd she have a special radar-like sense that enabled her to hear that name? She shook her head. *Get it together, girl.*

"He should be back from that hockey function by now."

What hockey function? Why didn't she know? She was Dan's friend. Even if she hadn't been acting much like it in the past five days, with her self-imposed absenteeism from next door.

"Maybe we should have him over for dinner tonight." The back door slid open, and Ange called to her. "Sarah? Do you mind popping next door to ask Dan if he'd like to come for dinner? It'd be good to catch up with him. Tell him anytime this week will be fine if he's busy tonight."

Sarah's mind raced through different responses: *Actually, I do mind. I hope he's busy. And I really hope Boyd isn't still there. Can't you text him?* She settled for, "Are you sure?"

Her aunt looked at her strangely. "Of course I'm sure. He's your friend, isn't he?"

"Yeah, he is." Sarah bit her lip. It was about time she started acting like it.

She wandered through the trees to Dan's lovely home only to hear the sounds of male laughter coming from the back. Heart dipping, she walked around to the deck. Dan sat with some men she didn't recognize. She took a step back, but one of them saw her and leaned over to Dan. Dan glanced around and stood up, beckoning her to join them. She sighed and slowly walked closer. Hopefully Dan's friends would be nice and kind like him, not disapproving like Boyd.

Dan smiled. "Hey, Sar. It's good to see you again."

Her heartbeat skittered at his smile. It was almost too good to see him. He wore the usual Leafs T-shirt, shorts, and bare feet combo, but he looked...perfect.

"Sarah, these are my friends from university, Rob and Jason. They're up for a few days to do some fishing."

Sarah glanced at the men. "Hello."

The darker haired one nodded, but the shirtless, tanned blond offered a broad grin. "Sarah. It's really nice to meet you."

Sarah briefly smiled, then turned to Dan. "I, um, just came to see if you wanted to come to dinner tonight, but obviously you'll be busy..." Her voice trailed off, and she studied her scuffed toenails. She really needed a pedicure.

"Oh. I promised the guys a grill tonight. We've got lots to catch up on."

She heard Rob's voice behind her. "Looks like we do, Danny boy. Looks like there's lots to fill us in on."

Sarah's gaze tangled with Dan's again. "Okay. Well, maybe tomorrow or the next night. Anytime is fine with Ange. And you know her, the more the merrier." She hoped Dan would come. Standing before him now only reinforced how much she'd missed him.

"Thanks. We'll aim for the day after tomorrow. We've a big fishing trip planned tomorrow, so we might even have some fish to bring."

"Okay. I'll let them know. Have fun." She gave a small smile and headed back, her steps slow, heavy with the disappointment that weighted her soul.

~

"So, who is she?"

Dan frowned as he steered the boat round the rocky outcrop jutting out into the lake. Rob's unbridled interest in Sarah had not abated through the past day and a half, which was kinda disturbing. Rob was a blond, blue-eyed manager in a Toronto car dealership and also something of a ladies man—which was good, as it often took the heat off Dan. Girls seemed to be attracted to Rob's Nordic looks, charm, and never-ending supply of new cars and forgot about Dan, which was just the way he liked it. Although, it had been gratifying to note that despite Rob's abs having been on display, Sarah had barely given him a glance.

"You didn't give much away yesterday, Dan my man."

"Down, boy." Jason's lazy chuckle broke in from the back of the boat. "She's obviously Dan's woman."

Dan rolled his eyes. Jason's recent engagement seemed to have made him see romantic outcomes everywhere. "No, she's not."

Rob perked up. "I'm not stepping on your toes if I ask her out?"

"No." Dan's stomach grew queasy. "But I don't think she'll say yes."

"Why not?"

Rob's self-confidence was something to behold. "I think she's a little wary of dating."

Rob shot him a smart-aleck grin. "Yeah, but that's you, not me."

Dan swallowed. Judging from Sarah's cool behavior post camp, maybe that was true. He'd thought time at a hockey skills camp in Toronto with Mike and Brent would help refocus him. It hadn't. Meeting Brent's wife again, seeing how the two couples got on, only drew envy and reinforced his desire for a certain other Aussie woman to pay Dan attention.

He steered the boat around another rocky headland, the huge pines standing to attention like soldiers.

"That's Sarah, isn't it? Couldn't miss that hair." Rob pointed out the figure on the little beach. He cupped his hands like a megaphone. "Yo, Sarah!" Rob started waving.

Dan's stomach knotted as she waved back then disappeared through the trees. He frowned as he steered closer to the dock. Rob didn't tend to take time to really develop relationships with girls, and there was a long string of disappointed ladies who'd been promised the world, gaining nothing but dust as Rob drove off alone into the sunset. He'd bet Rob was attracted to the thrill of the chase, the mystery of the pretty girl. Rob hadn't gotten to know her, let alone seen her give a proper smile. Wait until he did. Dan groaned.

Jason shifted over, an amused glint in his shrewd gray eyes. "You do like her."

"She's a friend." Dan frowned at Rob. "A good friend, and I don't want anyone hurting her. She's been hurt enough."

Rob shrugged. "Dude, if you're not gonna ask her out, I will."

As if she'd say yes anyway. "Fine. Ask her at dinner tomorrow night."

"Fine." Rob smirked. "I will."

. . .

THE NEXT DAY, after a solid morning workout, Dan headed next door. This was just a neighborly visit, to see if the walleye they'd caught yesterday would be helpful for tonight's meal. But when John informed him that Ange and Sarah were in town buying groceries, his level of disappointment told him something more.

He slowly walked back, reluctant to return to Rob's conversation. He was a funny guy, and it was good to spend time with guys who needed Jesus, but not as good as he'd hoped, even though he'd been looking forward to this catch up for weeks.

He stopped in the shade of a huge spruce. Since Sarah had arrived four weeks ago, they'd spent hours almost every day in each other's company. He'd missed her this past week. He'd missed talking with her, listening to her soft voice with that cute accent. He'd missed her smile, which had only come into full bloom recently. He'd missed the wrangling of spiritual questions that propelled him to study his Bible like nothing before. He'd missed her teasing and the sly, dry wit that came out at unexpected times. He'd even missed all those endearing clumsy, messy moments that made him laugh. His chest tightened. He really missed Sarah. He couldn't wait for tonight.

AFTER A LONG BUT enjoyable day of buying groceries and cooking up a storm, Sarah was putting the final touches on the table when a firm double knock came at the front door.

"I'll get it!" She moved quickly down the hall, hastily checking her appearance in the mirror. She smoothed down her hair a final time, then opened the door. "Hi." She smiled at the three men who stood before her. "Come on in."

Her eyes skated over Dan's guests to rest on the man himself. He looked so good tonight. The cheek stubble was gone, and he'd replaced the usual faded T-shirt with a nice shirt that complemented his chocolate-brown eyes. And with that smile, well, yeah, okay, she could see why he garnered so much attention from those girls in church. Her heart fluttered. He looked mighty fine—

Stop it! She mentally slapped herself. She wasn't supposed to be checking out guys, least of all this man who was her friend, who had only ever been kind to her. She turned to lead the way inside, staying quiet while Dan introduced his two friends to John and Ange.

As JOHN and Angela returned to the kitchen, Dan tried to settle into the small talk, but his mouth was on autopilot. Everything else was hyper-aware of Sarah, like his very pores were standing to attention. She looked so pretty. He'd only seen her in a dress one time, in church, but the bright blue color of this dress seemed to make her hair even shinier than normal and her skin sort of glow. And her eyes seemed extra sparkly. She looked extra good. Maybe he should tell her that.

"Sarah, you look gorgeous." Rob beat him to it.

Her cheeks turned pink at the compliment. Dan's heart sank.

ANNOYANCE HEATED SARAH'S CHEEKS. She'd tried hard to look nice, but Dan didn't seem to have noticed. She summoned up a smile as she led the way to the deck. Oh well, his loss. Her mind and emotions were awhirl with confusion these days as far as he was concerned. She'd missed him and thought maybe he'd missed her too, but now she wasn't so sure.

After the last boring week, it had been good to have something different to look forward to today. Once the shopping had been completed, she and Ange had ventured past a shop selling recycled clothes, and Sarah hadn't been able to resist this dress.

She'd also treated herself to a haircut and eyelash tint—it was amazing how just investing a little time in her appearance made her feel so much better. Some women were unrecognizable without their mask of cosmetics on, but she'd never been one for heaps of makeup. But venturing beyond the usual lip-gloss and mascara seemed to have done the job.

She glanced down at the swirly skirt. At least someone seemed to appreciate her efforts. This Rob guy must be sort of nice if he was Dan's friend, but he did seem a bit arrogant, like he expected all women to fall at his feet. Dan still hadn't said anything much to her beyond hello, although she could feel his dark eyes watching her again. She lifted her chin. Maybe if she were nice to Rob, Dan would realize what he was missing.

THE CONVERSATION over the delicious Greek-themed dinner was pleasant enough, although Dan was surprised to see Sarah respond to Rob's charm. He'd been so obvious, ignoring the rest of them as he asked question after question about places she'd travelled. Sarah was happily answering, laughing, and smiling away. Princess Charming.

Dan shoved the black olives to the side of his plate, but they weren't causing the queasiness.

Jason polished off the last of the moussaka, then scraped out the final piece of feta cheese from the bowl of Greek salad. He turned to his hosts. "That moussaka is delicious. A little different to what I'm used to."

"There's light sour cream in it instead of the usual cheesy sauce, seeing we all know Mr. Fit and Healthy has to watch his figure." Sarah finally glanced Dan's way, her smile fading. "Although, he hasn't eaten all his vegetables. No dessert for you, then."

He looked down at his plate. "I've never liked olives. But I loved the rest."

Ange smiled. "Sarah's a good cook."

Dan looked up in surprise. "I thought you said you don't cook."

Sarah's mouth lifted on one side. "I said I don't cook much. There's a difference." Her eyes caught his, her private smile making his heart dance for a moment until her gaze cooled and she turned back to the rest of the table. "I can cook, but Ange is such a fabulous gourmet, why try?" She shrugged. "It's okay to cook for you three, because you don't know any better."

Rob leaned forward. "I'd like to get to know you better."

Dan bit back a groan. He wished he had Rob's easy charm. Sarah was lapping it up.

Later, as John and Ange retreated to the kitchen to prepare coffee, Rob finally made his move. "I've really enjoyed tonight, Sarah."

She flicked a curly strand of hair from her eyes. "It has been nice."

"Are you free tomorrow night? Maybe we could have dinner together."

Her eyes lit up. Dan's sharp pang of disappointment made it suddenly hard to breathe.

HOPE FLARED BRIEFLY in her heart. Dinner over at Dan's filled her with anticipation. But that wasn't what was meant. She bit her lip at her stupid misread. Rob meant a date, with him. No one had asked her for a date for so long. After the accident, no one had dared, and she barely knew anyone in Canada. This was a Big Deal.

"I don't know." Rob was nice enough, but he wasn't... She swallowed. Perhaps this was one of those times to live a little, to not feel guilty. And after the ring episode, she was trying to not let the past control her so much.

She studied their faces. Rob's seemed hopefully expectant, Dan's face had blanked, and Jason was watching the exchange with a slight smile.

She snuck another look at Dan. If only he'd give some sign as to what she should do. *Be brave.* She cleared her throat. "What do you think, Dan?" *Tell me no, you don't want me to. Show me that you care.*

"Well, uh…" He cut a look at his friends, his gaze returning but not quite touching hers. "Sure. If you want. Why not?"

Why not? Her heart froze, her limbs suddenly heavier than lead. Emotion burned her eyes. She blinked it away. Affixed a stiff smile to her lips.

"She doesn't seem too keen, bro," Jason said to Rob.

"Yeah, better give her up as a lost cause."

Dan's words cut through her indecision. *What* did he think she was? A lost cause? She clenched her hands in her lap and turned to Rob. "Sure. What time?" How was that for nonchalant?

"Seven. We'll find the fanciest place around."

"Sounds good." Her gaze flicked from Rob's satisfied expression to Dan, who sat, shock written all over his face. Good. She smiled tightly and stood. "I'd better go help inside."

"I'll give you a hand." Rob stood and started clearing away the plates as she collected glasses. She kept the smile pasted on, ignoring Dan's gaze and the tightness in her chest that hinted that the Big Deal could well be a Big Mistake.

JASON LEANED FORWARD AS SOON as the others had moved inside. "Not what you expected?"

Dan shook his head, chest tight. She liked Rob? Never in a

million years would he have picked that. The night continued with coffee and baklava, but his heart wasn't in it anymore. Who was this woman? Sarah was transforming, emerging from her self-protective cocoon of sadness. He wanted to know her before she spread her wings and flew away.

But what was the point? He took another sip of his coffee and almost choked. Hadn't she admitted to Boyd that Dan was "only a good friend"? He'd thought maybe Boyd had misconstrued things, but tonight—in fact, everything this past week—had proved otherwise. Sarah had even asked for Dan's opinion, proving she really wasn't interested in him. He picked at the fringe of the tablecloth. *Lord, this hurts.* How dumb was he to have hoped—

"Dan?"

He blinked. "Sorry, what was the question?"

Dan worked to ignore the ache and maintain polite conversation with John and Ange, but pretty soon the pretense started to slip. He couldn't do this much longer. As soon as he finished his coffee, he scraped back his seat.

"Thanks for a great night." He gave Ange a quick hug and shook John's hand. "Nice meal, Sarah." He couldn't meet her eyes, just flicked a small smile in her general direction, then walked back through the trees, Jason and Rob trailing in his wake.

"She's going out with me!" Rob's gloating felt like fingernails running down the chalkboard of his soul. "Noticed you seemed a little put out there, bud."

Dan shook his head. "Just don't hurt her, okay?" It was like a piece of his grandmother's precious porcelain had just been given to a toddler.

Rob grinned. "Never."

CHAPTER 12

Why was it that every time she schemed and scammed, she later wished she hadn't? Sarah glanced out the Muskoka Shores resort's restaurant window to see the moon reflected in the lake. It was so beautiful and would be really romantic, if only she were out with the right guy.

She peeked at her dinner companion. She was a horrible person. *Horrible.* Pretending to be interested when the real reason she was out was piqued pride. Her gaze lowered to her plate. The hurt on being ignored by Dan the other night had quickly escalated into a type of roaring pain that had made her act in a way and say stupid things she didn't mean. It had been a little bit funny at the time, but now all she could remember was the way he'd left without looking at her. An evening she'd highly anticipated had ended up tasting like ashes.

She swallowed a piece of venison. Dinner out with Rob was nice—well, the food part was, anyway. After eating so much fish lately, it was a treat to finally eat something that hadn't swum. And Rob had tried hard, thoroughly complimenting everything from her hair to her shoes. But his charm, while flattering, made her uneasy. She got the feeling he'd probably spent lots of time practicing similar lines on many other girls. He was too smooth, too slick, too shallow. If Mr. Right ever did come along, he'd have to be able to plumb the depths of her heart, not just splash around on the surface.

"Dan was telling me how you met."

Sarah's head swung back to her date. Uh oh.

"You don't need to look like that." Rob chuckled. "He just mentioned how much you like to swim."

She exhaled. "I don't mind swimming."

"Something else we have in common."

"Something else?"

"We both like to swim and we both have excellent taste in the opposite sex."

Oh, puh-leeze. She struggled not to roll her eyes.

"Did I ever tell you about my champion swimming days?"

Sarah smiled sweetly. "No. But I'm sure you're about to."

He laughed. "You're real funny. I like a pretty woman who makes me laugh."

Sarah sipped her water and glanced around the resort restaurant for a clock. She slowly chewed the last carefully carved vegetable decoration as Rob kept on with yet another long story that invariably showcased himself as the hero. She attempted to look interested, but her thoughts kept drifting. She hadn't had a first date in such a long time. Stephen had been her first real boyfriend, and she'd never really gone out with anyone else.

She clutched the ring on her right hand as Rob laughed loudly again. *God, is this what it's going to be now? A whole lot of hurt and confusion and misunderstandings? How many Mr. Wrongs will there be until I finally meet Mr. Right?*

"So, Sarah, do you want dessert?"

She looked up guiltily into Rob's hopeful face and shook her head no. All she wanted was to go home and read a good book.

DAN HAD STAYED up waiting for the turn of headlights in the drive, trying to watch some lame action movie with Jason, but he couldn't stay focused on the ludicrous stunts, wondering all the while how the date was going. He felt edgy. Anxious, even. When Rob's sleek and shiny silver Porsche pulled in earlier than expected, the knots inside eased.

Rob moved through the door. Dan nodded, keeping his gaze on the big screen.

Jason glanced up from the movie. "How was it?"

"Good. We had fun. Food was great."

As Rob went on to describe tonight's five-star resort restaurant with water views, the food, and the dinner service, Dan fought the jealousy that rode hot and high.

"So, will you go again?" God bless Jason for asking all the right questions.

"Not sure. She didn't say too much."

Dan blinked. Since when did Sarah not have much to say?

Rob yawned. "Yeah, she was a bit tired or something at the end, and we didn't set another time." Rob made his excuses and headed upstairs.

Dan tried to ignore Jason's satirical expression and slight chuckle and make it look like he actually cared about the final scenes of the film. An ember of hope flickered in his heart. Maybe she wasn't as enamored as he'd believed.

THE NEXT DAY Dan made his way next door. Ange and John were out the front about to get in the car. "Hey, Ange, John. Is Sarah around?"

"She's out the back in the hammock. It seems to be her favorite place these days."

"Thanks." He made his way round the back, where he could

see Sarah slowly swinging, looking up at the pine trees, lost in thought.

"Hey, stranger."

She turned to look at him, unsmiling. "Hi."

"I came to ask if you wanted to come for a boat trip today. The day's perfect. Fish will be biting."

She stopped swinging and gingerly sat up, her green eyes cool. "What did you mean by saying I'm a lost cause?"

Uh oh. Judging by the blades in her voice, he was in trouble. "What?"

"The other night. Rob asked me out, and you said I was a lost cause."

"I didn't say that." He frowned. What *had* he said?

"You did." Her voice pitched higher, and she carefully stood. "You told him to give me up as a lost cause. Is that because you think I'm so pathetic that I don't want to have fun anymore? Or do you think no one would ever find me attractive?" She gulped. "I know I haven't always been nice to you, but I didn't think you could be so mean."

"Sarah." He inched closer. "I would never say you were a lost cause. I just meant Rob shouldn't bother asking you out. I thought you didn't want to go out on dates."

"I didn't." The green gaze dropped to the floor as her cheeks went pink.

The truth hit him like a slap in the face. She didn't want to go out with him, but Rob was a different matter. He squeezed air past the rocks sitting on his chest. "But now you do."

"I thought you told me to live a little, to not feel guilty if I feel new feelings."

He nodded but really only wanted to shake his head. Words clamped in his throat: *I meant I want to be more than just a shoulder to cry on, so don't feel guilty if you have feelings for me.*

"So if someone wants to ask me out, I might say yes."

"Even if they're not the right man for you?"

She snorted. "And you'd know?"

Dan sucked in a deep breath, trying to maintain an impassive face. "I know Rob, and I know he won't satisfy you. He's a nice guy, but not really suited for long-term relationships."

She choked back a hysterical-sounding laugh. "I kind of got that impression."

"So why'd you go out with him?" He took a step closer.

She turned away, and he gently moved her shoulders until he could see her face. Her eyes were wide, vulnerable, shimmering. "I just want to know that someone will love me again."

"Oh, Sar." He wrapped his arms around her, feeling her start of surprise, hearing her intake of breath. Yeah, he felt like that too. Could she hear how fast his heart was beating? She fitted so perfectly in his arms, her hair smelled so sweet—his heart was zinging all over the place. "Sar, you know there'll be many men who'd love the chance to love you."

"I don't know that. I'm not a man. I don't know what they see."

"Are you fishing for a compliment?" he murmured.

"You know I hate fishing."

His smile softened as he drew back. "Well, this man sees a sweet, beautiful girl who's been hurt by life and was lost, but now, with God's help, is finding her way back to being the person God made her to be." He tucked a stray curl of hair behind her ear. "She's kind, funny, a gifted singer, and has so many other talents I don't even know of yet. Why wouldn't someone fall in love with her?"

Sarah's big eyes were drinking in his encouragement. He stopped before revealing too much more of his heart. "Sar, if you think you're a victim, then others can start to view you that way too. But you're not. And guys are noticing."

"Guys?" Sarah's head tilted. "As in plural?"

Dan's cheeks heated. He had foot-in-mouth syndrome, for

sure. "Believe me, there will be plenty. Now, I need to know. Do you want to go out on the boat?"

"Okay. But"—a beat—"I'm bringing my book."

BRIGHT SUN DANCED across the sparkling water, a dazzling tonic for the turbulence of the past few days. Sarah had slathered on the sunscreen, and with a broad-brimmed hat and long sleeves, was doing her best to avoid sunburn as she sat, trying to read under the boat's canopy while the guys fished and swam. But the words were just black marks on the page, her thoughts too full of what had been said earlier.

Dan thought she was beautiful! A little thrill rippled through her. But no. Stop. Stuff that emotion back into its box. He was just being nice because, really, that was overstating things a *lot*. She'd settle for pretty. Occasionally. On a good day.

She peeked across at Dan as he laughed with Jason at the other end of the boat. He'd said she was funny. Did he mean funny *ha ha* or funny *peculiar*? Her sense of humor was a little warped at times, but some people seemed to like it.

The other qualities used to be true and maybe would be true again. At least she could agree with him on the gifted singer statement. She wasn't falsely modest about that. She'd been told for years she had a gift and had seen it at work, God using this part of her life to really touch people.

"Hey, Sar." She turned to where Dan stood at the back of the boat. "You coming in?"

She shook her head, then watched as Dan executed a perfect dive, swimming underwater until he was halfway to a floating platform the others had almost reached. A few more strokes and he pulled himself out of the water, looking lean, brown, and very...fit.

Sarah swallowed and looked back at her copy of *Persuasion*, but the words might've been in Chinese for all the sense she could make of them. She dropped the book back in her beach bag, sipped her water bottle, and settled back in the padded chair, facing away from the men, looking across to Lake Muskoka's far shore.

It was a beautiful day. The sky was clear save for a light dusting of cirrus, the water deeply blue, the green fringe of trees glowing jewel-like in the sun. Birds ducked and dived as the water gently slapped the side of the boat. Peace settled softly on her soul. She took a deep breath, then exhaled. Drew in another lungful of clean, fresh air. Her chest grew tight, and there was no room for the used-up air already in her lungs. It had to be released.

She closed her eyes. Maybe life was like breathing. Draw in the good; release the bad. Maybe all this time she'd been fighting, struggling for air, when God had wanted her to breathe in something new and fresh. Maybe all this confusion was kind of like God saying He wanted her to breathe Him in and let go of the past.

Let go and let God.

Humor plucked, and she opened her eyes. "That's funny, God."

The sun continued to bless her with warmth. Dan's words earlier had peeled open the truth already in her heart. She wasn't a victim of her past. She was Sarah Maguire, loved by God. And she really didn't need a man or an engagement ring to know she was loved and all right. With God, all *was* being made right. Here, in this beautiful part of the world, she really was getting better. And even though she might not feel like it all the time, the puzzle pieces of her life were slowly being put together again, revealing the person God had made her to be: loved, forgiven, unique, special, free.

She stared across the glistening water, where shadows chased sunlight. And inhaled: *more of You, God.* Exhaled: *less of me.* Did it again, as deep contentment filled her heart for the first time in a long time. *Thank You, God. Thank You so much for setting me free.* Blinking back emotion, she basked in the warmth of the afternoon sun, a smile dancing on her lips, peace in her soul. *God, You are so good.*

The guys' shouts grew closer, and she turned to watch them clamber back on board. She turned away as they started toweling themselves dry, but soon peeked back and caught Dan's gaze. His smile sent a bolt of warmth right through her.

"So, do you want to go out again?"

Sarah jumped, shading her eyes as she looked up at Rob, standing close by. "Um, I'm not sure."

"I had a lot of fun."

"It was nice, but…I don't think I'm the right sort of girl for you."

Jason's snort of laughter drew their attention. "Rob gets shot down."

Dan was watching them intently. Her pulse skittered, and she turned away as Rob, recovered from his initial fluster, resumed the joking around at his friends' expense.

Later, as Dan steered the boat for shore, Sarah surreptitiously studied him, noting the tiny whiskers on his chin, that pale scar on his jaw, those deep smile lines that made his grin so easy to return. The lake's cooling breeze ruffled his dark hair. Her heart skipped a beat. What if the plural was Dan?

He glanced over. "Have you had fun, Princess?"

"It's been great. Thanks for including me."

"No problem." He adjusted his sunglasses and grinned at her. "Glad you came."

As they wandered through the Canada Day markets in Huntsville, Dan's mind flicked back to the fishing trip a few days ago.

It was funny. Straight after the camp up until that day on the water, Sarah had been aloof, much like the ice princess he'd first known. But since then, she'd come alive with a vivacity she'd only hinted at before.

The fishing expedition seemed to have smoothed the waters between them whilst creating an undercurrent of something else. Expectation? Anticipation? Maybe it had been the feel of her in his arms. He hadn't been able to stop thinking about that these past few days. He exhaled. Thinking too much about that might get him into more trouble. Trouble with a capital S—that was Sarah, for sure...

"This is so cool! Look at all the flags!"

He smiled as Sarah roamed around the markets, eyes wide with excitement as she took it all in. Wandering through the stalls, she picked up one piece of memorabilia then another, a big grin on her face. Then she discovered the stand with maple candy and, of course, had to try some.

"Oh, this is so yummy!"

Jason shook his head. "Don't you have Australia Day celebrations back home?"

"Yeah, but this is different. I like different." She looked straight at Dan with a funny smile on her face.

His insides curled. Oh man....

They joined the crowd, listening to some official speeches followed by a rousing rendition of the national anthem. Even that gave rise to her excitement.

"Do you do that hand on your heart thing before games?"

He nodded. His uncle had fought in the Middle East; it was a sign of respect.

"Do you sing along or just act cool?"

He didn't have time to answer, as some little kid turned to look at him.

"Hey, mister, don't you play for the Leafs?"

All of a sudden, a bunch of kids came up wanting autographs, proof his hat and sunglasses hadn't exactly worked as disguise. But after an enjoyable morning flying under the radar, it did his ego good to have Sarah impressed by all the fans. Well, he hoped she was impressed.

"So, you really are a bit of a celebrity, then?"

He couldn't quite decipher the look in her eyes or the tone of voice. It was like she was measuring him for something and wasn't sure if he fit. She studied him a beat longer before turning to check on the nearby market stalls. His ego swiftly deflated, especially when she soon returned, more interested in the free cake on offer.

"There's cake!" She leaned close, her voice dropping. "Do you think they give it to just anybody, or do you have to be a genuine Canadian to get some?"

Rob grinned. "I think you're supposed to know the words of 'O Canada.'"

Jason laughed. "Go up to the table and try 'oat' your best Canadian accent, eh?"

Dan couldn't resist. "Princess, you're not just anybody. You're a somebody. Here, you can have your cake and maybe even eat it too."

"You're so funny."

But the smile his lame joke elicited had the power to make him feel like he was the wittiest man alive.

The blue skies and buzzing crowds continued. While John and Ange had strawberry scones, the rest of them checked out the museum, then enjoyed something from the barbecue while listening to a jazz band. Dan couldn't help but smile as Sarah mouthed along to the words.

He touched her arm. "You wishing you could be up there?"

"Not at all! I'm having too much fun watching."

When the band finished their second set, it was time for an agricultural exhibition.

"I can't believe she's getting excited by all this." Rob rolled his eyes at Dan as Sarah raced over to watch the tractor pull, the three men trailing in her wake.

She turned back to flash another smile at them. "I've never seen a tractor pull before, so I'm enjoying it, okay?" She turned back to watch the spectacle, her brand-new red Canada baseball cap clashing violently with her hair.

Happiness rose as high as an escapee pink balloon soaring to the heavens. Sarah was so fun to be with. She kept laughing at Rob's funny comments, chatting with Jason and finding out about his fiancée, and displaying the spunky sass he'd witnessed before. The fact that she coped with these friends gave him hope that she'd adjust to his family, who were visiting later this week, after Rob and Jason had left. Now *that* would be interesting.

Later, as dusk fell, they settled in at Avery Beach to watch the fireworks. Sarah sat on the red-and-green checked picnic blanket between Ange and himself, loudly slurping gravy as she hurried to finish her roast beef sandwich before the light completely faded.

He nudged her as they waited for the fireworks to begin.

"Your T-shirt looks like you've had fun today." He motioned to the roast beef gravy stain that had joined the cranberry juice and ice-cream spillage from earlier.

"Oh." Through the dusk he caught the flicker of a smile and her small shrug. She leaned in closer. "You know, you once mentioned you weren't always a gentleman. I have a confession to make. I know this will surprise you, but"—she leaned closer still and murmured in his ear—"I'm not always a lady."

He snorted with laughter as the sky exploded with a loud boom.

Dan glanced across. Sparkles of blue and red shimmered against Sarah's transfixed face. She tilted her head, and the bursts of color continued to play against her throat as her hair tumbled down her shoulders. She laughed and caught his gaze. "Isn't it pretty?"

Golden raindrops dripped from the sky. He stared at her instead. "Really pretty."

Sarah wrinkled her nose at him, just like he'd known she would. She leaned back on her hands, her fingers brushing his, sparking a heated shiver across his skin. "Oh, sorry." She moved slightly away.

"I'm not." He shifted his fingers to graze hers again in another nerve-tingling moment.

Sarah stared at him, green eyes wide as clouds of color boomed above to the cheers of the crowd surrounding them. But as she slowly smiled that gorgeous smile, it made him feel like he was the only person in her world.

And that maybe one day soon she'd reconsider that "only a good friend" comment.

CHAPTER 13

Rob waved at Sarah as he and Jason pulled out of Dan's drive to head back to Toronto. "I'll call you sometime!"

"Bye!" Sarah waved and turned to catch Dan rolling his eyes. "What? Think he won't?"

"History tells me."

"Out of sight, out of mind?"

"Pretty much." He shrugged, hands in the back pockets of his cargo shorts.

"Oh well."

"You don't sound too disappointed." His eyes—dark, intense—watched her carefully.

"Nope. He's not really my type."

"Really? He isn't?"

His overly innocent expression and tone drew her chuckle. "There's no need for you to sound so smug." Sarah shoved him off the step.

His dimples deepened. "There's no need for violence."

Sarah laughed. "I'm going."

"Speaking of going, I was, uh, wondering..." He glanced down and swallowed.

Sarah stared at him. Mr. Cool, Calm, and Collected was nervous?

Dan looked up again. "Do you want to go out for dinner?"

Oh! Her heart skipped a beat. Could he really mean—"As in...?"

His cheeks reddened. "As in, if you're needing dinner and want to go out and have some with me sometime, that'd be really nice."

"Oh." Yes! Who cared about going back to Australia or any other complication this could bring? "Are you asking me out on a date?"

His lips twitched up at the corners. "I've been told you might be open to dates."

"As long as they're not pity dates."

"Definitely not a pity date."

At that husky note in his voice, her tummy turned over. She worked to rein in the big smile she could feel slowly blooming across her face. "In that case, I think I'm definitely needing dinner."

"Tonight?" Hope filled his eyes. "Pick you up at six?"

He was so keen! Another thrill rippled through her. "I'd better go get ready, then."

"See you soon."

AT LAST. He was so glad he hadn't listened to that little voice in his head that always whispered his worthlessness. Sarah was going out with him! She must've finally decided to put her past behind her, and this was a sign from heaven that it was okay to proceed.

He fought to tamp down the excitement as he cleaned up

around the house. It was just a date. He wadded Jason's forgotten newspaper and lobbed it into the basket next to the fireplace. Grinned. Playing it cool? Nope, couldn't do it. What was wrong with being excited, anyway? This was his first real date in forever. And it would be great to go out with Sarah before his parents and younger brother arrived tomorrow. He needed to focus now to get things ready. He wasn't planning an early night tonight.

When the house was respectable enough, he had a quick shower, then got in his Jeep and drove next door. He knocked and was taken aback by the swift opening of the front door.

"Hi, John."

"Daniel. How are you?"

"Fine, thanks. You?" This definitely wasn't the easygoing man he was used to greeting. Then again, this definitely wasn't the usual thing for him. He couldn't even remember the name of the last girl he went out with. How long ago?

"Have a seat." John motioned to the lounge. "I'll cut right to the chase. When your friend Rob took Sarah out, Angela and I weren't too concerned. Anyone can see he doesn't think much beyond today. But you're a different matter." John leaned forward. "Sarah regards you as a friend, a good friend. No one has been able to get her to open up the way you have." John sighed. "She relies on you, Dan, so I don't want you messing this up. You'd better be thinking about the consequences beyond today. You got me?"

"I've been thinking about this for a while now."

"Good. As long as we both understand each other."

"I understand, sir. Loud and clear."

John's shoulders sagged. "Glad that's done. Ange wasn't too sure about this today."

"I'll be careful."

Ange entered the room followed by Sarah. "Careful about what?"

He ignored Sarah's question as he stared. "Wow, Sar, you look amazing."

She wore a green, hippie-style dress with bronze beads around the neckline. Her hair was caught up, with little wispy bits around her ears. Her eyes seemed bigger and her lips rosier. "Princess, you look beautiful."

She blushed. "Thanks." Her lips curved up as she surveyed him. "You look nice."

Dan grinned, then glanced at John and Ange, who still looked at him with barely disguised apprehension. His mouth dried. Surely they didn't think—

"Have a good time, you two."

John's comment dislodged the uncertainty. He turned to Sarah. "Ready?"

"Yep. Don't wait up." Sarah smiled at Ange and John and stepped out with him.

His heart tripped in anticipation. Tonight would be unforgettable.

THE RESTAURANT WASN'T in some fancy resort but a little café right on the water. Blue-and-white china adorned the café's yellow walls, and a big picture window revealed another boat entering Gravenhurst's little harbor, pulling into the wharf opposite. How sweet that Dan would think to take her here.

His consideration drew a fluttering in her veins, and she lowered her head to examine the menu. She couldn't help but contrast the two men who had taken her out in the past week. Whilst both were attractive men, Rob's charm was fairly obvious, his flattery as fleeting as his interest had no doubt been.

Dan was different. His care and concern over the past few weeks had taken some time to adjust to. She hadn't always liked what he'd said, but he was honest, and she now counted him as one of her good friends. Her lips twisted. Considering how she'd treated her friends back home, he was probably her best friend.

"Hey, what's that look for?" Dan lowered his menu and studied her. "If you'd rather go somewhere else, that's fine."

"No, this is great! I love that you're so secure in your masculinity that you'd take me to a tea shop." She leaned forward. "Some men would be threatened, but not you."

His eyes laughed. "I'm glad you approve."

She returned to studying the menu, or at least pretending to. "I was just thinking."

"About?"

"How nice this is. How nice you are." She peeked up as his smile lines deepened. Why did her fair skin always have to give away her thoughts? Not that her big mouth helped matters, either.

But Dan was *so* nice, with the best smile, and dimples, and laugh lines that always made her want to smile back. And he smelled *so* good tonight. Not that he'd ever smelled bad—even sweaty he still smelled good. But tonight, when he'd leaned close to help seat her—perfect gentleman that he was—she'd caught a whiff of his enticing aftershave. He'd smelled *really* good. "Really, really nice."

"I think I like the fact that you say what you think."

She looked up to meet his eyes filled with amusement. Oh no. How much had she said aloud? Embarrassment simmered in hot waves from her skin. "Well, what you see is what you get with me. I'm not too good at pretending."

He shifted forward and caught her hand, brown eyes intense. "I don't like pretenders."

She bit her lip, staring at him for a moment before glancing down to where he still held her hand, his thumb slowly caressing the thin skin on the back of her hand, each gentle brush sending her insides crazy. Had he noticed she wasn't wearing Stephen's ring tonight? Her fingers looked naked without the familiar glimmer, but it had just seemed wrong to be out on a date with Dan and still flaunting that ring. She'd left the ring at home for the first time ever today, but strangely, wasn't too bothered by its absence.

WHAT WAS the definition of the perfect date? Surely it had to involve good food, a good view, and good conversation with a good-looking woman. Dan smiled, mentally ticking the boxes: the food tasted delicious, the view was really pretty, the laughter hadn't stopped, and Sarah…Sarah was gorgeous.

The table near the big window overlooked the lake, and the early evening light reflecting off the water seemed to bathe Sarah in a golden glow. Her ruddy hair gleamed and held those little curly tendrils he wanted to loop round his finger. The hue of her dress seemed to make her eyes greener, and he loved the creaminess of her skin. And the way she kept blushing, it was like her face couldn't hide a thing—and so fun to watch.

"Hey, Sar."

She glanced up from her plate of roast beef.

"I like your dress."

"Oh! Thanks. I got it at the church's op shop."

"Op shop?"

"Oh, right, you don't call them opportunity shops here. A goodwill store? A place where they sell secondhand clothes?"

"A thrift store."

"That's it. I really appreciate being given a second chance, and I bet the clothes do too."

He stared at her as she swallowed another mouthful, his own plate barely touched.

"This is so delicious, Dan." She tilted her head. "What's wrong?"

"Nothing. It's nice to be with someone who doesn't care about the latest and greatest in fashion." Like his mom. He couldn't imagine her ever wearing anything hand-me-down, let alone admitting to it.

"Fashion?" Sarah laughed. "Clothes are clothes, aren't they? If you like something and you look okay in it, why go buy something else?" She leaned forward. "You know it's just part of a giant conspiracy to keep the world economy rolling." She patted his hand with both of hers. "Just don't buy into it."

"Conspiracy theorist, eh?"

"No. But I like to think I'm doing my bit for the planet. Do you know how many clothes get thrown away each year? Or how many people work in slave-like conditions just to make cheap clothes for westerners? It's actually way more environmentally and ethically responsible to wear recycled fashion."

See? This was why he found her fascinating. She brought such a different perspective to his world.

"Am I boring you?" she asked, a pleat in her forehead.

"Not at all," he assured.

"Oh, good. I know I can get on my personal high horse and ride far, far away. But I do care about these things." She placed her fork and knife on her plate. "It's actually quite refreshing to pick my own clothes. Back in Heartsong days we always had to wear a certain style, and let's just say I'm more of a hippie than a rock chick kind of girl."

However she liked to describe herself, she was definitely his kind of girl.

He glanced down at her hands. His heart tripped. She wasn't wearing Stephen's engagement ring. Surely that meant—

"So, there's something I want to know, Mr. Walton." Sarah leaned forward again, smiling that delicious smile at him.

"What's that, Miss Maguire?" He grinned at her. He could tell her anything.

"Why do you call me Princess?"

Okay, well, maybe not that. While she'd rediscovered a sense of humor, he didn't think she'd be quite up to the aloof ice princess explanation just yet. "Uh, I guess it's just how I think of you."

Eyes that had been warmly gazing into his a second ago cooled as she grappled with the weak response. Uh oh. He needed something else. "And isn't that what Sarah means? God's princess, or something like that? I'm sure I read that somewhere once."

Her eyes softened and he wanted to cheer himself. That had been close.

"That's why Mum and Dad named me Sarah." She smiled shyly at him, and his heart started doing flip flops again.

The conversation flowed easily, the friendship built over the past few weeks providing lots to talk about. It was the best date he'd ever had. Sarah was enthusiastic, witty, and challenged his ideas about lots of things. She wasn't like other girls he'd known, who'd always agreed with whatever he said. She definitely had her own opinions. They had to agree to disagree on a few topics, but the rest of the night was filled with banter and laughter until the restaurant had emptied of all other patrons and the wait staff was yawning and it was time to go.

The short drive home held a happy, contented kind of silence. Another sign that their friendship was genuine and didn't need chatter to fill in the holes. He pulled up outside the cottage and turned to face her. "This has been great. We'll have to do it again."

Her smile lit up her face. "I'd love to! I've had so much fun."

"Me too. I'll remember this date forever."

"Really?"

That soft, shy expression made him so glad he'd manned up enough to ask her out. He shifted in his seat, searching for a sign that she might be open to a kiss. The green eyes smiled and, heartbeat quickening, he inched forward.

"What's today's date? Living out here the days kind of blend together, and I can't remember what day of the week it is, let alone the date."

He knew exactly what she meant. "My family comes tomorrow. That's supposed to be the fourth. That must make today the third of July."

Sarah's breath hitched as she stilled, eyes wide. "The third? Really?"

He snuck a peek at the time-date display illuminated on the dashboard. "Yeah."

"No. Oh no." She placed a hand on her mouth, then bent, scrabbling for her handbag.

"Sarah, what is it?"

She shook her head, looking like she was going to faint. Or be sick. "I'm so sorry. I have to go." She stumbled out the door and up the steps and disappeared inside.

"Sar?" He scrambled from the Jeep and neared the house as an inner door slammed. Ange appeared at the front door, lines creasing her forehead.

"She just ran off! We were having a great time together and Sarah just ran away."

Ange sighed. "Today is Stephen's birthday. I thought she must have forgotten, because she hadn't mentioned it. I didn't want to remind her in case of this reaction."

"Oh." No. Stephen. Again. But how could he have known? After a half-hearted goodbye, Dan drove back home and parked out front, slumping over the steering wheel as rejection swirled. He squeezed his eyes shut. *Lord, I thought she was over him. Help her. And sorry for taking this so personally, but this kinda sucks.* He exhaled, got out, kicking at the gravel on the driveway before entering his big, lonely house.

~

THE KNOCK on the front door startled her from shallow sleep. Sarah slipped off the bed and carefully moved closer to her bedroom's front-facing window, where she could vaguely hear John's and Dan's voices. She hoped John remembered what she'd said earlier.

"She doesn't want to see anyone." John's deeper voice replied to something Dan said. *Thank you, John.* No, she sure didn't.

She bit her lip as Dan murmured something else she couldn't make out.

John sighed. "I know it wasn't anything you did. Just bad timing, that's all."

Another murmur.

"Okay. Bye, Dan."

Hidden behind her bedroom curtains, Sarah watched Dan go. Shoulders slumped, head down, he looked exactly like she felt: lonely, bewildered, sad.

Her heart twisted. Part of her—the trying-to-be-brave part—wanted to race out and apologize and try and make him understand. But courage cowered against the heavy confusion that had snuck up in the night. She couldn't rationalize her panic last night, only that it seemed like such a betrayal to Stephen's memory to have been sitting there on his birthday—that she'd forgotten!—having had such a fun date.

Wanting Dan to kiss her.

She hadn't been able to explain any of it to Ange or John apart from assuring them Dan had been the absolute, perfect gentleman. She leaned her forehead against the window and tried not to let the burn in her eyes turn to liquid. No. She'd finally started feeling like she was moving on only to realize that the ghosts wouldn't let her. She'd so enjoyed last night, and Dan had seemed to also.

Until she'd managed to spoil things.

Again.

CHAPTER 14

"*D*aniel. It's good to see you." His mother dropped a barely-there kiss on his cheek, then stepped back to survey him. And sighed. "But why do you insist on wearing such old clothes?"

His smile dropped a notch. "It's a vacation, Mom. It's about relaxing."

"Hmm." She arched a brow, then turned to totter up the stairs in her fancy heels and linen pantsuit. Dan bit his lip and turned to his father, who placed the last suitcase on the drive.

"Hey, Dad."

His father's deep brown eyes looked him over before he nodded. "Son."

Dan fought the trickle of rejection he'd always experienced in his father's presence. He should be used to this by now. "I'll bring in the bags."

His father nodded, walked up the steps, and disappeared inside.

Dan exhaled and bent to pick up his parents' expensive luggage set when a red sports car raced through the gates and down the drive. He straightened as the Corvette pulled up sharply, scattering gravel, then stepped closer as his younger brother got out of the car. "You know you're gonna have to rake that up later, stunt man."

"Later." His brother grinned, giving him a hug. "It's great to see you too."

"Been too long."

"Way too long. I'd almost forgotten what you looked like." Sam looked up at the clear sky. "Looks like an awesome day for fishing, right?"

"Perfect."

Sam nodded to the silver Mercedes. "What's the temperature like today?"

"Cold but calm. So far." Dan picked up his parents' bags as Sam popped the trunk and retrieved his gear. "Come on. I think we all need a coffee."

Dan closed his eyes and prayed for strength. One, two, three, four... He exhaled, opening his eyes to stare out the kitchen window to the lake, shimmering blue in the sunshine. Thank God for Sam. At least there was one person in the world that understood him, who he didn't need to try and second-guess or walk on eggshells with or have to explain himself to all the time.

His parents, however...

"Daniel? Are you serious about these drapes? They're starting to look a trifle dated. Surely it's time for new ones." His mother walked into the kitchen wearing her usual look of discontent.

"Mom, they're fine." He handed her a cappuccino. "Enjoy."

She grasped the mug, took a sip. The lines on her brow eased away in a rare smile. "Thank you, Daniel."

Warmth filtered into his heart as she moved back toward the lounge area. He wondered sometimes about his parents' love, both for him and for each other. Since making a ton of money ten years ago on the stock market, they seemed to have assumed new personalities, and most of the warmth he remembered had disappeared, along with the old house where he'd grown up.

Dan sighed. Everything seemed to be about appearances with them now: the best address, the latest car, constant redecorating, designer clothes. Not that it ever seemed to make them happy. Maybe it accounted for Luke being the golden boy in the family, with his join-the-dots life of academic excellence leading to an investment banking career and a perfect, pretty wife. Dan wasn't jealous, and it shouldn't bother him that his parents didn't understand his different priorities. Because, really, without God to live for, what else should he expect from them?

He wiped down the espresso machine, dumped out the coffee grounds, then put away the skim milk his mother used— right next to the regular milk he'd started buying for whenever Sarah came over. He chewed his lip. Despite the many coffees he'd made for Sarah, she'd never once wanted anything diet-like, always insisting full fat tasted so much better. But then, she never seemed to care too much about appearances, which was just another thing he liked about her.

A clatter announced his brother's arrival. "Hey, wanna come fish?"

Dan shook his head. "Love to, but Dad wants to talk investments."

"I know. That's why I'm getting outta here before he starts."

"Catch some for me, then."

His brother escaped outside, and Dan gave him a thumbs-up through the kitchen window before Sam headed toward the boathouse.

God bless Sam. These past few days had been fun with him around, fishing, catching up, visiting some of the nearby tourist-filled towns. The easy teasing reminded him of being with Sarah—relaxed, fun, connected. Dan shook his head. He really had to stop thinking about her.

"Daniel? Are you ready yet?"

Dan grabbed his coffee and headed back to where his father sat on the leather lounge, his head stuck in the financial pages of *The Globe and Mail.* Dan shifted the Joseph Prince book John had lent him weeks ago as he sat down opposite.

His father looked up. "Finally."

The next half hour was an endurance test of patience as his father peppered him with pearls of wisdom from the world of finance. Dan tried to stay awake, tried to look interested, but he did have an accountant—and a year of a business degree. He wasn't completely clueless.

"Now, Dan, did you invest in those shares as Luke recommended?"

Ah, no. Gave that money to a Haiti earthquake relief program. "Not yet."

His father sighed, shaking his silver head. "I don't know what it is with you. Ever since you joined that church, you've been ignoring sound financial advice and—"

The doorbell rang. *Thank God.* "Excuse me a moment." Dan leaped up and hurried to open the door. And stared. "Sarah! Uh, come in."

Flushed, hair half falling from a ponytail, she wore the same shirt and shorts she'd worn that first evening. She started talking as soon as she entered.

"Dan, I'm so sorry about the other night. I need to explain what happened." She walked toward the living room. "I was having such a great time, and thought you were too, but obviously I didn't know what date it was, and I felt so bad when I realized about Stephen, so I didn't—" She stopped. "Oh."

Mom and Dad looked up, a matched pair of shock and dismay. Sarah's bright pink cheeks deepened to magenta.

"Mom, Dad, this is Sarah Maguire. She's the niece of Pastor Angela, who lives next door. Sarah, these are my parents, Andrew and Helen Walton."

"Hello." Mother managed a thin smile. Dad didn't manage anything.

"Um, hi. Nice to meet you." Sarah gave his folks a weak smile, lifted a hand to smooth her hair, and stepped back. He caught the panic in her eyes before she started edging to the door. "I, um, didn't know you were here. Sorry for interrupting."

He stepped closer. "Sar, you're not interrupt—"

Sarah was gone.

~

How humiliating! She should never have gone. She walked the bike through the trees, trying not to stumble over exposed roots and slippery rock. His parents were there? They'd looked all coolly tailored in their color-coordinating linen ensembles, like they could entertain the queen at a moment's notice. And she'd rocked up dressed like this?

"Sarah! Wait up!"

She threw a hand through her sweaty hair. Why had she thought she needed to see Dan straight after getting back from town on the bike? She grimaced. All the long way in and back she'd planned her speech out to the nth degree—but hadn't bargained on his parents being there! Racing back outside, she'd glimpsed her bright red face in the mirror in Dan's hall—why did she have to have skin like this?

Dan quickly caught up without a single puff to show he'd just raced one hundred meters in fifteen seconds. Pro athlete. "You ran out! What's up with that?"

She dropped her gaze, studying the browning pine needles on the ground. "Look, I'm sorry. Sorry for running out just now. Sorry for running out the other night." She lifted her eyes to his. "I'm sorry I don't treat you very well."

"Sar—"

"I was out with you and I forgot him. I was there, with you, on Stephen's birthday, wishing..." *You'd kiss me.*

HE'D LOVE to know what she was thinking. "Princess."

She shifted, studying a nearby blue spruce as if it were the most fascinating tree in the world. He followed her gaze. Nope, not even a squirrel.

"Dan, it's too soon."

He swallowed the pain wadding in his throat. "It's never too soon for a friend."

"Friend." She seemed to consider that for a long moment, then sighed. "Friend it is, then."

Friends. Only a shadow of what he really wanted, but still, better than nothing at all.

She offered a small smile. "I didn't know your parents were here."

"And my brother. He's out fishing at the moment. Maybe you should all come for dinner tonight. You could meet my folks properly."

Her smile turned wry. "Are you saying I didn't make a good impression?"

"You don't need to impress me." His parents on the other hand...

Her head tilted. "You really want us to come tonight? All of us?"

"Yes. Come at six."

"Okay. Can we bring anything?"

"Just yourselves."

"Okay then." She nodded, as if convincing herself. "Thanks."

There was nothing to be nervous about. Sarah swallowed against the butterflies threatening to escape. They were just people. But still... *Jesus, give me some of Your strength.* She took a deep breath, trying to smooth the previously unseen wrinkles out of her white cotton dress—another goodwill find—while balancing the plate in one hand as they waited for their host to admit them.

The door finally opened. "You're here!" Dan welcomed her aunt and uncle, then gave her a warm smile. "Hey, friend."

"Hello." Caught in his smile, the nerves dropped away. Why did it matter anyway? As he'd just made very clear, she was his friend. And as much as she'd like to improve upon that first impression with Dan's folks, her security was supposed to be based on what God thought of her, not anyone else. Her shoulders relaxed as she followed them into the spacious living room.

"Mom, Dad, you remember John and Angela McPherson from next door? And you met Sarah earlier. This is Andrew and Helen, my parents, and Sam, my younger brother."

"Hello, Sam." Sarah forced her lips to stay up. "Your brother didn't tell me much about you."

Sam shot Dan a look, then turned back to Sarah. "He didn't tell me anything about you, so I guess that makes us even." He winked. "But whatever you want to know, I'm your man."

She snickered and the tension in the room dropped about a hundred watts. Sarah glanced across at Dan and smiled.

The ball of hurt Dan had been carrying in his chest since their date four days ago suddenly disappeared. "Come on. Let's have dinner."

God bless Sam—he knew how to break the ice. Much to Dan's relief, Sarah continued to loosen up as the meal progressed, especially after the delicious lemon cheesecake she'd brought had been complimented by everyone—even his mother, who usually never ate dessert. But the warm vivacity Dan loved about Sarah really sparkled to life a little later, when they moved to the lounge for coffee, and his brother started asking her all sorts of questions about Australia.

"I saw a documentary years ago on the Great Barrier Reef, and I've always hoped to go."

"Oh, Sam, you should!" Sarah's face lit. "I went once with my parents. Queensland is definitely the place to go if you want sand and surf. Tasmania is great for colonial heritage. Then there's the red center and Uluru."

Even his parents, who'd looked at him askance when he'd returned from racing after Sarah earlier, seemed to be warming to her, interested in her answers. "You seem to have done a lot of traveling, Sarah."

She nodded at his father. "My parents have worked with disadvantaged people for most of my life and taught me a lot about the need to understand and appreciate our world and the people in it." She smiled affectionately at Ange. "It certainly helps to have family living overseas."

Dan handed Sarah a mocha and the final coffee to Sam, then sank into the leather lounge next to Sarah, trying to follow the swirl of conversation as Sarah and Ange chatted with his mother and the men planned a trip for walleye.

"Dan let me borrow your book, *The Blue Castle.* At least I'm guessing it's yours and not Dan's." Sarah's gurgle of amusement drew his smile.

As his brother, Dad, and John started contrasting the benefits of inline spinners and crankbaits, Dan switched his attention fully to the women, who'd arranged an excursion to Bala's Museum in a few days' time.

His mother smiled at Ange and Sarah—even looked a little excited for once. "We'll have to go to Don's afterward. They make delicious scones."

"Helen, have you tried their butter tarts? There's nothing better."

Ange's expression reminded him of Sarah's intense enjoyment of the blueberry jam and that ice-cream sundae. Some things definitely ran in families.

Sarah's face was alight with enthusiasm. "That sounds like so much fun." She turned and caught his gaze. "Hey, Dan, we're going to see the Lucy Maud Montgomery museum! Isn't that exciting?"

"Sure is." *If you're a girl, maybe.*

She wrinkled her nose. "Obviously you're not a kindred spirit."

"Obviously you're a big fan."

She shrugged. "I grew up watching the movies every Christmas with my sister. It's a tradition. Anyway, you can't diss Anne. It'd be like me saying something mean about that Wayne Grotsky guy."

The laughter escaped before he could stop it. "You just did. It's Gretzky, Princess. And you can't compare a fictional character with the Great One."

She tossed her head. "Aren't they both supposed to be national icons?"

His mother nodded as Ange stage whispered, "Anne is a redhead, Dan."

"So-o-o, that explains it. You like her because of the color of her hair, don't you?"

She nodded, smiling. "We're rare and special, so treat us with respect, *friend*."

His heart skipped a beat as Sarah smiled that sparkly smile. Rare, special, that was certainly true. But friend?

Denial was useless. This friend thing definitely wasn't gonna work for him.

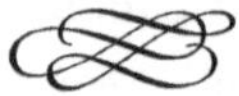

CHAPTER 15

Bala was another of the pretty towns on Lake Muskoka, teeming with tourists enjoying the summer sunshine. Sarah grinned at Sam as she tried to stop the double choc ice-cream cone from dripping onto her top. A shorter, stockier version of Dan, in his early twenties and sharing the family's dark hair and eyes, Sam was as laid-back and relaxed as his brother. He seemed to understand her—unlike his parents, who were far more serious and looked at her sometimes like she was a tropical parrot in the exotic bird exhibit at the zoo.

"She can't help it, bro. It's like a curse."

She looked up from the waffle cone to catch Dan's chuckle. "What?"

He pointed to her white knee-length skirt, now delicately spotted with brown.

She groaned. "I just don't understand how that always happens."

"None of us do, Princess. None of us do."

Oh well. She'd never manage to look all polished and put-together like his mother. Not that any of that mattered anyway, when she and Dan had agreed on being friends.

"So, are we ready for our pilgrimage?" Ange turned to the men. "You're certain none of you want to come?"

"We're going to check out the marina, maybe give one of those brand-new boats a test drive," John explained, hands up at Ange's raised brows. "We're only looking."

"Boys and their toys." Sarah snickered as she gulped more ice cream. A tiny piece of cone caught in her throat. She choked, wheezing, her eyes watering as she fought for breath before eventually coughing it up. Her cheeks sizzled as strangers turned around to stare.

Dan passed her his bottle of water. "You okay, Princess?"

She nodded and took a long swig, forcing a smile at the concerned faces. "Sorry." She turned to Ange. "Can we go now?"

After carefully swallowing the last of the cone, she followed her aunt and Helen to the Lucy Maud Montgomery museum. It was a fascinating place, filled with period furniture, a huge collection of first-edition books, and many things connected to Anne of Green Gables. The couple that ran it were Anne fans who'd discovered that the turn-of-the-century building had been a dining house for travelers, including the esteemed Canadian author and her young family, in the 1920s. This discovery had prompted extensive renovations, transforming a rundown house into the pretty, friendly museum it was today.

Almost two hours later, laden down with gift bags, they made their way down the lovely tree-lined street beside the Moon River, meeting up with the men at the assigned location —a picnic area near the famous waterfalls.

"Gee, Mom, did you buy the gift shop out?"

Sarah swallowed laughter as Helen sent Sam a look she'd seen her own mother wear. "I'm afraid most of it is for me. Well, actually, for my nieces and my mom and my sister."

"Admit it—and for you." Dan's eyes crinkled with amusement. "You look like you had way too much fun in there."

She smiled. He was getting to know her pretty well.

As they ate some of the delicacies purchased from Don's bakery—Helen and Ange were right: the scones and butter tarts were delectable—Sarah excitedly filled them in on all treasure they'd seen. "They even have the boat from the movie, the one Anne is sinking on when Gilbert rescues her!" The men stared at her blankly. "You know, in the first movie?"

Dan seemed to take pity on her. "Sorry, Princess. Never seen it."

"Don't think he ever will. Not a good look for his image." Sam's smirk at his brother faded as he sent her a considered look. "Although someone here might be able to persuade him."

Sarah's cheeks heated as all eyes fixed on her. "Uh, these éclairs are yummy, aren't they?"

WHERE HAD THE TIME GONE? Dan flicked open his phone and checked the date. Phone calendars didn't lie, did they? It was amazing how fast his vacation had sped by. Surely he didn't have to go back so soon. Now, with only a week to go, there was this weird feeling of incompletion. Normally by this time he'd be raring to go, the weeks of lakeside living so conducive to utter rest and deep refreshment that he was almost glad to get back to pre-season training and city busyness.

But not this year. He wanted to stay.

He glanced across at Sarah, engrossed in the James Bond film playing on the big-screen TV. Today's cooler, showery weather had meant fishing wasn't so enjoyable, and they still had quite a few James Bond movies to get through.

"Check out the shoulder pads." Sarah laughed. "Is that like what you guys have to wear on the ice?"

Sam snickered. "If we did, it'd be straight to the penalty box for reckless endangerment. Those corners could take out an eye."

Dan relaxed deeper in the chair. It was nice to see Sarah getting on so well with his favorite brother. Sam had stayed for a few extra days after their parents had gone back to Sunnybrook, and much of the time had been spent with Sarah.

Of course, it had led to the exchange of anecdotes he'd not always appreciated, such as when she'd read a newspaper article rating Dan's defensive skills near the top of the League. She'd made some comment that'd had Sam grinning.

"Dan has always stuck his neck out to try and protect the helpless." Sam had gone on to tell some embarrassing story about a broken-winged bird Dan had tried to help one summer long ago when he was a kid.

Sarah had turned to him, a soft expression on her face. "You're so sweet."

His heart had skipped even as he'd scoffed.

"He's so embarrassed." Sam had chuckled. "But then, Dan's always liked to be a hero."

"A hero who does Pilates," she'd said with a teasing grin.

"Bro, seriously?"

Dan had shrugged. "Keeps me flexible."

"Flexible for all sorts of activities, right?" Sam had said with a wink.

Dan had sharpened his gaze, shaking his head slightly. He was a different man now. How long until Sam realized?

Soft laughter from Sarah drew Dan's attention back to the screen as the camera panned around the décor of one of the villain's hideouts. He leaned across the empty space between them on the three-seater couch and poked her gently in the side. "What is it?"

"The movie just reminded me. I never asked you about your antlers."

"My antlers?"

She motioned to the chimney where the prized head of a deer his grandfather had killed years ago gazed impassively down. "I s'pose you're into hunting too."

Too? What was that about? "Uh, no."

"Really?" She shifted on the couch, eyes wide with surprise. "You don't hunt?"

Sam reached across to pass the popcorn bowl to Sarah. "He doesn't like guns."

She positioned the bowl precariously between them on the lounge and grabbed a handful of popcorn. "Really?"

Why? Was there something wrong with that? He had a gun in the cottage for the rare bear scare, but he'd never gotten it out of its secured box, let alone fired it.

"Why's that?"

"He thinks guns are too violent."

Thanks, Sam. Really appreciate it. Sarah's amused expression was disconcerting, as was the snicker she no longer hid. *Stop acting like a mute.* "What?"

"It's just funny. You're not into violence, yet you play hockey, which has to be one of the most violent sports on earth, and you like James Bond movies, which are full of crazy action scenes that aren't exactly gentle. I love it!" Smiling, she turned back to the screen.

Whoa. His heart skipped a beat. Did she say she loved—?

"What about you, Sarah? You don't seem to mind the James Bond violence either."

Sam's voice pulled Dan out of confusion. That was more like it—*thanks, Sam.*

Sarah flashed them another smile. "I'm a redhead. I'm genetically predisposed to get a little more fierce and passionate than some."

Finally Dan recognized his cue. "Really? I hadn't noticed."

"Thanks for not noticing."

"You're welcome."

As the movie shifted to another scene, he reached into the popcorn bowl at the same time as she did. The touch of her hand shot fire to his nerve endings.

Sarah caught his gaze, then leaned in closer to whisper, "I'm really glad you don't like guns. I don't like them either."

She turned back to the movie, but he couldn't remember what it was called anymore. Watching Sarah's animated face, every wince or flicker of enjoyment, was far more entertaining. She was way more appealing than any of James Bond's leading ladies.

But time was running out. Would she ever reconsider just being friends?

SARAH SAT at the dining table, trying to follow the conversation between Dan, John, and Ange, trying to smile and look interested while hiding the pain that was pooling in her chest. All week as she'd counted off the last things—the last boat trip, last day of fishing, final swim, final meal together—she'd not allowed herself to really think about Dan's departure. He had commitments in Toronto, he had to go, but she knew she would miss him so much. These past weeks had restored her soul and her relationship with God. She felt more like herself than she had in years. So much of that was due to Dan. He'd been such a good friend.

But honestly, who was she kidding? The touch of his hand was enough to make her tummy curl. His hugs, his smile, even the scent of his aftershave had some crazy effect on her senses. But as much as she liked him, there couldn't be any future there. He'd go back to his hockey stardom, and she'd go back to Australia to pick up the broken pieces of her life. She was so glad they'd agreed on the friends thing. It'd be stupid to think otherwise.

Dan finished his cup of coffee and pushed back his chair. "Well, that's it. I'm off."

"Bye, Dan." John stood and shook hands. "We'll see you in T.O. soon."

Ange gave him a hug. "Take care. Drive safe."

Dan glanced across at Sarah. "Walk me out?"

She nodded, stood, and followed him slowly down the cottage's hall, emotion clogging her throat, banding her chest.

They walked outside to the front porch, where she stopped while he stood on the step below. Watching pines glowed hazily as the leaves of the poplars shivered in a light breeze.

Sarah gazed into Dan's warm brown eyes framed by those thick, dark lashes. Tiny golden specks glinted softly in the late-afternoon sun. It was so much easier to see his beautiful eyes when his face was at her eye level. She swallowed and forced a smile. "Thank you for all your help, Dan. You've been such a good friend. I feel heaps better, and I couldn't have done this without you."

She bit her lip and looked down. What else could she say? What would be the point of admitting how much he'd come to mean? One day she might visit Toronto, but by then he would've forgotten all about her. Her chest was tight, her stomach felt like it was full of rocks, and for some reason she desperately wanted to cry.

Be brave.

She looked up, willed her lips to curve. "I wish there was a way I could show my appreciation."

"I'm just glad you're feeling better." His expression was serious. "I've enjoyed getting to know you these past weeks."

"Maybe some of the time you did. I know I'm not exactly low maintenance."

"Maybe I like a challenge."

"Well, lucky you! Challenge is my middle name." Her smile slipped. Her heart ached so much it was getting hard to breathe. Best to do this quick. "Bye, Dan."

She leaned forward. Just one hug was all that was required. She wrapped her arms around his broad shoulders and squeezed lightly, his scent tugging her senses as he hugged her.

"Don't forget me," he whispered.

She blinked back moisture. "I won't."

She moved to kiss him on the cheek, but he shifted his head slightly so her lips found his mouth. Instead of the quick peck she'd intended, her lips softened, clinging to his.

Oh…

Her eyelids fluttered closed, and she melted into him, reveling in the tender strength of his arms around her, the faint taste of coffee on his lips, the masculine roughness of his jaw. His arm slipped around her waist, his hand sliding through her hair as if he'd been longing to touch her.

Heat curled in her stomach, and she pressed closer, savoring the rush of nerve-tingling potency melding their lips together. She was kissing him. He was kissing her. She was sinking into blissfulness—

No. Guilt spiked at her first kiss since Stephen's death, a kiss unlike any she'd known before. Her eyes snapped open. She broke contact and pulled back, breath shaky, limbs trembling.

Dan blinked. A deep smile curved his lips. "That was…quite a thank you."

Her cheeks grew magma hot as she dropped her gaze. "Sorry, I didn't mean to do that." Sarah took a pace back, another, then turned on her heel, shame chasing her as she raced inside and slammed the door to her bedroom and huddled on the bed. She touched her burning lips, her heart quivering between self-reproach at kissing someone other than Stephen, desperate longing for the impossible, and remorse for leaving Dan out on the front steps alone.

WHAT HAD JUST HAPPENED? Dan stared at the closed door, heart pounding as he exhaled in a vain attempt to calm the sensations pulsing through his brain and body. That kiss had been amazing. After almost two weeks of minimal contact, Sarah's little hug had sparked his whole body to life. But when he'd turned to say something and her lips had touched his—

Oh man.

Her lips had been so soft, so sweet, so yielding, he'd barely been able to breathe. The spark that had always been there had kindled into this fire rushing through his veins. As the kiss had grown in intensity, his arms had slid around her, cradling her waist and her soft, soft hair in a perfect embrace. Perfect—until a stray thought wondered if she imagined it was Stephen she was kissing.

His heart clenched. Was that why she'd apologized? If only she had meant to kiss him.

He blinked, almost dizzy at the thought.

Should he pound on the door and demand an explanation? Somehow he didn't think that would go down well with John and Ange. And hadn't Sarah made her thoughts pretty clear anyway? But how could she kiss him like that and it mean nothing?

Indecision kept him rooted, one foot on the step, one foot one the ground as he waited, hoped, and prayed that Sarah would reappear. That she'd smile and he'd see tease. That she'd draw near again and finally agree to give them a chance. And maybe they could kiss again...

The cooling shadows pressed in, the door stayed closed, and his heart and hopes wilted. So that was no, then. Or was it more a case of not yet?

Regardless, he should probably leave before John questioned why he was still here.

Somehow, he made it to his car and drove away. He barely noticed the road as the past two months replayed in his head, that kiss—that kiss!—cutting across everything to make him re-analyze it all. Far from being the relaxing, peaceful vacation he'd anticipated, he'd been pulled and pushed and challenged by Sarah. Despite all their differences and a loitering sense that he was never going to be good enough for her, he was captivated.

Captivated. Sam had been right when he'd smirked at him before driving home yesterday. "Dan, I've never seen you look so gooey-eyed about a girl before." He'd smacked Dan on the shoulder. "Good to see."

Gooey-eyed? Dan frowned. This friendship felt a lot more solid than goo. Being with Sarah made him feel assured, more able to be himself, more like the man God wanted him to be: strong, fearless, a warrior.

But as he neared Toronto's urban sprawl, the questions began. Were they just friends after all? Had this been a pale imitation of a summer romance? Did she really like him, or was he just a substitute for a dead man? He rubbed a hand through his hair. Where would this go? Where *could* it go? How long was she staying, anyway? With everything they'd discussed, why had they never talked about that?

His stomach twisted. If Sarah went back to Australia and he never saw her again…

CHAPTER 16

"It's a gorgeous day," Ange said, leaning against the deck's balustrade.

"Mmm." Sarah gently swung in the hammock. Muskoka was as beautiful as ever, but for some reason it seemed like the color had been dialed down.

"You miss him, don't you?"

She'd tried to act nonchalant, but her aunt's wise eyes saw too much. It was crazy how much during this past week she'd longed to see Dan, had kept half expecting him to suddenly appear at their back door or down by the beach. She even missed the putter of his boat. At least that had been a sign that Dan was nearby. Nope, this ache was ridiculous, and she couldn't afford to indulge it any longer.

She shrugged. "He's been a good friend." Despite the chats, the hugs, and that accidental kiss, it couldn't possibly be more. She'd come here to try and heal from a relationship, not ricochet headlong into another.

"Sarah, it's been over eighteen months. It's okay to have... feelings for someone else."

What were those feelings anyway? "I like him, but I just don't know."

"He likes you too." Ange's patient face creased into a smile. "He's a good guy. Stop worrying and over-thinking things and trust God."

Trust God? Easier said than done. Sarah rubbed at the dull ache in her forehead. At least she wouldn't be seeing Dan again for a while, his work and training commitments keeping him busy in Toronto. Maybe by then she could sort out this mess of emotions she was in. She'd barely slept the last few nights thinking it through.

Ange peered at her. "You know we'll visit the city a few times in the next few months. And Dan will likely come here. He usually gets some time off at Christmas."

Christmas? That seemed years away. "I wasn't necessarily thinking I'd still be here by then."

"Oh?" Ange pulled up a chair and sat. "Have you something to get home to?"

"Mum and Dad."

Ange's eyes lit. "Or they could come here. Wouldn't you like to experience a white Christmas?"

Well, yes. But not if this awkwardness with Dan still lingered and he was nearby. "You could mention it. You know Dad always needs time to warm up to ideas."

"I do." Amusement creased her aunt's eyes. "I remember how long he took to propose to Lindy. She was almost ready to pop the question herself."

"He needs time to adjust to new things, to think through all the ramifications."

"Not unlike some others I know, eh?" Ange teased.

Sarah rolled her eyes, but it was true. "I just like to be sure."

"But even then we can't guarantee things, can we? A person can plan their course, but it's God who establishes their steps."

"Is that another way of saying 'let go and let God'?"

"I certainly don't mean give up and do nothing. But I do think too many of us cling so tightly to wanting to control every possible outcome that we forget we're supposed to be living by faith, not by sight." Ange smiled tenderly. "God loves you, Sarah. He has good plans for you. Let go of the fear and the need to be in control, and trust Him."

Sarah nodded, throat cinching as the words tumbled through her heart. She exited the hammock to give her aunt a hug. "Thank you."

"Anytime," Ange said, patting her back. "It's good to know I don't need to write sermons to be able to preach."

"Amen," Sarah said. "Speaking of preaching, when does John want that missions presentation for church?"

"Yesterday?"

Oops. Someone might have been enjoying her vacation a little too much. "I can finish it today."

"I'm sure he'd like that. I'm heading to the church shortly, so I'll mention it when I see him at the office."

"Um, can I come?" Doing something productive had to be better than feeling lonely here. "I can help if there are things needing doing."

Ange's eyes lit, but all she said was, "That would be fine. I'm sure John will find you something to do."

An hour later they were in John's office in the former minister's house, which had been converted to ministry use when John had taken on the position five years ago after moving from the city. Former bedrooms were church offices, the living spaces used by various groups for meals or small functions. The décor was faded and somewhat mismatched, suggesting the priority was on people, not appearances.

John clicked through the slideshow Sarah had started weeks ago. "So, do you think you could give a presentation about this on Sunday?"

"You mean actually speak out the front?"

"It's not like you haven't done that kind of thing before."

True.

"And it's not like you need to focus on this." He paused the slides on a picture of Stephen.

She stared at the image, the paler face amid a sea of brown-skinned children, all grinning at the camera. Stephen's last missions trip. After which he'd proposed.

"We could be in ministry together, Sarah," he'd said. "You with your teaching, me with my medical degree."

It had been hard not to get swept up in his plans—he'd always been strong-minded—and it had only been when he'd started urging her to switch her focus from music to English teaching—"It's much more practical"—that she'd realized just how much his personal goals had begun to swamp hers. Thus the source of their argument on that last, fateful drive.

Memories whirled, and she blinked, suddenly woozy.

"Sarah? You okay?"

She sucked in a breath and slowly exhaled. "Yes."

"So you'll do it?"

Do what? Oh, the talk. "Uh, sure. How long would you want me to speak for?"

"Five, ten minutes. Whatever you think best."

Not at all was her version of best. "Two minutes it is, then."

"I'll take what I can get. Oh, that reminds me, do you think you'd be interested in joining our music team here?"

"Let's not get carried away now, John."

His lips tweaked with good humor. "Think about it and let me know."

"That, I can do. Now, what's happening with the admin area? I noticed it's a little messy out there." She gestured to the adjoining room, where a desk sign proclaimed *Church Secretary* but with no secretary in sight.

"Ah. Trudy is on vacation in Alberta seeing her grandkids.

I'm supposed to get a newsletter together, but it's not really something either Ange or I enjoy."

"Lucky for you, it's something I enjoy." The trifecta of purpose, ministry, and creativity. "May I?"

"Really?"

"I've done it for Dad lots of times. I know how challenging ministry life can be, and you and Ange have been so good to me, so it's the least I can do." She seated herself at the desk. "Now, show me how to turn on this dinosaur of a computer, and tell me what you want included."

THE NEXT DAYS passed in a welter of reading, church work, therapeutic stretching, and swims. The loneliness induced by Dan's absence gradually lessened as she slowly got to know more of John and Ange's congregation—people like Serena, who worked in the events department of Muskoka Shores, and Jenny, whom she'd met weeks ago at the Pilates class and who wanted to know when Sarah would return.

"That silly young instructor got dismissed—apparently she yelled at one of the resort owners' wives, who didn't appreciate being embarrassed—and now we're back to Francine, who led it before. She's much more understanding. I hope you'll come again."

"That'd be good," Sarah agreed. She probably should stretch more than her body wanted to. They settled on a Friday class, which ended up going so well she thought she might check out the Tuesday session as well.

Sunday's service came, and Sarah did her talk, and apart from one moment when she needed to pause to clear emotion from her throat, she managed okay. Unlike the musicians, who played the songs at a dirge-like pace or in keys way too high for the congregation to sing. When John eyed her with upraised brows halfway through the last hymn, she nodded.

Later after lunch, a potluck affair that proved surprisingly enjoyable as she chatted with congregation members, John finally cornered her. "So you'll join the music team?"

"What exactly would be involved? I don't want to go stepping on anyone's toes."

"I think Doug and Enid would welcome some younger blood."

"Would they really welcome someone five decades their junior?"

He chuckled. "I'm sure they will. And it's only *four* decades, at least in Doug's case."

"Sorry, my mistake."

"Sar, I'd love to see some newer music. I'm not expecting Heartsong quality—"

Just as well.

"—but if you could look at our folders and add to what we have, we'd really appreciate it. Don't worry, I'll chat with them. To be honest, I'm sure they'll be relieved to have someone else take the reins."

The way he said that, like he thought she would be staying forever, hastened her to say, "You know I haven't decided yet when to go home. I don't want you thinking I'm committing only to leave you in the lurch in a few months."

"Sarah, we'll gladly take whatever you can give, whether that be for a few weeks or the rest of the year. God has gifted you, and I know we'd be blessed by those gifts."

Her uncle might be a minister, but he was also president of the Guilt Sarah into It Club. Yet even so, a tug within demanded she say yes.

A search through various files revealed a music ministry mired in last century, which wouldn't be so bad if the songs were played in the key of singable. And judging from the congregation's youthful age, it seemed her uncle might not be the only one to appreciate a change in repertoire.

Ange only confirmed this later at dinner when Sarah worried aloud about stepping into the role, suggesting that perhaps Sarah could perform an item. "Which would likely only reiterate just how much we need you."

John saw the wisdom of this, and gave Sarah carte blanche to choose a song. "Or write one while we're away," he said, a twinkle in his eye.

Yeah. Right.

Guest speaking roles at a ministry conference drew John and Ange to Parry Sound the next day, a visit that would take until Saturday.

"You're sure you can manage on your own?" Ange said with pleated brow.

"Thanks to you I now have a phone, and Dan let me borrow the bike, so I'll be fine."

"You can always drive my car if you want."

"Thanks, but the bike is fine." If she couldn't always remember which way to look for traffic while bike riding, then driving a car was a potential disaster.

"Well, be careful."

"What's the worst that can happen? I might see a bear?" Sarah laughed. "I'm a big girl. Don't worry, I'll be fine. See you on Saturday night."

"Okay then." Ange stepped closer and wrapped Sarah in a warm hug. "Love you, Blue."

"Love you too." Sarah kissed her on the cheek. "Have a good trip."

She stood on the front porch, waving goodbye until their sedan disappeared around the corner. She exhaled. The afternoon sun beat down relentlessly, stilling the breeze that made the pines sing. Five days on her own. Time to think. Pray. Play the piano. And maybe somehow figure out what she was supposed to do with the rest of her life.

And how to get over Dan.

. . .

SARAH WRAPPED her arms around her knees, sitting on a boulder as sunlight played catch-and-kiss with the water. The sun warmed her back, slowly drying her hair from the quick dip she'd taken before. The blues of lake and sky lulled her senses, and she closed her eyes.

These past days had been great. Emailing her family and sponsor girls—and Georgia—meant her love tank felt near full, and she'd spent so much time playing the piano and singing—reminding her of Heartsong days—that a deep sense of contentment was growing again.

She gently massaged the ache in her fingers caused by practicing scales and arpeggios. Music. Why had she ever stopped? Music fed her soul—its creativity life-giving and the discipline it demanded strangely therapeutic. She'd prayed about John's request and scribbled down some chords and words as she used to do. Hopefully he'd like the song.

She took a deep breath of pine-scented air, then slowly exhaled. Quiet walks and swims, exercise, and early nights had continued restoring her body and mind. She'd finally finished reading the other Jane Austen novels waiting for attention. *Northanger Abbey* and *Mansfield Park* weren't her favorites but were entertaining diversions.

A loose thread on the caftan she'd bought earlier in the week begged to be pulled. A relic from the 70s with its swirls of orange, green, and brown, it did her figure no favors, but at least it kept the sun off her skin. She stretched back on her hands, the rock's texture gritty to her touch. Time helping at church and time alone in the afternoons had also provided lots of opportunity for long talks with God and reading the Bible. More and more she was starting to release some of the expectations she'd had on herself, learning to forgive and let go of some of the pain and guilt she'd been carrying. It was as if the Holy

Spirit was there, whispering freedom through the shaggy pines, bringing release to her spirit and soul.

It also allowed time to contemplate the messy situation that was Dan. He hadn't contacted her since that fateful goodbye—obviously he was too busy or too shocked to call. That was probably for the best anyway. Despite Ange's words, she still wasn't sure if she was ready for a new relationship. She'd been slowly letting go of Stephen. She didn't want to use Dan to try and get over her past. Relationships on rebound never worked out.

She groaned. Was that what that kiss had been about? Had she just been using Dan to recover? He'd been a good friend, but she'd apparently lost that friendship with a misguided, mistimed attempt at romance. No. It was better to just try and forget…

A car door slammed. She opened her eyes and looked up, catching the glint of a windscreen over at Dan's. A wild throb of excitement pulsed through her body. He was here? She stood, dusted sand off her legs. Should she change? The caftan was kind of ugly, and her hair definitely needed to be brushed—not that Dan ever seemed to mind what she looked like. She smiled, pulled her damp hair into a rough ponytail and jammed her hat on instead, then hurried next door, trying not to skip.

Oh. She peered through the trees, her feet stumbling to a pause. That wasn't Dan's car, unless he'd bought a yellow coupé recently, which didn't seem to mesh with his unpretentious style.

Who was here then? There was a faint murmur of voices. Sarah glanced over to where the sound had come from, her eyebrows shooting up as a dark-haired woman in a skimpy hot-pink dress wandered down to the jetty. Who was that?

Sarah edged closer to a nearby spruce, hiding as the woman laughed. She peeked around, but couldn't see anyone else. Dan wasn't there. Was he?

So, who *was* that? Why was she here? Did Dan even know?

Sarah frowned, then started walking again. Was this what people did around here, just gatecrash empty houses? How rude!

"Excuse me!"

The woman turned a beautifully made-up face toward her. "Yes?"

Sarah cleared her throat. "Um, are you supposed to be here?"

The woman lifted a perfectly plucked brow. "I beg your pardon?"

"Do you know you're on private property? Have you got permission to be here?"

The woman looked her up and down, and Sarah was suddenly conscious of how pale and peculiar and *old* she looked in comparison to this perfectly polished Instagram-worthy creature. The brunette tinkled a small laugh. "How sweet of you to be concerned. I'm sure Dan will love to know he has such good neighbors looking out for him."

Sarah blinked. "You know Dan?"

The woman waved a hand. "We've known each other for years. He's such a lovely guy, a real sweetheart. I love him to bits."

Sarah's heart dropped. Was she Dan's girlfriend? Did Dan love this woman to bits too?

"He's totally gorgeous, don't you think?"

Sarah swallowed again before croaking out, "Totally." She turned to go.

"Excuse me? Sweetie? What's your name?"

For some reason she didn't want this woman to know her name. No way did she want her to tell Dan about Sarah, the plain girl-next-door, poking her nose into his business. Especially after Sarah had kissed him when obviously he'd been keeping this beauty pageant wannabe a secret.

The woman placed a perfectly manicured hand on one perfectly toned, perfectly tanned leg. "Your name?"

A clump of damp hair dangled into Sarah's face. She stared at it, swallowed, then managed a croaky "Blue."

The woman raised a brow. "Well, I'll let Dan know of your concern as soon as I get inside."

What? Dan was here? And hadn't bothered to see her? Pain snagged her breath. "I've got to go."

The woman nodded. "Enjoy your day."

Sarah forced her stiff lips into a semblance of a smile. "You too."

Her heart grew heavier with every footstep that led away. Was this woman really Dan's girlfriend? And if so, how could he have acted like he had all summer long? How could he have *kissed* her? Was he just a player after all, but in a league way beyond anything Rob could aspire to? She stumbled over a tree root. Shook her head, as if she could force the whirl of images and words and hopes—and that kiss!—to somehow make sense now they'd crashed into miserable reality.

At least one thing was clear. She didn't need to worry about whether Dan cared about her or not. She blinked against tears. He obviously didn't.

CHAPTER 17

The phone chirped its tinny version of *Für Elise*. Sarah swallowed the last Hershey's Kiss with a gulp, then looked at the screen. "Hi, Ange."

"How are you, Blue?"

Sarah took a breath, hoping her voice wouldn't betray her. "It's all good here. You?"

Ange chatted briefly about the conference. "Sar? You sure you're okay?"

"I've, uh, got a new neighbor." Her chest tightened like it did every time she thought about the bikini model staying next door.

"At Dan's?"

"Yep."

"I know he sometimes lets people use his place." A small sigh. "Dan has always been something of a fixer."

Breath suspended. Was that why he'd hung around? He'd wanted to fix her? A memory flickered, something Sam had said about broken-winged birds. He'd tried to warn her too, that Dan had something of a hero complex...

"Sar? You still there?"

"Yep."

"Are you okay?"

"Yep." Sarah forced out a shaky laugh. *Change the subject.* "Haven't seen any bears yet."

"Oh, but there's been reports of bears! It's been on the news. Sar, you need to take—"

"Care, yes, I know." Sarah closed her eyes. Okay, dumb choice of topics. "I'm being careful. But honestly, Ange, can you imagine a bear wanting to pick a fight with little ole me?"

"I don't think they're too fussy about who—"

"Ange, I'll be fine. Say hi to John for me, okay?"

"Will do. And Sar, please take care. I'd hate to see you hurt."

"I'll be fine, Ange. Thanks for calling."

"Okay then." A sigh. "Bye, Blue."

"Bye." Sarah stared out the window at the bikinied bombshell who'd staked her claim on the beach for the day. She bit down on her trembling lower lip. Good thing Ange wasn't here, otherwise she'd see just how hurt Sarah was already.

"OH MY GOSH!"

Sarah looked up at the supermarket's blonde cashier, whose nametag read *Rochelle – how may I help?* She followed the fakeeyelashed gawk to the store's entry where a tall, dark-haired man was pulling a basket from the pile near the door. Dan. Her heart fluttered.

Stop it. She stepped behind a tall stack of soup cans handily positioned near the checkout and swiped her hair up into a low bun, wishing she had a hat as well. Red hair never made it easy to blend in. *He doesn't want to see you, remember? You were just a summer distraction. A project.*

"Excuse me?" She thrust the bread, milk, and carton of eggs

closer, but it was no use. Rochelle was mesmerized—and definitely not too helpful right now. Sarah wiped sweaty palms on the back of her shorts. She had to leave before Dan saw her and she was forced to smile and pretend everything was okay.

"Oh, I swear, he's so yummy." The shop assistant licked her lips. "But I read online he has a girlfriend."

Sarah's heart cramped. A week ago she could've believed she was that girl. Now she knew better.

"Such a shame." The blonde shook her head. "Guys like him never go for girls like us."

Us? Sarah bit her lip. Imagine if Rochelle knew Sarah had kissed him.

Rochelle sighed. "I bet he has women throwing themselves at him all the time."

Sarah's skin crawled. Was that how Dan had seen things? She was just another girl who'd thrown herself at him?

Rochelle shook her head, then slowly started scanning the items. "Those guys are all the same. Won't even say hello to you unless you're a supermodel." She glanced over Sarah's shoulder, her face darkening as she scowled. "See what I mean? Look at her. Typical hockey-player fare."

Don't look back, don't look back—

Sarah glanced over her shoulder. Her mouth dropped. So it really was true. She watched as brunette Barbie from next door drew close to Dan, flicking her long hair over one bare, tanned shoulder as she touched him on the arm, whispering something to him before laughing. He smiled down at her.

Sarah swallowed. "Would you mind hurrying, please? I really need to go."

Before Dan could see her. Before she could be humiliated even more.

~

DAN GLANCED AT ELLA. The brunette hadn't stopped talking since he'd met her down the street an hour ago. She'd been gushing about his house, the location, the cute town.

"And Simone and Jace?"

"They're feeling so much better about things now. Thanks to you." She squeezed his arm. "I'm so glad you could come."

He shrugged. "I'm doing a hockey clinic with Brendan and Marc." In two days. In Peterborough. Visiting Muskoka was just a roundabout way of getting there. He smiled to himself. Real roundabout.

"The people around here are so sweet." She laughed. "I met someone the other day who obviously has a huge crush on you."

He studied the health information panels on the boxes of cereal. How much sugar?

"Dan?" Ella nudged him. "Don't you want to know who I'm talking about?"

He shrugged. Who cared? As soon as they finished restocking supplies he had an important date he'd been looking forward to all week. Anticipation rippled through his stomach.

"She was so funny—like a little guard dog but dressed like a bag lady." Ella plunked a can of tomatoes into the basket. "Her name is Lou, Sue, something like that."

Dan frowned. "I don't know anyone of that name."

"Ha! I knew she didn't know you."

Why was Ella keeping on with this? "What'd she look like?"

"She's fair." Ella shrugged. "Fair to middling, anyway." She giggled, then turned blue eyes on him. "Oh, and she's British."

"Nope. Don't know her."

Thirty minutes later they were back on the road to his house. Trees flashed by. His heart caught as they passed the section where he'd spun out all those weeks ago. He shook his head. What a fool he'd been…

They rounded another corner. "Look! There she is." Ella pointed ahead. "That's Lou."

Dan squinted and saw a familiar bike, halted in the middle of the road, its familiar-looking rider standing frozen. Dan frowned. Lou?

"What on earth is she doing?" The Jeep drew closer. Ella gasped. "Oh my goodness!"

Dan's heart stopped. Sarah stood in front of a black bear.

COULD A BEAR SMELL FEAR? Could it hear her heart slamming against her ribs? The bear had lumbered out onto the road before she'd had time to turn, and now it kept staring at her, those deep, dark eyes impossible to fathom. Should she run away? Stand still? Look it in the eyes? She gripped the bike handlebars more tightly. What had that newspaper article said about bear attacks?

The bear took a step closer.

Oh, God! Help me!

Bear safety tips flickered into memory: Identify if it's a black bear or a grizzly.

I don't know, God! I'm an Australian. Help!

Sarah inhaled slowly. The newspaper had said Muskoka had black bears. But this one didn't exactly look black, more a reddish color. What was she supposed to do?

The bear stretched up on its hind feet.

Oh, God! Sweat prickled her neck. Her head pounded. Getting hard to breathe...

Be brave.

She planted her feet more firmly to stop her knees shaking. Sucked in another breath. Just because a bear stood upright didn't mean it was angry. It might only be checking her out. She bit back a hysterical laugh. Maybe she wasn't Dan's ideal woman, but apparently she could still attract some attention—

Stop it! Focus. The bear examined her before dropping to all fours and lumbering closer, its huffing breath thunderously loud. *Oh, Lord, save me!*

She vaguely heard a sound behind her but couldn't look in case the bear decided to pounce and eat her. Was she supposed to stand still or run away? *Run away!* Run!

Be brave.

No. Sarah took another deep breath. If she ran away, it would chase her. She had to either scare it off or play dead. She gritted her teeth. She was a high school teacher; she could do scary. She took a step forward, clutching the bike's handlebars in a death grip. "Rahh!"

The bear stopped. Tilted its head to one side like she was a crazy woman.

"Go away!" She took another step. "I'm warning you, don't mess with me, mate!"

She exhaled. Yelling like this was liberating. She pinged the bike's bell, then took another step closer. "I've had it up to here with try-hard tough guys, so don't start something unless you're gonna finish it!"

The bear stared at her, refusing to move.

"Go away! Why can't you be like every other man on the planet and just leave!" Sarah gulped and swiped at the tears in her eyes, her voice shaking. "Please, please leave me alone." How pathetic did that sound? *Lord, I really don't want to die now.*

Gravel crunched behind her. Her heart skittered. *Oh, God! Don't let it be another bear!*

BEEP! BEEP!

She jumped. The bike clattered to the ground. Groceries smashed. The bear took a step back.

BEEP! BEEP!

"Go on! Get!"

The voice sounded so far away. Sarah watched as the bear, as if in slow motion, ducked its head, growled, then backed away before slowly disappearing into the undergrowth. But was it really gone? Was she safe? Black dots wavered in front of her eyes. The world tilted—

"Sarah!"

She blinked. Dan's face hovered above hers. His hands were on her arms. Warm hands. Cold heart. She took a shallow breath, shivering. Blood thudded in her ears.

He leaned closer. "Sarah, Sarah, look at me."

She looked up. Brown eyes peered anxiously at her.

"Focus on me."

His eyes held warmth, tenderness, kindness.

"Breathe."

She sucked in a breath.

"Now exhale."

The world steadied. She took another breath.

"That's good." He wrapped his arms around her. "Oh, Princess, I was so scared."

Sarah shut her eyes and let herself be held. His strength. His scent. His lips in her hair. His heart thudding loudly in her ear. She was safe. It was all so familiar and so right…

"Lou?"

And so wrong.

Sarah opened her eyes and stared at the beautiful brunette who gazed at them wide-eyed. Oh. As much as she'd like to burrow into Dan's arms and hide here forever, he wasn't available. Not for her, anyway. She blinked back tears.

Be brave.

She took another breath and pulled back, away from the false security Dan's arms offered, turning from him. She offered the woman a shaky smile. "Actually—"

Dan chuckled behind her. "Ella, this is Sarah."

The brunette lifted a brow. "Sarah?" Her features sank into a frown. "So who is Lou?"

Sarah wanted to groan. "Uh, no one."

"I don't get it." Ella placed a hand on her hip as her frown deepened.

Plastic rustled behind Sarah. Fresh panic shot through her. The bear? She turned.

Dan looked up from collecting her scattered groceries. "Princess, I think your eggs are kind of scrambled now."

"I don't care."

Nothing mattered much anymore. Except getting away from this gigantic mess of confusion and going home.

DAN CAREFULLY PICKED up the pieces of a smashed bottle, trying to focus on something other than those shivers that kept shooting up his spine. That moment when the bear had stopped in front of her... He took another deep breath and slowly released it. *Thank You, God.*

He glanced over to where Sarah was picking up the bike. "Sar, tell me you're not thinking of riding back."

She still wouldn't meet his eyes, ignoring him as she swung one leg over.

He stood up and grasped her arm. "Sarah. No."

The green eyes finally looked up at him. Fear mingled with something else—wariness? Disillusionment? She shook her head slightly.

He took a breath to control the spike of panicked temper. "I'm driving you. Get in the Jeep."

She dropped her gaze.

"Sar, if you don't get off the bike, I'll pick you up and drag you over there. Don't think I won't."

He finally noticed the trembling hands and gentled his voice. "Sar, please?"

She sighed, then slowly got off the bike and stood, looking dazed. He gently guided her to the Jeep. Ella opened the back door, and Sarah climbed in and sat, the vacant expression the same one he'd seen months ago.

He touched her arm and winced. "Sar, you're icy cold. Here, put my sweater on."

She didn't move.

He handed the broken bag of groceries to Ella, then reached past Sarah to grab an old sweatshirt, zipping her into it, flinching each time he felt her cold skin. After placing the bike in the back, he drove back to the house, eyes peeled in case the bear made a sudden reappearance. He'd need to report this encounter to the local authorities. He glanced in the rear vision mirror. Sarah's expression hadn't changed. "Hey, Sarah."

No reaction.

"I swear, she told me her name was Lou," Ella muttered from the front seat.

He tried again. "Sar."

Still nothing. He frowned and swung past his driveway to John and Ange's little cottage. He pulled up. "Here we are, Princess."

"Princess?"

He ignored Ella, collected the bag, and opened the door. "Come on, let's get you inside."

He gently grasped Sarah's arm and led her round to the back. Two steps up, then onto the back deck. "Got your key?"

She nodded, slowly fished it from her back pocket, and handed it to him. He unlocked the door, slid it open, then led her inside to the lounge. "Sit while I make you a cup of tea."

Sarah obeyed.

He put the water on to boil and turned as the floor creaked behind him. Ella.

"Dan? Is there anything I can do?"

"Can you find her a blanket? I think she's in shock."

A short time later she was back, holding out a plaid woolen throw. "Anything else?"

He shook his head. "If you want to head back, I'll be there soon. I just want to make sure Sarah is okay."

She frowned, then nodded and disappeared.

Dan poured in the boiling water, steeping the tea bag until it was the muddy brown color Sarah always insisted on. He took it in to the lounge, where Sarah sat huddled under the throw. "Here you go, caffeinated just the way you like it."

Her eyes briefly met his as she accepted the steaming cup. "Thanks."

"You're welcome." He squatted before her and tucked a loose strand of hair behind her ear.

She flinched and pulled back. "Please don't."

"Sar, what's wrong?"

"Don't touch me, Dan."

Huh? He leaned back on his heels. "Okay, well, I'll be back later."

"No, don't." She shook her head. "I can't...I don't want to see you anymore."

What? Dan slowly stood. She wasn't thinking straight. "I just need to check on Ella, but I'll be back soon. Sit tight, okay?"

She didn't answer. He cast her a final glance, then carefully closed the door and headed back to his house.

SARAH TOOK A SIP OF TEA. Perfectly made. She bit her lip to stop the tremble. Why did Dan remember things like that? Didn't he realize it was paying attention to the details that made her feel so special? How could he do that, then run back to Ella? Why didn't he want Sarah instead? What was wrong with her? Her chin quivered, her chest grew tight. Who was she kidding? What was right about her?

She hung her head as tears leaked from her eyes, tracking down her cheeks to splash into her teacup. Salt trickled into her mouth. She pressed her lips together to hold in a sob.

Be brave.

She sucked air through clogged nostrils. *Breathe.* She lifted her chin. That's right. She was not going to feel sorry for herself. She took another deep breath and exhaled. Anyway, Dan was a grown man. He could see whomever he liked. And of *course* he'd want someone uncomplicated and baggage-free, especially if she looked like Ella—they were perfectly matched, right down to their clear, honey-tanned skins. She glanced at her freckled, sunburned arms. She could never rival Ella in the looks department.

She took another breath. What was the point in even thinking like this when she'd be leaving soon anyway? How stupid was she to think two such different people would ever be able to make a go of things? And wasn't she just one of his Mr. Fix-it projects anyway?

Another breath. Resolve strengthened. She lifted her chin. She'd just have to do the noble thing and let him go. Not that she had any choice in that, apparently. He'd already made his choice and gone. Maybe she should take a leaf from his playbook and go too.

The thought settled, firming into substance as a memory prodded.

Be brave.

Eyes blurry, she picked up the local newspaper, flicking through its pages until she found the advertisement she'd recalled. She pulled out her phone and dialed the number, clearing her throat until her voice reached something approaching steady. Sure, she could do this on the internet, but there was a finality about hearing herself own her decision.

"Hello? Yes, I'd like to book a ticket to Sydney, please."

"Sydney, Nova Scotia?"

"No. I need to go home." Sarah's breath caught. "I need a plane ticket to Sydney, Australia."

CHAPTER 18

"*D*an, thanks so much." Ella stared up at him, her big Bambi eyes blinking. "It's been so wonderful to stay here."

"You're welcome. I'll be praying for your cousin." He glanced at the occupants of the car and lifted a hand. "I hope the radiation helps."

"Thanks." She pushed to his tiptoes and kissed his cheek. "See you soon."

He summoned a smile. "Bye."

As the car doors slammed, he glanced surreptitiously at his watch. This had taken longer than he'd wanted, but he still had time… A final wave and the yellow car finally turned out of his drive. He raced back inside, grabbed his wallet and keys, and got in the Jeep.

An hour later he was at the cottage's back door, heavy laden. He knocked on the door. "Sar? Sar? You in there?"

No answer. He quietly slid open the glass door. "Princess?"

He glanced around the dim room. Late afternoon shadows stretched across the floorboards. He could just make out the blanket-covered figure lying on the couch.

"Hey, sorry I took so long." Dan held out a bag of groceries. "Replacements. You don't have to have scrambled eggs now." He peered at her more closely, then placed the bag down. "Sar?"

She didn't move. One arm was stretched along the couch, red hair splayed across her face as she slept. He knelt beside her, touched her hand. He frowned. Too cold. He grabbed the blanket from the other couch and gently laid it over her. Her breath caught, and he thought she'd stir, but no, the soft, steady breathing resumed. Sarah was out.

He sighed. He should've gotten here sooner.

Dan slowly shifted back and sat on the coffee table, knocking a note pad and pink cell phone to the floor. She had a phone? His stomach churned. Why hadn't she called? He picked up the note pad, glancing at it absently before pausing at the page that curled open.

Flight details. Booking confirmation number. His heart froze.

Thoughts whirled in his brain, the jigsaw of pieces shifting into a new sequence, presenting a picture he'd never noticed before. Boyd had been only half right. Maybe Sarah had liked him once upon a time, but instead of being a mere rebound, time apart had obviously made her think twice, as her words earlier had attested. And here was the proof.

Sarah didn't want him. She'd rather be on the other side of the world.

DAN LAY on the dock's still-warm boards and stared up into the heavens. A thousand white pinpricks dotted the blackness as, somewhere below, frogs gently burped their goodnights. He placed his hands behind his head as the horror of the day continued swirling in his brain.

God, I really need You.

He closed his eyes. A vision of the bear and Sarah resurfaced.

He shuddered. So much for being tough—that first moment he'd seen the bear had paralyzed him. He'd felt helpless watching, not wanting to startle the bear into doing something dangerous. Ella's panic in the Jeep hadn't helped matters, either. He'd almost had to shake her to get her to pay enough attention to know when to honk the Jeep's horn when he finally eased outside. He wrinkled his brow. What had Sarah been yelling? Something about men leaving?

His heart caught. Was that what she'd meant—she was glad Dan had left? His heart stung. That fitted with her reaction later, when she'd barely coped with him being near.

God, I don't understand. He swallowed the emotion clogging his throat. *How could I have gotten her so wrong?*

And she was leaving. Running away again. His heart hitched. Had she even mentioned leaving to John and Ange? Somehow he didn't think so. Sarah was just like so many other women, who'd say one thing then do another, deceiving him. Again.

A loon's anguished cry pierced the night. His skin crawled. It sounded like a woman's scream. He grimaced. Not that he'd heard Sarah scream like that today. Actually, come to think of it, he'd hardly heard her say anything today—apart from yelling at the bear.

Yelling at the bear. His lips twitched. He shook his head, his amusement slipping as another shudder engulfed him. What if she'd been attacked—or worse, killed? His mouth went dry. What if there was no more Sarah in his world? He stared at the twinkling night sky. *God, thanks so much for keeping her safe.*

Muskoka's steady orchestra of insects and amphibians continued thrumming until that eerie cry punctured the night again. Dan shivered. Funny how something could seem so ominous when it was just part of nature. Things could be so different than what they seemed.

His heart skipped a beat.

Sarah had been in shock today. What if leaving was just part of that shock? What if…

He sat up. What if she did care about him? If he didn't try and patch things up soon, there really would be no more Sarah in his world.

He glanced over to where the cottage hunched, dark and still.

Tomorrow. If Sarah told him about going away, she'd prove she could be trusted. And he'd prove she would never have to run away again.

SARAH YAWNED. Her eyelids cracked open as morning light poured through the living room's back windows. Why was she lying here on the couch? Why hadn't she gone to bed last night? Rubbing at the sleep grit in her eyes, she stared blearily at the coffee table, then slowly sat up. At least that explained the pain in her neck. She squeezed the tense muscles in her shoulders. So needed a cuppa. Another yawn escaped, and she stumbled to the kitchen and put the kettle on to boil.

As she reached up to get a mug she almost gagged. Ugh. She *really* needed a shower. She glanced down at Dan's hoodie and frowned. Why was she wearing that? Memories from yesterday resurfaced, and she gripped the edge of the kitchen counter, as if its solidity could give her strength and help stop the trembling. *Thank You, God. Thank You, God!* The boiling water rumbled loudly as she finally got her breathing under control.

She sucked in a deep breath and cringed. Tea could wait, but this horrid schlumpy feeling of stale grossness couldn't wait a moment a longer.

An hour later, showered, caffeinated, and breakfasted, Dan's top drying outside in the sun, she felt like a new woman.

Warmth and food had chased away the fear, and connecting with God through music would help settle her spirit even more.

The piano stool screeched as she sat down. Her fingers moved automatically into music from old Heartsong Collective days before shifting to the chords and melody of the new piece of music from four days ago—before she'd noticed Ella over at Dan's. She shivered. Nope, not going to live there. "God, I need to give You some thanks and praise instead."

She started again at the top of the song, choosing to focus on what was good, what was true, what was praiseworthy. Today was a new day. Fresh, with no mistakes in it. Yet. *Thanks, God.*

So what if Dan didn't care? God cared. *Thanks, God.*

And she didn't need Dan or anyone else to rescue her all the time. God was her rescuer. *Thanks, God.*

And she needn't worry about her future, either. God would sort it out. *Thanks, God.*

And soon she'd see her parents again, which would be great —even if it was slightly earlier than she'd anticipated. "Thanks, God."

As if her spirit caught the echo in her ears, her focus shifted, slowed, stilled. Words from weeks ago resonated. Thankfulness. There was still so much to be thankful for. She sang through the song again, blocking the whisper of disappointment that had previously murmured on the outer edges of her soul. The words filled the room, her mind, touching her heart and lifting her spirits. She played the last chord and bowed her head. *Thanks, God, that You're with me, that You love me and have good plans for me. Help me remember—*

Cr-e-e-a-k-k.

She jumped. Looked up. Through the curtained back window hovered a broad, dark shape. Breath snagged. Was it the bear? How did it know where she lived? After yesterday's incident she'd meant to doublecheck the garbage cans, but she'd been too exhausted. *God, help me to be brave.*

She tiptoed into the kitchen and picked up a large frying pan. Banging something loudly was supposed to keep bears away, wasn't it? If necessary, she could always bang it on the nose.

Something clattered to the ground outside. Her heart picked up pace, and she wiped damp palms down her skirt. The cottage was a little flimsy—could a hungry bear get in here? Why was he so attracted to her? Why couldn't Dan be more attracted—?

No! Stop thinking like that. Stay focused. *Be brave.*

She peered out through the curtains. The shape had stilled. Was it trying to figure out how to get in here? Oh, if only she had a gun! Hypocrite. But a gun might be useful in scaring it away. *Oh God, please keep me safe!*

The shape moved. Oh no, it was coming to get her! Should she hide in the bathroom? Would it find her there? *Lord, what do I do? I used up all my courage yesterday!*

Knock knock.

Her breath escaped in a rush. Bears didn't knock, did they? Oh, what a goose she was! Her heartbeat slowed its wild thumping, and she peeked past the curtain.

Oh. No.

Wincing at herself, she slid the glass door open.

"Hi." Dan's smile seemed strained. There were shadows under his eyes.

"G'day." She forced herself to meet his gaze as a mental video of the time she'd thrown herself at him replayed, swiftly followed by a vision of him and Ella laughing together at the store. How could she have ever thought he liked her? She fought the cringe. And no way was she telling him that she'd mistaken him for a bear. He'd be laughing for a month.

He glanced down at the frying pan in her hand. "Did I interrupt your breakfast?"

"No."

He stared for a moment, then gave a flicker of a smile. "Is that the latest in bear protection?"

"How did—?" His eyes filled with amusement, and she lifted her chin. "What do you want, Dan?"

The laughter in his eyes softened as he slouched against the doorframe. "I wanted to know how you slept last night."

She lifted a shoulder. "Lying down. On the couch."

His smile grew lopsided. "You're cute."

Cute was such a downgrade from beautiful. But was it any wonder when he had the gorgeous Ella staying in his home? Her chest wrenched. She pasted on brightness. "Would you like a coffee?" She turned and headed into the kitchen. "I need one. You look like you need one too. Or do you need to get back?"

He shook his head.

Sarah frowned. He didn't want a coffee, or he didn't need to get back to Ella? She shrugged and dumped in enough ground coffee to perk up an army. Darn. She sighed, tipped it out, then measured properly before adding the just-boiled water.

Be nice. "So, what's Ella up to today?"

"Don't know."

He didn't know what his girlfriend was doing? What kind of man was he? Irritation rose as he sauntered over to lean against the fridge.

"You know, you never did tell me how you slept last night." He smiled. "No dreams about big bad mice or mean teddy bears?"

"I don't know. I slept." She whirled around. "How did you and Ella sleep last night?"

The words echoed horribly around the room as his face paled. "No. No, Sar, you've got it all wrong. She's not stay—"

"What do you call it, then?"

A muscle in his jaw twitched. "Ella is a youth leader from my church in the city and—"

"A youth leader who likes to parade around in her tiny bikini—"

"Who I let stay at my house with her cousin and her cousin's husband who has just been diagnosed with terminal cancer. I guess Simone's been staying inside with Jace." He shook his head. "He's pretty sick."

Her jaw dropped. Oh no. No. She took a step back, hand to her mouth as her breakfast threatened to reappear. "Dan, I didn't know."

"Now you do."

"Those poor, poor people." Sorrow kneaded her heart. "Why didn't Ella say anything?"

"Would you tell a stranger all that?"

No.

He pushed a hand through his hair. "Ella, Simone, and Jace left yesterday afternoon." He sighed. "I was just trying to help them."

Of course he was. Mr. Fix-it had been at it again. The wind picked up outside, rustling the trees. She turned to hide the sting in her eyes, concentrating on the French press as she slowly pushed the plunger down. "I'm sorry for jumping to conclusions."

"That's okay." A beat. "Sometimes I get things wrong too."

She peeked up, caught the shadow in his eyes. "We make a good pair, then."

He nodded. "I always thought so too."

He'd *thought* so? Past tense. Sarah bit her lip. Past. Not present. Nor future.

CHAPTER 19

*D*an stared at her. Green eyes gazed warily back. Even the dust motes seemed weighted with tension. Sarah seemed to feel it too, because she picked up their mugs and headed to the living room. He sat on the couch opposite where she sat on an overstuffed armchair, knees up, nursing her mug in a white-knuckled grip.

He took a sip and blinked. Despite Sarah's efforts earlier, it still contained enough kick to power a small city. He swallowed and looked up to catch her wrinkled nose.

Sarah shook her head. "It's a little strong."

"Just helps us know we're alive."

"That's for sure."

At the glimmer of her smile, a knot in his chest eased. "I hate arguing with you, Sar."

"Me too." She sighed. "It's a shame I'm so good at it."

"Yeah."

A beat. "It's a good thing you're so patient, then, isn't it?"

"Yes, it is."

"And that you never get upset or misunderstand things."

"Never."

Her mouth twitched. He joined in her laughter as it chased away the earlier strain. They finished their coffees in silence, as if words would break the tentative truce between them.

She put her mug down. "Thanks for the groceries. You must've dropped them off while I was asleep."

He nodded. "So, what have you been up to this morning?" His gaze flicked to the notepad still lying on the coffee table from last night. *Please tell me what you're planning.*

"Oh." Sarah swallowed. "Uh, John asked me a while ago about something." She picked up the notepad. "He wanted to know if I'd play something at church."

His heart leaped. Was she going to stay? "When will you do that?" He held his breath.

"I'll probably play at tomorrow's service." She shrugged. "I need to do it while I still have some courage."

He laughed. Confusion filled the green eyes that looked his way again. "Sorry, Princess, but you seem plenty courageous to me. Not everyone yells at bears."

Her smile flashed. Her gaze fell. "Well, it's one thing to play here by myself, another in front of others."

"Do you want me to be your audience? I'm really happy to—"

"No! I haven't even played for Ange and John yet."

"Come on, Sar. It's just me. Be brave."

Her eyes widened. She bit her lip, then slowly nodded. "Only if you don't look at me."

He couldn't promise anything. It'd be really difficult not to look.

Sarah moved to sit at the piano, her fingers poised above the keys. She glanced at him once, sighed, then refocused on the sheet music in front of her. Then she began to play.

The piano music trickled over his soul, soothing away the tension that still edged his heart. She'd admitted some plans, but still, would she admit to leaving? He chewed his lip. Was she going because she'd thought he was interested in Ella? How could she think that? How obvious did he need to be?

She started singing and everything else dropped away. The words were so powerful, so real, it was like a tiny slice of heaven was in the room. He'd seen icy Sarah, spunky Sarah, broken Sarah, but this was another side to her...this honest, gentle, spiritual side. Like a diamond, she kept revealing further facets the more he got to know her.

The music poured through her fingers and voice, reflecting her soul, and the words—all the brokenness, the hope, and the healing were there. He was reminded of the YouTube clips he'd seen her in—but this was different. Although unpolished, it felt much more genuine, connecting with his heart in a way that moved him deeply. He blinked back an unfamiliar burn in his eyes as she played the final note, the sound ringing off the rafters.

The glance she shot him was shy. "What do you think?"

He couldn't speak. Could only stare.

"Oh, Dan." Her face went all soft. She moved to perch on the coffee table, leaning closer with that gorgeous smile. "Are you getting a little emotional, tough guy?"

He cleared his throat. "You're amazing."

The tease in her eyes disappeared, replaced with vulnerability. "So, it's okay, then?"

"Way more than okay." How could she not know that? "I've never heard that song before."

Sarah shrugged. "That's because I wrote it."

"Really?"

She nodded.

"Like what you did for Heartsong Collective?"

Another nod. "You've heard some of that music?"

Admit he'd spent way too many nights watching and re-watching all the videos he could find of her? That even though it was worship music, he'd still found her energy and vibrancy mesmerizing and strangely sexy? "I think you're amazing. The song is really, really good, Sar. It's beautiful. I can't wait to hear you perform it in church."

She bit her bottom lip as indecision wavered in her eyes. *God, please help her to trust me and tell me the truth.*

"Dan?"

"Yes, Princess?" He picked up her hand.

"Am I a project to you?"

"A what?"

"A project. Somebody you felt you had to fix."

"Where'd you get a crazy idea like that?"

She looked down. "People say you have a tendency to be a bit of a hero."

He frowned. "Who said?"

"Sam, Ange, Boyd."

"Really?" Huh. "They all said that?"

"Maybe not always in so many words."

He leaned closer and touched her cheek. "Sar, I only ever want to see you happy."

She glanced up, a small smile playing around her lips. "Come on, admit it. Maybe a little bit of a hero complex?"

He shook his head. "I couldn't be your hero yesterday."

"But you were. You scared the bear away when I froze." She shivered. "I was so frightened."

"Yeah, but you didn't show it." He swallowed. "If you stay in Canada long enough, we'll have you wrestling bears in no time." *Please stay, please stay.*

Her eyes widened. "Dan, I…" She bit her lip.

He held his breath.

"Oh, Dan, I've missed you so much." She flung herself into his arms.

He wrapped her close, drinking in her scent as her hair tickled his nose. "I missed you too. I'm so glad you're safe," he murmured. "I've never been so scared as when I saw that bear."

She shuddered. "I'll never look at teddy bears the same way, that's for sure."

"I couldn't believe it when I saw you shouting."

"Oh." She squirmed slightly. "Did you hear any of it?"

"Not really." He felt her shoulders relax. "Is that a good thing?"

The murmur from his chest sounded suspiciously like *maybe*.

He grinned, then leaned back, gently tilting her chin. "I still don't get how you can be scared of a mouse yet can face down a bear."

"Maybe it comes from hanging out with you so much. All your toughness must be rubbing off on me."

He lifted a hand to trace her cheekbone with his thumb. "I don't think so, Miss Maguire. I suspect you've always been a lot tougher than you look. But then, that's not difficult"—his fingers slid to the back of her neck—"when you look so..."

Her face lifted to his, her green eyes enormous, her lips soft and enticing. Their last kiss had been so amazing. His heart danced in anticipation.

He drew close and brushed the softest of kisses across her mouth.

Heart tingling, he drew back, smiling as she slowly opened her eyes.

"Oh." Her cheeks glowed. "So, you're really not interested in Ella, then?"

"Never was, never will be."

"And you don't have any girlfriends stashed away somewhere?"

"Of course not."

"And I'm not a little summer project for you after all?"

Words weren't going to cut it. He would have to show her. Even if it took the rest of his life. He picked up her hand and kissed the back of it, smiling as she caught her breath. He glanced up. "Sar, what are you doing today?"

"John and Ange come back late tonight, but I don't have anything planned."

He smiled and stood, tugging her up. "Good. Because I do."

LAKE MUSKOKA SPARKLED as they sat enjoying a late lunch at the Moon River Lookout, a classy restaurant in Bala with an amazing view over the water. After dining alone these past days, eating something she hadn't prepared was a treat in itself, and having someone to talk to was nice. But for that person to be Dan… Her heart was full.

"Are you enjoying that, Princess?"

Sarah glanced up. His smile had that usual melting effect on her insides. Was he even better looking than two weeks ago? "I love it."

Something flickered in his eyes, and she caught her breath. Tried to relax. Smiled. "I've never heard of Muskoka salad until today, but this is really delicious. And these ribs!"

He laughed. "I do like a woman who enjoys her food."

"Well, you must really like me, then!" She blinked. "I mean, I really like food, so…" She frowned. "I don't think I said that quite right."

Dan's smile grew tender. He gently picked up her hand. "I think you said it right the first time."

She looked down at her lap. This was terrible. She had to tell him. *Needed* to tell him. She couldn't let him keep treating her like a queen when she was leaving. In three days.

"Hey, Princess." She glanced up. His gaze was warm. "What are you thinking about?"

"I, uh…" She swallowed. "You never told me what you've been up to these past weeks."

Disappointment flashed then disappeared. "Been busy with training and team stuff. We've got a bunch of new guys that'll stir things up." He shared about an upcoming hockey clinic he'd visit with some teammates, helping out young kids with their skills.

"You're such a kind man."

He flushed. Ha. Big tough hockey player was embarrassed.

"So, Sar?" She looked up from where she was trying to chase down an errant cherry tomato. "Tell me about Lou."

Oh. "I, um, don't think Ella heard me properly."

"Yeah, even with your accent *Sarah* and *Lou* sound kind of different."

She wrinkled her nose. "Well, if you must know, I was having an insecure moment, and didn't want this fabulous-looking woman peering down her nose at me."

His brow creased. "Fabulous-looking woman?"

"Ella. Is she a model or something?"

Dan shrugged. "I don't think she's that pretty, but then"—he reached across to hold her hand—"she can't hold a candle to you."

God bless him. He even seemed serious. She ducked her head. "So anyway, I just said my name was Blue."

"Blue?"

She shrugged. "Ange calls me Blue sometimes. *Blue* or *bluey* is an old Aussie slang expression for a redhead. It's meant to be ironic but a sign of affection."

"Affection, huh?" His eyes darkened, and he leaned closer to rub a lock of her hair between his thumb and forefinger. "Blue it is, then."

That look of intention. Nerves fluttered through her body like a dozen tiny wings.

He reached for her hand. "Let's go, Blue."

They spent the afternoon pottering around Bala's shops. He'd insisted on buying her souvenir after touristy souvenir, saying she'd need them for when she went home. The way he looked at her when he said that—a kind of searching question—

made her heart sore. She bit her lip. She needed to tell him. Must tell him. She had to be honest. He deserved nothing less.

DAN HANDED her into the boat. Sarah placed the packages on the floor, then settled into the seat next to his at the front. Soon they were slipping past Bala's outskirts and heading out onto Lake Muskoka's sparkling blue.

Beauty was everywhere: the trees, the reflections in the water, the perfect sky. She drank it in. She could only imagine how pretty it would be in autumn. Leaving so soon, she'd never see this again. Her eyes blurred. Never see Dan again. She gulped back the emotion. Did she really have to go?

She took in a deep breath. Yes. Despite all his kindness toward her, Dan had never really said anything about the future. And despite his denials about Ella, it was obvious there would be a long line of girls willing to step into his arms. She winced.

"Sar?"

Thank God for her big Jackie O sunglasses that hid emotion. "Yes?"

"What's wrong?"

"Nothing."

"You sure? You've been a little preoccupied today. You're not still thinking about scary teddy bears, are you?"

"No." She managed a chuckle she hoped gave the impression of ease, but the tenderness in his face suddenly made the truth so much harder to say. How could she hurt this man who'd always been kind to her?

Dan steered around a heavily wooded peninsula, and his familiar red boathouse came into view. She was running out of time. He steered closer to his dock. Killed the motor. Threw the rope around the pole. Stepped out. Held out his hand.

"Here you go, Princess."

His smile had always made her respond in kind. But she couldn't right now.

She stood on the dock, waiting as he finally finished securing the boat.

"Hey, Dan?"

Be brave.

She swallowed. "There's something you should know."

AFTER WAITING ALL DAY, suddenly he didn't want her to say it. The perfect Muskoka afternoon would be wrecked by such a disclosure. He gestured to the bags. "Want to put them away first?"

"Uh, sure."

Five minutes later they were on the cottage's back deck. Sarah was picking at her fingernails.

"Sar?"

She glanced up.

"You want to talk here?"

She shook her head.

"At my place?"

She shook her head again. Seemed she didn't want to say what he didn't want to hear either.

He stepped closer. "The dock?"

She nodded. She slipped her hand into his, and they slowly walked to the dock. He loved the feel of her hand—small, delicate softness entrusted to his care. He glanced across as they passed the large pine's shadow. The late afternoon sun caught the golden strands of her hair, setting them on fire. Her face was pale—that wasn't anything new—but the resolute look she wore was different from the usual openness in her face.

They reached the dock and walked slowly to the end. "This

is one of my favorite places." Dan stopped and turned. "It's a good place to sit and talk or pray."

Sarah sat, the long hippie-style skirt spreading around her in a pool of green and purple. She took off her sandals and stretched out her legs, her scarlet-painted toenails pointing toward the distant twinkle of lights across the indigo lake. She leaned against his shoulder. "This is nice."

"Yeah." It was a mild evening, and the day's heat had made the boards warm to touch. He waited for her to speak while dusk slowly stole over the far horizon. The sun was setting, creating a pink-and-gold light show in the clouds.

"I really enjoyed today, Dan."

"Me too." He picked up her hand, threaded his fingers through hers.

"That's what makes this so hard."

He braced internally. *Lord, I really don't want her to go.*

"Dan." She finally faced him. "I'm going home on Monday."

His grip tightened. Finally—she was being honest with him. Yes—he could trust her. But she had a look on her face that suggested she still really intended to go. His heart tumbled with emotion. Did she truly want to leave?

"Why?"

"Because I've booked my ticket."

"That's not a good enough reason, Sar." He attempted a smile. Failed.

"Because summer is over and I need to go home."

"What do you need to go back for?"

Silence enveloped them, the quiet only broken by the gentle lapping of water and the occasional splash of a fish. Sarah looked down, her bright hair shielding her face.

He leaned closer. "What would you say if I said I need you here?"

She glanced across, wide-eyed.

He gently squeezed her hand. "What if I said I'd finally

found a girl who I want to get to know more, and that I'd like to get to know her here rather than from opposite sides of the world?"

"Dan, I—" She shook her head slightly. "No. It could never work."

"Why not?" He brushed her palm with his thumb, releasing a shiver of heated energy. Did she feel that too? "I like you." What a feeble expression for the depth of his feelings. "I really like you, Sarah."

"Dan, I really like you too, but—"

"I haven't felt like this about any girl before, and I'd really like to know where this can go." He swallowed. "I know things haven't been easy for you, but I won't hurt you, Sarah. Can we take things slow and see what happens? Please?"

He waited in the silence that followed, his heart in her hands.

She glanced down at their entwined fingers.

"Sar? Would you want to be with someone like me?"

She looked up at him. "Someone like you?" She wrinkled her nose. "No."

No?

"Why would I want someone *like* you?" She smiled and touched his face. "Not if I could be with someone who *is* you. Someone so sweet and kind and patient and wonderful." Her fingers traced heat down his jaw, ending at his lips.

His mouth went dry. She couldn't know how enticing she was. "So, will you stay?"

"You really want me to stay?"

"Of course I do."

Time seemed to hold its breath as she searched his face.

Finally, she nodded. "Ange and John said I can live with them for as long as I want. I'll see if my ticket can get postponed for a while."

His heart hummed with hope. "How long is a while?"

"Long enough." Her expression melded into tease. "But you might need to promise to come visit me occasionally."

"I can do a lot better than occasionally. Toronto isn't too far, or you can come visit me in the city. There's plenty to see there."

"I bet." She turned to face the lake glimmering under rose-colored clouds. "But I don't know if anything can ever quite compare with Muskoka. I love it here."

"Me too." He wrapped his arm around her shoulders, tugging her close.

SARAH LOOKED DOWN at her naked fingers. The past was done. The future swirled with possibilities. She stretched her fingers that rested loosely in Dan's large, tanned hand, where they looked so small and white.

He picked up her hand, kissing the back of it, then held it gently, carefully, securely, like she was precious and treasured. Her heart thrilled. This tough man was tender. *Wow, God, I never expected this. You're so amazing, aren't You?*

Dan smiled that melting smile again. She twisted closer to him. Honesty demanded complete openness. "But, Dan, I need to clarify something." She swallowed. "About how our last day ended?"

"What's that?"

"You know kissing you was an accident, right?"

He slowly smiled. "I know it was—at first."

Her cheeks warmed. "I'm not in the habit of throwing myself at guys, just so you know."

"Really? I never would've guessed. Not from the way you've made it so easy for me to get to know you this summer."

"You don't want a girl who's easy, do you?"

He stared, a muscle twitching in his jaw.

"I didn't mean that! Oh my goodness!" She squeezed his hand and smiled as the last rays of gold sank into violet water.

"Sar…" She glanced up. Dan was gazing across the lake, his expression strained. "You know nobody's perfect, right?"

Her laughter faded at his serious expression. "Of course I know that. I know I'm definitely not perfect." Her stomach tensed. And if this relationship continued for as long as she hoped, he'd definitely learn just how far she fell short. "But I also know we're forgiven. And that makes everything okay."

"Good." His shoulders dropped. "I don't want you to be under any illusions about me, especially when the hockey season begins."

"And what does that include? Groupies? Late night parties?"

He nodded slowly. "There's some of that."

Really? Oh. The breeze picked up, wisping hair across her face. He picked up a strand and smiled, tucking it behind her ear with a caress that spoke of strength and security and hope for whatever lay ahead.

"Speaking of accidents"—the brown eyes begged a question that she answered with a smile—"this won't be one."

And he bent his head and kissed her, a heart-singing, wondrous promise for the future.

The next two months passed in a blur of wonder. Wonder that she was still here in Muskoka, wonder that Dan liked her, wonder that God might still have good plans for her life.

Her item at John and Ange's church had resulted in Enid and Doug practically begging her to take on the music, and had led Dan to say some sweet things before he'd needed to drive to a hockey event in Peterborough, then attend a friend's wedding in North Carolina. But it wasn't anyone's compliments, rather the sense of utter rightness, the knowledge that she was once more doing what she'd been put on this planet to do, that made her soul truly smile for the first time in nearly two years.

So she'd started leading music in John's church and had been surprised and encouraged by the number of kind comments she'd received. She'd even had some of the teens in the congregation ask if they could join too, seeing the songs now had words they understood. John had given his approval, so now the music ministry duo was approaching a team more like she was used to, with the addition of a couple of guitarists as well. Who knew? The way they were going, they might even one day score a drummer!

But it showed once again that God was gracious, God was good, that He had everything under control. And yes, maybe Ange was right and Sarah didn't need to over-think things. Maybe she could relax and just enjoy the moments gifted to her.

A shiver of anticipation rolled over her, and she glanced at the blurring trees on the highway to the city.

"Excited?" Ange asked.

"Yes." Over the past weeks she'd felt a return of the zest and enthusiasm that had once colored every day. She woke each morning with anticipation, with thankfulness for what the day would bring. Since Dan's return to Toronto, she'd visited a few times, staying with Ange's in-laws in Mississauga and enjoying the chance to see the sights and see Dan. And now to be heading back to the city for her birthday...

She wondered what he had planned for tonight.

THE LIGHTS WERE DIM, the music soft, this restaurant in Little Italy perfect for tonight. The past few months had flown. As training had ramped up, they'd squeezed in dates around Dan's busy schedule—movies, dinners, and occasional adventures made more fun by Sarah's wide-eyed enthusiasm. And all the time, Dan kept discovering layers to this woman, clues to her past, deepening the fascination Sarah twirled around his heart.

He leaned forward, smiling as Sarah daintily slurped her linguine marinara. Every so often she'd slurp loudly and glance up. The candles made it hard to tell if her cheeks were pink, but their flickering shadows did something magical to her eyelashes and hair.

"So, Princess, are you enjoying your birthday?"

She nodded. Slurped. Smiled. "This is so delicious."

"Not too ordinary for you? Now I know you've eaten African food." He raised an eyebrow. "In Africa."

A recent revelation from their trip to Niagara Falls: she'd been on a missions trip to Zimbabwe and seen Victoria Falls.

"Mealie-meal sure doesn't taste like this, Dan. And while seeing baby elephants in the wild was cute, I quite like the view here, too." She raised her brows at him and then winked.

Okay, he really liked this flirty side of her. It reminded him a bit of Mike's wife, Bree, with her open affection and sassy comments at Beau's recent wedding. Except he'd never felt anything remotely romantic for Bree, which was the total opposite of how he felt about Sarah.

"What are you thinking about?" she asked.

"You. See, I quite like the view right now too."

"Oh, you do, do you?" She waved a hand at the rustic terracotta walls. "I didn't think this would be your cup of tea, but okay."

"Granted, it's not quite as dramatic as the view from the CN tower," he admitted. Another revelation from last weekend: Sarah hated heights.

"Lake Ontario at sunset was pretty spectacular, but I prefer my feet on the ground."

He couldn't say the same. These past few weeks, his heart had skipped way in front of his head. It was hard to take things slowly when Sarah kept bringing extra joy to his world. His favorite moment of their trip to the falls had been when the boat had lurched, causing Sarah to slip, and he'd had to wrap his arms around her—*had* to—as a Japanese tourist snapped their photo. His phone screensaver was now the image of them both grinning at the camera, her hair drifting to one side in the moist breeze, safely ensconced in his arms. He could stare at that image forever.

"Dan, are you going to finish that, or do you need help? I'm surprised you haven't finished already, seeing you love eating as much as you do."

"So sue me. It's an occupational hazard." He pulled his plate closer, smiling as she snitched a ravioli square.

He liked that she enjoyed food as he did. He liked how they could talk about all sorts of things yet never run out of conversation. He liked how she noticed people, like the men fishing at the falls. He liked listening and watching and learning her.

"Are you ready for your present now?"

She lit up like a kid at Christmas.

"Is that a yes?"

"I don't do cool, calm, and collected. It's not in my DNA."

"I like your DNA just fine the way it is."

As he handed over her gift, uncertainty trickled through him. It'd been hard to know what to give her. Sarah wasn't into glitz, definitely wasn't sporty, and he didn't want to give her something that signaled a depth to their relationship they hadn't reached yet. He'd finally settled on a framed print of Lake Muskoka in the fall, the colored trees rising through the mists. It was evocative and appropriate, given the time enjoyed there.

She unwrapped the purple tissue paper, her breath catching. "Oh, Dan, how beautiful! Oh, it's exactly right. Thank you so much."

Thank goodness.

"And it's flat, so I can pack it easily when I go home." Her smile slipped.

Dan's spirits sank. He wasn't ready to think about her leaving yet. She'd changed her flight to New Year's Day, but even that felt way too soon.

Sarah read the photograph's nameplate aloud. "Muskoka Mist." She glanced up. "You chose well. I'm sure all that crying I did contributed to some misty conditions in Muskoka."

"Sar, I didn't—"

"Hey, it's okay. When I'm home I'll look at this and

remember how much I 'miss' Muskoka." She laughed at the silly pun, and Dan smiled with her.

"Look at it and remember me too, sometimes."

"I will. Sometimes."

Her cheeky look drew his chuckle.

Later, after kissing her goodnight at John's parents', he drove home to his apartment, his thoughts turning to the coming weeks. Training camp, then five preseason games back-to-back. Practice and travel wouldn't allow much time to be together, let alone dates like this. But at least she'd finally get the chance to see what his job entailed. He couldn't wait to hear Sarah's opinions on the sport he loved.

"AND HE SCORES!"

Loud music thumped through the Air Canada Centre, the Friday night crowd dressed in blue and white loudly cheering the Maple Leafs' first goal to tie the game. Sarah looked around at the crowded stands, the charged atmosphere. She knew something about crowds and fans from her Heartsong Collective tours, but this was next level. Imagine if Christians worshipped God the way these hockey fans cheered on their team.

The game continued, and she kept her gaze on Dan's number sixty-seven jersey as he defended his team's goal. All his off-season training now made sense. The sprints, the weights, the stamina-building bike rides. The puck slid from the Vancouver stick but was intercepted by Dan's fellow defenseman, who passed to him. After a swift look, Dan shot it to a forward who was already skating toward the Vancouver goal.

John shouted in her ear. "See how Dan cleared the puck? That's one of the things that makes him so good, his ability to read the play." He stood and cheered, then turned to her. "See that?"

Sarah nodded even as her stomach tensed. Sure, there were skills on display, but mostly, she saw a bunch of guys crashing into each other while she wondered about potential injuries. Dan's role as a defenseman meant he was often in the thick of it, barging into skaters from the opposite team, slamming them into the side as he worked to prevent them from getting near his net. Those big shoulders and strong chest that made her feel so protected when he hugged her were being used to inflict damage on others. Pride in him mingled with concern. She wasn't sure how she felt, nor could she understand half of what was done or said.

"Go Dizzy!"

Ange leaned closer. "That's Dan's nickname." She smiled at Sarah's raised brows. "Walt from Walton, Walt Disney, now Dizzy. Or maybe it's something to do with how fast he skates. I can't remember."

Sarah turned to look at the girl who'd called out. She was wearing a tight blue-and-white midriff top, holding up a large sign with—her phone number on it? How wrong was that?

The siren blew, and the crowd dispersed for further refreshment. "How are you finding it?" John glanced over.

Best aim for diplomatic. "It's nothing like what I'm used to."

"There's a lot to take in."

That was for sure.

She focused on Dan as he skated back on for the start of overtime. John was right: Dan *was* skilled, with a focused intensity so unlike the easygoing Mr. Wilderness she'd known in Muskoka. She rubbed her forehead as if she could press these new revelations into place. *God, please keep him safe.* He wasn't in the boards as much as some, but still, how many bruises would he have at the end of a game? Did he ever get concussions? She watched Dan block a shot, then reverse into an opposing forward, who tumbled over Dan's back in a cartwheel. The crowd stood to their feet and roared. "Hip check!"

Sarah gasped. Dan flicked a look back at the forward, who was moving gingerly. "That poor man! Will he be okay?"

"Sure. Zac Parotti is tough." Her uncle stood. "Come on, Leafs!"

Dan picked up the puck, passing it to a teammate who shot and scored, but the siren didn't blare, and the referee denied the goal, much to the vocal dismay of the crowd. Sarah cringed at some of the comments, especially about the referees. "They take it so seriously. It's only a game, isn't it?"

Ange laughed. "Don't say that too loudly here. Hockey is what many Torontonians live and breathe."

Scoreless overtime led to a shootout, which was pretty nerve-racking, as was the post-game crush as the disappointed crowd exited. Dan had already explained he had an away game tomorrow and would catch up with her after church on Sunday. But after tonight's events, Sarah wasn't sure what she'd say when she finally saw him.

"Hey, Sarah."

"Patrik! Hi." She gave the Swedish student a hug, offered Boyd a smile. *Be nice.* "How are you, Boyd?"

"Great."

He didn't look it. His sour expression suggested he'd rather she be anywhere else. But Dan had invited her to his city church, and she was glad to have a peek into another part of his world. Even if the large congregation meant neither she or Ange had seen him yet, although she had seen Ella from afar, and been introduced to Boyd's not-quite-girlfriend Joanna.

"Sarah?"

She turned. Georgia stared at her, open-mouthed, standing

next to Travis. "Georgia! Hi, sweetheart!" She hugged them both. "How are you, Travis?"

"Um, good," he muttered, red-faced.

"I didn't realize you went to church now."

"We go to the youth church here," Georgia said.

The youth service that ran simultaneously with the regular morning service. She'd enjoyed the music and the preaching today, and could well understand why Dan worshipped here.

"And how are you, Georgia? Really?"

"Better." Georgia's eyes, her smile, proclaimed it true.

"I'm so glad. I've been praying for you." Sarah hugged her again. Who cared what Boyd thought about her hugginess? This was so necessary.

"It's a family thing," a voice said behind her.

She spun, saw Dan's amused face as he gestured to where Ange was hugging a friend. Boyd rolled his eyes, but his small smile indicated amusement. Or at least resignation. Maybe one day he'd accept her.

But she didn't have time to wonder further as Dan scooped her up in a big hug that said exactly how he felt about her. She closed her eyes, holding him tighter as she savored his scent, his strength, his nearness.

"Hi."

"Hi." Her nerves fluttered away as she pulled back to sink into the depths of his smile. "You played well."

"You enjoyed the game?"

"I've never been to any great big sporting events like that before. People got so loud. How do you manage to concentrate?"

"It's actually kind of good. We feed off the energy of the crowds, which is why home games are so important."

One they'd lost, followed by another loss in Ottawa. "I'm sorry you didn't win."

He shrugged. "It's a game. Win some, lose some."

She nodded, her mind turning over his philosophy. It seemed a little strange to devote so much time and energy to a game that could simply be shrugged off. But his ability to let it go, to release disappointment easily, was something she could learn from.

Later, after lunch with Ange, John, and the others, she visited Dan's apartment. Sixteen floors above downtown traffic, it was quiet and afforded some nice city views from the living room and balcony. She pressed her forehead against the glass, gazing out at the red and gold trees dotting the cityscape.

"It's really starting to look like autumn now."

He moved behind her, pointing out various landmarks and the blue-gray sliver of Lake Ontario. His hand trailing down her arm and his body heat behind her drew a tingling awareness that they were alone and the fresh realization to take care and not invite temptation. She forced herself to move, ducking under his arm and going to the kitchen. "What's that awesome smell?"

"I made lamb shank stew for an early dinner before you leave. Hope that's okay."

"Of course it is! It smells amazing. I love lamb, and you know I've always liked your cooking."

"You mean my cooking or me cooking?"

"Either. Both."

He laughed, drawing her to sit in the living room with its ubiquitous leather lounges and expensive entertainment system. "It's good to have you to myself for a while."

"It's good seeing where you live, being able to imagine you here when I'm away."

"About that." He sighed. "I told you my schedule, didn't I? I've got a few long road trips coming up between now and Christmas, so I won't be able to spend as much time with you as I'd like."

Especially seeing she was two hours away and reliant on

others to drive. She'd driven Ange's car a few times in Muskoka but wasn't yet ready for city driving. Which only made these times together more precious. "I'm happy to get as much time with you as I can." She leaned up, pressed a kiss to his jaw, heard his intake of breath. "Will you get a chance to come back to Muskoka soon?"

"I hope so." He tugged out his phone, checked his calendar. "I have Thursday off. Are you busy?"

"One benefit of volunteering for John and Ange is that I can set my own hours. I can be free."

"Great. I'd love to spend the whole day with you again."

"Me too."

THE NEXT FEW days rushed by as Sarah worked hard to complete her work in order to keep Thursday free. Now Trudy was back, Sarah's focus had shifted from admin to helping reorganize the charity store that filled what used to be the front living room of John's former home. She'd happily volunteered her time to sort and style the displays to look more inviting as well as be with customers and ring up sales. This, combined with some music tutoring and songwriting, filled her days with purpose, like it had in Heartsong days or when she used to teach.

Thursday arrived, and Dan joined John and Ange for a late breakfast before whisking her back to his place. She moved out to stand on the deck and took a deep breath, filling her lungs with the earthy scent of crushed leaves intermingled with the smell of the pines. How heavenly. Sighing, she turned to encounter Dan's amused expression. "You like it here, Princess?"

"Oh yes. It's like coming home!" She caught Dan's widened eyes and felt her cheeks heat. "I mean, it feels so familiar. I didn't mean your place specifically is like my home, because obviously it's not." Dan's smile grew lopsided the more she babbled. "Although it's such a great house, but I don't want you to think that I think your home is my—"

Stop. Just stop. Now. She clamped her mouth shut and turned to face the water.

Dan snickered. "I like you, Sarah Maguire."

She peeked past her hair. "I like you too, Daniel Walton."

He grabbed her hand. "Come inside and I'll make you a coffee."

"Is that so you can hear more stream of consciousness from moi?"

"I like the effect sugar and caffeine have on you."

As Dan powered up his espresso machine, Sarah sat on one of the comfy armchairs in a nook behind the dining room, gazing out through the trees to the calm lake beyond. Imagine if fairy tales really did come true and she could live here. Her heart fluttered. How amazing would that be?

"Here you go, Princess."

She jumped, almost knocking over the blue coffee mug Dan had placed on the wide armrest of her chair. One sip of the creamy coffee and she almost purred. Yum. Yet another thing Dan did well. "Oh, that's delicious."

He smiled and leaned closer, dark eyes caressing her face. "Sar…"

Her breath caught at his husky tone. Oh-h-h. Was he going to kiss her? Dan was such a gentleman they hadn't really kissed since the last time they were here. She smiled invitingly and leaned forward to be within kissing range.

"Sar, I'm going to do a quick check on the place. I'll be back in a minute, okay?"

Oh. "Uh, sure." She slumped back, shaking her head at her silly misread as he disappeared. It was weird figuring out all this relationship stuff again. Dan was so different to Stephen.

She leaned her head back against the padded headrest. Dan

was so good, so kind, so patient, so godly. Whoever married him would be so lucky. She wished—

No. As if that would ever happen.

She bit her lip as the questions started clamoring. Where *was* this going? Her stomach lurched—probably shouldn't have had that second croissant at breakfast. But how could this work when she was leaving for Australia in a few months?

And what did all this mean about her relationship with Stephen? She'd always thought Stephen was her soul mate. His earnest, intense nature had fascinated her, and she'd been flattered when he started paying her attention, then proposed. But now that she wasn't wearing grief's heavy glasses, she could see things more clearly. She'd been so insecure—ha, like she wasn't now!—but now she wondered whether she'd grown stifled by his seriousness and tendency to act superior.

After he died, she'd forgotten all this. Stephen had instead become a type of saint.

She frowned, remembering when he'd wanted her to quit Heartsong to have a "real" job, and how she'd blindly followed, rarely voicing her opinion, until that final argument when he'd suggested—or was it demanded?—that she change her teaching focus. Now she could see her compliance had shackled her, reduced her to a shell of who she really was, unlike her robust discussions with Dan that only seemed to strengthen their relationship. And now, here she was, three years older than that girl who'd finally said yes to Stephen's proposal, but feeling decades wiser. And lighter. And more free to be herself...

She scooped out the remaining froth with her finger and licked it clean, then placed the cup to one side. Outside, a maple leaf delicately arced its way to the ground. How would things have turned out if Stephen hadn't died? They'd be married now. She'd still be teaching, doing her regular church commitments, and planning for babies.

Babies. She wrapped her arms around her knees. A sudden streak of pain raced through her as her eyes filled. *Oh God.*

THE PATIENT TICK of the old wooden clock on the mantelpiece was the only sound breaking the deep stillness of his cottage. Dan leaned against the doorframe, studying Sarah as she sat in front of the window, her legs pulled up on the lounge, her face a parade of emotions, her initial delight melding into pensiveness.

She looked so at home there, her bright hair gleaming in a stray sunbeam contrasting with the dark leather. She shifted slightly, and he caught the tiny smile wedged in the corner of her mouth. She was so expressive, yet sometimes still so hard to read.

His heart warmed as he recalled her rambling comments earlier. It was nice that she liked this place like he did. He'd never invited a woman to come here alone with him before. Those few times when Sarah had come before didn't really count—they hadn't been involved then. But now, she just seemed to fit, like she was meant to be here, part of his life, part of his future.

Future? His chest tightened. He really, really liked her, loved spending time with her, loved so many things about her, but actually *love* her? Really? He hadn't felt this way. Ever. But as Pastor Josiah and the guys in the online Bible study always emphasized, love wasn't just about feelings. Love involved choices. It meant choosing patience and kindness, believing the best, enduring. Wasn't love supposed to be self-sacrificing? He'd seen that firsthand with Jai leaving Chicago to follow his now-wife to San Jose. Mike, Brent, and Beau had demonstrated real love too. So this was serious. He couldn't lead Sarah on. And if he did love her—and, miracle of miracles, she actually loved him back—what could follow but the big *m* word?

He swallowed, trying to ease the sudden dryness of his throat. Why was this so confronting when it was everything he'd been hoping for and praying about for years? Maybe it was the questions that still hovered over her future. Maybe it was the questions from his past. He stared out the window for a long moment before stepping closer.

"Hey, Sar." She jumped, suggesting she'd been as deep in thought as he. "Are you ready to go out on the boat?"

"Um, sure." Contemplation lifted and a teasing glint replaced the brooding of before. "You gonna try and catch some fish?"

"What's this 'try' business? I can catch plenty of fish. Sometimes."

She stared at him for a moment, amused, before a strange look crossed her face and she turned away. "Yeah, there's plenty of fish in the sea…or the lake, as the case might be."

"Uh huh." He frowned. What was going on?

Whatever it was, she seemed to shake it off as they made their way down to the boathouse. Dan handed Sarah in, completing the necessities until he could finally power up the motor and start moving through the water. Sarah zipped up her jacket over her blue woollen sweater, rewrapping her cream scarf against the cool lake air as his house grew smaller. The sun glinted on the water, and the dizzying array of tree color was breathtaking. As they passed a particularly scenic stretch, Dan killed the motor, and they drifted in silence. Dan moved to the back of the boat and sat next to Sarah. This was one of the prettiest sections of the lake, unmarred by any sign of human habitation, and she was obviously moved, blinking as if trying not to cry.

"Are you okay?" he asked, threading his fingers with hers.

She nodded. "There's just something about perfect beauty that overwhelms me sometimes. It happens with music too. I hear a series of chords and it's like my soul is moved on some really deep level. I think it's God, just letting me know He's the creator of beauty."

Dan studied her face. "He certainly is."

Pink washed across her cheeks as she squeezed his hand. "Muskoka in autumn is so lovely."

Sure was. He wrapped an arm around her. But what had gotten her emotional before? "So you're not worried about anything?"

"No. Why?"

"You just seemed a little concerned about something back at the house."

"Oh, that." She bit her lip.

She didn't want to tell him. That could be a good sign. Or not. No point wondering. "Sar, I don't want you feeling sad when you come to my house."

"I wasn't sad about your place. Not at all. I love it here! That's the problem."

"How is that a problem?"

"It's just too perfect! You're just too good." She glanced away.

His gut tensed. Too good? If only she knew.

"You're so good to me, and I wish I could stay forever here with you, but I can't, and I don't know where this is going, and it got me thinking about Stephen and how things happened with him—"

As Sarah took a breath, Dan could feel a mental eye roll coming on at the mention of Stephen's name again. *Let the dead man rest in peace already.*

"Dan, I really like you, but I don't know if you would ever really want to be with someone like me, and—oh, I've just said way too much now, and I feel really embarrassed, so I'll just shut up and pretend you didn't hear all that."

Dan shoved a hand through his hair. Sarah liked him, liked his place, wanted to be with him—that was all good. But she still wasn't sure if he liked her? And what did she mean about Stephen and things with him?

"Listen, Sar." He waited until her gaze met his again. "I thought I'd made it clear before, but I'll say it again. I like you. I like you more than any woman I've ever known. You're interesting, talented, challenging"—a small smile crept onto her face—"and you intrigue me. There are so many layers to you that I just want to spend time with you so I can know you more. I'm not sure what will happen when you go back home, but I definitely want to keep building this—"

Friendship? Relationship? Romance? No. It was time to take things more seriously.

"I want you to come with me to my parents' next Monday for Thanksgiving. Will you come?"

The thought had only just crossed his mind before he blurted it out. Being with his family for Thanksgiving wasn't a casual event. Thanksgiving ranked up there with Christmas as far as important family occasions went, and inviting a girlfriend was akin to declaring your engagement. Luke had only invited Marguerite after they were engaged. This was a big deal, and he'd be facing questions.

"Really?" Sarah took her sunglasses off and searched his eyes. "You really want me to come?"

As he nodded, the tension on her face melted away. "That'd be so good."

He returned her smile. Yeah, this would be a Thanksgiving to remember.

TODAY HAD BEEN MAGICAL—THE perfect Muskoka day. After the morning boat ride, they'd enjoyed a long lunch at Muskoka Shores resort, and the rest of the day had been really relaxing. They'd taken the long way home, puttering into tiny coves, Sarah in a constant wonder of oohs and ahhs as they discovered one perfect scene after another. The afternoon light cast a soft golden glow over the foliage, as if God had put a special camera filter over Muskoka to draw out its beauty even more. Dan glanced down at Sarah. Much like the sunshine brought out hidden hues and ruddy tints in her hair. He twirled a strand around his finger.

She shifted slightly and glanced up, her green eyes sparkling. "You right there?"

He nodded. Yeah, he'd been right for months now. This, being with Sarah, holding her tucked under his arm as he let the boat drift for a while, listening to her musical voice—this had *right* written all over it.

After carefully securing the boat for the winter season, they spent the rest of the afternoon mooching about on the deck, talking, laughing, enjoying the mild sunshine, until the late afternoon chill edged around their jackets and Sarah shivered. "I'll need to go back soon."

"But first we have a sunset to watch. Want to go inside or down to the dock?"

"The dock, of course."

They held hands and lay on the warm boards as the sky melded into pink and orange and gold, staying until the darkening sky revealed the first of the evening stars.

Sarah propped herself up on an elbow and gazed down at him. "Today has been fantastic," she murmured. "I'm so glad you made me come."

"I *made* you, did I? I don't recall you protesting too hard, Princess."

Her smile stole his breath. After that last kiss, he'd forced himself to hold back, struggling with desires that demanded satisfaction. But she was so lovely, so close, so tempting...

He slowly brushed his thumb down her face, enjoying the smoothness of her skin, then reaching the softness of her lips.

"You know, I don't think I've met anyone with quite your coloring, Sar. I think you've bewitched me."

"Are minister's daughters supposed to do that?"

"This one has." In the dim twilight he could just make out her deep green eyes as they widened then softened as she leaned her face to within a breath of his.

He tilted his head until he could almost taste her smile. He paused, anticipation tingling through his body, then pressed his mouth to hers. Her soft lips were warm and responsive as her body relaxed against his, her hand sliding up his jaw into his hair. He wrapped an arm around her waist and tugged her closer, his senses heating as their kiss deepened. Oh man. She felt so good, smelled so good, tasted so good…

Some dim awareness of a promise made long ago told him to stop. He ignored it, enjoying the moment and Sarah's eager response too much. But the stubborn voice kept at him until he could ignore it no longer, and he pulled away with a gasp.

He had to get upright. Now. Before there was any more trouble. He edged away and staggered to stand, heart hammering loudly, before pulling up a confused-looking Sarah. He blew out a frosted breath. "I think I like you a little too much. Kissing you like that—" *I just want more.* "Sorry, Sar."

A beat. A heavy-lidded smile. Then, "I'm not very sorry."

His lips tweaked. Part of him wasn't either. "It's getting late. I think I'd better get you home."

Before the magic of her kisses proved too much temptation.

And before he could lead her astray.

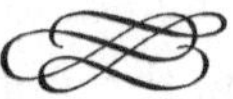

CHAPTER 21

Sarah sat in the passenger seat, fiddling with the lacy ends of her scarf, nerves pattering through her veins.

Dan glanced across. "So, are you ready for your first Thanksgiving?"

Her heart skipped a beat. The way he'd said that made her wonder if there'd be more. "It sounds fun. I'm so glad your parents are happy to have me come."

Dan bit his lip.

Oh. Was *happy* overstating things?

"It'll be fun," he said, almost absently.

Was he worried about today too? "Dan?"

"Sorry. You want to know about the food?" He glanced at her, his tension fading as he grinned. "But of course you do." As he negotiated the heavy Thanksgiving traffic, he described the meal and some of the traditions that usually took place. They pulled up outside his parents' large Tudor-style house. Sarah's eyes widened. It looked three times as big as her parents' home. She checked her appearance in the visor mirror again.

"You look great," Dan assured her.

She hoped so. She'd suspected today would be formal, so had

dressed in a teal jacket and black skirt to improve upon the last few impressions she'd made. Dan got out, racing round in the brisk October breeze to hold the door open for her, holding her hand as they walked up the short bricked path together.

Sarah took a deep breath, tugged her jacket down, then smoothed her knee-length skirt whilst checking her tights for any snags. She tentatively patted her hair. Hopefully it would stay up in the French roll she'd attempted. It was a big deal for Dan to have invited her today.

The door opened. "Daniel!" His mother gave him a hug, then turned to Sarah. "And Sarah. Welcome to our home."

"Hi, Mrs. Walton." Was Sarah expected to hug her too? She moved forward and gave his mother a light hug, but the stiff shoulders soon indicated her mistake.

Helen stepped back. "Oh!" Why did Helen's smile feel like a frown? "Come in."

Spirits sinking, she followed Dan and his mother inside. He paused in the entryway to draw her close. "Don't mind Mom. She always gets a little stressed at Thanksgiving."

"Why?"

"She likes things to be perfect." He shrugged. "Come on. Let's go find everyone."

Sarah followed Dan into an elegant cream-and-gold living room that looked to have been styled by *Home Beautiful*. She greeted his father and younger brother again before being introduced to his paternal grandparents and an uncle. Another couple entered the room. The tall man looked to be in his mid-thirties and shared the same dark hair and brown eyes as Dan and Sam, but his smile seemed even cooler than Helen's.

"So, you're Sarah."

Her heart double-thumped. Obviously people had been talking, and it didn't sound too promising. *Be nice.* "And you must be Luke. Hello."

He nodded, then turned to his brother. "Daniel."

"Luke." They shook hands.

That was all? No hug like with Sam? Didn't they get on?

A sophisticated blonde dressed in a cream suit and pearls that made her look like Helen Walton's mini-me stepped forward. "Hello, I'm Marguerite, Luke's wife. It's nice to finally meet one of Daniel's girlfriends."

Sarah shot Dan a quick glance. "One of? How many do you have?"

Sam snickered in the background. "Only one he brings to Thanksgiving."

The tension in Dan's face dissolved as he smiled. "Only one, period."

Marguerite sat and motioned for Sarah to join her on the leather sofa. "Sarah, I understand you work in schools too?"

"Yes." Sarah quietly exhaled. Finally, some common ground. "What do you teach?"

"Oh, no. I'm the financial manager of a private school in Vancouver."

Okay. A lot in common there. Was the room getting warm or just her? Sarah removed her jacket, but the long, puffy sleeves of her green-and-purple top caught on one of the jacket buttons. Oh no. She looked up. Eyes politely glanced away. She tried wrenching it loose, but it wouldn't budge. Her cheeks heated. Sweat trickled down her neck.

Dan crouched in front of her. "Hey, Princess." He grasped the jacket and fiddled with it for a moment, then gently unhooked it. "There you go."

"Thanks." Sarah leaned close and whispered, "How embarrassing."

He murmured "Only if you care what others think."

She took a deep breath and turned back to where the rest of his family gazed at her like she was a circus clown at a business meeting. *Be brave.* She smiled at Dan's dad, seeming to catch him off guard as he nodded back.

Helen gave a thin smile. "That's an…er, unusual blouse, Sarah."

Sarah rubbed damp hands down the sleeves of the paisley silk top. Admitting that she'd found another goodwill treasure didn't seem like it would go over too well right now. "I wasn't expecting it to have attachment issues."

Silence. Then quiet chuckles from Dan and Sam.

Helen looked like she didn't know whether to smile or frown. "Excuse me while I go finish preparing."

Sarah stood. "Would you like some help?"

"No, thank you, dear." Dan's mother disappeared.

Sarah sank uncertainly back on the lounge. Didn't Helen like her? Dan picked up her hand, kissing the back of it before leaning close to her ear. "Don't take it personally. My mom never admits to needing help." He smiled. "Kinda reminds me of someone else who once told me she didn't need help. Remember?"

Oh. "That was a long time ago." She smiled, relaxing into the assurance she saw in the depths of his eyes.

The conversation veered to the stock market, real estate, and other money-focused things. Sarah perched on the edge of the seat as she watched the family interact. It was so different to her family dynamics. Everyone here was very serious, polite to the point of coldness. Dan and Sam seemed to be the only ones with a sense of humor. How had they managed to escape being so starchy?

Dinner was announced and they were ushered into the dining room, Dan seating her next to him. The table was set with a linen tablecloth and napkins, special pieces of crockery, and an abundance of cutlery and wine glasses that produced an expensive-sounding *ting* when she bumped one accidentally. A huge turkey sat in pride of place in front of Dan's father, surrounded by assorted fragrant dishes begging to be devoured —or photographed for a food magazine.

Andrew Walton cleared his throat and glanced around the table. "Thanksgiving is a time to remember things that we are thankful for. But please, keep it shorter this year."

He shot Sam a look that made her wonder just how thankful he'd been on previous occasions. Dan's hand found hers under the table as people started sharing. This was a nice custom, and she was grateful for so many things. When it was Sarah's turn, she murmured something about being thankful to have the opportunity to come to Canada and find hope and healing. She squeezed Dan's hand. It was his turn now.

"I'm thankful for meeting Sarah." A beat. "She's an amazing woman, and I hope you'll all grow to love her as much as I do."

WHOA. He hadn't meant for that to slip out just yet. Had intended something far more romantic and private. But there was just something about how right she looked next to him at the family table with his loved ones looking on.

He glanced at Sarah. Her eyes widened, then her gaze faltered. His words had taken her by surprise as much as everyone else at the table. He bet his cheeks were as red as hers. Oh well. No one would be in any doubt now about how he felt.

SARAH FOUGHT for self-control as her heart pulsed wildly, joy threatening to burst out in disbelieving laughter. Dan loved her? Was he for real? Despite her messed up life and the constant challenges she sent his way, he loved her? She squeezed his hand, felt his fingers slip through hers, and listened with half an ear as Sam finished sharing something.

Luke cleared his throat. "Marguerite and I are very thankful"—he paused, as if waiting for a drum roll—"for the new addition that will be joining our family in May next year." He sat back, the huge, proud smile on his face echoed in every face around the table. Obviously this was the place for big announcements, and it seemed this really *was* considered good news, unlike the startled looks that had greeted Dan's statement.

Sarah smiled across at Marguerite, mouthing *congratulations*. How special! What a blessing. What a joy—

Her smile froze. Gladness teetered, then nose-dived. Her gaze fell. Dan might never be able to make that same joy-filled statement if she remained in his life.

"Sar, would you like some cranberry sauce?" Dan asked, holding out a gold-rimmed white saucer filled with rich red fruity goodness.

She nodded automatically, swallowing past the heartache in her throat. "Thank you."

The roast turkey and side dishes were delicious, the conversation pleasant enough, but the rest of the day was a struggle as she battled the irrational jealousy that kept spiking whenever she glanced at Marguerite. *Just smile. Talk. Breathe. Act normal.* But it was getting harder by the minute.

She felt as fragile as glass, ready to shatter if someone looked at her the wrong way. Plates emptied as the conversation continued, and a dull thump began in the back of her head. She sipped her water. *God, I really need Your grace right now. This is so hard.*

"That was delicious, Mom. Thanks." Dan smiled across at his mother.

Sarah nodded. "Thank you, Mrs. Walton."

"You're welcome." Helen sighed and eased back in her chair, looking more than a little drained. "It's always nice to reach this end of the day."

Poor thing. Was all the hard work worth it if Helen was exhausted at the end? Sarah stood. "You've worked so hard. I'll go start cleaning up." Ignoring Helen's half-murmured protests, she picked up several plates and headed to the kitchen, where she was soon joined by Dan and Sam. She was thankful for the distraction as they talked hockey and loaded the dishwasher whilst she carefully washed the glasses, the pain pooling in her heart and head easing a little now she was away from the baby-focused conversation at the dinner table. Maybe it would disappear when they made their farewells and she could finally escape.

~

Dan adjusted the air-con and looked across at Sarah in the front seat. "That better?"

She nodded, her recently discarded scarf on her lap. "Thanks."

He gazed affectionately over at her. Today had gone so well. Everyone had seemed to love Sarah, and she seemed to have relaxed more too. It boded well for the future. "So, did you have fun?"

She nodded. "It was good. It was nice to meet Luke and Marguerite. They…they seem excited about becoming parents."

"Oh yeah." His super-serious brother was so excited at the thought of being a dad. He and Marguerite would be good parents, although they'd probably be overly strict. Dan's stomach tensed. His parents' enthusiastic response about their first grandchild made him wish—

"It's good news." Sarah's comment interrupted his remorse.

He pushed aside regret, gave a quick smile. "Sure is. I love kids." He studied her as they waited at a red light. Imagine being the father of Sarah's children. His heart skipped a beat. She'd make a great mother. She was so fun, enthusiastic, and smart. He could just see them now: little girls with their mother's red locks, little tough guys he could teach hockey. A family filled with laughter and love.

Whoa. Seriously? He'd said he loved her—but marriage, fatherhood, the whole works? She was only here for another two months. What then? Boyd's long-ago words about thinking with his head resurfaced. Memories of his past seeped in. His stomach churned. There was still so much unknown.

~

THE SUBURBAN LANDMARKS slowly became familiar once again as Sarah mulled over Dan's comment at the dinner table. Probably he'd only meant he loved her as in liked her a lot, just as earlier he'd declared how much he loved his mother's baked dinners. As nice as he'd been, as much as he seemed to have enjoyed kissing her last week, he couldn't really mean he loved her in a romantic forever sense. Could he? How could she ask him to clarify his comment anyway?

She'd always believed that saying *I love you* was one of the big moments in a relationship, when one was sure of the other and willing to commit to a future. Dan saying it like that had caught her by surprise, unprepared, and she now felt almost obliged to say it back. But then, he hadn't actually said those words to her, so probably this was just another flight of her too-active imagination; something that likely wouldn't matter when reality bit all too soon.

Her feelings tilted into sadness again about his brother's news. It *was* great news for Luke and Marguerite, but a secret part of her wanted to cry about the fact that she'd likely never have that opportunity. Especially as Dan loved kids and was excited about becoming an uncle.

Should she say something about her inability to have children? She bit her lip. Like that was an easy topic to slip into conversation. And Dan hadn't said anything beyond *I love her*—to his family, no less, not even to her! It wasn't like he'd declared he wanted to marry her. Besides, the doctors hadn't definitely ruled out her ability to bear children, only advised that the accident and surgeries had likely affected it. She pressed against the ache in her forehead. But then, Dan had once said he didn't like pretenders, and she wanted to be honest. *Oh Lord, what's best for Dan?*

Too soon, he'd pulled up outside John's parents' home and killed the engine.

Her insides churned. "Thanks for inviting me along today. It was fun." Mostly.

"My folks like you." His steady gaze cut through the doubts.

"I like your family too." Mostly.

"I think today went really well."

She nodded mutely, a marionette doll with a painted smile. Today *had* gone well. At first.

He threaded his fingers through hers. "I don't really know when I'll next get to see you. The first big road trip starts tomorrow, which means I'll be out of action for a while."

"But we can still text or email."

"And call or FaceTime." He stroked her cheek, tracing fire. "I love to hear you speak."

He sure wouldn't like hearing the awful revelation she'd had at the dining table. Should she say something now?

Be brave.

But before she could speak, he bent his head and kissed her, and she closed her eyes, content to let the worries subside in the pleasure found there. His lips caressed hers gently, feather-like promises of passion that slowly intensified, growing more demanding. She slid her hands up along his jaw into his thick hair and shifted forward in her seat, pressing herself as close as she dared as the kiss deepened, growing urgent before he pulled away.

She drew back, lightheaded, breathing hard. "I guess that kiss will have to be enough to keep you going."

"It'll keep me going," he rasped, then exhaled. "It's probably a good thing I won't see you for a while."

Probably. It would give her time to rein in these wild emotions and consider just how best to share this latest piece of awesome information about her past.

"Come on. I'll walk you in."

They exited and he grabbed her hand and walked her inside. They were getting to know John's parents pretty well with these visits, John's dad proving to be as big a Leafs fan as his son.

Sarah watched the conversation, answering automatically when Ange asked how she'd enjoyed Thanksgiving with the Waltons. But her heart and mind kept twisting, turning, trying to figure out what to do. Tell Dan she couldn't have kids? Let things slide a while longer until she knew whether this relationship would last? What was best for Dan?

On the car trip back to Muskoka with John and Ange, she pleaded exhaustion from a big day and closed her eyes, still thinking, thinking, thinking. Later, in her room, she found Stephen's ring and tried it on, wondering if placing it back on her ring finger would spark any sense as to what to do. It didn't. It was just another piece of jewelry now.

What should she do? Had she missed her opportunity to be honest today? She wouldn't see him for weeks now, and this wasn't exactly a conversation she could have over the phone. *God, give me wisdom. Help me do what will be for Dan's best.*

And with that prayer on her heart and lips, she slept.

CHAPTER 22

The next weeks flew in a haze of flights, games, bus trips, training, flights, training, and more games. Dan had found a new energy, his time with Sarah at Thanksgiving only solidifying his cause, prayer and reading God's word further reinforcing this. Two were better than one, and now that he'd found the other person he wanted as part of his two, he couldn't wait to make it come true. This had necessitated a special trip, when the team had been in New York, for something that he hoped she might like to wear this Christmas. That wasn't too soon, was it? Then maybe she'd feel like she didn't have to leave in the new year, and she could stay forever in his house she'd said was like coming home.

Home. He could just imagine it: Sarah's vivacity lighting his world, welcoming him back after a road trip. Kids, a dog, the whole package. He smiled.

"Yo, Dizzy, what's got you smiling, man?" Matt Reynolds, star forward for the team, snapped a towel at him. "You got a lady friend?"

"Didn't know you knew any women," Marc Valesky, the Leafs' number one goalie, grinned from his dressing room stall.

Brendan Jordansen, Dan's fellow rookie defenseman from Pittsburgh days and probably his closest friend on the team, raised his brows. "You got a girl?"

"Yeah."

"Nice! It's been a while. Wow, not since that chick from Pittsburgh, remember?"

His stomach squeezed. Oh, he remembered.

"What was her name again? Lisa? Lana? A hot tamale?"

Yep, that's what he'd thought back then too. Stupid him. Thank God for His forgiveness and grace.

Later, as the team bus drove back through LA traffic to the team hotel, memories of his younger exploits kept bobbing to the surface, like lake mud swirling through clear water. What would Sarah say if she knew about his past? Should he tell her? God might have forgiven him, but would Sarah—innocent, loved-Jesus-since-a-child Sarah—be so gracious? He wasn't sure.

The thought she would reject him kept his mouth closed when they next Skyped, a too-quick call due to his miscalculation of time zones, giving him a glimpse of the challenge of a truly long-distance relationship should she return Down Under. But would she even want to stay in contact with him if she knew the whole shameful story?

"Dan? Are you okay?" He seemed tired tonight, or worried, a little crease in his brow.

"I'm fine. The Kings are tough to play at home."

Sarah nodded like she knew which team he meant. She thought the Kings were based in Los Angeles. Or was that the Ducks? Or was she getting confused with a kids' movie?

"So, Sar, tell me what's happening with you."

"Did I mention my parents are coming for Christmas? They

got an excellent deal and booked to come visit in mid-December and stay for Christmas. It's their first trip to Canada in thirty years. They're so excited!"

Dan's eyes crinkled. "Did you learn excitement from them?"

"Why, Daniel, whatever do you mean? No, this"—she gestured to herself—"is all me."

He grinned at her, and her heart scampered. This evening's Skype call would have to end soon—he'd called too late and it was past midnight here in Muskoka—but she was grateful for the distance that allowed more time to sift her thoughts and emotions. Things could be hidden behind a screen that couldn't be hidden in real life. And she still hadn't really figured out how to introduce the topic that haunted her future. Despite near-constant prayers, she remained unsure, the churn in her heart blocking any real certainty save the sense she should speak with him. Soon. And in person.

"Sar?"

"Oh, sorry. I was just wondering when you were coming back."

"Late Saturday. Hey, can you come see me on the Sunday? We have the day off, and I thought we could see a show."

"Oh, I'd *love* to, but that Sunday I'm rostered on music."

"Ah. Well, maybe I could come see you."

"That'd be good." She forced a smile. Maybe by then she'd have figured out what to say.

His first Sunday back, and Dan was stuck in chilly Toronto. Sarah had canned their date, pleading sickness that she didn't want him to catch, and she'd begged him not to visit.

She had at least agreed to FaceTime, and he noticed she seemed a little less vibrant than the last time. Maybe the cold snap that had brought the season's first snow was getting to her.

When he asked her, she sighed. "The snow is pretty, but I don't mind admitting I'm looking forward to warmer weather when I get back home."

"You know you don't have to leave at the end of the year."

"I think your government might disagree. My visa expires January second."

He chewed his lip. "Well, maybe we'll just have to have some time together over Christmas."

"Didn't I mention it before? Ange and John are having Christmas here in Muskoka with my parents."

Then when the heck would he ever see her? An idea sparked. "Maybe I could convince my family to do the same."

"You think they would?"

If God did a miracle. "I can ask. Hey, that reminds me. There's another team function coming up next weekend. Can you make it?"

She pulled back from the screen, peering at something beside the computer. "Would you believe it, but no."

Figured. Didn't she want to see him? Sometimes he wondered whether she even loved him. She still hadn't said it yet. "How about November twentieth? There's a charity function that I'm going to, and partners are welcome." He forced a chuckle. "Might help convince some of the guys that you're not just my imaginary girlfriend."

"They don't think that, do they?"

"They're not used to seeing me with any girl, so I'd love for them to meet you."

She checked again. Slowly nodded. "I think so."

"Great!"

"And you accuse me of over-excitability," she teased.

"I like your version of over-excitability."

She smiled, the first real smile of this call. Tension lining his chest released. "Oh, and can you save New Year's Eve?"

"The night before my flight leaves?"

The night before she'd leave with his heart. "There's a party at a big hotel downtown for the team, and I want you there as my date."

She hesitated. "I'll have to see what Ange and John's plans are. I think there was talk of staying in the city with John's parents again, with the flight so early the next day."

"That would work. I don't mind kidnapping you until sunrise if necessary."

"Good to see those stalker vibes I sensed weren't too misplaced."

He snorted with amusement, remembering her comment from months ago. "I promise you'll have fun."

She nodded. "Are these things fancy? Do I need to dress up?"

"Most do, but some just wear business casual. Everyone is pretty nice and normal."

"Looks like it's back to the stores for me."

He leaned closer to the screen. "I'm really looking forward to seeing you, Princess."

"You too." She coughed.

"I hope you feel better soon."

"Thanks. And I hope you'll stay well. Talk tomorrow?"

"Can't wait."

She smiled and blew him a kiss, the call finished, and he stared, head in hands, at the blank screen, his emotions churning in a never-ending cycle of yearning, frustration, desire, and regret.

THE GLITZY HOTEL ballroom held a myriad of men and women in evening dress chatting, eating, laughing. Sarah munched on the arancini ball the waiter had just scooped onto her plate and swallowed some more pride. Okay, so maybe her assumptions about rich people were misplaced after all. The players and business people she'd met tonight really did seem to care about Toronto's needy, donating outrageous sums to provide for a women's shelter downtown. Maybe she was more like Elizabeth Bennet than she liked to admit, happily judging individuals and a whole stratum of society before getting to know them. *Judge people? Moi? Surely not.*

"What's with the smile?"

Dan hovered back into view, another mocktail for her in hand—delicious concoctions of juice with fruity decorations. She didn't need any extra kick from alcohol. Life was kicking along just fine, thank you very much. Attending a cocktail charity function in freezing cold Toronto in November was not something she'd thought she'd ever do, but hello, here she was. These days there was a lot she was doing that she never would've anticipated a year ago.

Sarah studied Dan, etching his features in her mind for future reference: his tousled dark hair, his long-lashed dark eyes, and his strong, smooth jaw complete with scar. Her throat cinched. Only six weeks, then she'd be leaving the country. What would he say when she told him? Tonight still had not provided time to talk privately.

"Princess?"

She refocused with a start. "Oh! Sorry. I was just looking around at your friends here thinking, wow, Dan sure knows what he's talking about. They actually do seem normal and nice. How's it feel to be Mr. Right?"

Whoops. Hadn't meant to say that. Like that. At all.

He drew closer, eyes alight with mischief, all shadows gone. "Mr. Right, eh? Well, I don't know, Princess. You might need to fill me in on what you mean by that."

Dan tucked a loose strand of her hair behind her ear, smoothing it with a caress that made her shiver inside. "I, uh, just meant…"

He smiled. "No, don't spoil the illusion."

ILLUSION. That's what it was all right. Dan kept the smile pasted on for the rest of the evening, but that night, after taking Sarah home, sleep was impossible as his mind tracked through the past few weeks.

She was so right, so good, just so nice, and he? Despite what she'd said tonight, he knew he really was Mr. Wrong. An illusion. A fake. Sure, she'd had her issues, said stuff, done stuff that had made him want to scream in frustration at times, but at least she was working through things.

She was changing, willing to admit to mistakes, willing to trust God with the future, whereas he? Dan groaned aloud as that now familiar ball of guilt made its presence felt again. How could he ever admit to her the massive mistake he'd once made?

WHY WAS it that going somewhere for the first time always seemed to take longer than the return journey? After John escaped the snow-snarled traffic and finally parked at Lester B. Pearson International Airport, Sarah almost slipped on her way in, so great was the excitement. How many other twenty-nine-year-olds would be this excited to see their parents? But then, she'd always scored high marks for enthusiasm. And after all that had happened over the past six months, there was so much to catch up on, so much to tell.

She waited at arrivals, jogging from one foot to the other. Finally, her mother's dark red hair signaled their entrance.

"Lindy!" Ange raced to give her a huge hug. Maybe excitement did run in the family after all. Sarah hugged her dad before finally taking her turn with her mother.

Her mother's arms wrapped around her, a cocoon of security and peace.

"I've missed you, Mum."

"Oh, sweetie, you look so much better. We could hear it in your voice, but to see you!" Her mother's voice quavered, and she pulled back, turning to Ange and John. "Thank you."

"It wasn't us," Ange smiled. "God did it using a certain someone, hey, Blue?"

Her dad turned. "Do you mean that sports man? I'm looking forward to meeting him."

"Daniel is a fine young man." John's assertion calmed the question in her father's eyes.

Her mother's smile held familiar tenderness. "I can't wait to meet him. You're a different person to the girl who left. It's like you've been brought back to life."

DAN KNOCKED AT THE DOOR, stomach roiling. He felt like such a phony, dressed up in a suit to make a good impression on the church minister and his wife. But if they could see the way he was now, maybe they would cope with his money. And, ultimately, his past.

Sarah answered the door, a bright smile on her face. "Hello!" She drew him inside to the warmth. "Ooh, it's so cold out there!"

Her big hug and quick kiss helped calm his nerves. "I've missed you this week, Princess."

"Oh, me too. These road trips are kind of tough, aren't they?"

"Florida wasn't so tough."

"Stop boasting." Her laughter held more ease than he recalled hearing before.

"Sar?"

At the voice coming from the lounge, her eyes widened. "Are you ready to meet my parents?" He nodded, and she grabbed his hand. "Come on, then."

Dan smiled a quick hello to Ange, John, and John's parents before recognizing Sarah's features in the auburn-haired lady before him.

"Mum, Dad, this is Daniel Walton. Dan, these are my parents, James and Lindy Maguire."

"So, you're Daniel." Sarah's mother's eyes were a little teary, even as she gave a warm smile and hug. "Thank you for being a good friend to Sarah."

"My pleasure, Mrs. Maguire."

Sarah snickered. "It wasn't always a pleasure, was it?"

He grinned, relaxing a little more. "You've definitely made my life interesting these past six months."

Her sudden sweet smile made his heart leap.

Her father's brows rose. "And you play sport?"

"Yes, sir. I'm in the Toronto Maple Leafs hockey team."

"Ah." Still that look, as if Dan was being measured for worthiness. "And you're a Christian?"

"Yes. Almost eight years ago, just after I turned twenty-two."

Sarah's father nodded and invited him to sit, then began asking other questions about Dan's Christian experience, and soon they were chatting freely. How nice to be talking about important stuff and not the usual trivia that filled his own family's conversation. He relaxed into the sofa, watching Sarah sparkle as she laughed with her mother and aunt. Dan caught Sarah's eyes and winked.

HER CHEEKS HEATED. It was so great her parents were getting on with Dan, especially her hard-to-please father. He was usually warm with people but had always been pretty fussy with the guys in his daughters' lives. So far the conversation had centered on faith, although they'd touched on Dan's family and work situation too. Muskoka had been mentioned, and Dan had even invited them all to visit his cottage during his pre-Christmas break.

"I like your Daniel, Sar," her mother said later, after Dan had left to go prepare for a game.

"I like him too. He's so sweet and gentlemanly even Dad should approve."

Her mother sipped her tea. "But you're leaving soon."

Sarah sighed. "I don't know how a long-distance relationship is going to work." Or even if it should work. She swallowed. "He's so busy with games and travel and training he won't have time to miss me." She bit her lip. Would it be a case of out of sight, out of mind? She'd seen the girls all too keen to get his attention. Would Dan fall when temptation was so blatant?

And what did that mean when the future he wanted wasn't one she could give? Breath caught. *God, give me wisdom.* Maybe there'd be a chance to talk when he was in Muskoka.

"Oh, sweetie." Sarah's mum smoothed a recalcitrant strand of hair away from Sarah's face. "Judging from the expression on that man's face earlier, he'll be missing you, more than you realize."

Sarah could only push out half a smile. "I hope so."

CHAPTER 23

"So, you've never made a snow angel." Dan chuckled as Sarah danced around in an effort to keep warm in the snow. With five days off before their Boxing Day game in New Jersey, he was glad to be here in Muskoka, glad to have had time with Sam and Sarah and her family before the rest of his family arrived tonight. Especially with Sarah looking up at him like that.

"Of course I haven't." She clapped her gloved hands to warm them. "Growing up, I only ever saw snow like this"—she motioned to the idyllic scene around them—"on the movies, so you need to show me what to do."

Man, he was going to miss her. For weeks now he'd tried to be thankful and make the most of things, and a game every second day had been fairly effective distraction, but it was impossible to ignore the calendar. In ten days she'd be gone. This joy Sarah brought into his world would be so hard to lose. He shook his head. He was going to miss her so much.

"You won't? Oh." Sarah's bottom lip pushed out. "I'll have to ask Sam."

Sam. Yeah, Sam's presence was definitely not required right

now. He'd already made his presence felt, wondering aloud yesterday why Sarah wasn't sharing Dan's bedroom.

Once her parents and his family had decided to come to Muskoka for Christmas there hadn't been enough room for everyone to stay. He knew his folks and Luke wouldn't cope with extra guests interrupting their special Christmas festivities. Having Sarah stay was challenge enough. Having her family visit for a meal was pushing it. Having her family stay with them? Forget it.

So Sarah's parents were staying next door with Angela and John, while Sarah and Sam had stayed at his place last night. His parents were due later this evening, and Luke and Marguerite came tomorrow. Once upon a time, the confusing transport and accommodation arrangements had made sense, even if his unsaved brother couldn't understand.

As Dan's guts had twisted and his sweat glands had worked overtime, Sarah had gently explained something about being a Christian and not sleeping with any man until she was married. Dan had shaken his head imperceptibly as Sam shot him a look.

"But isn't that old fashioned? Who cares, anyway?"

"I do."

And Sarah's smile at Sam had seemed to close that conversation. But who knew what he'd say next time? Nope, Sam definitely wasn't needed now. Not when Dan wanted—needed—every drop of her attention himself.

He brushed snow off her green toque. "No, I'll show you. But just so you know, making snow angels is usually more of a little kid kinda thing."

She grinned. "I promise not to tell, oh great mature one."

He poked his tongue out at her and flopped on the ground to demonstrate.

· · ·

"THAT WAS SO MUCH FUN!" Sarah's face glowed red from the laughter and exercise of the past half hour. "The cold really makes sense if you get to play in lovely snow."

"It's pretty nice, isn't it?"

"It's Muskoka. Of course it's nice!" She patted the final creature into shape. "There. You like?"

He laughed. "Princess, that's kinda freaky looking. What is it supposed to be? A dragon? A squirrel? I can't tell."

She pushed him. "It's a snow kangaroo, of course."

He snickered. "Of course."

As she tried to push him again, he sidestepped and caught her around the waist, smiling down into her laughing eyes. "I like making snow angels with you." He hadn't had this much fun since he was a kid.

She tilted her head. "And snow animals?"

He kissed her nose. "Even weird snow animals."

She laughed and took a step back. "I love it, but I'm getting cold. It must be hot chocolate time!"

"Must be." He held her hand as they slogged through deep snowdrifts to the path that led back home. Warm light spilled through the windows onto the snow-covered deck.

She shook out a glove as she opened the door to the warmth. "I'm sure I've got snow in places that I really shouldn't." She took another two steps, then stopped.

Dan peered around her. His parents had arrived and were standing by the fire, looking at them in surprised alarm.

Awesome.

He turned to give Sarah an encouraging smile, plucked some sticks and dirty leaves from her hair before turning back to his folks. "Hi, Mom, Dad. You're early."

～

THIS WAS SO NOT how she'd wanted to appear. Sarah swiped at her messy hair, pushing it off her sweaty brow, wishing once again her skin didn't glow like hot coals after exercise. Oh well. Little Miss Perfect she'd never be. "Hi, Mr. and Mrs. Walton. It's good to see you again." Not really. Not like this. But a girl had to be polite, especially when crashing her boyfriend's family's Christmas.

"Sarah, it's nice you and your family could come."

Andrew Walton's tone didn't exactly ooze sincerity, but Sarah smiled anyway. "I love Muskoka. It's such a beautiful part of the world. I can't believe I'm going to experience my first white Christmas!" She grinned at them, and their faces relaxed slightly. *Just be yourself*, Dan had said concerning his parents. *Just be natural.*

"We've never spent Christmas away from the city, so this is something different for us too." Helen looked a little worried.

"I'm sure we'll all have a lot of fun."

At Dan's comment, his father gave Sarah a stiff smile. O-kay. That must be her cue. She made her excuses and left to clean up. After a super quick shower, she returned, pausing at the entrance of the living room to check her appearance in the hall mirror. Dan never seemed to mind what she looked like. It was a shame the same couldn't be said about his parents.

"And who decorated the tree?" Mr. Walton's deep voice came from inside the room.

"We all did. It looks great, doesn't it?" Sam said.

She inched closer and glanced over to the corner of the living room, where Sam had been playing some computer game for ages. What was it with guys and computer games?

"Don't we have a tradition—? It just looks a little, I don't know, tatty."

They didn't like it? Her heart sank. Yesterday had been so much fun as she, Dan, and Sam had argued about what constituted the perfect tree, eventually finding one in a far corner on

Dan's property, cutting and dragging it in. After finally getting it to stand almost upright, they'd realized there were no decorations. Sarah had suggested making decorations themselves, and she'd painstakingly written each family's name on a cheap bauble from town. She'd thought it'd looked festive and cheery, particularly once they'd added the popcorn strings. Obviously not everyone agreed.

She entered the room and stood near the roaring fire, trying not to feel like the intruder she really was as all eyes swung to her. "I'm going to duck next door so you can all catch up. I'll see you later."

With a smile but unable to meet anyone's eyes, she'd almost made it to the front door when Dan hurried over, grabbing her hand. "Hey, Sar, don't go. Mom and Dad need to taste your shortbread." He turned back to his parents. "Sarah's a great cook."

She glanced over. They didn't look convinced. Maybe Dan thought that too, for he slung an arm around her shoulders, murmuring in her ear, "Please don't go. They just need some time to adjust."

"I don't want to stay if I'm not welcome," she whispered.

"I want you here."

She gazed up into his steady brown eyes. "Well, I won't be too long then."

"Want me to come?"

"I'll be okay. Besides, I think they need you to stay."

Regret followed her refusal minutes later. Trudging through the thick snow by herself wasn't as fun as it looked on TV. Hallmark movies had a lot to answer for. Her boots kept sinking up to her knees, so it was actually kind of exhausting, but the ice-laced trees and the little cottage all cozily aglow with lights were so pretty it almost made her forget the tension at Dan's.

Breath escaped in a white puff. Thank God for families who were willing to go with the flow. Her parents were reveling in their time with Ange and John, the size of the small cottage meaning Sarah had given up her room so her parents could stay there, while she stayed in one of Dan's guestrooms. Mum and Ange were enjoying reconnecting, and it was nice they could do so while she spent time with Dan and Sam.

After yesterday's early start and careful drive on icy roads, they'd bought provisions, done the firewood thing, decorated the tree, then cooked before her family came over for a meal. They'd played some silly board games that had been heaps of fun and finished really late. Today had been a nice chance to relax. *Had* been. She sighed. She hoped they'd all feel better soon.

~

"THAT WAS DELICIOUS, SARAH."

Dan squeezed Sarah's hand as her face pinked with pleasure at his mom's compliment concerning the berry pie she'd made.

"Daniel was right. You are a woman of many talents, and with such pretty hair."

"I'm supposed to have some Irish or Scottish blood, aren't I, Mum?"

Lindy nodded even as his dad frowned. It had proved an interesting meal, the two sets of parents with little in common, his pastors, Sam, Sarah, and himself. Somehow, their stilted attempts at conversation had chiseled off the initial frost and, with Luke and Marguerite's arrival tomorrow, the parents had at least found a mutual interest in grandchildren. Apart from Sarah being a little subdued during that conversation, everything had seemed to be going well, until the heritage comment.

"You don't know?" his father asked Sarah.

Dan stifled a smile. His dad could proudly trace his lineage back to pre-Confederation English settlers and loved boasting about some of his forebears. He caught the sparkly tease in Sarah's eyes as she turned to his father.

"I think we may have convict blood in us somewhere, too."

"What?"

Sam unsuccessfully hid a snicker at their father's bug-eyed reaction. Even their mom looked aghast. Uh oh.

"Andrew, numbers of Australians have ancestors who first arrived in the colony on the first and second fleets," Ange said. "Many of them were convicts sent to the colonies from England for petty crimes committed in order for their families to eat. Today, most people see such ancestry as being a little like the colonists on the *Mayflower*—cause for pride in their tenacity in coping with a harsh and very different environment."

Ange's explanation seemed to go some way toward appeasing his dad, although he still looked at Sarah doubtfully. Dan squeezed her hand again. He should probably mention his father's lack of a sense of humor.

Sarah smiled sweetly. "I don't think our history should define us, as a nation or as individuals."

Dan's dessertspoon fell with a clatter. She said that now, but wait until she learned about his past. John's sharp eyes caught his, and he nodded faintly toward the kitchen.

Dan stood and started collecting empty plates and bowls, then met his pastor in the kitchen. After Dan had briefly explained his dilemma, John pursed his lips, frowning.

"I think it's wise to say something soon. I hate to admit it, but secrets like that have a way of coming out."

Dan exhaled. He hated to spoil this special time, but, "I'll do it soon, I promise."

CHAPTER 24

"So, have you ever ice-skated before, or is this another one of those 'No, I'm an Australian' kind of things?"

Dan's teasing eyes pulled out the truth. "I skated a couple of times way back when," Sarah confessed, thinking back to her youth group days. "I bet you can guess just how good I am."

He groaned, even as he finished pulling the laces tight on the old skates that used to belong to his mother. "I'm looking forward to this."

And yep, she was pretty sure she'd lived up—or, more literally, down—to his expectations, spending most of the next hour either sprawled on the thick blue ice or yelling, "Don't let me fall! Don't let me fall!"

He'd said they were lucky the lake had frozen so much already, allowing them to skate. She wasn't so sure it was such a good thing. Skating wasn't as easy as Dan made it appear. Despite his best efforts to help her stay up, she'd still managed some spectacular falls. There'd definitely be bruises tomorrow.

But it was fun. At least for him. Dan wasn't bothering to hide his amusement. "You just gotta learn how to fall gracefully, Princess." He shook his head. "It's bringing back memories.

Remember that first evening at the cottage? You, in the hammock, reading?"

Oh, that. Why did he have to remember those moments? Couldn't he remember the times she'd behaved, well, slightly more gracefully?

He did some fancy move, ending up skating on his knees to where she was rubbing her elbow as she attempted to sit up after falling yet again. "But I have to say that this time, I've fallen for you."

"You do have to say that." But though the words held tease, the smirk wouldn't come. The sweetness of his face only inches from hers caught her heart in knots. As for his smile...

Dan leaned in closer, the weak afternoon sun still able to find gold in the depths of his eyes. "Why's that?"

She caught her breath. *Because you're so special, so kind, so good, so patient, and I appreciate so many things about you and have for months. You're everything I could ever want. I love you. I don't want to go home and don't want to admit something I think may hurt you very much....* She swallowed. "I'm going to miss you so much, and I'll need to remember that you care."

"PRINCESS, I CARE." So much that it hurt. He cupped her face in his hands and gently caressed the cheekbones before tracing her lips with his thumbs. He leaned in, touched her nose with his, then kissed her. Her mouth was warm, soft and sweet. He wrapped a hand around the back of her head and kissed her more ardently, with just a hint of the desire he felt. A dizzying kind of kiss that had them both coming up for air, looking at each other in a dazed way.

He exhaled. "Princess, I love you. I love you so much that I've tried not to think about how you're going so soon, because I don't want to spoil the time we have together." His throat thickened with what he still had to say.

"Oh." A shy smile filled her face as her eyes sparkled like priceless jewels, clear and true. "Daniel, I love you too."

At last! *Thank You, God.* The gift she'd just given him was better than any other he could ever receive. Contentment flowed as a sappy grin refused to be restrained. He loved her and she loved him. All was finally as it should be. He wrapped his arms around her, holding her tight, enjoying the scent of her, the softness of her hair, everything he would miss as soon as he admitted—

"Am I interrupting?"

YES! Sarah wanted to scream as she looked up to see Sam holding a couple of battered hockey sticks, a puck, and a smirk. She sighed instead. These Walton men certainly had timing on their lives. Bad timing, mostly.

Dan studied her and she forced a smile. "It's okay. You two have fun."

He helped her up to a handy rock, where she sat as the two brothers scrimmaged. They dodged and faked, looking like kids having the time of their lives, not two grown men in their twenties. They were really good. Well, Dan was really, *really* good. Not that she was biased or anything.

"Hey, Sar, are you cold sitting there? I can teach you some hockey moves if you want to warm up."

Ah, no. Much preferred his previous method of warming up. Cheeks aflame, she looked down at her skates. How did she undo them? "I think I'm kinda done."

"Then so are we." Dan nodded to Sam, and they skated over. Sam tugged off his skates, grabbed the sticks, and disappeared.

Dan gave her another warm smile, then kneeled to help her

again. He took his beanie off, and his lovely thick, dark hair was all mussed up. It *needed* her to smooth it down. She yanked off her gloves.

Oh. His hair was so soft and velvety. She shivered. This suddenly felt way too intimate, and from his startled glance, he must feel the same. She traced along the planes of his cheeks until her fingers caressed the slight stubble of his jaw. He'd stopped trying to free her feet and was watching her, intently.

"You having fun, Princess?" The smooth baritone had roughened into a timbre she'd never heard.

She nodded, gazing into his eyes until he exhaled, broke eye contact, and finally finished tugging the boot free.

"So you like being out here, then?" His voice was still husky but had steadied to something approaching normal. He glanced up at her again.

"Yes." Maybe a little too much. She was so glad Sam had disappeared.

"Good." His smile was full and warm before he kissed her again, then wrapped her up in a long, long hug. Oh, she loved this man. When he next gazed at her, his eyes had shadowed again. "Sar, there's something I really need to talk to you about. Tonight, after dinner."

Her insides suddenly tensed. There was something she needed to say too. "Okay."

~

"This salmon is amazing, Dan. You're such a good cook." Sarah smiled at him, then turned to the rest of his family, who sat around the dining table. "Isn't it just fantastic to be here, inside and warm, enjoying such yummy food? I love Christmas!"

Her vivacity chased away the strain that had arrived with Luke two hours ago. Dan watched his family relax as Sarah's natural warmth drew them out of themselves.

"Christmas has always been my favorite time of year too," Sam said.

"Why's that?" Sarah tilted her head, her hair glowing in the candlelight.

"I guess I like us being together." Sam's cheeks flushed. "It's nice."

"I agree. Family is so important, isn't it?" She turned to Luke. "How about you, Luke? Which is your favorite holiday?"

As Dan's salmon disappeared, Sarah skillfully drew each family member out, and the warmth he'd craved for years in his family began to flow like sweet honey. Even his mom and dad seemed to have finally found a sense of ease, proof indeed that Christmas was a time of miracles. Now he hoped for one more: that Sarah would be okay—would still love him—after he finally shared about his past.

Sarah turned to his parents again. "I hope you all know how much I appreciate being here. Thank you again." She turned back to Dan and gave that sparkly smile that made him catch his breath. "I'm so glad I'm here with you."

He gazed at her, his personal cheerleader, the one who stirred his heart and his family, the one who helped chase away the shadows of his soul. He smiled. "Me too."

SNOW FLURRIES DANCED outside the picture window overlooking the lake. The wild wind outside made this quiet moment so special. The little alcove here was about as much privacy as they could safely get. His parents and Sam were busy catching up with Luke and Marguerite, but right now Dan needed Sarah alone. His heart pounded, twitchy with anticipation. Dinner had been just an appetizer before the main event.

Dan wrapped an arm around Sarah and drew her closer. She glanced up, smiled, and pressed her lips to his jaw. He sucked in air, his heart racing. Did Sarah know the effect she had on him?

Maybe it was just as well he was going back to T.O. tomorrow. That kiss on the ice before, then when she'd touched his face, had been intoxicating. And today had to be the day she finally admitted what her kisses had confirmed long ago. But as awesome as that had been to hear, it had just made other things more difficult now.

"I love you, Dan."

Her words infused confidence that rippled to the edges of his soul. He'd never get tired of hearing that. "I love you too." He squeezed her hand. "I know it's a day early, but I have something for you."

Her eyes lit. "Oh! We're exchanging presents! I have something for you too. Let me run and get it."

She jumped up and disappeared before he could argue, returning shortly with a medium-sized gold-wrapped box and a big grin. "I hope you like it." She leaned forward, kissing him lightly on the lips. "Merry Christmas, Daniel."

Dan slowly read the card, took his time to unwrap the present. Tonight had to be drawn out. He wanted time to create the memories he'd later treasure. He smiled at the digital photo frame, already loaded with photos from their time together. It was a visual record of their relationship, from the early fishing days, to the camp, Niagara Falls, the CN tower, the charity event. There were even a couple of candid ones from today's funny ice-skating lesson.

She nudged him. "Sam took that photo, then helped me load it. He's good value, your brother."

"This is amazing. I didn't know you'd taken so many pictures."

"I'm a tourist, remember? Anyway, I've seen the attention you guys receive, so I figured you'd probably need reminding once I'm gone."

She didn't mean that, surely. "Sar, there'll never be anyone I could love like I do you."

"Really?"

"Really." He kissed the back of her hand. "I have something for you. It's just a little something, though." Small, but it said a lot. He handed over the small pale blue package. "Merry Christmas, Sarah."

It was shaped like a jeweler's box. Her mouth dried. Was this what he'd wanted to say? Surely he wouldn't. They'd only known each other seven months. That wasn't enough time to know for sure. She looked up into his eyes. "Dan, I—"

"Just open it."

With a growing sense of panic, Sarah slowly opened the box to encounter a magnificent cluster of diamonds winking at her. "Oh, Dan." *No. It's too soon.*

He was watching her carefully, and she lifted her eyes to his, drinking in the chocolate warmth, before looking at the diamonds again. "It's so beautiful."

"I wanted something so you'd remember me and remember how much I love you."

She couldn't stop the hysterical gurgle. How much had he spent? It was almost too gorgeous. "It definitely makes a statement." A forever kind of statement.

She pulled it from the box.

Oh.

It wasn't a ring but a pendant. She glanced up. Dan was still closely watching her. She couldn't reveal how silly her initial assumption had been, so she hugged him, resting her cheek against his, closing her eyes to savor the slight roughness of his jaw and that aftershave that made her swoon. "Thank you." She couldn't believe this man. Remember how much he loved her? This gift ensured she'd never forget. She wrapped her arms around him tighter. She felt almost giddy.

He eased back. "You want to try it on?"

She nodded, and he carefully extracted the pendant and underlying chain from the box, the delicacy of the workmanship magnified by his strong hands. He lifted up her hair, sending shivers down her spine when he touched her skin as he clasped it on.

She turned around, and Dan's expression went all soft. "Princess, that's just how I imagined it. You look beautiful."

THE DIAMOND CLUSTER nestled at the base of her throat—her beautiful, creamy throat housing her amazing voice, in that little well that looked like it was made for kissing. It was a pretty amazing piece of jewelry, with a price tag to match. God bless the NHL—and his agent, who'd negotiated his contract. Anyway, she was worth it.

Sarah was looking at him with shining eyes. He couldn't spoil this moment with confessions from the past. "Come on." Grabbing her hand, he led her to the dining room, where the conversation among the rest of his family was still going strong.

"But didn't you want to..."

Dan shrugged. "Later." Like maybe never. Why'd she have to know anyway? She didn't need to know everything. Their entrance stopped the chatter as his family all stared at the necklace.

"Wow, Sarah, that son of mine has chosen well."

"Now that's a rock and a half! How many carats?"

While it was a nice change that his father and older brother were pleased with something he'd done, it meant more when Sam, Marguerite, and his mom exclaimed over the photo frame. Sarah had chosen well. The dark wood frame would work well either here or in his apartment in the city. But it was the photos that drew the most comment.

"Oh look, you two look so happy!"

"How much did that fish weigh?"

"That's taken up the tower, isn't it? You look like I felt—scared stiff!"

Sarah relaxed and chatted, every so often touching the pendant as if to check it was still there, filling them in on some of their adventures these past few months. Dan watched her wistfully. He hoped she'd hold on to these good memories. He'd give anything to change the past.

CHAPTER 25

Sarah leaned past her mother to look through the back passenger window, watching the postcard-like scenery flash by. Dark pines contrasted with the white glare of snow, interspersed with the occasional red barn. It was so pretty, so typically Canadian. She sighed.

Ange turned to her. "I know it's squashy. We'll be there soon."

"I don't mind. Sitting between you and Mum just helps me feel really close to you."

Her mother laughed. "Sounds like you enjoyed your time at Daniel's."

Sarah sighed again. "It was fantastic. And I'm so glad that you got the chance to come here. Muskoka is so pretty, isn't it?"

"It is lovely. But very cold."

"That's for sure. Hey, John, could you turn up the heat back here, please?"

The hike in temperature went some way to diminishing the chill in her feet.

"You and Daniel seem happy together."

Sarah smiled at her mother. "He's just amazing. He's so kind and honest and such a gentleman. Did I show you the necklace?"

"A few times, dear."

Sarah bit back a smile. Okay, so she'd been a little excited.

"He seems quite serious about you, judging by that gift."

Sarah glanced at her father in the front passenger seat, his mild expression not giving any cause for concern. "Dan loves me." Her voice grew softer. "I love him too."

Her uncle exchanged a glance with her aunt. What was that about? John sighed. "Just remember nobody's perfect, Sar."

"I know that." But Dan was pretty close. She bit her lip and looked outside at the snow-burdened trees. He wasn't perfect, but neither was she. Guilt streaked through her chest. Despite having had a few opportunities to talk privately, she hadn't wanted to spoil what little time they had together with such an epic bomb of an announcement. Besides, she almost dared to believe he might just love her enough to look past her short-comings and still see a future with her. Anyway, hadn't everyone wanted her to move on? Who better to move on with?

DAN GLANCED around the hotel ballroom filled with the happy hum of his teammates and other people here to celebrate the new year.

"Dan, my man!" Matt Reynolds slapped his shoulder. "How's it going?"

"Great. Just great."

"Gettin' a star for last night's game has gotta feel good, right?"

"Sure." He could count on one hand the number of games when he'd been considered worthy of star status by the League. He only hoped Sarah was impressed.

"Gotta love some old-school hip-checks," Reynolds continued. "The way you laid into Guillemette was pretty fun to watch."

"Wasn't personal." He'd apologized to Ryan for the big hit afterward, but his Bible study friend had brushed it off, understanding what playing hard meant.

Dan forced a smile as Reynolds started going on about the game they'd won against Edmonton last night. It was a mask he'd worn many times in recent days. He was the world's biggest fake. He might've won a star, but it didn't really matter. He wasn't happy. He hated the small talk. He didn't want to be here. All because this woman he hadn't even known seven months ago was going away, leaving a massive hole in his heart.

How could he have ever thought she was an ice princess? He'd had her so wrong. She was more like the sun. Everything from her hair to her smile to her kiss made him warm inside. How would he cope when the sun moved away?

Sarah looked up from her conversation with the coach's wife, caught his gaze, and smiled. He returned it even as his heart protested. Sarah was leaving. He was staying. And as John kept reminding him, if he was as serious about this relationship as those diamonds suggested, Dan still really needed to talk to Sarah.

SARAH DUSTED the icing sugar off her new dress. How did people eat these pastries without making a mess? Yet another one of life's little mysteries.

"You look gorgeous. That dress looks amazing on you."

She smiled up at Dan, glad she'd bought the vintage designer wrap dress in its striking pattern of amethyst, turquoise and ochre. It was nice to leave him with a good impression. She'd barely seen him since Christmas. He'd been busy with training and last night's game, so she'd put her last few days to good use:

packing, saying goodbye to friends like Georgia, and shopping, which had necessitated repacking.

She stepped closer. "What, this old thing?"

He drew her close, his hand stroking the back of her neck. Breath suspended as he leaned close to her ear. "Seems like a pretty new thing." With eyes lit with laughter, he handed her the price tag that had been attached to the back.

"Oh." Her cheeks were hot—what a surprise. "What can I say? I was excited about coming. I didn't have time to check."

He grinned. "You do excitement well, Princess."

"Do you think many people saw it?"

"Nope. Your jacket hid it before."

"Oh well." She laughed. "You know, it's not the first time that's happened." She leaned closer. "When I first started teaching I had parent teacher interviews, so to make a good impression I went out and bought a new suit. It was only halfway through the night that I discovered the tag was still swinging from my arm. I'm *such* a professional." His snort of laughter drew some curious glances. "So, thanks for looking after me."

"Anytime."

Her heart sank, but she kept the smile pasted on. *Anytime* couldn't last much longer; she had a plane to catch in just over twelve hours. Twelve hours? How could everything that needed to be said be shared in such limited time? Whilst glad she was attending the Leafs' New Year's Eve party, she was equally glad they were only staying for a few hours. She didn't want to share Dan a moment longer than necessary.

A tall figure moved into her line of vision and gave Dan a man-hug before kissing Sarah on the cheek. "Hey, good to see you again, Sarah."

She smiled. "Hello, Brendan. Happy almost-new year."

"Have you met my fiancée yet?" He drew forward a petite blonde. "Candice, this is Sarah."

Candice smiled at Sarah. "That's a gorgeous pendant."

"A gorgeous man gave it to me." She caught Dan's cheeks turning red. So adorable.

Another couple joined them, and she was introduced to Matt Reynolds and his very pregnant wife. She froze, the reminder of what would never be spearing guilt within.

"Hey, Sarah, you're the first girl I've seen Dizzy with in years."

Dan's smile grew tight, and he glanced at his watch.

"Hey, Brendan, what was the name of Dizzy's last girlfriend?"

Sarah glanced between Dan and his teammates. Why did he seem so tense?

"Lana something, wasn't it? From Pittsburgh, I think."

Had she heard that name before? Maybe it had been on one of the online forums she'd "accidentally" visited, when she'd googled *Daniel Walton's girlfriend* and come across a site filled with pictures few missionary daughters would likely have seen. Women dressed like that? Women talked about others that way? Had Lana been one of those names mentioned?

Regardless, he didn't seem too thrilled to be chatting about an ex, so she smiled and grasped his arm. "I'm reliably informed that I'm the only girlfriend at present."

Even if it might not last much longer. She sucked in a breath. Better get this over with. "Do you mind if we leave soon?" she whispered to Dan before apologizing to the others. "My flight leaves early tomorrow."

"You're sure?" Relief edged Dan's eyes.

She nodded, and they made their farewells. The thumping music was still echoing in her ears when they arrived back at John's parents'. They had graciously allowed Sarah's family to join John and Ange before their flight tomorrow, and Sarah figured spending these last few hours with Dan here would be wiser than at Dan's apartment. Who knew what she might be tempted to do on her last night with him?

Ange and Sarah's parents were seated in the front room, enjoying a final opportunity for conversation before tomorrow's early morning airport departure. "Did you have fun?"

Sarah nodded. "I enjoyed it, but I'm glad we left when we did." She had plenty of time now to talk with Dan. Or maybe they could just take the time to kiss—

"We plan on staying up all night, seeing as the flight's so early tomorrow." Her parents looked so pleased with themselves.

"You're such party animals," she teased.

"I figured it might help us sleep on the plane tomorrow. That flight's so long," her father said. "You're welcome to join us."

"Maybe later." Sarah dragged Dan away.

"We'd like to spend more time with you, Dan."

"Yes, sir. We'll talk later."

Tension roiled through Sarah's midsection as they sat on the little lounge wedged in the corner of the dining room, picking at a plate of leftover cheese and crackers.

Dan wrapped his hand around hers. "So, you enjoyed tonight?"

"Yes. It was good to go out. I can't believe how different I feel compared to this time last year." Last year. On the first anniversary of Steven's death. She'd remembered the anniversary this morning, had prayed for his parents, but though her mood had dipped, she no longer felt the roar of pain. *Thank You, God.* Her scarred heart was healing.

"You're certainly a lot happier than you were six months ago."

She shifted closer. "Thanks to you."

"Thanks to God." His eyes were sober.

"Well, God used you." Sarah's heart swelled. "You know I'm going to miss you, Mr. Walton."

"I'll miss you too, Miss Maguire." But his smile didn't reach his eyes.

"I'm sorry I won't be here for your birthday."

What to give the man who had everything, or at least could afford to buy whatever he wanted? Something personal that would make it hard for him to forget her. Her Heartsong experiences had shown the possibilities of basic recording using her laptop and the church sound system. She'd managed to record onto a USB flash-drive a selection of songs he'd said he liked, along with a couple of songs she'd written, and mix them using a program on her laptop. It was very personal, revealing her heart, and she hoped he liked it. She'd given the finished copy— and a CD of the same, mostly because she'd gotten to design the cute cover—to Ange for safekeeping until she could give it to Dan on his birthday in two weeks.

"If you call me, that will make the day special enough."

"Of course I will." She closed her hand on his and squeezed. The moment stretched, her heart pounding with intent. She was leaving in just a few hours, and this was her final chance to say what really needed to be said.

His grip tightened, his brow grooved. Was he okay? Her stomach tensed. After listening to what she had to say, he soon wouldn't be.

DAN WET HIS LIPS, his pulse thundering in his ears. *She's leaving. She's leaving.*

"Dan? Are you okay?"

"Sar, I don't want you to go. Please stay."

"You know I can't."

"Stay with Ange," he blurted. "Stay with me." *Marry me.*

"Dan, I—"

He couldn't bear to hear her protest, so he pulled her near

and pressed his lips to hers. Sarah sighed as their kiss length-ened, twining his hair in her fingers and kissing him deeply, more deeply still, twisting in her seat to press closer, closer, even closer.

He'd never forget the feel of her lips, the softness, the sweet-ness, the sense of breathing her in. Her lips were so inviting he pulled her as near as he dared, but still she didn't resist. *Oh man.*

His lips teased hers apart and all he was aware of was this moment of melting intimacy. This was so nice, so good, too good. His senses whirled, screaming at him to stop, until finally he wrenched away, lungs heaving. "You kiss way too good."

She touched her swollen lips, which curved upward. "Are you complaining?"

His lips felt weighted as he attempted to echo her smile. "It just leads to trouble."

"It doesn't have to."

But it had. The secret pressed in, heavy on his heart, up, filling his mouth. He wanted to say, needed to say, was almost out of time to say—

"Dan, I love you."

"I love you too, but…"

"But what?"

Oh, Lord.

It was time for the truth to come out.

CHAPTER 26

Sarah shivered. Something was very wrong. Dan was holding her hand tightly, but his hand was clammy and he wasn't looking at her. She could faintly hear the television in the front room, tuned to New Year's Eve celebrations from around the world. She'd already seen the spectacular Sydney Harbour Bridge fireworks several times throughout the day. North America now awaited its turn.

She glanced at the kitchen clock. Only twenty minutes until midnight. What did Dan need to say that was so important? He wasn't going to ask a certain question, was he? Anyway, if that were the case, he'd be happier-looking, wouldn't he? Not looking like this, like he wanted to be sick.

Although she well understood that feeling. She pressed against the dull ache in her forehead. She'd barely slept the past few nights, her stupid fears about what she needed to say and the coming separation making it hard to find rest. When they'd kissed earlier she'd found it so hard to let go, as a kind of desperate hunger for his lips had made her embrace him in a way she never had before. It was just as well Dan was such an honorable guy; these sensations she had when with him made her feel almost wanton, definitely not like a minister's daughter. *Thank You, God, that there are still gentlemen in the world.* She squeezed his hand, noting his flinch before he lifted her hand to his lips, giving the back of it a lingering kiss.

Her insides tensed. She really had to speak to him now. But Dan wasn't happy. Why? "Dan?"

He turned to face her.

"What's wrong?"

~

DAN SWALLOWED. He couldn't bear to destroy these last few hours together with the truth. But maybe she'd be okay. He'd been praying she'd be okay for months now. "There's something I've been meaning to talk to you about."

"Oh, Dan, there's something I need to tell you too—"

"Please, let me go first." He had to get this out. Any interruption might lock the secret in his heart forever. "I wondered if I should even tell you, but when Brendan mentioned it tonight, I realized secrets have a way of coming out. And I want to be completely honest with you."

He squeezed Sarah's hand one more time. "No one knows this except the people involved, and John and Ange. I told you something of it before in Muskoka. You asked me about forgiving myself and, well, it was about this."

"Okay," she said slowly.

"I was young, brash, and full of myself." He tried to tiptoe through the memories, picking out the ones that were real yet didn't expose him too much. "As you know I didn't grow up in a Christian home, didn't really think too much about God, and didn't care much about what I did or the results of my actions. When I got drafted, I went to Pittsburgh, playing there until I got traded to Toronto nearly eight years ago." He swallowed. "Lana was a girl I got to know too well."

Sarah watched him warily. "Too well? You mean—?"

He rubbed a hand through his hair. "I wasn't a Christian, but I knew better. I just didn't care." He swallowed, then just said it. "I got Lana pregnant."

He hung his head so he wouldn't have to see the accusing look accompanying the gasp he heard. He had to continue, get it all out now, while he still could. "I wasn't thinking, just got caught up in the heat of the moment, and…it happened."

He chanced a quick glimpse at Sarah's face, then wished he hadn't. She'd paled, staring at him with shocked, wide eyes. "You're a father?"

Dan shook his head. "Lana only told me when she started to show after four months. She'd kept it hidden—I think she thought maybe I'd marry her or something." Another intake of breath. "I was twenty-one, my career was just taking off, I was in the midst of talks about being traded back here, and then this happened. I didn't want it, even asked her to have an abortion."

He winced again at Sarah's gasp.

"She refused. I got desperate, said I'd give her money to just go away, but she wouldn't. It went on for weeks. I even prayed and asked God to take the baby."

Another sound of shock.

"I know I was selfish, but I was so desperate. Then it happened." He swallowed. "At seven months she went to a doctor's appointment, and they told her the baby had died. Just like I'd prayed."

He blinked back tears at the memory of that awful time. Lana had told him about his perfectly formed tiny son whom he'd never wanted, never wanted to see until it was too late. Even though he intensely regretted all that had occurred, he still wished the innocent life had been spared. *Lord, forgive me.*

Ange wandered into the kitchen, laughing at a comment from someone in the front room. She filled up a jug of water before noticing them huddled in the corner. "Hey, guys, you okay in here?"

Dan looked up. She must have realized what was going on, as her mouth rounded into an O. Ange cast a quick glance at Sarah, who sat with her head propped in one hand, before shooting him a compassionate look and slowly exiting.

"Sar?" He reached for her other hand, but she moved it away, the action enlarging the ache in his heart. He had to finish this, even though he knew the longer he talked the more she hurt.

"I couldn't say anything to my folks or the guys on the team." His voice cracked. "It was horrible. I was here, trying to deal with this, trying to figure out all this stuff to do with a new team. My head was a mess, and I was open to anything that would help. I'd known Boyd since high school, and when he asked me to church I finally said yes. I met John and Ange, told them my story, and found God. Later, I joined the online Bible study group, which helped too." Dan swallowed. "I'm so sorry, Sarah. I should have told you this before, but I... I didn't know how. I didn't want to hurt you."

He glanced up only to see her shocked face staring at him in disbelief. Her eyes...oh man, her eyes looked so, so sad, as if the light that had been there these past six months had been totally, irrevocably extinguished. The diamonds mockingly twinkled at her throat.

She hated him. The innocent minister's daughter didn't understand. Wouldn't understand. Cheers of "Happy new year" came from the front room.

He swallowed. "I know this is hard to hear, but I'm so glad we don't have any more secrets between us."

～

Oh, Dan, if only we didn't. Her eyes burned. So this was why he was so keen to be a dad. He'd made some poor choices in the past—who hadn't?—and eight years of regret had strengthened into cause. He wanted—no, he *needed* to have a chance at fatherhood. His confession, which he obviously thought so challenging, challenged her for quite a different reason. Any doubt about her decision had just crystallized into certainty.

God?

No answer, but a peace that this was right stole across her.

She exhaled. Lifted her head. Stared ahead at the cream kitchen cabinetry so she wouldn't see his face and lose her nerve. Allowed him to repossess her hand.

"Sarah, I'm so sorry I disappointed you. I know I'm not perfect."

Her lips pressed together. How many times had he warned her he wasn't perfect? And had she listened? No.

"Sarah? Please say something."

Her throat felt scratchy and raw. "I...I'm so sorry, Dan. It must have been so awful."

"Yeah." He exhaled brokenly, as if the weight of years was gushing free.

Compassion surged and she shifted to wrap him in a hug. "It's okay," she whispered, inhaling his enticing scent through clogged nostrils. "We all make mistakes, but God forgives us."

His clasp tightened into fierceness, as if he needed her understanding. But he didn't, she realized. Not really. He might have been a Christian for a number of years, but he needed to know God's mercy. To truly *know* God's grace. Her eyes filled, and she pressed her head against his neck. Just another thing she'd pray about for him when they were parted.

"I love you," he murmured.

"I love you too," she replied automatically. And because she loved him, she had to say this now. His pain only renewed her purpose, strengthened her resolve to finally share the secret blazing in her chest. The secret she should've shared after

Thanksgiving. The one that ensured she couldn't be part of his future. *Lord, help me.*

She eased back, swiped at the moisture leaking from her eyes.

"Hey, I didn't mean for this to make you cry."

"It's not that," she murmured.

"No?" He wiped at a tear, his face softening. "You mean us being apart? It's okay. We can do this long distance."

She summoned a smile. No, they couldn't. Not if she was choosing his best. "You sound like you're looking forward to being a father one day." Her casual tone was a relief. Surely he'd never guess the depth of emotion beneath that simple statement. Her heart sank as his face lit up.

"Sure. I'd love to be a dad." His dark eyes flickered with emotion. "I can't wait until I have kids. I see the older guys in the team when they bring their kids in, and I'm really looking forward to being able to do that too."

Sarah's smile stiffened, and she turned away to pull the clip out of her hair, allowing it to fall forward to hide her face. This was it. What she needed to share was going to hurt. She couldn't be part of his life anymore if having kids was his dream. And after all he had done for her, it was time to truly be unselfish and think of Daniel and his desires before her own. *But, God, my heart is breaking in two all over again.*

WAS SHE REALLY OKAY? He'd kind of expected her to lose her cool, to not understand, but she seemed strangely calm. That had to be good, right? Anticipation throbbed. Maybe this was his second chance. Maybe this was God's way of finally redeeming the dark hole of his past. *Please, Lord...*

But dreams of little children calling him *Daddy* paused at Sarah's continued silence.

"So, Sarah, how about you? Do you want to be a mom one day?"

She didn't answer for the longest time. Maybe she hadn't heard him. "Sar?" He reached for her hand, which lay limply in his grasp. She still wasn't looking at him. "Sar, what is it?"

There was a tiny pinched noise she was making now, like she was trying to breathe over pain. He recognized that stiff set to her shoulders too; it held the same fragility she'd shown the first time he'd met her.

"That's the thing, Dan." Her voice was faint. "I don't even know if it's possible for me to have kids." She removed her hand from his. "The accident messed me up a fair bit inside, and the doctors don't know if I'll ever be able to fall pregnant, let alone have children."

No. *Lord, no.* He stared straight ahead at nothing, fisting his hands as if it would help him rein in emotion. He took a deep breath, then exhaled really slowly. No. God couldn't be so cruel as to let him finally fall in love with someone only to never let him be a dad. His dearest dream couldn't be gone.

He knew now how precious each little life was, what a blessing children could be, that they were a gift from God. He wanted to be able to impart the God stuff he'd learned over these past years, to raise kids who were free, who lived loved and didn't always need to try and earn their father's approval, like he'd always felt he'd had to. To never have that chance...

Fresh regret warred with a surge of intense envy of his brother. *God, this isn't fair.*

He glanced across at Sarah. What would this mean for her? He hoped he'd been able to hide his distress in time.

∼

SHE'D SHOCKED HIM. His knuckles had gone white and his jaw had tensed, his slight Adam's apple dipping as he swallowed. "Sarah, I—"

Sarah held up a hand. An imp in the back of her mind sang like a game show host: *but wait, there's more!* She blinked it away, her voice satisfactorily cool as she answered. "I've had almost two years to adjust to this, so I understand this is a lot to take in." She took a deep breath. *Be brave.* "I think it best we break things off, because I don't think our relationship should continue when it means you might miss out on your dreams. I mean, I know you haven't promised anything, but I just don't want to hurt you any more."

Lord, being unselfish is so *hard.* She couldn't look at him. One brief glance had been enough to show his pale face, his stricken eyes.

"What? No, I don't get it. I don't understand."

"I'm just not the right woman for you." Her eyes filled. *God, help me keep it together.*

"How can you say that? Sar, I love you."

"You say that now, but what happens if this—if our relationship does continue and one day you resent me? I couldn't bear that. I love you and don't want you to miss out on your dreams. So you need someone else—"

"No. We can work this out. Just talk to—"

"Dan, we can't," she whispered. She reached to unclasp the necklace.

"Sar, what are you doing?"

She held out the necklace, but he refused to take it, so she let it fall on his lap. "I can't take this."

"Sarah, please. This doesn't have to be the end."

"It does with me if you want kids. I'm not going to get in the way of your dream."

∽

SHE COULDN'T BE SERIOUS. There had to be another reason. Maybe it was his confession earlier. "Sar, you'll never know how much I regret all that happened with Lana."

"I'm getting some idea."

"Sar, I promise I haven't seen Lana since back then."

"You haven't?" Her brow furrowed. "Why not? You should. She must've been as devastated as you. She's probably been carrying this pain as well."

Was she seriously suggesting he go visit his ex? There had to be more to this. "Sarah, I really don't want to talk about the past. I want to have a future with *you*."

HER HEART WITHERED at his look of hurt. But she had to stay strong. Be unselfish. This was for his good. "I'm sorry." She stood. Forced her feet to stay as he shot upright, when all she wanted to do was run away. *Run away!*

"Seriously? You're just gonna leave? After everything, this is how it ends?" His voice cracked. "What did I do wrong?"

"It's not you, Dan, it's me."

His laughter was brittle. "That has to be the lamest line ever." He reached for her hand. "Sarah, please talk to me."

"Dan, I'm so sorry. I didn't mean to hurt you." *And I'm praying that one day you'll understand why I'm doing this.* She mustered a smile. Took a step back. "Goodbye."

"Wait. You don't want me to take you to the airport anymore?"

"What's the point? So we just break up again?"

"I don't want to break up. Sarah, please—"

"I love you, Dan, but I can't be part of your future."

He grasped her hand. "Princess."

She stilled, eyes on his fingers wrapped lightly around her

wrist. Slowly his fingers unpeeled. "Goodbye," she whispered before fleeing to the sanctuary of her room.

ANGER PUMPED THROUGH HIS VEINS, driving him to pace, to move to follow her up the stairs, but he hesitated at the realization her dad and uncle a room away might have a problem with that. Stuff it. He hurried up two stairs at a time, then took a guess that the closed door was hers.

"Sarah?" He tapped on the door. "Are you in there?"

No reply.

"Sarah? Please. We need to talk. Don't shut me out." He banged a little harder.

The door remained closed.

He tried the door handle, but it was locked. Disbelief whooshed through his chest. "I thought you loved me," he rasped, knowing he sounded pathetic and desperate, resisting the urge to pound on the door. He didn't want to raise attention from those downstairs. Neither did he want to barge in. Not when there were too many explanations needed already. Maybe that's what had freaked her out, and the awkward intensity of the moment meant she'd felt the need to escape. "I'll go downstairs and wait for you, okay?"

Still no sound from within. Was she even in there? "I love you," he said desperately, forehead against the door. And he did, he always would, no matter how far away she might be.

A sound on the stairs shifted his attention to John's dad. Dan straightened, inched away from the door, shot for a smile that wouldn't make him look shady.

"You okay there, son?"

"Yes, thanks, sir," Dan lied, obeying the implied request to return downstairs.

Nauseous and feeling dizzy, Dan returned to the kitchen and

slumped on the couch where only a few minutes earlier he and Sarah had been passionately kissing. Seriously? How could she kiss him like that only to dump him the next minute? Or had that been her goodbye kiss?

He bent over, head in his hands, and groaned, the sound echoing through the kitchen. What a stupid way to end things. He closed his eyes, breathing deeply, trying to calm his rapid pulse, clasping his hands to stop the shaking, his mind a whirl of confusion. For all her messy explanation, it still wasn't clear. What had she meant by saying she couldn't be with him? Was she still hung up on Stephen? He felt like an ulcer wanted to explode in his stomach; he was starting to hate the dead man. He hissed out a breath and shook his head. No, this wasn't just about Sarah's past; it seemed to be about the future. But what? What had her exact words been? What had she said? What had he done wrong? Would she come down and properly explain?

"Dan?" Ange's soft voice drew his attention to the door. "Are you okay?"

Nope. He had the weirdest feeling he'd never be okay again.

"Where's Sarah?"

"Upstairs."

Her brow knit as if she'd heard the tremor in his voice too. "You told her?"

"Yeah. Then she told me."

The lines on her forehead deepened. "Told you what?"

"Did you know she can't have kids?"

"What?"

He'd take that as a no, then. He pulled the necklace from his pocket. "She gave this back. Told me she wants to break up."

"Oh, Dan."

"Then she ran upstairs, wouldn't open the door to talk to me. I thought she loved me, but…" He managed a broken laugh. Yeah, he felt as stunned as Ange looked. "I've got no idea what to do."

"Let me go talk with her."

"You can, but I think her mind's made up." Emotion clutched his chest, and he glanced away, breathing slowly to regain control. "She doesn't want me at the airport. Doesn't want to see me anymore. I don't know what to do."

"I'll talk to her. I'll get her to call you, okay?"

He nodded, but her words seemed devoid of any certainty. "Yeah, well, just in case that doesn't work, can you give this to her mom for safekeeping?" He poured the necklace into her hand. "I can't explain this to them right now. It's too, too—" He swallowed, once more overcome with the rawness of it all.

"I will. Make your goodbyes, and I'll text you as soon as I've talked with Sarah."

"Thanks."

"Don't give up, Dan." She offered a wry smile. "You know she's always been a little more passionate than other people."

One of the things he loved about her. He nodded. Moved to the front room. Put his defense face on. Deflected their queries about Sarah's absence, instead offering his best wishes for their safe travels.

"Are you coming to the airport in the morning?" Lindy asked.

"I have a flight to Montreal." Later in the day. But they didn't need to know that. Nor that their daughter wanted nothing more to do with him. His chest physically hurt with the effort to keep the ache contained.

"I can understand Sarah might wish to say her goodbyes tonight rather than in the morning." Lindy smiled gently, and he could see her daughter's likeness. "Sarah's probably too upset to be down here right now."

Dan's gritted-teeth smile slipped. Yeah, but not for the reason Lindy thought. "Well, it's been good to meet you. Happy new year." The words tasted hollow in his mouth.

"You too, Dan." She hugged him, then he shook Sarah's dad's hand.

"I'm sure we'll stay in touch," James said.

Yeah, nothing to be sure of there.

"If ever you're in Australia—"

"Thanks." He couldn't do this anymore. Any second the mask would slip. "Bye."

He escaped the house and hunkered in his Jeep, turning on the engine to blast warmth through the vehicle. But he didn't move. Instead, he watched his phone, waiting, waiting, for Ange's text. As soon as it came, he'd hurtle straight back in there and kiss Sarah until she saw sense.

Two minutes passed. Five. Ten. He shivered. Cranked the heat higher. What would people say if they saw him out here? Would someone call the police?

"Come on, Ange," he muttered between prayers God would soften Sarah's heart.

The shriveled remains of his pride begged him not to text Sarah, but desperation demanded he did. I LOVE YOU. PLEASE TALK TO ME. DON'T GIVE UP ON US.

No answer came. Another five minutes passed, ten, fifteen, despair gnawing a little harder with each tick of the clock. Should he return? Pound on her door until she spoke with him?

His phone blinked with a message and, half-crazy with trepidation, he read it.

SORRY. SHE'S ASLEEP. WILL LET YOU KNOW WHEN I TALK TO HER.

Ange.

His heart splintered a little more. Looked like barging in there wasn't gonna be an option. Maybe it really *was* over now.

His body trembled, as if it now finally understood the magnitude of what had just happened, the agitation spiraling outward from his very core. He blinked back emotion and gripped the steering wheel as if it held a lifeline to sanity. It couldn't be true. It couldn't be over. They couldn't be done. *God?*

No answer. He heard nothing but a yawning howl of desolation.

Eventually, conscious he'd need to be at the airport in eight hours, he forced himself to drive through the snowy streets as the mocking sounds of "Happy new year" came from a few straggling revelers.

Once home, he huddled on his bed. But sleep wouldn't come. He pulled the blankets closer, staring into blackness.

Happy new year? It was anything but.

CHAPTER 27

$\mathscr{E}$verything about this felt wrong. Sarah stared, bleary-eyed, at the bleak cityscape as they drove to the airport. Last night's conversation had replayed on a continual loop, rendering sleep impossible, her tears and memories of Dan's strained face and broken voice constant reminders of the pain that she'd caused. Ange had tried to talk to her, but she'd pretended to be asleep. What could she say? Trying to be unselfish only seemed foolish now. And she was tired, *so* tired of keeping her emotions in check.

This morning's rush had allowed no time to talk. Now, as they passed various landmarks, she tried not to recall the special moments that had meant so much. Not that restaurant, not the hockey games, nor the time up the CN tower—no, she wouldn't think about that. Instead, she listened to non-committal comments about the weather and traffic until they finally made it to the parking station.

Their tickets were processed, and after hugs and more good-byes, they boarded the plane. It was so cold. Too cold. She wrapped another too-thin blanket around her. Flicked open her phone where his messages still dwelled: I LOVE YOU. PLEASE TALK TO ME. DON'T GIVE UP ON US.

She loved him. Which was why she'd done this. For his sake. *Lord, help him see that.*

"You okay, princess?" her father asked.

But the reminder of the pet name just made her tears leak more.

DAN OPENED his eyes and stared out the plane window. Everywhere was stark, snowy whiteness. His eyes burned at the brightness, so he shut them again. His eyes were too tired from no sleep, his brain too blurry from grief, and his heart…

His heart was numb, like deep frostbite had taken hold overnight. He couldn't coherently answer any questions from his teammates about last night, so he'd plugged in his music and feigned sleep. Fortunately, some of the others seemed to be tired from last night too, snoozing in their wide, private plane seats on the short flight to Montreal.

But he bet nobody craved rest as much as he did.

"SAR? ARE YOU AWAKE?"

Sarah blinked sleepily at her mum, then gazed around the cabin. She'd forgotten how long these flights took. By the time all their connections were accounted for, it felt like they'd been traveling in a glorified tin can for days.

She stared out the plane's window as the Pacific blue ended at high sandstone cliffs before the sprawl of houses began. She just wanted, needed, to be home.

Her mother leaned closer. "Sar, you want to tidy yourself up a bit?"

"You worried they won't let me back in the country?"

She slopped her hair into a ponytail. No point looking like someone to concern the security people at the airport. She didn't want more delays.

She deplaned and did the usual arrival routine, but the lack of sleep combined with the awful memories hiccupping in her soul had left her feeling almost tipsy, drunk with exhaustion and grief. When they finally got through customs, she nearly cried in relief as she saw Rebekah waiting for them.

"Hey, sis." Rebekah wrapped her in a big hug, her strawberry-blonde hair tickling Sarah's nose. "It's good to see you."

"You too."

Rebekah moved to hug her parents. "Joe and the girls are at the beach, so I'm free to be your chauffeur now. Have you got all your bags?"

Sarah wearily followed her parents and sister to the car, half listening as they shared about the past few days. She stared vacantly out the backseat window as heat steamed off the road and the browned grass and shrivelled plants of limp gardens flashed by.

It was weird being back. Summer, not winter. Cars driving on the left, not right. Everything felt a little off-balance—wrong, not quite right. But the sight of the two-story home brought comfort: familiar smells, remembered sounds, shared memories. And nothing beat her own bed and pillow. But rest still proved elusive. After thirty minutes of closed eyes and no sleep, she tiptoed past her parents' bedroom and made her way downstairs.

Rebekah looked up from a magazine. "Couldn't sleep?" Sarah shook her head. "Want a cuppa?"

Sarah followed Bek to the kitchen. She sat at the table as Bek sliced fruit cake and soon placed a steaming cup of tea in front of her. "Thanks."

Rebekah took a sip and gazed at her. "So, how are you?"

"Okay."

Her sister's brows rose.

"Well, not great."

Sarah filled her sister in on what had happened with Dan. How many days since her world had shattered? Crossing datelines and so many time zones made everything feel extra weird. She finished explaining and couldn't help but notice the pleat in Bek's brow.

"Wow. That's a big call. I didn't expect you to see it that way."

Sarah frowned. She hated to ask, but if she didn't ask Bek now, she'd worry the comment for the next few days until her sister finally explained. "What do you mean?"

"I'm actually kind of impressed. We both know you can get pretty emotional at times, so I'd have thought you'd be all upset that he hadn't lived up to your Mr. Darcy ideals."

"He made mistakes. God forgave him. And I...I want what's best for him."

"What if you are God's best for him?"

Her heart stuttered, but she folded her arms. "He wants kids, Bek. I can't have kids."

"How do you know?"

"Rebekah Elizabeth—"

"Calm the farm, Sarah." Bek held up a hand. "I'm not suggesting you did anything. I'm sure Dan was a gentleman."

Sarah thought back to the times they'd kissed, the passion that'd always ignited in her belly, and how every time, it had been Dan who had stopped things progressing further. A shameless *I'm not very sorry* sprang to mind, and with a guilty heart, she looked at her sister. "He was." She, on the other hand...

Bek sipped her tea and eyed her. "So does this mean you've sworn off all relationships, or are you just going to look for a man who doesn't want kids?"

"What? How can you say that? I don't want anyone else."

"So let me get this straight. He loves you, and you love him, but you don't want to be with him. Yeah, makes perfect sense."

Sarah propped her head in her hands and closed her eyes. It must just be jet-lag-induced tiredness that made her reasoning seem so blurry now. Something about him needing to know the depth of God's mercy rather than papering over the heart cracks via a relationship with her. "It made sense over there."

"So did you talk to him about this or just dump it on him and run?"

She winced.

"I'm gonna take that as a dump and run, then."

"Bek, I'd really appreciate a little more understanding now."

"I bet you would," her sister continued relentlessly. "And I bet Dan feels the same."

Her heart panged. Oh, he'd need to know God's mercy, because she sure as heck wasn't displaying any. Her eyes opened to see the cake sitting on the table. A memory flared of something Dan had once said. *Here you can have your cake and eat it too.*

No. She couldn't. She wiped at a tear.

Bek grasped her hand. "Sar, from everything you and Mum and Dad have said, it's obvious he loves you."

Maybe he had, once upon a time. He probably didn't anymore.

"And he's patient."

True.

"And he's kind."

Hold on. He wasn't exactly Saint Daniel. "It doesn't change the fact that he wants to be a dad and I can't give him that."

"Did he propose?"

"No," she said in a small voice. And now he never would. Her chin quivered, and her eyes filled with fresh tears.

～

THUMP!

Dan gritted his mouth guard as he shoulder-slammed Tyler Woletsky into the boards at Madison Square Garden. The past couple of games, several members of opposing teams had been on the receiving end of his personal frustration. He wasn't really proud of it, but the coach seemed pleased with his ramped-up level of intensity, and the points he'd received had been good. He skated back to position, intently watching the play. A chirp from New York's Jenner saw Dan shove him, something that could've escalated into punches if Dan hadn't pretended to not hear the expletive that dropped from Jenner's mouth. Instead, he skated past, focused on the game, yelling encouragement to his teammates as sloppy play and agitated Rangers resulted in a powerplay for Toronto. Tim Carruthers, New York's captain, pointed to the bench, which saw Jenner skate away, shaking his head. Tim might be captain of one of the Original Six teams, but Dan didn't envy his friend now.

The powerplay began, and Toronto's extra man advantage saw New York hustling as they tried to prevent Dan and his teammates from scoring. He focused on managing the puck at the blue line, moving it to the shooting lane for Brendan to bang it home. Andrei Novak stopped him, shooting the puck wide, forcing Dan to collect it off the boards as the two minutes counted down.

He needed to stay dialed in and concentrate on hockey. He needed all the distraction that tough workouts and hard, physical games could provide. He skated back into position at point, ready for the puck when it finally slid his way.

He stopped, steadied, and slapped the puck toward the net, hoping his teammates' traffic in front would confuse New York's goaltender. The red light above the net flashed, the space filling with the crowd's boos.

"Goal!" Brendan skated up and thumped him on the shoulder. "Nice one, man."

Tyler skated past, offering Dan a nod that said no hard feelings before commiserating with his teammates.

Dan skated off to the side to fist-bump his teammates. He grabbed a seat on the bench, glad to suck down another energy drink, and watched the replay on the Jumbotron. But his teammates' cheers and the applause felt empty tonight.

He watched the action on the ice for another few minutes until his final shift. Skate, hit, scramble for the puck, another hit, blocked shot, clearing shot, then watching the play down the other end of the ice for the last minute of the third period. He tried to be excited that the team finally had some momentum going its way, but honestly, there were more important things in life.

The siren sounded, signaling the end of the game. They'd held off the Rangers by a goal, so there were some relieved faces from the coaches.

"Good game, Dizzy."

"Thanks." He should be happier, but all he wanted was to be away.

He followed the team down the tunnel, handed his stick to the equipment staff, stripped off his gear, and headed to the shower. The hot water massaged away some of the aches, but not where it really hurt. But then, what could help soothe the hollow spaces of his heart that had been carved out by a certain girl?

He closed his eyes. This past week had been like a bad dream. He still couldn't figure out what had happened. His memory kept playing tricks on him until he was no longer sure what had even been said. Had she really said something about not being able to have kids, or was that just another part of this nightmare? No kids? He couldn't even begin to start processing how he felt about that.

He wasn't ready to call her yet either. The road trip meant he'd barely had a moment alone, and anyway, he didn't know what he could say. Not that she seemed to want to talk to him, having ignored his texts and emails. And who else could he talk to? Boyd? Hardly. He couldn't very well say anything to his family. How humiliating. The first woman he ever tells his family he loves dumps him two months later. Why hadn't he kept his mouth shut and played it cool instead of getting caught up in her excitement like that was something he could do too? And as for confiding more in John and Ange, fat lot of good that would do. They'd be on Sarah's side for sure.

The questions and uncertainty swirled around his brain like a whirlpool. The more he thought about it, the further he got sucked into insecurity, and now he was drowning in dark doubt. And seriously, with his background, he should've known it couldn't work out. She'd grown up with missionary parents, had traveled the world singing praise songs to Jesus. She'd always be too good for him. She would never really understand him. He groaned. Questions from the past kept bubbling up, boiling lava below the surface, but he didn't have the emotional energy to face them just yet. Why had he ever thought someone like Sarah could fall in love with him? Who had he been trying to kid?

"Dude," Brendan called, "you're gonna drown in there."

Dan switched off the water, toweled off, and changed into street clothes. He glimpsed himself in the bathroom mirror, barely able to recognize the man staring back at him. Haggard. He'd never really known what that word meant, but he bet he looked it now. It was like he'd aged fifty years. Fatigue lined his face, shadows underscored his eyes, and it was like his mouth had forgotten how to smile. Smile? How could he ever smile again?

He was a ghost. Numb, frozen, emotioned out. Walking, talking, somehow even playing hockey, but nobody could really see him. Somehow he'd kept it together enough this week to fool his teammates, who seemed to think he was experiencing some sort of extended New Year's hangover. A few more discerning others like Brendan and Marc attributed it to Sarah's return to Australia, and his coach had looked at him strangely a couple of times, but still, no one really knew. Thank God the road trip meant he'd skipped the online Bible study this week, and the travel schedule hadn't permitted time to talk with Beau or Tyler.

Marc walked into the dressing room. "Hey, Dizzy, how you doin'?"

Dan nodded but ignored the question. "Good game, man."

The goalie fist-bumped Dan, then wandered out to face the barrage of media—media Dan was super glad to avoid.

Dan grabbed his phone and wallet, glancing down at his phone. His stomach clenched. He hadn't had the heart to change the screensaver yet, so Sarah's gorgeous face still smiled at him. How was he doing?

His chest grew tight, and he flicked his phone off, shoving it into his back pocket.

Thank God for hockey. The road trip had kept him busy, the physicality of the games against Beau's team, Montreal, then the Rangers demanding his full attention. But it was only the years of training that meant he could operate on autopilot; his brain and body knew what to do. But he still felt this distance, like he was watching his life through Plexiglass. He'd love to feel anything, but his heart felt dead.

CHAPTER 28

Sarah shifted self-consciously on the seat, staring at the carpet, the brown, cream, and navy swirls as familiar as the freckles on the back of her hands. This first week back in her father's church was strange. Everything had changed, yet nothing had. Once again she was sitting in the same church seat, surrounded by the same people, the first Sunday of a new year, feeling like her heart, her life, had shattered.

She mouthed along to the songs, half-listened to the announcements, frowned at a typo in the church bulletin, then glanced up, her heart shrinking in horror. Dad had a tradition of allowing congregation members to share during communion, and now Hugh and Heather, Stephen's parents, stood at the microphone. After Stephen had met Sarah on the PNG mission trip, he'd switched churches. His parents had followed and joined the church not long after.

"We asked to share today," Stephen's dad began. "As many of you know, our son was killed in a car accident just over two years ago."

As he took a deep breath, Heather smiled at Sarah gently. Emotion burned Sarah's eyes, and she looked down again.

"These past two years have been very difficult, as no doubt you can understand, but in recent weeks we've felt like God has been showing us something we believe He wants us to share with you all."

Heather read from notes. "Lamentations is a book we've gained much comfort from. In chapter three, the author describes how he feels down and despondent because bitterness and affliction seem to surround him."

She looked up and caught Sarah's eyes again. "We understand that feeling only too well. But"—she read from her notes—"verse twenty-one gives such encouragement: 'Yet this I call to mind and therefore I have hope: Because of the Lord's great love we are not consumed, for his compassions never fail. They are new every morning; great is your faithfulness.'"

Hugh took over again. "On this first Sunday of a new year, we want to encourage you all to remember, God loves you, and no matter what your past year has been like, God is doing new things. The past is done; it's time to embrace the new. Our prayer is that this year we all might grow closer to Him so we can extend God's mercy, grace, and forgiveness to those in our world."

The assistant minister then led the congregation in communion, but Sarah's heart had snagged on Hugh and Heather's testimony. Throughout the remainder of the service, the words kept resonating: *Extend God's mercy, grace, and forgiveness to those in our world.* Surely this applied even to those on the other side of the world.

Lord, touch Dan. Heal him.

Despite the sticky heat of January that the ceiling fans did nothing to abate, Sarah shivered.

DAN SHIVERED. Muskoka was so cold. But maybe that was just the state of his heart. The empty bleakness of Muskoka in winter seemed so appropriate these days.

At least he was away.

He was tired of speculative looks from his teammates and friends. He was tired of pretending to Josiah and the Bible study guys that he was okay. He was tired of phone calls never being answered, of sending texts and emails that never received a reply. He was tired of this gnawing pain, as bitter as the breeze outside on the snow-capped deck.

Dan stared out the window as the wind tossed the trees, sending showers of snow to the ground. Even John and Ange's support was starting to grate. There was only so much "let it go" encouragement he could cope with. Now he had to do it.

After wrestling with how to escape, he'd eventually screwed up enough courage to ask the coach for a day's personal leave that—thank God—he'd been granted. He glanced up as gray clouds banked ominously above the lake.

A cold draft ruffled the pages of his Bible. Dan flicked back to the middle. In Psalms he found the hurting, contrite David, and though David's trials had been vastly different to his own, it seemed a similar brokenness. Many times David had despaired, yet the songs he'd written showed that as he'd chosen to thank and praise God, his perspective had changed.

Dan's lips twisted as a conversation he'd had with Sarah months ago dimly echoed. Thankfulness. He shook his head. More practice-what-you-preach time. Why had he ever thought he knew so much?

Psalm thirteen stood out for some reason. He tried to read on, but his eyes kept wandering back. He reread it, David's words about feeling forgotten, feeling sorrow, feeling overcome by his enemy, resonating through his soul. Yeah, David knew what he was talking about, for sure. Not that Sarah was his enemy, although she definitely wasn't acting like his friend right now. He read verse five aloud. "'But I trust in your unfailing love; my heart rejoices in your salvation. I will sing the Lord's praise, for he has been good me.'"

David seemed to have changed his tune, gotten more hope-filled. Dan studied the psalm again as his heart stirred. *Lord, I'm trying to trust in Your mercy. Help me remember Your salvation.*

It was strange how he could remember so much about the day he got saved, but his soul was so quick to forget how bountifully, graciously, and generously he'd been dealt with by God.

His memories flashed back to that horrible time when he'd first prayed that prayer. Maybe his pain now wasn't just because of Sarah rejecting him; instead, it was a symptom of deeper issues unresolved. And regardless of what happened with Sarah, he needed—he *needed*—to get this sorted out once and for all. Was God's grace big enough to cover his sin? Really? He might've talked the talk for years, but did he really believe God had forgiven him for what he'd prayed?

"I don't deserve it, God," he rasped. "I prayed You'd take my son's life."

Moisture bled from his eyes as his heart wrenched again. How many times had this memory crept in, guilt and regret slithering to poison his faith?

"Lord, help me."

His gaze fell to the page. To the words *unfailing love.* God's love didn't fail because of his stupid, selfish prayer. Did it? Had it?

No.

No. Trusting in God's unfailing love meant trusting Him despite Dan's own weakness. It wasn't like his sins had ever taken God by surprise.

Just that thought swelled new emotion, and he wiped his eyes, grateful he was alone so nobody need see the wreck he was. So much for being cool, calm, and collected. He wasn't tough. Not at all.

But somehow, right now it didn't matter. He'd rather look like a fool than play pretend a second longer. He needed his heart healed. Once and for all. *Lord, help me.*

He glanced at the verse again. Dan was saved, just like David had been. And if David could be forgiven for adultery and murder, then Dan could know he'd been forgiven too. But knowing it and *knowing* it had always been two separate things. That could change today.

"Lord, help me know I'm forgiven, once and for all."

He stilled, the emotions buffeting inside gradually easing, as his attention snagged on verse six, on David's challenge to worship God despite his circumstances. Maybe Dan just needed to sing like David had. Not that Dan really wanted to. But verse six indicated it had been more an act of David's will, a choice. Maybe Dan could try out his rusty pipes anyway.

"Amazing grace, how sweet the sound, that saved a wretch like me, I once was lost, but now am found, was blind but now I see..."

White puffs of condensed air told of the sub-zero temperature outside. Good thing no one else was around to hear him; his singing sure wasn't in Sarah's class. But strangely, the words seemed to have extra impact. He *was* saved. He *was* found. God's grace truly was amazing. And even though the bitter cold rushed into his throat, the rawness felt good. Maybe this was a bit like David, out in the wilderness, singing where only God could hear him—only with a vastly different climate, of course.

Dan continued declaring God's mercy, forgiveness, and love out loud. It was weird, but praising God in the midst of pain was actually working. Hearing his own voice declare God's promises was reverberating in his soul, clarifying his beliefs, solidifying his faith. That nullifying X for failure he'd always felt branded on his soul really had been turned on its side, cross-shaped.

Somehow, the more he sang, the more he seemed to truly

hear, like his spirit latched on to truth. He *wasn't* a failure. He was forgiven, branded eternally with a cross. These past years were testament to God's grace, and he didn't have to keep carrying his shame, because Jesus carried it for him. God's grace meant the old was gone, his sins dealt with, and because of what Jesus had done, as far as God was concerned Dan was whiter than the snow that gleamed outside. He *was* clean. He *was* forgiven.

Breath escaped as a rush of gratitude and thanks expelled regrets and guilt. He scrubbed his face with his hands, feeling drained but somehow like his heart was lighter than it had been for years. Maybe not everything would work out as he wanted, but Sarah's leaving had at least led him to this release. *God, thank You for Your forgiveness. Thank You for turning things around for good.*

The leaden sky opened, but the gentle padding of snow felt like a hug. Who knew what other miracles lay in his future?

Help me to trust You. And please—he swallowed—*bless Sarah.*

SARAH SAT AT HER LAPTOP, staring at the long list of unopened emails. Most were from Canada, which meant most would need to stay unanswered for a while longer. The past days had been too busy to deal with questions from the other side of the world. And until she had clarity about her relationship with Dan, she wasn't up for emailing anyone else. And while she prayed for him constantly, she sure wasn't up for emailing him.

She shook her head. No. Emailing was no way to sort out this mess. What she had to say had to be said, needed to be spoken aloud. Not that she could talk to him very easily either. Those first few days she'd been exhausted from grief-enhanced jet lag. Then the Leafs' schedule indicated he'd be away on a road trip, which made it challenging to know if he was traveling, training, playing, or resting. Time zone differences just complicated everything so much more, so she still couldn't have talked to him, even if she'd wanted to.

Which she hadn't.

But the whirl of questions and regrets kept dancing around her soul, refusing to settle. She couldn't take much more of this uncertainty. She'd need to do something soon.

Just not now.

Sarah stood up and stretched to release the kinks from her body. She moved over to her bedroom's window, gazing out at the summer haze that had settled across terracotta and gray rooftops as the cicadas burst into evening song. She drew in a deep breath and caught the tang of the eucalyptus leaves from the old gum in the backyard. Her lips lifted. Who'd have ever thought she'd be glad to smell that particular scent after a gum tree's role in the accident? But then, God had a way of turning things around, didn't He? Just like He had after last Sunday's service.

She leaned her head against the wooden window frame as memories stole to awareness again. After the congregation had disappeared to the function room for a welcome home lunch for her parents, she'd spent some time down the front just talking to God. Who was she to think she knew better than God, that she could actually know what was in her future? Surely if she claimed to trust God, she needed to trust Him with every aspect of her life.

Tears had filled her eyes, silently spilling down her face. Maybe she'd missed the actual beginning of the new year, but any day could be a fresh start as far as God was concerned. She'd sat down the front and finally, tearily, let God have His way.

Okay, fine, God. I don't know what You want from my life, but it's Yours. Whatever You want. But it'd be great to know what You do want.

There'd been no great booming voice from heaven, only a gentle whisper in her soul. *Trust Me.*

Please help me trust. I don't want to live in my emotions or out of my fears. And help Dan. I think I've broken his heart.

The special lunch had been going on for some time when she'd finally made her red-eyed appearance only to be met at the door by Heather and Hugh. Up close, she could see how much they'd aged in these past two years.

"Hello, Sarah. How are you?"

She'd forced a smile. Since Stephen's death, there'd been this new awkwardness with his parents. It had been so hard to speak to them, wondering what was safe to talk about. Now it felt even harder.

"Your mum and dad have kept us in touch with how you've been going overseas. You're looking better."

What had they told them? What could she say? She was better. Time away had given her perspective, but falling in love with Dan had given her hope. She couldn't say that, wasn't even sure if it was true anymore, so she'd kept it simple. "I feel a bit better."

"You know we only want the best for you." Heather had gently grasped her hand. "We've been praying for you, Sarah. This new year, don't keep living in the past. Stephen wouldn't have wanted you to do that. Go, do what you need to do to have the life you feel God wants you to lead."

Her patient face held wise eyes that said she knew more than she could say. Heather's gentle hug had made Sarah's eyes sheen with tears while her heart writhed at their empathy. It wasn't like she'd needed their permission, but their blessing brought further release. Mercy-laden release. For whatever the future might hold…

Knock knock.

Sarah turned to see her mother standing at the door.

"Sar, what are you doing?"

"Oh, just thinking." She rubbed her bare arms.

Her mother moved to stand next to her. "Are you worried about the job?"

Sarah shrugged. "Not worried about the job, exactly."

Her mother's eyes studied her seriously. "Are you thinking about what this means for your future with Dan?"

Sarah's eyes filled as she nodded.

"Oh, Sar." Her mother drew Sarah into a gentle hug. "Remember what I told you just before you left for Canada?"

Sarah nodded against her mother's hair. "Be brave."

"Sweetheart, you can trust God with your future. With all parts of your future. Which means your job, your relationships, including Dan."

She shook her head. "I really hurt him."

"He knew you had to leave."

"No. I broke up with him, Mum."

"What?"

With a broken voice, Sarah finally explained about that last painful night in Canada.

"Oh, Sar." Her mother clutched her closer. "Why didn't you say anything to us?"

"It hurt too much," she whispered.

Her mother stroked her hair. "Love is hard. Loving others is hard. I understand your reasons, but Dan..." She sighed. "Poor Dan."

Moisture spilled from Sarah's eyes. "He can't love me anymore."

Her mother drew back, studying her with compassion. "God has placed within you such passion, which can be a double-edged sword at times, can't it?"

She nodded. How easy it was to live in emotions.

"Part of that is the capacity to love richly and deeply, which is a wonderful trait." Her mother's arm tightened around Sarah's shoulders. "But remember, God has also given you strength and the ability to think clearly. Sar, I know you'll make the right decision, and whatever happens, you will face it with courage and grace."

Sarah swiped at the wetness on her cheeks. "I'll try."

Her mother hugged her. "I'm always here if you want to talk. Do you want to talk?"

Sarah shook her head. "I think I know what I have to do."

Her mum gently patted her cheek, then moved toward the door. "Dinner will be ready in twenty minutes."

"Okay. Thanks, Mum." Sarah exhaled, blew her nose, and moved back to her laptop, the screensaver displaying a photograph of her parents. *Thanks, God, for Mum and Dad.*

She opened up the updated résumé and application letter she'd sent off three days ago and reread them again. Nope. They both seemed clean of errors. She bit her lip. If she got the job…

On Monday, her father had received a phone call after which he'd looked at her curiously. "That was Mr. Phillips from the local Christian Community School. The music teacher is on maternity leave, and the replacement teacher suddenly had to move to Tasmania to care for her mother, and he was wondering if I knew of anyone who could fill in for the next two terms on such short notice." He'd smiled. "What do you think I should say?"

Sarah had stared at him. Was this some of God's direction? Hadn't she prayed about that only the previous day? If so, it must mean Dan was out of the equation.

Fighting back the roar of emotion, she'd nodded stiffly. "I guess it can't hurt to send my résumé in."

Her father had smiled gently at her. "And we keep trusting God, that He'll work everything else out, in His timing."

Sarah had exhaled. Yep, she'd sorely needed that reminder. No more living in sorrow. "We trust God."

The last few days had been a rush of résumé updating, applications and interviews, and catching up with more family and friends, leaving little time or emotional capacity for much else until now.

She flicked over to her emails again, and bit her lip as her mother's words sang in the back of her head: *courage and grace.* Maybe she should read them.

Be brave.

Sarah finally clicked and opened the messages. The more she read, the more her heart twisted.

Tomorrow was Dan's birthday.

CHAPTER 29

*D*an got to church late and settled into a seat near the back, behind Brent Karlsson's parents. Last night's tough game meant his body needed all the rest he could get, and he didn't mind missing the mandatory meet and greet time at the start. The songs were good reminders of his time in Muskoka, recalling the need to trust God and praise Him regardless of the circumstance. That was important, especially when he spotted a redhead near the front. His heart thudded. She'd come back for his birthday?

But no. The woman had moved, her profile revealing a stranger. The sharp shock of disappointment stayed with him through the rest of the announcements until John's guest-preaching sermon helped remind him of what he was here for. Later, after Boyd, Patrik, and other friends had come up and done the happy birthday congratulatory thing, Ange found him.

Her face was troubled as she held a small package in her hand. "Dan, I know the past two weeks have been tough, but John and I want you to know we're praying for you, and for Sarah." She gave him a sad smile. "I don't know if you've heard from her?"

He shook his head no, and her shoulders slumped.

"Sarah gave me this to give you for your birthday. Happy birthday, Dan."

He unwrapped the blue tissue paper to discover a CD and USB flash drive. The CD's cover was a picture of the two of them months ago at Niagara Falls, the obvious joy on their faces and the way Sarah fitted in his arms as they grinned at the camera causing a fresh stab of pain. He blinked, willed the burn away, then looked up.

"She put in a lot of hard work to make that for you. I know it may be hard to listen to now, but..." Ange bit her lip.

He forced a smile. "I won't throw it away." How could he? No one had ever done something so meaningful for him. And even if he couldn't have her, at least he'd have a permanent record of how she'd once felt about him.

He made his escape to sit in the car. Took a deep breath as he plugged in the USB and waited for the sound to begin.

"Hi, Dan! Happy birthday! I hope you enjoy this, and I hope you have a wonderful day. I wish I was there with you. I love you!"

He swallowed the roar of pain. Her voice sounded so happy he could almost see her smiling at him. Sarah introduced the first song, one of his favorites from church. The congregation was making their way to the parking lot, so he drove off to meet his parents and brother at a restaurant for lunch, vacillating between smiling at the corny jokes and the way she sang, to despairing that he'd never see her again. He sat in the restaurant's car park until the last song had finished, praying to maintain his composure over the next few hours. Playing Sarah's songs before meeting his parents had been a really bad idea.

He got out and met his folks inside, managing the small talk and even a few smiles through the first courses, murmuring his appreciation for his parents' and Sam's gifts as dessert was served.

His mother leaned forward. "So, what did Sarah give you?"

At least he could say something. "She gave me a CD she made. It's awesome."

"A CD?" His father's lip curled.

"Yeah, she wrote all these songs, played them, sang them, recorded them…" His voice trailed off. "It's really special."

"That's nice, dear."

His mom's condescension dug defensiveness on Sarah's behalf. "Did I ever tell you Sarah was part of this famous music group called Heartsong Collective?"

"Really?" Sam looked mildly interested.

"Yeah. They toured the world, did a bunch of albums she wrote songs for. Her songs are sung in churches everywhere."

At the mention of churches, his dad's face tightened.

"I see. So, how is Sarah?" His mother looked at him expectantly.

Oh God. "Uh, I haven't spoken to her for a while."

"Really? She hasn't contacted you for your birthday?"

Lunch threatened to reappear. This was awful. He could either let them think badly of Sarah or tell them the truth. He sighed. It was time for the truth about his past to come out anyway. He kept it short, only too aware of the shock and disappointment evident in their faces. Happy birthday indeed.

His father shook his head. "Why didn't you tell us, son?"

He shrugged. "I didn't know how to. I'm sorry." When would the apologies stop? When would his father's disappointment end?

"I can't believe this is the first we're hearing of this. This is important. This, this…Lana woman could've taken you to the cleaners! You could've ruined your career."

"Dad." How could his father see it like this? It was dollar signs all the way with him.

"I'm sorry, Daniel," his mom said. "We liked Sarah—and her

parents, for that matter. I know you cared about her, and I'm sorry she won't be part of the family one day."

Dan blinked. "You really liked her that much?"

"Yes, we did."

What—even Dad approved of her?

His father nodded. "She was a little forthright at times, but on the whole Sarah seemed like a lovely, sweet, innocent girl. I'm not surprised she left you, considering what you did."

Dan wanted to roll his eyes, but that wouldn't go down well. "Dad, it happened years ago."

"Maybe it did. I think you should count your lucky stars you escaped so lightly."

Dan shook his head. "It wasn't lucky stars. I'm not proud of what I did, not happy about any part of it, but I am glad that it made me realize who God is."

"God?" His father snorted. "I don't want to hear about any more of this God nonsense."

"Dad." Dan fought to stay calm. *Lord, help me say this right.* "God has brought me more peace and joy than anything—more than hockey or money or anything else. I'm more...more me because I know who God is."

"That's nice."

His insides writhed. Mom's encouragement sounded so patronizing.

His father pushed back his chair and stood. "Daniel, I hope you've had a nice birthday, but I've had about enough now. I think it's time for us to go."

"Okay. Bye, Dad." Dan swallowed the rejection.

"Bye, dear. Happy birthday." His mother gave him a little hug before following his father outside to the car.

Dan exhaled noisily, slumping back in his chair away from the table. Why couldn't his parents be more like Sarah's, with all that warmth and huggy stuff? He wished—

Nope, no good wishing.

He turned to Sam, who'd watched it all silently. "You going too?"

"No. It's your birthday, Dan. You still need to celebrate."

"I'm not really in a celebrating kind of mood."

"Well, I'm here for you, bro."

Dan blinked back the burn in his eyes at his brother's compassion as Sam continued. "I guess I get it now. I've always wondered what it was that changed you." Sam shook his head. "My memories aren't great. I know I was struggling with school, but I do remember you changing from being an arrogant S-O-B to someone almost completely different." He grinned. "I liked you more after."

Dan managed a wry smile. "I liked myself more after meeting God too."

"So…" Sam hesitated. "Can you tell me more about…about this God thing?"

Dan blinked. Wow. So not what he'd expected. But hey, if God wanted to use Dan's failure to bring Sam closer to Him, who was he to argue?

Over the next couple of hours, they slowly picked at their desserts, drinking copious amounts of coffee as they continued their discussion at a slightly more private table next to a big window where they could watch the snow falling outside.

Sam looked at him seriously. "You still love Sarah, don't you?"

A giant ball of heartache lodged in his throat. He could only mutter a raspy, "Yes."

Sam was thoughtful. "Maybe I'll have to have a word with this God of yours, see if He can change her heart or something."

Dan clenched his jaw to avoid tearing up again. That wouldn't be cool for his baby brother to see. "You do that. I need all the help I can get."

·　·　·

AFTER WATCHING a stupid action movie with Sam that had finished far later than he'd wanted, Dan finally felt ready to face his lonely apartment. Funny. While today hadn't been the best of days, his brother's new interest in God was nothing short of amazing. He'd even promised to think about coming to church sometime.

Dan pushed out a smile, recalling a prayer made not too long ago in Muskoka. Something about God somehow turning things around for good?

He unlocked the front door and threw the keys on the side entry table, noting the missed calls on his phone, which he'd earlier switched to silent. He bet one was from Luke. He always tended to ring him late on his birthday, like he'd forgotten and been reminded by his wife or Mom and now felt obliged to call. Dan grabbed a bottle of water, then pressed speaker and settled down on his favorite couch that overlooked the city lights. Sure enough, Luke's voice soon filled the room, wishing him a good day. Nothing deep or terribly personal—they didn't have that kind of relationship—but it was still nice to hear.

Luke's message clicked off, and Dan stared out at the cityscape. *God, help my family know You.* The birthday congratulatory messages continued: Mike, Beau, and a few other Bible study guys, Brendan, a friend from college, a manager from the club. Most people these days were too busy to care to send much beyond an impersonal text or email, so it was nice to actually hear a voice if he couldn't see them. Then the next message came on.

"Hi, Dan, it's Sarah."

His heart clenched and he sat up straighter, as if it would help him hear better.

"I, uh, wasn't expecting to get your voice mail…"

She made a noise halfway between a nervous giggle and a sigh, and he was instantly transported back to those early days, back in Muskoka, when she'd look at him with sassy tease. He blinked. *Stop it. Don't go there.*

"Anyway..." There was a long pause before her voice resumed again, lower in pitch and more controlled than the breathiness of before. "I wanted to wish you a happy birthday. I guess it's getting late there, but I hope you enjoyed the day. I don't, I don't know—"

The message clicked off. Dan groaned, then pressed the next message. What didn't she know?

"Um, hi again, it's still Sarah. Gee, your voice mail doesn't give much time to leave a message, does it?"

Why didn't she get to the point? This was agony.

"Anyway, I...I don't know if Angela gave you the CD I made, but if she did, then I hope you know...that I still mean everything I said on it."

Dan's heart began a crazy pitter-patter.

"I...I love you. I'm so, so sorry for how I treated you before I left."

Her voice dropped to a whisper, and Dan leaned closer to hear.

"Please forgive me. I understand if you don't want anything to do with me, but in case you still want to be my friend, I'll be sitting by the phone today, thinking of you and praying for you. I...I miss you heaps."

The message stopped abruptly. He scrolled to see if there was more, but no, that was it. He quickly replayed it, listening again to the sound of her magical voice, his brain tumbling over the information, trying to make sense of it all as hope battled doubt.

Dan pushed his head into his hands, staring at the phone like it was Aladdin's lamp and Sarah could suddenly materialize from it. He glanced at the clock and winced at how late it was already. He had training tomorrow, but if this phone call went the way he prayed for it to go, the lack of sleep would most definitely be worth it. He pressed recall and the +61 international code flashed up followed by a long series of numbers, then he heard the double dial tones.

∼

SARAH LAY with her head on her arms, the prayer never far from her lips. Ever since laying her heart on the line several hours ago, she'd been whispering Bible verses and praying in a futile attempt to not allow the worry to crowd in. Surely he would have got the message by now. She'd calculated the time differences. It was late there. He must not want to speak to her. Jagged pain speared her heart, and she closed her eyes. *Oh God, it must be too late.*

Her phone's jangling ringtone woke her. "Hello?"

"Sarah?"

She swallowed. *Please, God.* "Dan?"

"Yeah."

Her heart danced a jig. *Thank You!* "How are you?"

"Okay."

No, he wasn't. He sounded cold, stiff. Didn't he want to speak to her? Not that she'd blame him if he stayed cool toward her forever. But then why had he called? "Did you have a good birthday?"

"It was okay." He sounded so distant. And not just because of the number of miles that stretched between them.

"I…I guess you got my message. I miss you."

He sighed and Sarah filled with sudden fear. She'd done so many dumb things and apologized so many times. What if he didn't want her friendship anymore?

"And I miss you."

"Really?"

"Of course. But Sarah, I need to know. Why'd you call it quits?"

Her eyes filled. "Dan, you're the nicest man I've ever met." She didn't qualify it; it was true. His mix of joy and playfulness balanced beautifully with a caring, serious side. He'd proved himself patient, honest, and kind over and over again. Stephen paled in comparison. "I love you, and I really, really appreciate all that you've done."

"But?"

Her chest tightened. Truth time. "But when you asked me about whether I wanted to be a mother one day, well"—she swallowed—"the doctors aren't sure how much internal damage was done in the car accident, so I don't know if I'll ever be able to have kids." She sighed. "I felt so envious of Marguerite." The shame was so deep. "And you were so excited, and obviously do want kids, and so, at the risk of sounding presumptuous, there's not much point being together if we want different things."

There was a long silence before he finally spoke. "Don't you want kids?"

"Well, yeah, of course I do, one day. But that would take a miracle! And if I can't, then I don't want you to miss out. Especially now I know..." She winced.

"Now you know about my past," he concluded.

"Yes," she whispered.

Silence ticked away, begging her to break it. "Oh, this is so awkward."

He gave a short bark of laughter. "Actually, awkward is being dumped without a proper explanation."

Ouch. Why couldn't he see what she meant? This was for his good. She dragged in a breath. "Dan, you should just move on and find someone who can give you what you want in life."

"Like who? I don't want anyone else."

Did that mean he still wanted her? *Don't be so stupid.* She swallowed. "I'm sure there's someone out there." Sarah forced her lips to move up even as her heart sank lower.

"See, Sarah, that's the problem. I thought I'd found someone nice, someone who I even dared to tell my family that I love. But she doesn't love me." He sounded so sad. "I wish I knew what I did wrong."

"Dan, you've done nothing wrong."

"Then why?"

How to explain the hesitation she felt had come from God? She considered words, then tossed them back into the torrent of unutterable things cascading through her head. *Lord, help me, please!*

Dan offered a raspy sigh. "Maybe I'll never be good enough for you, but at least I know now that God really has forgiven me."

He did? Her eyes filled. *Oh, hallelujah!* One of her taut heart-strings eased.

"So, that's what it is, then." His voice was flat. "I'm not good enough for you."

"No! No, you're way too good for me. But don't you see? I don't want to get in the way of who you should really be with. I want you to be able to"—she almost choked on the word—"to be a father and have your dreams come true."

He exhaled. "So it's not me? It's not my past, the fact I'm not Mr. Perfect?"

"I think you're pretty perfect," she said in a small voice. He had to be to put up with her.

He sighed. "Sar, as hard as it may be for you to believe, I want *you*. God does miracles all the time. Anything's possible with God."

"I know."

"Do you? Because if you did, you'd be willing to trust Him with this, like I am."

His words pummeled inside. Was she really so weak in her faith? *Lord, forgive me. Help me trust You.*

A beat stretched into two, three. "Sarah, I love you."

Her throat cinched. "You do?"

"Yes. And I want to be with you, regardless of what it means for the future."

"Oh, but Dan, I could never ask you to make such a sacrifice—"

"You're not asking. I'm telling you what I want. Sar, I love you. You can trust God. And you can trust me. Sarah, we can work it out. But we need to talk about things and not just run away when things are difficult."

She nodded. Realized he couldn't see her, so murmured, "I know."

"Why do you run away?" he asked softly.

She chewed her lip. Had she always done this? No. "I used to be braver," she admitted. "But for months when I was in hospital, I had to lie there while people gave me bad news. I had nowhere I could go and hide. Because of my injuries, I couldn't even turn over in bed and hide my tears when they told me Stephen had died and I'd missed his funeral. I hated not having even basic privacy to do that."

It had been awful, like she'd been trapped in a snow-globe, everyone watching her in all her vulnerability while her life had been shaken again and again. But there'd been no pretty sparkles falling. Only tears.

"People didn't want me to cry much either, worried I'd lose my strength and not focus on getting better. So now, if there's something that bothers me, I try to get away if I can. I hate feeling helpless," she confessed.

"I don't mind the tears, Princess. I just don't want you running. We need to talk about things, okay?"

"Okay." She sniffed.

"Are you crying?"

"No," she said, wiping at a stray tear.

"Are you sure?'

"No."

"Don't cry, Princess. It's all good. We're all good."

"Are we really?"

"Really."

Oh. She closed her eyes as her soul played the "Hallelujah Chorus." *Thank You!* "I know I'm not great at trusting God, but I am trying. Very trying, apparently."

He gave a wry laugh not exactly filled with genuine-sounding amusement.

"I always thought low maintenance was something to aspire to, but it's just not me. I'm afraid I'll always be more passionate than some. Besides, where would the challenge be?"

SARAH'S last comment drove home the memory of another prayer. How many months ago had he been complaining to God about the lack of women who piqued his interest? He'd wanted a challenge. Just hadn't realized Sarah would test him quite so much. His mouth lifted at the corners. God sure had a funny sense of humor.

She continued. "I remember someone once describing you as being someone who didn't like to back down from a challenge."

"Really?" The lip tweak grew as his own words were quoted back at him.

"I guess I took it too much to heart. I thought I'd become your ultimate Aussie challenge." Her laugh crossed with a sigh as she dropped her voice. "Dan, please don't ever back down."

His throat thickened. "I won't," he rasped.

"I know it's hard to tell sometimes, but I do, I really do love you, Daniel."

His eyes blurred while his heart lifted higher than it had for weeks. He swallowed to get his voice under control. "I love you too, Sarah." If only he could be there, to see her, hold her, read her face and know that everything truly was okay. "Hey, Sar, can you put me on video call?"

"Sure."

Seconds later, his screen showed her sitting in what he guessed was her sunshine-filled bedroom, hair in a high ponytail, her drawn features relaxing to echo his small smile. Another knot in his soul released.

She exhaled. "I really am trying, you know, to not do the whole emotional thing. Rebekah, my sister, is right. It's not fair on you."

"Sounds like I'll have to meet your sister."

"I wish you could. She seems to be a fan of yours."

"Long-distance fan, eh?"

"I reckon you'd get on pretty well. You both don't mind telling it like it is. Darn it."

"So does this mean if I email you again, you'll actually reply?"

She laughed. "You should check your emails more often, bud."

"Hold on." Dan tapped open his phone to find a whole bunch of unopened emails, most of which were from her. He opened the first, a big *I'm sorry*. The second and third were similar… She must have spent the day replying to each of his emails. Cute. He returned to the call. "Thanks, Sarah. Today hasn't been the easiest of days, but it's finished on the right note."

She propped her chin on one hand, green eyes wistful. "I wish I could be there to give you a big hug and a bigger kiss so you know exactly how I feel."

How he wished for that too. But with training starting in a few short hours, he needed to save that for his dreams. After wishing her goodnight, he lay on his bed reliving the past half hour. His birthday had miraculously turned into a happy one after all. *Thank You, Lord.*

CHAPTER 30

Everywhere Sarah went it felt like she was the lead in a Disney musical. The sun shone brighter, flowers looked like they might burst into song, small children laughed, and old people smiled. Hope danced in her heart as her spirits soared, and it was all she could do not to skip across the quadrangle at school or sing at the top of her lungs.

Even Mondays at work—never the easiest of days, for who didn't prefer weekends after all?—were good, this school proving better than some she'd taught at. The staff and parents, even the students, were so supportive, and she'd been enjoying teaching this Year Seven class these past two weeks. They were practicing on their keyboards today. Thank God there were enough headphones for everyone. Listening to twenty kids trying to thump out a tune was a headache and a half waiting to happen.

"Delivery for you, miss."

She looked up from her desk where she was marking a quick quiz. And gasped. The bunch of red roses was big enough to make every excitable twelve- and thirteen-year-old stop and stare in open-mouthed amazement. "Wow, miss, someone really loves you."

"You think?"

She raised her eyebrows at the perpetrator of that comment.

"Sorry, miss."

Sarah drank in the fragrance of the vivid blooms, moving some roses aside to discover a small envelope. After encouraging the class to get back to their songs, she opened the card.

Happy Valentine's Day - and every day.
I love you, always. Daniel.

How? Oh. She'd wondered at her mother's secret smile this morning. Dan must have organized this with her. Her heart glowed. How thoughtful was he?

Every teacher in the staffroom seemed to have heard about her amazing bouquet, and it set the mood for a really good day. Then later that afternoon at home, she discovered a small package on her bed. She carefully unwrapped the paper to find a velvet bag, like one might see from a jewelry store. Heart racing, she opened the drawstring and, through blurry eyes, saw the diamond pendant complete with a note.

Please wear this and know how much I love my princess.

She blinked back happy emotion.

Her mother's voice came from the door. "Dan gave it to Ange, who gave it to us, even though she didn't tell us what was inside. He sent the note later."

Oh-h-h-h.

That night, she video-called him, gushing about the roses and especially the pendant and note. "You're a man of faith, aren't you?"

"How do you mean?"

"Believing we would be together."

"We didn't come this far not to be together. This long distance thing might be hard, but it won't be forever."

Please, God, no.

"Hey, that's the door. I wonder who's calling so early? Back in a sec."

She waited, heart thrumming as she desperately hoped it was what she'd planned. Given the time zones, the only way they could spend any of Valentine's Day together when he had a road trip and a game tonight was for her to stay up late while he snatched time first thing early in the morning before heading to the airport. And if all went to plan…

She heard a murmur of voices, a laugh, then the closing of the door. A few seconds later, she saw him holding his own bunch of flowers. Yes!

He smiled. "Someone sent me roses."

"Really?"

"I wonder who?"

"Maybe there's a card."

His lips hitched up. "Maybe there is." He searched through the fancy wrapping—it appeared the florist had a little too much raffia-love—and found a small envelope. Glanced at her. "You know, nobody has ever sent me roses before."

"No one?"

"Well, actually, now I think about it, a couple of crazy fans sent me some a few years back, but that doesn't count."

"Indeed it does not," she said firmly.

"So, I wonder who sent these?"

She grinned, and he laughed.

"Remind me never to play poker with you, Princess. Your face can't hide a thing."

"Go on, read the card," she begged.

He opened the white envelope and drew out a piece of paper, then looked at her. Oh, thank goodness everything seemed to have worked out well. It was one thing to have imagined how this could go and quite another to see all the little arrangements falling into place.

"I wasn't expecting a letter," he murmured.

"Obviously, someone who loves you *very much* must have arranged this."

His eyes met hers, and she knew a savage longing to be there.

"I wish you were here with me," he said.

"I wish you were here with *me*."

"Yeah. Your pictures make it look way warmer there than here."

"It's our school's swimming carnival tomorrow, so we're glad to be spending the day at the pool when it's sunny. Those things are never too much fun when it's rainy or cool."

He nodded, his gaze returning to the words she'd penned several weeks ago, before sending it express mail to the Toronto florist for inclusion in Dan's bouquet.

Dear Daniel,

I found an old baby name book a few days ago and looked up your name.

Did you know that Daniel means "God is my judge"? I love that, because if God is our judge, then we know we are judged according to what Jesus has done. God judges us according to His grace and love, so no one else's opinions need really matter. God sees you and He loves you.

I know you live up to your name so well, displaying love and grace to those who don't deserve it, having been on the receiving end so many times (hello). Thank you.

I love you so much, and I appreciate you more than words can ever say, my darling Daniel. And I hope you know you really are MY darling Daniel.

Yours forever,

Sarah

She watched his face as he read her words, the tenderness there renewing warmth inside. He rubbed his lips, head tilting a little, before his gaze crept up to meet hers.

"Sar."

She couldn't read his expression. Was it too much? Too gushy? She was trying to not live out of her emotions so much, but it didn't mean she couldn't express the fullness of her heart to someone she trusted, someone who had proved to hold her heart like a precious treasure.

"I really wish we weren't going to Vancouver today."

Huh?

"I wish my plane was going straight to Sydney instead."

She sighed. "Me too."

"One day," he promised.

"Can't wait."

"Hey, thanks for the flowers, and the note," he said, holding up the paper. "I'm going to put this somewhere where I'll always see it. I've never thought about my name in that context before, but you're right. So right."

"Miss Right?" she teased.

His dimples flashed. "Absolutely."

His intense look fluttered her insides. "I'll be praying for you, and for me, to know this more and more. It's so good to know that God sees us through what Jesus has done. The stuff of the past is covered by His grace."

"And the stuff of the future, too, so we can trust Him," he reminded her.

She nodded. How she loved this man.

"Speaking of, have you done that thing you said you'd do?"

"That's later this week."

"I'm really proud of you, Sar. And remember, whatever happens, God's in control."

"Just as well, huh?"

"I need to go get ready soon, but hey, just so you know, this is my best Valentine's Day ever."

"Mine too." Stephen had never really believed in Valentine's Day, thinking it too commercial. But she wasn't about to let any such principles get in the way of feeling the love.

"Hey, I love you."

She touched her pendant. "I love you. I hope you have a great day. And crush the opposition."

He laughed. "That's my girl. Talk soon?"

She nodded. "Whenever you can."

Even with the fourteen-hour difference in time, they could make this work. Dan was right. God's grace was big enough to cover the past and their future.

Now was the perfect time to be brave.

Sarah lifted her chin and, for the final time, went through the email message again. Satisfied it said all she needed to say, she started typing the address, copying it to the others who also needed to hear her words. Courage seemed more familiar these days, likely an effect of spending time with Dan, who encouraged and believed in her. And now she knew how short life could be, well, what was the point in not trying? One life on planet Earth, a brief dash between her birthdate and death before eternity. Why not make the most of this short space and do all she could? Hence the email today, one of apology, regret, and, she hoped, a second chance.

She reread it, attached the sample, then, hands shaking, pressed return and heard the swoosh as it raced through cyberspace to land at a particular inbox on the huge church campus not too far away.

"God," she exhaled, "whatever You want. If not this, then that's okay. I trust You."

She clutched the diamond pendant at her throat, and her

heart steadied. Whatever happened, she was putting herself out there. The days for shrinking back were done.

⁓

"HEY, IT'S DAN THE MAN!" Vancouver's Chris Thomas exclaimed as Dan joined the Bible study Zoom call. "Good to see you."

Dan smirked. "I wasn't sure if you'd say that after the last game."

"Dude, I'm just glad to have survived the puck blast intact, and that you didn't hip-check me the way you did poor Zac. What'd you eat before the game? Rocket fuel?"

"I hope your wife forgives me for the scar."

"She will." Chris touched his newly decorated cheek. "One day."

Dan lifted a hand to the other guys to a chorus of heys and hellos. It seemed a Monday night when nearly everyone was there, even though the online Bible study crossed four time zones. Brent, Tim, Beau, and Tyler were all on Eastern time like him. Chicago-based Pastor Josiah Abrahams, who often led the study, was on Central time, as was Luc Blanchard from Winnipeg. Calgary's Mike and Edmonton's Ryan Guillemette were on Mountain time, then Chris and Jai Mullins were on Pacific time, in Vancouver and San Jose respectively.

"Anyone else think we're getting so big we may need to split this group?" Mike said. "Maybe have a separate one for those of us living over here in the Western Conference."

"Dude, I love living in San Jose, but making these times gets a little hard," Jai confessed.

"Yeah, I bet that has more to do with your new wife than any time zone issues," Tyler said with a waggle of his eyebrows that brought a round of laughter and Jai's red face.

"Time zones can be a killer," Brent said. "I remember trying to juggle things when Holly was in Australia. I'm so glad she's here with me now. Man, that's far away."

"Sure is," Dan agreed without thinking.

Brent's head tilted. "Now that sounds like the voice of experience. Who do you know on that side of the world?"

Dan chewed his lip. He hadn't really told any of the guys about where things were at with Sarah. But he supposed there was no time like the present. So he told them, to a chorus of catcalls and tease.

"So, tell us more," Chris demanded. "What's she do, where does she live. Deets, man. Spill."

"She's a music teacher, works in a high school—"

"Oh, so she knows how to keep you in line," Tyler razzed.

"She lives in Sydney," Dan continued.

"Cool city," Brent said, nodding.

"How'd you meet?" Ryan asked. He and Luc were now the only two single guys in the group.

He told them, which led to more teasing about loving your neighbor and the like.

"I'm happy for you, Dan," Josiah said. "He who finds a wife finds a good thing."

Dan choked. "We're not at that stage yet."

"Yet?" Tim asked.

He needed to change the subject, and fast. "So about tonight's study—"

"Nah, we want to know more about this chick," Chris said. "Sorry, Pastor Jo."

"It's fine." Josiah lifted his hands. "I want to know more too."

Ten expectant faces waited for Dan to speak. Oh well. Here went nothing. "Have you heard of Heartsong Collective?"

There were a few nods. "My wife loves their music," Beau offered.

"Bree does, too," Mike said.

"We often use their songs here in church," Josiah said.

"Yeah, well, she's one of their main songwriters. She used to tour with them a few years ago, took some time off, and is now writing for them again." Dan felt a ping of pride that she'd faced her fears and sent that email last month. Heartsong's powers-that-be had immediately sent back confirmation that yes, they'd love to meet with her and see how things could progress. Sarah's excitement when she told him had been next level but slightly tempered by questions of what this could mean, because she didn't want to necessarily tour with them again.

"But if they were to ask you?" Dan had asked, not liking the trickle of selfish fear his question produced. If they wanted her to tour, what would that mean for them?

"Then I'd have to see where things go," Sarah had said. "There are others who join for occasional events, so maybe something like that could work out again. But that's a lot of ifs. The fact they're wanting me to submit songs is what's really important."

"Wow," Mike said now. "That's so cool."

"For real?" Beau asked. "What's her name?"

"Sarah Maguire." Dan's chest might've expanded a little as he said her name. How awesome to think someone like her loved someone like him.

"Are you serious?" Tim asked. "Lacey's listening in, and she says she *loves* Sarah's music."

"Maggie says the same," Beau added with a nod.

"Dude, is this her?" Chris asked, holding up his phone.

An image of Sarah from years ago, dressed like a rock star, arms high as she led worship in front of thousands, filled Chris's screen.

"Yeah, that's her." He'd seen that video so many times it was burned into his brain.

"Wow," Ryan said.

Luc whistled. "She got a sister?"

"Yeah, but she's married."

"Luc, you look sadder than a kite in a hailstorm," Beau teased. "Don't worry, you'll find someone soon."

The other guys laughed at Luc's rolled eyes and crossed arms.

"Or maybe not, if that's how he tries to charm the ladies," Tyler said to a round of snickers.

"That's cool, Dan," Jai said. "I'm real happy for you."

"Thanks. She's pretty awesome," Dan confessed.

"Sounds like we'll need to get together sometime and have all these wives meet your girlfriend," Tim said.

"That'd be good. Maybe sometime in the summer might work."

The study finally started, discussion about praise seeming particularly pertinent today. Dan had so much to praise God for, so much thanks for His grace toward him.

The meeting concluded, prayer requests were offered and prayers were prayed, then the conversation veered to hockey stuff, as some of the guys had to leave due to family or other commitments.

"Yeah, no surprise, but we're not tracking to make the play-offs," Dan admitted.

"Maybe you could come to the Philippines with me," Mike said. "We're running another MPFG missions trip, and anyone who wants to come is very welcome."

Dan's chest sparked with interest. "Sarah's parents were missionaries in Papua New Guinea."

"Wow. I don't even think I know where that is," Luc said.

"Maybe you should both come," Mike suggested.

"When are you talking?" Dan asked.

"May. June. We're pretty flexible but will need to lock in flights soon and make sure we've got all the necessary paper-work filled out."

"Send me details and I'll pray about it," Dan said.

"Me too," Luc said.

"Oh, I have to go," Jai said. "Allie's just driven home from work, and she'll be super excited to meet your Sarah one day, Dan. But hey, just putting this out there, I'd really like to see another group for those of us more in the northwest. Just in case anyone else is interested."

"That'd work for me," Chris said.

"And me," Mike agreed.

"We could be the Northwest Ice division," Ryan said.

"Would that include Winnipeg?" Luc asked.

"Do you know your geography?" Brent scoffed. "You know that Winnipeg is virtually in the center of North America, right?"

"It is?" Luc sighed. "Guess that's a no."

"I'm sure we can make allowances," Josiah said. "That is, if you guys want me to be involved."

"You know we do," Jai said. "You and me started this thing, so we can continue it."

"For sure," Mike said. "Gotta go. I'll be in touch about the missions trip, okay?"

Dan nodded and joined the chorus of farewells, his heart thumping with anticipation. His hockey season might be drawing to a close, but it looked like God might have plenty of exciting things still left in store for this summer.

CHAPTER 31

Only a few days to go. The past school term had flown by. Sarah changed the date on the board, tidied her desk, picked up the assessment tasks requiring marking, then locked the door.

She collected her bag from her desk in the staffroom. "Bye, Suzy. Have fun tonight."

The languages teacher smiled. "Thanks for the birthday flowers."

"You're welcome."

"Enjoy your afternoon."

"I always do!"

A smile lit Sarah's heart as she got in her car for the short drive home. School had been such a blessing these past three months. Smaller class sizes meant she could get to know her students better, which helped with classroom management. As the school's only music teacher, she did have a higher demand placed on her for programming purposes, but that was good. It stopped her thinking about how much she missed Dan.

She parked in the driveway, gathered the papers, her bag, and jacket, and headed inside. The house was quiet. Her family must still be out. She switched on the kettle, stroking her pendant as she waited for the water to boil. After making a cup of tea, she headed upstairs, threw her bag on the bed, then sat at the computer.

Nope. No new emails. She fought the disappointment. Dan had said he'd be busy. In between training and games, he was planning a trip to the Philippines after the season to visit a missions organization his friend Mike Vaughan was involved with. He'd sounded so excited. His first mission trip.

Her smile drew into a sigh. The crazy clashing schedules of work and time differences meant Zoom calls and FaceTime were a rare treat now. She missed Dan's smooth voice. She missed his arms around her. She missed his gorgeous eyes. She'd stare for hours at the photos she'd taken and the beautiful picture he'd given her and remember happier times.

Sometimes she'd get up super early to try and watch his games over the internet, even though the distorted images and sound fluctuations made it a challenge to see or hear anything about her Dizzy. She'd even visited the David Jones department store in the city, tracking down that aftershave he wore just so she could be reminded of him. Her mouth twitched. How desperate did that make her?

But she *was* desperate! Sure, she knew how to put on a nice suit and a big smile, but inside she was dying of Daniel deprivation. God was still on the throne, anchoring her soul, but day by day, this yearning to see Dan only intensified.

Sarah took a deep breath and exhaled. One day. Maybe in July, when she had mid-year school holidays, he could visit. That'd be *so* good. She quickly emailed him the idea, then sat back in the office chair, twirling her hair round her fingers. Dan would be busy for the next few weeks with his final games and other team commitments, his trip preparations, and of course his family stuff, like Easter, then being a fantastic uncle for his soon-to-be-born niece or nephew. It was probably a good thing

Luke and Marguerite lived in Vancouver, otherwise Dan would always be over there babysitting, his emails made him sound that excited. She smiled. She hoped Marguerite and Luke liked the koala toy she'd mailed them as her gift for the baby.

A yawn escaped and she stretched her arms. At least the April school holidays were only three days away. She'd never been accused of not fully appreciating her holidays, and this time round, with Easter being so late, she was even more eager than usual. After having had so much time off over the past two years, it'd been really hard to maintain the concentration and physical demands teaching placed on her. That, combined with the extra work of composing songs to contribute to Heartsong, had meant her every waking moment was full of focus. Thank God she'd said no to touring with them when they'd asked. Writing songs was enough, especially when she was trying to be wise with her energy levels. Two weeks of sleeping in and lazing around sounded like gold.

The front door banged, followed by the stomp of little feet racing up the stairs.

"Aunty Sar! Aunty Sar!" A little golden-haired girl tumbled into the room, closely followed by an even smaller version. "We saw elephants today at the zoo!"

Sarah hoisted her nieces onto her lap, giving them a cuddle. "Hey, possums. Were they like the ones in the photos I showed you?"

"You better believe it, Blue," Joe said from the door. "All the girls would say on the way there was 'We're gonna see elephants like Aunty Sar!' Then when we were there, it was 'Can I ride on it? My Aunty Sar has ridden on elephants.'"

Sarah laughed at her brother-in-law's comical expression. "So, you enjoyed the zoo?"

Rebekah appeared with a yawn. "Some of us enjoyed it a little too much. Mum and Dad have collapsed on the couch downstairs, and I won't be far behind."

Rebekah and Joe had hastily arranged this visit a few weeks ago. They'd taken the girls out of school a few days earlier than their Easter break and were leaving just after the coming Easter weekend. Sarah gave the wriggling bundles on her knees another squeeze. Yep, after the last few days, she totally understood Bek and Joe's need for rest. She loved her little nieces, but two weeks of peace and quiet?

Priceless.

~

TWO MINUTES TO GO. Dan glanced at the Jumbotron as the seconds ticked down. This, the last game of the season, his last chance to impress before closing out his eighty-second game. So far he remained goalless, but at least tonight was tracking to a win. Tomorrow was locker clear-out and media interviews, but now required the last dregs of his focus.

Montreal turned the puck over, and Matt Reynolds scooped it up and headed to Montreal's net. Beau Nash stretched wide, and the puck hit his chest armor and was snatched up as the siren blared.

Dan joined his team in celebrating the win, something for the awesome Toronto fans who loved this game as much as he did. He nodded to Beau—he'd catch up with him later—and joined his teammates in lifting his stick to salute the fans as the lights flashed and the music boomed through the arena. He skated to the side and tossed his gloves to one small glasses-wearing girl wearing his number, then pointed to another kid before carefully passing his stick over the glass to the beaming boy. He loved the fans, loved their passion for this sport. Was anything better than this game?

Well, something—someone—was. He bit back a smile, thanking the equipment staff as he headed down the tunnel for the last time this season.

The next two hours with his teammates in the locker room held a mix of celebration and commiseration that they'd left it too late to find their form, but hey, it was done, and they'd shake it off and prepare for the next season. And he'd cheer on Mike, Brent, Chris, and Luc, all of whom were in teams in the playoffs. That was okay. Dan had other plans.

Thoughts of those plans lit his chest with warmth during the drive home as he remembered Sarah's latest email. She wanted to see him? She sounded as keen as he. He'd been surprised at the lengths she was going to to prove it, though. Getting up at 4 a.m. just so she could watch his games? When she'd told him that, he'd been lost for words. He'd told Boyd, who'd just smiled and mumbled something about "must be true love." Well, yeah, it certainly seemed like it. It was nice to see how interested she'd been in each game, even if some of it was concern over potential injuries he may receive. No, God really was working things out for good.

Even with his family. Maybe his father was never going to show him much affection, but since news of his past had leaked to Luke, his older brother had become far more considerate. He'd even flown over a week or two ago for a quick visit, ostensibly to watch a game but really to talk with him afterward about how Dan was feeling about the upcoming birth. They'd had the first real, open, honest discussion of their adult lives, and although things had gotten a little tense at times, it had been really good. Luke had even asked him to be the baby's godfather. The fact they even wanted a godfather still blew him away. Who'd have ever thought Luke could be that sensitive?

Luke's visit had reignited a desire to finally talk to Lana. He'd mentioned it to Sarah, who'd been hugely supportive, so he'd tracked Lana down, spoken to her, and learned she was now married with two kids and most definitely not mired in regret.

"I can't believe you called me," she'd said.

Dan could scarcely believe it either. But he was glad he had. A tiny crack in his heart that had splintered open after New Year's Eve now felt wholly healed.

And then there was Sam. He still hadn't taken that final step, but he was so close to faith now. His brother's interest in God and occasional attendance at church had spurred Dan on to investigate other ways to get him involved. When Mike had mentioned something a few weeks back about a team heading to the Philippines, Sam had leaped at the opportunity to "go help the kids," as he'd put it. Dan smiled. Helping others usually had a way of rebounding to help the helper. *God, help Sam.*

Yeah, God was definitely working things out for good. And tomorrow, once his final team and media obligations were done, all his energies could be devoted to his international adventures. It was going to be awesome. Joy lit his chest. He couldn't wait.

"ATTENTION EVERYONE: Sleeping Beauty has finally awoken."

Sarah made a face at her sister before yawning hellos to everyone else sprawled around the open-plan living area and dining room.

"Well, it sure wasn't Prince Charming this time." She cast a significant look at her early-bird nieces on her way to boil the kettle for that very necessary first cup of tea of the day.

"This time?" Her sister raised an eyebrow.

Sarah rolled her eyes. "Anyway, I'm entitled to some extra shut-eye. This past week has been full on." She'd been so busy with assessment tasks and papers to grade and preparation for next term that, coupled with the extra entertaining their house-guests required, meant the days had seemed extra long. And yesterday's early morning Good Friday service hadn't helped the lack of sleep factor either.

At least the rest of the day had been quiet. With everything apart from churches shut, there'd been little to do apart from eat hot cross buns and enjoy time with her family. And with Rebekah, Joe, and the girls headed back to South Australia in a couple of days, it was nice to spend time with them instead of being limited to the usual early morning and evening rush of school days.

"Blue, we'll get out of your hair and take the munchkins to the park," Joe promised before escorting all his girls out the front door.

God bless Joe—best brother-in-law ever.

Sarah ate her breakfast whilst reading the paper at the dining table, idly noting her mother seemed to be planning an extra nice dinner for tonight, complete with pavlova. Mmm, pavlova. "Do you want some help, Mum?"

"No, sweetie. Bek can help when they all get back."

Her father folded up his paper. "Sarah, if you're offering, I could do with a hand."

"Sure." She swallowed her toast. Vegemite was nice, but Muskoka blueberry jam…

"We have to go into the city." Dad grinned.

Odd. Dad smiled. He didn't grin.

Her mum lifted the bowl of whipped egg whites. "You might want to freshen up, hon."

"What's wrong with what I'm wearing?"

"That tracksuit isn't fit for outside, let alone picking up a guest from the airport."

She blinked. "Are you seriously having someone else come and stay?" She'd been so looking forward to some much-needed quiet time. Now someone was intruding. It felt like Muskoka again. She bit back the sigh. There was no point getting emotional.

"Yes." Her mum was carefully shaping the pavlova and didn't look at her. "Bek's family head back to Adelaide on Monday, so we'll be a bit squashed for a couple of nights, but then it'll be fine. Now, hurry up and get changed."

Oh well. She walked upstairs and stared at her closet. She should be used to visitors, the hospitality trait her aunt was famous for running strong in her mother's genetic makeup also. Since returning from PNG, her parents had often opened their home to provide emergency accommodation, and their beach suburb and guestroom was always popular with missionaries on furlough from overseas. Over the years it had necessitated a number of trips to the airport, where she'd helped her dad collect the visitors. It always worked out quicker and cheaper to do the tandem run, one person circling the parking lot while the other met the traveler. She wasn't out to impress, but got changed anyway, returning in skinny jeans and a plum-colored top. "Better?"

Her mother looked up and smiled. "Much."

When they got to the airport, Dad asked her to hop out whilst he began the well-practiced circling technique. "Look, we're running a little late. If you could just wait at arrivals, I've told him to look out for an attractive redhead holding this sign. He's tall, got brown hair and eyes and an accent. Don't worry, I'd trust him with my life. I'll be round again in a moment." He thrust a sign bearing the name *Maguire* at her, quickly driving off, ignoring her protests.

"Dad!" Sarah stood there as the car disappeared. How bizarre. She slowly made her way to the arrivals lounge. She'd had to hold signs before at the airport, but usually her father gave her more information about the person she was meeting.

International visitors were slowly making their dazed way in, the long-haul flights taking a toll. Yep, she definitely knew what that felt like. She stood at the end of a long line of chauffeurs patiently waiting with the names of their guests printed boldly on their posters, half-heartedly holding the sign, busily scanning for a tall, brown-haired man.

Hello? What was Dad thinking? Half the people walking through could fit that description. Was he one of the Indian missionaries they'd had stay before, or maybe someone from Africa? A litany of houseguests from over the years flashed through her mind. This could be anyone!

She took a deep breath. Not gonna get upset. But still… She shook her head before noticing a figure moving closer in her peripheral vision.

"Hey, Princess."

CHAPTER 32

He got a second to glimpse her startled wide eyes and hear the gasped "Daniel!" before she threw herself at him, pressing herself close in a giant bear hug like she wanted to be in his skin. "Oh! I've missed you so much!"

Yeah, he kind of got that impression. He wrapped his arms around her, drinking in her scent and nuzzling her bright hair that glowed against the purple of her shirt. He closed his eyes to the curious gazes around them, holding on tight. Everything was finally being made right in this moment.

She murmured something, and he had to duck his head to hear.

"But what are you doing here?"

"I've missed you. I had to see you again." There were some advantages to their season having finished early. As disappointing as missing the playoffs had been, it had allowed extra time to see her.

She touched his stubbled jaw. "It's so good to see you."

"You too." He cupped her face in his hands and touched her lips with his, kissing her the way he'd been dreaming of these past lonely months, sliding one hand up into her soft hair, wrapping the other around her waist. She responded by squeezing him tight for a long, lovely minute before breaking away.

"Whoa. You make me feel dizzy." She placed her hands on his chest and took a steadying breath. He knew exactly how she felt. "My dad—"

Dan grinned as she blinked, finally connecting the dots.

"You're staying with us! And Mum and Dad know! Oh!"

"You're on vacation for a couple of weeks, so I figured now would be a good chance to hang out. That is, if you're not too busy."

"No!" She hugged him again. "I'm never too busy for you!"

Her smile, her laughter, these spontaneous hugs, this exuberant joy in her face—he'd missed it so much. He had to kiss her again.

After another delicious moment, she pulled away again. "But I thought you were coming in July!"

"Couldn't wait that long, Princess."

She still looked stunned. "And what about the Philippines?"

"I'm heading there next month, after Luke's baby is born."

They wheeled his bags out to the entrance, Sarah's dad soon pulling into the loading zone, a broad grin on his face as he parked and opened the door.

"Like your surprise?" he asked his daughter as they drew near.

Sarah's cheeks pinked as she glanced across at Dan and smiled. "I love it!"

After shaking hands with James, Dan stowed his bags, then settled in the back seat, holding hands with Sarah as her dad drove them back to their house.

Sarah still seemed dumbfounded. "But when did you sort this out?"

"A few weeks ago, when it became clear we weren't making the playoffs."

She squeezed his hand, eyeing her father in the rear vision mirror. "Dad, you're so sneaky! I didn't know you and Mum could keep such a secret."

Her father laughed, and Dan grinned before a yawn escaped.

"Are you tired?" She shot him a sympathetic look and squeezed his hand.

Oh yeah, but he couldn't let her know just how little he'd slept. Massive excitement levels hadn't made falling asleep an easy task, then there'd been the usual passenger and plane service noises. Dan kissed the back of her hand. "Tell you what, that flight's long."

"It is, but I'm so glad you're here!" Her green eyes shone in delight as she almost danced in her seat.

His smile grew sappy. Oh yeah, that long flight had definitely been worth it.

HE WAS HERE! Sitting next to her! Here! She couldn't stop looking at him, and he seemed similarly afflicted, staring back, big grin fixed in place. Yep, the same dark hair, beautiful brown eyes, and that smile that made her insides wobble. This was just the nicest surprise ever. Seeing him made her world complete. His arms around her, his lips on hers—it was all so very right.

They soon arrived back at her home, collecting his bags to walk inside where her mother greeted him with a hug. Rebekah, Joe, and the girls were introduced next. Sarah bit her lip. How would her big sister act? She'd been so excited at the news of their reconciliation.

"Good to meet you." Rebekah gave her a wink, then a none-too-subtle thumbs-up as Dan was introduced to Joe and the girls. Sarah rolled her eyes at her sister.

They moved to the living room, chatting about his trip and making small talk for a while. Dan glanced around the room. "I didn't realize there'd be so many people here." He spoke to her mother. "I don't want to be any trouble. I'll go stay at a hotel."

"You can stay in my room tonight."

Oops. Not quite what she'd meant to say. Her cheeks heated at the startled looks thrown her way. "I mean, I'll sleep on the couch."

Dan turned to her. "Sar, you can't do that. I'm guessing I'll be so tired I'll sleep anywhere. I'm happy with the couch."

"Daniel, we've got it sorted. We know that flight is exhausting, and you won't want to be interrupted by little people in the morning. Stay in Sarah's room for the next two nights; she'll sleep on the couch, then on Monday when Bek and Joe leave, you can have the guestroom." Her mum gave a decisive nod and quick smile.

The rest of the day passed in catching up and cuddling. That night they enjoyed a big barbecue outside under the vine-covered pergola. Dan seemed to be settling in well, despite his exhaustion, laughing and joking with Joe and the girls and chatting amiably with her parents and Bek. Sarah smiled. He seemed so comfortable, fitting in with her family like he belonged. As they ate the steak, prawns, salad, and pavlova, they discussed their plans for the next two weeks. Everyone offered their opinions about what to see and do until Sarah could tell the noise was starting to overwhelm their guest.

She leaned closer to him. "Is there any place you want to go? Or are you happy if I take you to some of the best tourist spots?"

She tried to contain the shiver as he smoothed her hair behind her ear, his eyes warm. "I'm happy anywhere, Sar, as long as I'm with you."

~

DAN WEARILY SETTLED into the freshly made bed, glancing over at Sarah's bedside table. Amongst the perfume, jewelry, and knick-knacks, she had a silver frame containing the identical photo from their visit to Niagara Falls that she'd used for his CD. The joyous smiles pictured raised an answering one from him. How good to be finally here.

A gentle tap came at the door, and Sarah poked her head in at his answer.

"Hi, I just wanted to check everything is okay."

"Couldn't be better." He sat up in the bed. Her eyes widened and she glanced away. Oh. Should've worn a top. He tugged the covers up higher. "It's safe to look now."

Sarah peeked apologetically. "I'm not used to seeing a man in my bed."

"That's good to hear. But you know"—he offered a sly smile—"when you get married, you'll need to get used to it."

Her cheeks pinked. "But I'm not. So the sight of you there is a little distracting."

They stared at each other with matching smiles as she maintained her distance from the door. At a sudden door slam, Sarah straightened up from her slouch against the doorframe. "Um, I need to get some things. Do you mind?"

Dan shook his head, watching as she hastily gathered some clothes and began to exit. "Hey, I just remembered, I do need something."

She turned to him expectantly.

"I need a goodnight kiss."

SARAH'S PULSE CRESCENDOED. Having Dan here still seemed bizarrely unreal, like some long-held dream actually coming to life. She'd dreamed about kissing him for months now, but with the desire arcing between them, she didn't want to create a problem...

"Sar, I'll be a gentleman. Just one kiss."

She moved closer, then leaned down, smoothing a hand down the side of his face, gently touching the scar on his jaw, smiling into his eyes. "Dan, thank you so much for coming. I'm so glad you're here. I love you." She quickly kissed his forehead, then straightened up. "Sweet dreams."

She laughed at his expression as he grumbled. "That's not what I meant."

"Just one kiss, you said." She smirked. "Goodnight."

"G'night."

Later, when everyone else had gone to bed, Sarah and her sister drank tea and munched their way through a family-sized block of Cadbury's milk chocolate as they chatted, Dan being the chief topic of conversation.

"I like him, Sar. He's nice, great with the girls, and not bad looking at all."

Sarah swallowed at the memory of his naked chest. Even though she'd seen him without a top on before, when they were swimming months ago, it'd felt so much more intimate seeing him like that in her bed. Her cheeks warmed. Why did he always have this effect on her?

Her sister continued thoughtfully. "Both Joe and I were thinking, he's different to Stephen but probably better suited to you."

"How so?"

Bek sighed. "I don't know if I should say this, but there were times when Stephen seemed a little too controlling, like he wanted you to do things according to his agenda. That's why you quit Heartsong, right?"

Sarah nodded. "If you thought that, why didn't you ever say anything?"

"Because you loved him. And I love you and wanted you to

be happy. But I don't think you were as happy with Stephen as you are with Dan now."

"Dan's the best."

Her sister nodded. "You seem way more relaxed with him than I remember you being before. He's good for you."

"I love him, Bek. And he must really love me if he's come all this way."

"You think?" Her sister laughed, then took another sip of tea. "I think it says a lot that Mum and Dad arranged all this with him. They obviously approve."

"I'm so glad." Sarah smiled across the dining table at her sister.

Rebekah grabbed her hands. "Sarah, after all you've been through, you deserve to be happy. So be happy. Don't try to second-guess things. Dan loves you. So take this time and enjoy it."

Sarah nodded, exhaling slowly, remembering Ange had said something similar before. "I still have this fear that I'll sabotage things or something will go wrong."

Rebekah looked seriously at her. "Sar, keep trusting God. I know you've really had to learn this the hard way, but just keep trusting that He'll work things out."

"I'll try."

"Now, have some more chocolate."

Sarah laughed and reached for another piece.

FASCINATING. Sarah looked like a sleeping, flying Supergirl, lying on her stomach on the lounge, one arm outstretched, the other clenched in a loose fist. Especially with the cherry red blanket bunched up around her head, then tumbling loose around her shoulders like a cape. Her eyes were buttoned shut, and she had the edges of her mouth tucked up like she held a special secret. Cute, cute, cute.

Dan leaned back on the couch opposite the one where Sarah lay. Happiness glowed within. He still struggled to believe he was actually here. Doubt had queried whether things would be as easy as before, but as soon as she'd smiled at him at the airport, all fears had vanished. Her smile always managed to chase away the dark edges of his soul.

He wrapped the throw he'd found lying on the end of the couch around his shoulders, warding off the cool of early morning. When he'd woken way too early—gotta love such different time zones—he'd read his Bible for a while, then after throwing on some warm clothes to beat the pre-dawn chill, he'd come down to watch Sarah sleep. It seemed like a great way to not waste a second of being in her company. The different bird song and the first glimmers of sunrise hitting unfamiliar trees and buildings had been a little disorienting at first. But the peace and serenity of early morning was always good, no matter where he was in the world.

"She's kinda cute when she's asleep, isn't she?"

He started and looked up. Rebekah stood nearby, amusement on her face.

"I couldn't sleep in either. I'm the Easter bunny this year, so I have to put the eggs outside in the garden for an Easter egg hunt when the girls wake up. But first I need a cuppa. You want one?"

Maybe this need for tea was an Australian thing. His hesitation elicited a small laugh from Rebekah. "Don't worry, you won't be missing anything. Sarah's been like that since a kid. She always takes ages to get to sleep, tossing and turning and twisting the bedclothes inside out. She then burrows into the pillow and doona until she can't hear anything, but once she's asleep, heaven help the person who wakes her up." She chuckled. "You're Canadian. Think bear with sore head."

He nodded, thinking back to the morning after Sarah's bike

fall back in Muskoka. Yep, the warning on her PJs was necessary. Crabby was only part of it. He joined Rebekah in the kitchen for the cup of tea and was soon able to glean all other sorts of useful information…

Once Rebekah moved outside to begin placing the foil-wrapped chocolate Easter eggs, he shifted back to his position on the couch. Sarah moaned something from underneath the blanket. He shifted to sit on the coffee table, hunching closer to the figure sprawled on the lounge. "What's that, Princess?"

She pulled back the blanket and yawned. "Don't believe everything you hear." Sarah gave him a sleepy smile. "It's called self-preservation. I cover my ears so I don't have to hear her girls. They're *so* noisy."

He laughed as the shrieks and stomps of little feet overhead attested to that truth.

THE MORNING'S Easter service and subsequent lunch were another fascinating insight into this family, so different to his own. Sarah and her sister had performed an item, their voices harmonizing perfectly for the rendition of "Amazing Grace." James led the service, warmly extolling each person to live free and forgiven, fully embracing the new life Jesus had died for. It was almost like a personal vindication from the minister regarding Dan's own history, and he'd looked up several times to see if James was referring to him in particular.

But no, this grace thing, so contrary to his own father's, was just part of the Maguires' life. They'd even invited anyone from church who wanted to come for lunch to do so. The end result had been another rowdy but happy and relaxed affair, attended by several lonely people from church including a single mom and her baby, a couple of elderly gentlemen, and other people he met for the first time at lunch.

This, apparently, was normal. His mom would die of shock if asked to do something like this, but Lindy just seemed to take the extra guests in her stride. The day for her was about people, not whether the table was set fancy or not. The Maguires just practiced what they preached. Grace. Acceptance. Love for others. And, it seemed, love for him.

Later that afternoon, after the guests had all left and the cleaning was finished, the sisters looked at each other, then at him with matching smiles. "I think it's popcorn time!"

"Uh oh." Joe shifted from where he'd been building a Lego castle with his six-year-old daughter. He glanced across at Dan with a look of amusement. "I know that look."

"What?"

Joe stood, giving his daughter a tickle before making a show of looking at his watch. "Would you look at the time?"

"Joseph, don't think you're getting out of things that easily."

He kissed Rebekah's cheek. "Sweetheart, once was enough. Jonno and Andy are waiting for me. Anyway, I've already been initiated. You need to focus all your energies on Dan here."

Sarah drew closer with that gorgeous smile on her face. "Daniel, if you want to hang around, then it's time to let you know about one of the traditions in the Maguire household. Every Christmas we watch a movie, but because I was away we've had to wait until now to watch it *together*." She made a face at her brother-in-law. "And now they're old enough, it's time to indoctrinate Rebekah's girls."

"A movie?" He shrugged. "Sure, okay."

Joe laughed. "Not just any movie, my friend."

Uh oh. "What movie?"

Sarah smiled. "*Anne of Green Gables.*"

"Seriously?"

Sarah nodded, a delighted smile on her face.

"I've been had." He turned to Joe. "Help me out, man."

"Sorry, mate, no can do. When I found out what Bek and

Blue were planning, I made my own plans to catch up with some friends from uni."

"I can't believe you deliberately organized something to get out of this." Rebekah's friendly quarrel with her husband finished with Joe's laughter as he exited the room.

Dan shifted his attention back to Sarah. "How long is this movie, Princess?"

She held up three fingers.

"You're kidding me, right?" He groaned. "You know this will look really bad if the guys find out."

"I won't tell if you don't." She plopped down next to him, nuzzling his jaw with her lips. "But just think how proud your mum will be."

He rolled his eyes, but as she snuggled next to him, yeah, well, okay, he'd put up with it. He'd put up with anything. The movie music began, and the girls, and even Sarah's mother, who'd now joined them, were all entranced.

"Isn't Prince Edward Island just beautiful?" Sarah sighed. "I'd love to go visit one day."

He'd been to Nova Scotia a few times for hockey stuff, but never to PEI, so it was interesting to see settings that looked like they should be familiar. It was obviously very familiar to Sarah, who seemed to sparkle with anticipation during any scenes with the redheaded heroine and Gilbert, even mouthing along with the words. Watching her was even better than the movie. He tugged her closer. "I love this about you."

She dragged her eyes away from the screen. "What?"

He shook his head, chuckled softly, kissing the back of her hand again before turning back to the screen. And as she burrowed closer, his smile grew.

"See? It's not so bad, is it? Your masculinity isn't being threatened too much."

He snickered. "Yeah, I still love spittin' and fightin' and stuff."

He drew her closer as she laughed, looping a little curl at the base of her hair around his fingers.

She tensed, then slowly smiled again. "Well, that's good to know. I don't want Mr. Tough Hockey Man getting all soft and turning into a pushover. That wouldn't be cool."

He smiled back. Didn't she realize? She'd pushed him over a long time ago.

CHAPTER 33

*D*an sat across from Sarah at the modern waterfront restaurant, the last rays of sunset glowing through the large window causing the diamond at her throat to sparkle. These past two weeks had been awesome. It didn't seem right he had to return home so soon. He'd loved visiting different places, checking out the sights, doing things like the Harbour Bridge climb, seeing the Opera House from the Manly ferry, and visiting Taronga Zoo.

But the best parts had involved getting to know Sarah and her parents more. The times spent in their home, at church, visiting some famous city sights, and then away for a few days in the Blue Mountains, had proved really good opportunities to appreciate James and Lindy, their down-to-earth nature and conversation. It still amazed him just how encouraging they were of his relationship with their daughter and how comfortable he felt with them, despite everything. They definitely were supportive. He smiled.

Sarah put her fork down and swallowed, a blissful look on her face. "These scallops are sensational."

"So you're not completely over seafood, then?"

"You're obviously not." The smile slid up her face as she eyed his plate of barramundi and salad. "Still Mr. Fit and Healthy, huh?"

"Sorry, Princess, that's not gonna change in a hurry."

"Maybe not. But have you seen the desserts?"

He laughed at her characteristic enthusiasm as she subtly motioned to the couple at the table nearby, who were being served decadent sweet creations.

"It's okay, Sar. I promise, we can have dessert."

She grinned at him, and his heart tripped. *And if you keep smiling at me like that, you can have anything else you want too.*

Later, ambling hand in hand along the harborside path, his eyes refused to take in the famous view, so fixed were they on the woman beside him. Sarah was radiant tonight, her long hair cascading in waves down her back, her creamy skin aglow. The simple black dress elegantly showed her figure, and she wore some strappy heels that made her slightly taller. The moon was full, shining down on the harbor as the small waves washed against the sand of the little beach nearby. The time was right.

Dan stopped and gazed into her clear eyes. "I wish I didn't have to go back tomorrow. But Luke's email today made it sound like their baby will come a little earlier than expected. I guess I'll be seeing my little niece or nephew pretty soon. That'll be good."

"That will be so special for you all."

Dan observed Sarah carefully, but her eyes remained unclouded at the mention of the baby. Gratitude to God bloomed in his chest. He took hold of her hands. "Sarah, you know you're my favorite person in all the world, don't you?"

Her smile lit up her face. "How funny! You're my favorite person too!"

He took a deep breath. "Sarah, I love you. I've missed you so much, and I don't want to be separated anymore." He touched her hair, smoothing a wayward strand. "Will you come back to Canada with me?"

~

Sarah's heart started beating staccato, her thoughts twirling at his invitation, yet also torn by her contracted obligation. "Of course I'd love to go back, but I have a job to finish here. That doesn't finish until the end of June."

"Come in July then. We could spend more time together. That'd be awesome. Maybe even take a vacation together."

Her eyes widened. "What do you mean take a vacation together?"

"Well, we kinda vacationed together in Muskoka."

"Yeah, but we weren't 'together.' We were with John and Ange for most of that. What are you suggesting?"

"You're right. We'd need to get married first."

Breath stalled, her body tingling in a dozen heart-rippling thrills. "What?"

His chocolaty eyes softened even more. "Sarah, I love you so much. Will you marry me?"

Sarah blinked, trying to absorb his words. She hadn't expected, hadn't dared dream this would happen. He wanted to marry her? Low maintenance woman would've just said yes. She so wasn't that woman. "Are you for real?"

"Yes." He touched her cheek. "These past few months I've realized how much I need you in my life. Missing you was like an ache that never stopped." His fingers slid down her arms before repossessing her hands. "When you told me you didn't want to see me again, part of me felt like dying. The times we've been apart have just made me realize how important you are to me, how precious life is, especially when we live so far apart. And I don't want to be apart from you anymore. I love you, Sarah. I need you."

"I love you too, but…" Her brain was definitely operating in low gear tonight. "What do you mean you need me? I've seen how I've needed you, but how have you needed me?"

He gazed at her steadily, his lips curving as he answered. "Sar, you've challenged me, stretched me, helped me really live out what I believe rather than just say stuff I haven't lived. You're good for me. You're smart, you're talented, you're kind and joyful, you're beautiful, you're funny, you're everything I want in a wife." His voice grew husky. "I know I'm not the perfect man, but I am yours, and all that I am, and all that I have, I want to share with you." He lifted her hands and kissed them. "I love you, Princess. I want to be with you."

Oh-h-h-h. Sweetness sang through her spirit. "I want to be with you too."

But…they'd never talked about this. Ever. Had they? She frowned. No. Surely she'd remember that conversation! Dan was standing there, heart in his eyes, just wanting an answer.

Her mind ran faster. She loved this man. Loved his kindness, his generosity, his faith, his honor—and it didn't hurt that it was all wrapped up in such a handsome package. But despite the thrills rushing through her, she couldn't make an emotional decision, not with something as huge as this. And not when she feared that in missing her, he'd lost sight of the big picture, of what being married to her would actually mean.

She slowly exhaled, watching his expression carefully as she asked the question that loitered around the edges of elation. "But what about kids?"

"Sar." He gently squeezed her fingers, then trailed his hands up her arms to cup her face, his dark eyes intent on her. "Sar, I love you. You are more important to me than anything. If we can't have kids, then God will help us deal with that. But you never know, things might be fine. Regardless, God knows what's best, so we have to trust Him. And hey, there's always adoption."

Sarah gave a hysterical gurgle of laughter.

He smiled. "What?"

"You're ridiculously good to me."

"That's because I love you."

DAN TOOK a step back so he could gaze at her face, her lovely, green-eyed, sweet-lipped face. As she stared back, he watched the uncertainty melt away and confidence stretch across her features in a smile.

"Yes."

Yes...what? Yes, she knew he loved her? "Yes...?" he repeated slowly, his heart thumping more crazily than it had last week when he'd stood on the edge of a cliff called Govett's Leap.

"Yes, I'll marry you."

"Really?" Fierce joy threatened to consume him, but he had to stay patient a little longer.

"Yes." Her lips tilted up one side. "But you'll need to ask my dad for permission. He's old fashioned that's way."

He smiled. "Already done."

"What? When?"

He pulled her closer. "Yesterday, when you were cooking with your mom. I had a heart-to-heart with him. They've given us their blessing."

He slipped the ring from his jacket pocket and kissed the inside of her wrist as he drew her hand close. He smiled at her gasp as he gently pushed the ring on her finger, the moonlight catching the deep fire of the beautiful diamonds that perfectly complemented her pendant. Yeah, this particular investment had been so worth it.

"Oh, Daniel!" Sarah threw her arms around his neck. "I love you so much!"

He pulled her tight, swinging her around in a whirl of exhilaration that left them both laughing, before he steadied them again, caressing her beautiful face. "I love you."

"I can't wait to marry you," she murmured, her breath mingling with his as she drew closer.

Dan pressed his lips to hers, drinking in her kiss, her affection, her joy-filled commitment to their future, even as his heart marveled at God's grace and kindness. He didn't deserve this, but God was a redeemer and a restorer of broken things, able to turn mourning into dancing, heaviness into joy. He pulled back with reluctance, leaning his forehead against hers, breathing in her fragrance, reveling in the wonder of it all. "Remember when we first met, and I asked where you belong?"

She nodded. "And now I'm here, with you," she whispered.

"In my arms, where you belong." Dan's clasp tightened again, his fingers entwined in the softness of her gorgeous hair. "Thank God we met in Muskoka, eh?"

Sarah leaned back and gave him that heart-stopping smile. "I thank God every day."

"As do I." He stole another kiss. Then another. "My Muskoka Blue."

THE END

To catch a glimpse of Dan and Sarah's wedding and discover more romance in Muskoka, please check out *Muskoka Shores*. And if you want more hockey, please see *Fire and Ice*, the first book in the new Christian hockey series, Northwest Ice.

Thank you for reading *Muskoka Blue,* the sixth book in the Original Six Christian contemporary romance series, which combines my love of ice hockey with appreciation for the cities that comprised the NHL's original six teams. This is a much-edited version of the second book I ever wrote, and is based on my visit to the beautiful Muskoka region, so it's a thrill to see it now being read by others. If you've enjoyed this book, please check out the special bonus Blue Mountains chapter available for newsletter subscribers. I also have some pictures from my visit to Muskoka (and the Blue Mountains) on my website at www.carolynmillerauthor.com/the-original-six-romance-series

Reviews help other readers find new-to-them authors, so if you can spare a moment to write a quick review at Amazon / Goodreads / your place of purchase, I'd be very grateful.

If you've enjoyed this taste of Muskoka, and want to catch a glimpse of Dan and Sarah's wedding, then make sure you read *Muskoka Shores,* part of the Muskoka series that continues with *Muskoka Christmas.*

Please make sure you check out the other books in the Original Six hockey romance series, a sweet & swoony, slightly sporty Christian contemporary romance series.

The Breakup Project
Love on Ice
Checked Impressions
Hearts and Goals
Big Apple Atonement
Muskoka Blue

If you're a hockey fan you might also want to read *Fire and Ice*, the first book in the new Northwest Ice series, releasing in 2023.

I'd love for you to check out my other books and to sign up for my newsletter at www.carolynmillerauthor.com where you can be the first to learn all my book and contest news, and discover more behind-the-book details and photos.

A huge thank you to the following people for their encouragement and eagle eyes: Ros, Jacqueline, Jenny, Meredith, Kim, Bea, Brittany, Rebekah, Kaye & Becky - I appreciate you all so much! Big thanks to Nisha (for inspiring the use of several pithy sayings) and the ladies in my Facebook group, Carolyn's Books & Friends, for all your support in helping promote my books.

ABOUT THE AUTHOR

Carolyn Miller lives in the beautiful Southern Highlands of New South Wales, Australia, with her husband and four children. A long-time lover of romance, especially that of Jane Austen, Georgette Heyer and LM Montgomery, Carolyn loves to write contemporary and historical romance that draws readers into fictional worlds that show the truth of God's grace in our lives.

To find out more about Carolyn's books, and to subscribe to her newsletter, please visit www.carolynmillerauthor.com

You can also connect with her at

Dusk's Darkest Shores

Midnight's Budding Morrow

Dawn's Untrodden Green

Regency Brides: Legacy of Grace

The Elusive Miss Ellison

The Captivating Lady Charlotte

The Dishonorable Miss DeLancey

Regency Brides: Promise of Hope

Winning Miss Winthrop

Miss Serena's Secret

The Making of Mrs Hale

Regency Brides: Daughters of Aynsley

A Hero for Miss Hatherleigh

Underestimating Miss Cecilia

Misleading Miss Verity

'Heaven and Nature Sing' from the Joy to the World Christmas novella collection